SUFFOLK LIBRARIES

2 8 APR 2021

Please return/renew this item
by the last date shown.

01473 351249 | help@suffolklibraries.co.uk

www.suffolklibraries.co.uk

Make a donation to support our work at
www.suffolklibraries.co.uk/donate

The Green Man's Silence

The Green Man's Silence
Juliet E. McKenna

WIZARD'S TOWER

Wizard's Tower Press

Trowbridge, England

The Green Man's Silence

First edition, published in the UK September 2020
by Wizard's Tower Press

Hardcover ISBN: 978-1-913892-03-6

Cover illustration and design by Ben Baldwin
Editing by Toby Selwyn
Design by Cheryl Morgan

http://wizardstowerpress.com/
http://www.julietemckenna.com/

Contents

For Steve

Praise for the Green Man Series

Praise for The Green Man's Heir

"... any way you look at it, the book is a delight from start to finish. [...] It's one of my favorite books so far this year." — Charles de Lint in *Fantasy and Science Fiction*

"I read this last night and thoroughly enjoyed it, more please!" — Garth Nix on Twitter

"I really enjoyed this novel!" — Kate Elliott on Twitter

"Juliet McKenna captures the nuances of life as a stranger in a small town in much the same way as Paul Cornell does in his splendid Lychford series, with the local gossips, the hard-pressed police, the rampaging boggarts and rural legends come to disturbing life. Thoroughly enjoyable; a UK fantasy author branching out (oh god, sorry for the inadvertent and terrible pun!) and clearly having a great time doing it. Highly recommended." — Joanne Hall

"So far up my street it could be my house." — K.J. Charles on Goodreads

"*The Green Man's Heir* is a thoroughly engaging, at times almost impossible to put down, tale which, despite besides its titular character, is peopled with an impressive array of interesting and intriguing women." — *The Monday Review*

"After a stumbling start, I found myself unable to put down *The Green Man's Heir*. If you're looking for a book to read on your summer holiday, then this is it." — Charlotte Bond via The British Fantasy Society

The Green Man's Heir is a straightforward fantasy story, with a lively pace and characters who wonderfully come alive. It starts as *Midsomer Murders* set in the Peak District but with added supernatural element and turns out to be the book you won't put down because you enjoy it too much." — *The Middle Shelf*

"I hope this turns into a series. I'd love to read more about Daniel's adventures." — N.W. Moors in *The Antrim Cycle*

"And she has absolutely nailed it. This is a complete and utter joy." — S.J. Higbee in *Brainfluff*

"I'm certainly on board for reading more such novels." — Paul Weimer in *Skiffy and Fanty*

"Brilliant concept, compellingly told" — Virginia Bergin on Twitter

Praise for The Green Man's Foe

"I loved *The Green Man's Heir*, and while I expected to thoroughly enjoy *The Green Man's Foe*, I did not expect it to be even more satisfying than its forerunner. Which was foolish of me, I admit – I should know by now that McKenna is more capable of outdoing her previous tales in a series." – *The Monday Review*

"If you've read the first book then I'm pretty confident you're going to love this one, and if you haven't read the first one then you need to remedy that straight away." – Naomi Scott

"This is one of my outstanding reads of the year." – S.J. Higbee in *Brainfluff*

"*The Green Man's Foe* is a great addition to what is becoming a great series. I was entirely caught up in it for a couple of days. It is a must read if you have enjoyed the first one, and a great reason to start on this series if you have missed it." – *The Middle Shelf*

"*The Green Man's Foe* is a tasty serve of mystery and myth that has done quite enough to cement this series as one I'll be reading and cheerleading for from now on." – Imyril at *There's Always Room for One More.*

Chapter One

I'd never been to the Fens before. Work's never taken me to that part of the country, and whenever I take some time off, which isn't often, I head for forests and hills. That's what I know and where I feel at home. About the only thing I did know about these low wetlands around the edge of the Wash is there's a distinct lack of high ground or woodland, so I had no reason to visit the area.

At least, that's what I thought I knew. Driving over to Ely in early January, I could see far more trees than I expected. They were mostly willow and poplar, judging by their leafless outlines against the pale blue sky. There was an awful lot of sky, and that made me feel oddly exposed. I could see a long way ahead, as well as a surprising distance away on either side of the road. That wasn't just because the trees were bare at this time of year. There were precious few hedges and the roads were raised up well above the level of the surrounding fields of rich black soil. There was pretty much nothing to obstruct my view.

I kept my eyes on the road ahead regardless. Even what I would usually consider gentle bends were well signposted with lines of black and white chevrons. It wasn't hard to see why. Wide ditches ran between the roads and the fields and there was sod all by way of a verge if a vehicle needed to pull off. The ground fell away down steep, grassy slopes, and I had no idea how deep that darkly shining water might be. So it was a safe bet that getting things wrong on one of these sharper corners would be a very bad idea, even driving my Land Rover. I was glad it was a dry, sunny day, though that meant the Landy's heater was struggling to keep up with the chill.

I passed through a few small towns, or rather, I skirted them where enough land had been reclaimed to support a bypass and retail parks for supermarkets, clothes stores and coffee shops. Church spires showed where the medieval hearts of these settlements could be found. As I drove on, I began to see the way that the villages marked out what passed for higher ground. That's where the churches were, along with substantial, white-painted concrete water towers that now bristled with electronics to serve as mobile phone masts.

The older houses along the winding streets showed what must have been the limits of seasonal flooding when those churches had been built. Clusters of more modern developments from successive decades showed how these towns and villages had expanded as the surrounding land was drained and farmed. I wondered about problems with damp regardless. January's weather had been dry so far, but the past autumn had been very wet and the ground was sodden.

The low sunlight gleamed on water standing in the furrows of the ploughed fields.

The satnav and the road signs told me when I was getting near Ely. I didn't really need them. I could see the cathedral's towers from way off. It stood on the highest ground for miles around. It wasn't hard to see this small city had been all but an island before the wetlands here were drained.

Inevitably that meant the roads were narrow and twisted once I got off the bypass. The route directing modern traffic to the centre through residential streets must have made sense to some town planner but didn't seem at all obvious to me. Now the satnav did come into its own as I followed the directions to the car park that Finele Wicken had told me to aim for. I found it easily enough and was pleasantly surprised to find parking was free. I grew up on the Warwickshire–Oxfordshire border, where tourist towns like Stratford-upon-Avon charge cars an arm and a leg in hopes of persuading visitors to use the park-and-ride buses.

I got out and locked the Land Rover. Helpful black iron finger posts directed me through alleys cutting between Victorian terraces and along a street bounded by a tall brick wall. I soon found the cathedral, which was even more impressive close up, along with the medieval Bishop's Palace, which now housed a school.

I took out my mobile and rang Fin as I walked a bit further on. 'I'm here. Standing next to a cannon from the Crimean War.'

'You made good time. Can you see the tea room?'

I looked around. 'Yes.'

'Okay, I'll be with you in a few minutes. Go in and grab a table.'

'Okay.' I was already walking towards the tea shop where she'd suggested we meet. Getting a seat might be a challenge at the height of the summer tourist season, but it wasn't going to be a problem today. There was only one couple having a late lunch when I went in.

The woman behind the counter looked up with a hopeful smile. I didn't go too close. I do try not to loom over people, but it's not always easy at six foot four and taking XXL in most clothes.

'Good afternoon. Please, sit anywhere you like.' She came over with a menu.

I opted for a table for four by the window. The list of drinks on offer was ready and waiting in a plastic stand by a little vase of silk flowers. 'Thanks.' I took the menu from her. 'I'm meeting a friend. She'll be here in a minute.'

Her smile broadened. 'Let me know when you're ready to order.'

I was trying to decide between a hot sausage sandwich and a ham-and-cheese toastie when the bell over the door rang. I glanced up to see Finele

11

coming in. She looked as gorgeous as ever, even wearing an old duffel coat, with her nose red from the cold wind. She was carrying a couple of shopping bags and dumped them on a spare chair as I stood up. I was wondering about kissing her when she leaned forward and kissed my cheek first.

'How's your family? How was Christmas?' she asked as she sat down.

'Great, thanks. Quiet, you know. Just the three of us.' I shrugged as I took my own seat across the table.

It's not as if my family particularly celebrates Christmas, not since I left school. When I was a kid, fitting in meant turning up at carol concerts and the village Christingle service. When it comes to religion, though, my dad's an agnostic like me and winter solstice is what matters to my mum. She likes to watch the sunrise and sunset with both of us, if I can get home for the day. As a dryad, she's sensitive to the turn of the year in a way Dad and I can't begin to imagine.

Fin grinned as she pulled off her woolly hat and ran a hand through her pale blonde hair. 'That must have made a nice change. How did the December weekends' opening at Blithehurst go?'

'Absolute f—' I swallowed what I had been going to say, as swearing would have shattered the tea room's peace and quiet like a dropped cup. 'Mayhem.'

Fin laughed. 'So Eleanor was pleased.'

'Delighted,' I confirmed.

That was an understatement. Eleanor Beauchene – pronounced 'Beech-en' – is my boss. She's responsible for making sure the Staffordshire manor house that's her family's ancestral home pays its way as a tourist attraction and garden centre. The growth of Christmas markets here, there and everywhere had convinced her we should make a bid for some of that cash. She suggested it to the staff just before the house's usual closure for the winter at the end of October. Most people had welcomed the prospect of the extra pay. We'd had November to plan everything, and then we'd spent December setting up and running a winter fair in the manor on Saturdays and Sundays. The garden centre by the car park had flogged Nordmann firs and holly wreaths. The res-taurant had opened up to sell mince pies and mulled wine alongside the usual menu.

I'd been kept busy. The first job had been moving furniture out of the great hall, the picture gallery and the other rooms open to the public. Then I'd been heaving tables and chairs around for the artisan food stalls and other crafts people Eleanor had signed up. I'd also been making a shed load of wooden decorations and children's toys to go with the usual ornaments and trinkets I make for sale as Blithehurst's resident carpenter, joiner and woodworker. They'd sold as fast as the mince pies. I'd barely kept up with restocking the manor's sales tables for the next market, even working flat out on the weekdays in between.

Heading home on Christmas Eve had been a massive relief. My dad's house is out by the nature reserve where he's been a warden for years. When I'd got there, I'd stood by the Landy in the darkness for a quarter of an hour, just to feel the silence of the night and the woodlands before I went in. I've always been a loner. Those weekends dealing with clamouring Christmas crowds had been unpleasantly demanding.

Before either of us could say anything else, the lady from the counter approached. 'Do you need a few more minutes?'

'I'll have the sausage and chutney bap, please, and tea.' I offered the menu to Fin.

She waved it away. 'I'll have the tuna melt, with filter coffee please.'

I looked across the table as the lady made a note on her pad and took the menu away. I wanted to ask Fin all sorts of questions, but that meant starting a conversation that neither of us would risk other people overhearing.

'How are things going in Somerset?' I asked instead.

Finele's based in Bristol but her work as a freelance freshwater ecologist takes her around the country doing all sorts of things. In this case, a water authority was considering reinstating a river that had been drained or diverted for some reason or other a decade or so ago. Someone needed to assess the likely consequences of restoring the flow. The consultancy Fin ran with her sister had tendered and got the job.

'Good.' She nodded decisively. 'Very good. I think they can go ahead without any problems, though obviously we'll be monitoring the situation on an ongoing basis.'

I guessed that would keep her busy. That must be good for her company's cash flow. It was less good from my point of view, as that would keep her in Bristol while I was now firmly rooted in Staffordshire.

I was trying to work out where our relationship might be going. Was this even a relationship? Friendship? Friendship with benefits? We'd met back in the spring and we'd certainly become friends as we faced a dangerous challenge together. We'd seen each other a few times after that, and by the time Halloween came around we'd been ready to spend the weekend together in a cosy Cotswolds bed and breakfast. That had been everything I'd hoped for and more. Then Fin had got the Somerset job and Eleanor had announced her plans for Christmas opening. Both of us had been so busy for the last couple of months, we'd barely managed a weekly phone call.

I'd been wondering if she was trying to let me down gently. Then she'd rung just after Christmas to say her mother wanted to invite me to stay for a few days in the New Year, as long as Eleanor could give me the time off. I'd said yes, obviously, as soon as it was clear Fin would be there as well. Nothing ventured, nothing gained.

Eleanor owed me the holiday, so that was no problem. In fact, she said I could have two days off for each one that I booked against my official allowance since I was taking leave out of high season. So I had driven across the country from my dad's house now that the Christmas break was over and everyone was going back to work. But now I was here, I wasn't at all sure what I was doing. All I did know was I really didn't want to screw this up.

Our lunch arrived and the food was good. That helped ease the qualms in my stomach. We ate, and as I emptied the teapot for a last half-cup, I nodded at Fin's shopping bags. 'You had things to do in Ely then?'

She shook her head. 'Not really, but Mum gave me a list when I said I was meeting you here. I went over to see my dad this morning.'

I wasn't sure what to make of that so opted for a safer topic. 'I could have come straight to you. I'm sure the satnav would have got me there.'

'I'm not.' Fin grinned. 'Digital maps have no idea which routes are passable in the summer but are going to flood in the winter, once you're off the main roads and out in the fens. The locals have plenty of stories about visitors heading off along some drove or other because the satnav told them to, and ending up bogged down.'

I recalled a few adventures of my own in rural areas. 'Okay. Better safe than sorry.'

'Besides, I reckoned you'd have some questions before you meet my mum.' Fin finished her coffee and looked me in the eye. 'How about we pay the bill and go for a bit of a walk?'

I could see what she wasn't saying. She was ready for that conversation that neither of us wanted other people overhearing. Quite apart from anything else, they would think we were both insane.

We paid for our lunch, left the tea shop and walked towards the cathedral, across a broad and empty green. I wondered where to start, and decided on the easiest option first. 'So where does your dad live?'

'Out towards Littleport. He's a farmer, like his family before him.'

'So he and your mum...?'

I couldn't think how to phrase it, but Fin understood what I was asking.

'They met when they were both in college. They were in love for a while, long enough to have me and my sisters, but secrets are no good for a marriage.

They were already drifting apart when Mum moved back home to help look after her grandparents. Time passed and we stayed on in the Fens.'

Fin shrugged, but I could see that had been more painful than she was saying.

'They kept on good terms for our sake, and I think Dad would have tried again, but Mum found splitting up made her life – all our lives – so much easier. I can't argue with that.' She managed a rueful smile as we turned left and crossed a busy road.

'I can imagine.'

That was the thing we had in common. Something neither of us had found in other relationships. I genuinely could imagine the complications in Fin's life. We both have one foot in the ordinary human world and the other in the realm of folklore that most people think is just stories for kids.

My mother is a dryad, a centuries-old tree spirit who fell in love with my dad when he was volunteering at the nature reserve where she cherished the oak trees. That means while I'm as mortal as the next man, I can see dryads and naiads and the other creatures from myths and legends. A whole lot of things live their own very different lives unseen alongside oblivious humanity.

Fin can see these things too. That's because she's a swan maiden. It's straightforward enough, on one level at least. Her family can turn themselves into swans when they want to, or need to, as long as they have safe hold of the feathers that are bound up with that mysterious power. It cuts both ways. Look up swan maiden myths and there are far too many stories about those feathers being taken away, usually to force their obedience to the men who desire them. So Fin and her sisters, aunts and mother keep that side of their nature a secret. That's a definite complication when it comes to relationships.

My parents' situation had been far easier, since my mum could masquerade as a mortal woman easily enough and my dad had no close relatives to ask awkward questions. It had just been the three of us in a cottage outside the village, by the nature reserve, while I grew up. I'd accepted the world as I found it. I'd soon learned what I could and couldn't share with my class mates, who couldn't see the same things as me. I'd never thought much about it until I realised bringing a girlfriend home to meet my parents was out of the question.

We were walking down the narrow High Street by now, with modern shops fitted into the old buildings. What had once been part of the cathedral's monastery ran along our right-hand side. This road must have been a tight squeeze when everyone travelled by foot, horse or cart, and it was definitely not suited to cars.

'So, in general, how has your family...?'

15

For a second time, I couldn't work out how to ask what I was curious about. I'd read everything I could about swan maidens since I'd been introduced to Fin. Another dryad, one who knew her, had realised I needed help to deal with a creature from malevolent myth. The thing is, though, folk tales can help with killing monsters, but they're not a lot of use when it comes to the practicalities of modern life for people like us.

Once again, Fin could see what I wanted to know. 'It's not always been that complicated, certainly not in the so-called good old days. The girls would go off into service or find other work in Lynn or Peterborough, maybe head further afield once the railways arrived. A few years later, they'd come home with a baby or a toddler, along with a wedding ring and the sad tale of a hus-band who'd died of some sudden illness or who'd been a soldier or sailor lost far away in a war. The British Empire was never short of ways for people to die unexpectedly. Sometimes that was even true, and regardless, people just didn't ask many questions. Life did get trickier for my grandmother's generation, as bureaucracy and better record-keeping arrived, but when single-parent fam-ilies got more common things got easier again. These days, there are lots of options. One of my cousins used a sperm bank to have her two kids.'

She glanced at me as the High Street opened out into a market place at the top of what was undeniably an actual hill.

'If anything, it's always been harder for the boys, unless they could find a wife from one of the old Fen families with nereid or merfolk blood, who'd understand their twin nature. They tended to go off and make their way in the world alone, rather than risk fathering children who'd discover they could turn into birds when they hit puberty. Life's got easier for them though, these days. My cousin Will tells girlfriends there's a weird genetic disease in his family which he won't get but he doesn't want to pass on. No one ever asks him ques-tions after that.'

'Right.' As I'd read up on the relevant myths, I'd been surprised to find quite a few stories about men who could transform themselves. But most books are still more interested in the sexy swan maidens, and the stories of men being driven mad with desire for them. I knew Fin attracted more than her fair share of attention, whether she wanted it or not. That was something else we had in common. Dryads have been seducing mortal men for millennia, and thanks to my mother's blood, I would never go short of sex, if that's all I was looking for. I'd come to realise that cut both ways too. There's a world of difference be-tween a quick, fun fuck and making love.

Apart from that, I was glad that the only things I would pass on, if I ever even had children, would be a tendency to be well over six feet tall, the robust good health that means I'm hardly ever ill and every chance of living for close to a century. That's what my mother says, anyway. Along with the ability to see the supernatural, of course, as well as good night vision and a talent for mimicry that a jackdaw would envy. Okay, I'd pass on quite a few advantages. Not that I was at all sure I wanted kids.

We walked on down the hill past restaurants and shops and soon reached a substantial river. The Great Ouse, according to a sign. The waterside was clearly laid out for tourists, and it would be a nice place to come in the summer. For now, though, the firmly moored canal boats and cabin cruisers were shrouded with tarpaulins. Apart from a few dog walkers, we were the only people around. A small flock of Muscovy ducks waddled towards us, clearly hoping for food. When we didn't have anything for them, they wandered off, muttering among themselves. I wondered if Fin understood what they were saying, but decided not to ask.

I looked at the opaque green waters sliding past beneath the wide sky. 'You mentioned nereids. Have you ever met one?'

That was a creature I'd only encountered in books. The offspring of a river spirit and a mermaid or merman. Something to be wary of, I reckoned. While I didn't share my mum's deep-rooted mistrust of naiads, I knew exactly how ruthless freshwater spirits could be in pursuit of their own interests.

Fin shook her head. 'You?'

'Hardly. I grew up about as far away from the sea as it's possible to get in this country.' Added to that, we'd always spent the school holidays at home, so I'd never done the whole bucket and spade, sandcastles, paddling and collecting sea shells routine as a kid. Visiting the coast as an adult, I didn't feel I'd particularly missed out.

Fin gazed across the water towards a marina and a sprawl of boat sheds. Whatever lay beyond them on the flat, grassy land was hidden behind clusters of willows. 'My gran used to talk about one she met from time to time as a girl. They don't have as much to do with ordinary people since they can't transform themselves as completely as naiads. That makes it harder to blend in. Sea folk can't transform themselves at all, apparently. These days though, the only trace of mermaid or merman blood around here is when babies are born with a couple of fingers or toes webbed together. That's dealt with surgically easily enough, so no one thinks anything of it any more.'

'Right.' And if those children grew up to see supernatural creatures, I guessed most kept that to themselves, to avoid ending up in a mental ward. That's what Eleanor Beauchene had done, until the Blithehurst dryads who'd grafted themselves into her family tree a few centuries ago had enlisted me to help her deal with an unexpected menace to them all. I hadn't expected to get a permanent job out of that, but I wasn't about to complain.

Fin looked over at the sinking sun. 'Let's make a move. I'd rather get home ahead of the rush-hour traffic.'

We walked a bit further along the river and then cut back through a small ornamental garden that celebrated the history of the local eel industry along with the Queen's golden jubilee. Crossing the road on the far side, we followed the path that led us back uphill through a sizeable grassy park. With the trees bare of leaves, the views of the cathedral were stunning. There were enough medieval buildings left to make it pretty easy to imagine what this place must have looked like when the monks were in their heyday.

Fin paused by a bench and pointed at the cathedral's roofline. 'That's the Octagon there in the middle. Originally there was a central tower, but that came crashing down in thirteen-something-or-other. They realised the foundations weren't up to rebuilding it in stone, so the King's carpenter designed the lantern structure using wood instead. He used eight massive oak trees, apparently, with their trunks for the frame, and braced with beams slotted into the stonework.'

'I wonder if he had any help with that.' Specifically, I wondered if that skilled craftsman, whoever he had been, had shared the benefits of dryad blood when it came to working with wood. Knowing my mum's people would also have helped him find the trees he'd needed without getting on their wrong side. You really don't want to piss off a dryad.

That wasn't all I was wondering. Ahead on our left-hand side as the path cut through the park was what could only be a Norman castle mound. I remembered making a motte and bailey out of papier mâché and stirring sticks nicked from a coffee shop for a project when I was at school. Since then I'd learned things you won't find in any history books. According to the Blithehurst dryads, one reason that the Normans invaded was to drive out the wyrms and other malevolent creatures that flourished in England's medieval marshes. Those monsters had been protected by the Saxons, who used them to serve their own ends. These days, I look very differently at the fantastic coiling creatures in archaeological discoveries like the Staffordshire Hoard.

That was one reason the dryads had enlisted Fin to help me when I'd faced a shape-shifting lake monster in the Cotswolds. They knew she came from the Fens, where such things had once been found. Looking at the metal representation of a giant eel in those ornamental gardens back over the road had sent an unexpected shiver down my spine. It looked unpleasantly like the creature I had fought last summer, desperate to stop the bastard thing killing anyone else. I could certainly have used one of the barbed, three-pronged eel spears that made up one of the sculptures we'd passed by the river.

I turned to her and asked the question I'd been avoiding. 'Have you any idea why your mum has invited me to stay?'

18

Fin looked thoughtful. More than thoughtful. A crease appeared between her eyebrows. 'Honestly, no, I haven't. I wish I did.'

Chapter Two

Fin's little Toyota was in the same car park as the Land Rover. She told me to follow her, but handed me a printed map of our route in case we got separated. I soon realised that was a very good idea.

As the daylight faded, there was a lot more traffic than I expected. Modern farming may not use much labour, but these people were coming home from jobs somewhere, and there weren't that many main routes for them to use. There were also a fair few tractors out and about, some hauling trailers or heavy machinery that slowed up everyone at roundabouts and junctions. Add the HGVs coming or going to the agricultural processing plants we passed, and keeping sight of Fin's red car soon became a real challenge as other drivers kept slipping in between us.

There were fewer vehicles the further we got from Ely, but as the dusk deepened, the sky clouded over. I got more and more paranoid about knowing exactly where the edge of the road was. With so little roadside vegetation, there just wasn't the usual feedback from the Landy's headlights. I hadn't realised how much I take that for granted, driving at night. Lights from oncoming cars weren't necessarily any guide to the line of the road either. Without hedges to block my view, they could be on the far side of some field that the tarmac was swerving around and I'd never know it. The wet autumn meant that any little black-and-white posts with reflectors were dulled to uselessness by months of muddy spray from passing tyres.

I found myself driving quite a bit slower than usual. That didn't suit the locals used to tear-arsing along roads they could probably drive blindfold. That was all very well, but stupid bastards were coming in the other direction doing exactly the same. I had to brake hard a couple of times to let a gap open up between me and Fin for some prick who was desperate to overtake but hadn't realised there was another car ahead of my Land Rover. They pulled out without a clear view, confident they could make it before the oncoming lights arrived. When they realised their mistake, they just floored the accelerator instead of tucking back behind the Landy and waiting for a safer chance.

Thankfully Fin was paying attention in her rear-view mirror. The second time that happened, she found enough space to pull over and let the wanker in the Audi rush past to whatever was so important. I slowed and flashed my headlights to let her take the lead again.

As we went deeper into the countryside, the sky cleared. Moonlight silvered flooded fields where ditches and rivers had overflowed. The roads followed the wide banks that held back the rest of the waters. Glowing windows marked out isolated houses down in the farmland, and I was startled to realise just how far some of them were below the water level. We drove alongside a straight stretch of brimful river, and I could see any breach in these banks would drown buildings down on the other side of the road completely. I really hoped Fin's family didn't live somewhere like that. I couldn't turn into a swan, paddle out of a window and fly away if I woke up to find a flood filling my bedroom.

I had put the address into my satnav, but Fin was right to tell me not to trust it. More than once it tried to insist I turn off down a muddy track. A bit later we passed a sign saying the road I was supposed to take was closed by floods. That obviously happened often enough for the local authority to have pre-painted instructions ready to set up. I didn't try to read the directions, concentrating on following Fin.

Thankfully I soon saw a sign to the village where she lived. Saw Edge St Peter. Buildings appeared, strung along what I realised was one of those shallow ridges of higher ground. We passed a corrugated-iron barn with a yard of gleaming tractors and harrows secure behind a high wire fence with a padlocked gate and security lights. The farmhouse itself was a square Victorian building. The doors and windows were covered with metal plates, and a red-and-white sign warned trespassers that the property was alarmed. That looked a bit ominous, but the row of farmworkers' cottages that we passed next was being renovated. A patch of land between them and the next house was divided up with rectangles of brickwork and concrete. Footings for a handful of new builds were waiting for spring and the better weather for work to continue.

After a couple of light industrial units looking oddly out of place, we reached the village proper. Houses of pale brick showed lights behind curtained windows. Cars were parked along both sides of the road beneath well-spaced street lamps. There was enough space for a couple of side streets, and then a village green opened up ahead. Another road arrived from somewhere in the darkness to make a crossroads which must have been there for centuries. On this side I could see an ancient church to my left and an impressive Georgian house flanked by shadow-hung trees to the right. The church faced a pub called The Wheat Sheaf on the opposite corner of the crossroads. The big house overlooked a small convenience store and another shop with its windows shuttered.

Fin's Toyota braked in front of the church to let a Ford out of the pub car park. Then she went straight over the crossroads, past signs indicating a vehicle weight limit and telling me there was 'no through road'. I followed and noted the street name. Fen End. We were nearly there.

I was caught by surprise when we did arrive. A crescent of modern bungalows was tucked behind the pub, and 1930s semis had been built around the water tower opposite. Further on, where the tarmac gave way to a gravelled track, I wasn't expecting to find a long, low building of old russet brick with tall chimneys rising from a mossy slate roof. As Fin parked to get out and open the solid black wooden gates to the yard beside a line of outhouses, I saw the date carved into the stone slab set above the front door's lintel, lit by a modern lamp. So this was Venturer's House, and it had been built in 1657.

Fin came back to the Toyota, drove into the yard and stood there to beckon me in. I parked beside a mud-splashed VW. As soon as the Land Rover was through the gates, she walked around to shut and bolt them. So we weren't going in through the front.

The kitchen door opened and the light from inside showed me a bit of the patio between the house and a well-kept garden. The kitchen itself took up maybe a third of the building's length overall, with a dark window to the right showing me there was a utility room or something similar right at the end of the house.

I got my bag and followed Fin inside, careful to duck under the low door frame. I saw the kitchen ran the full depth of the house from front to back. Blinds were drawn over the windows overlooking the road we'd taken to get here. It was a sizeable room with an old, scuffed tiled floor, more than big enough for a six-foot table and chairs as well as fitted units on three sides. A vast inglenook fireplace took up the inner wall, where an Aga stood beside a modern cooker. I would have to watch my head on the exposed beams though.

Fin's mum stood by the table. She offered me her hand. 'Daniel. I'm Helen Wicken. I hope you had a reasonable journey?'

Given the family resemblance, there was no question that they were related. Where Fin's hair was pale blonde, Helen's was as white as, well, as a swan's wing. That didn't mean she was old. I wouldn't have put her at more than mid-fifties. She wasn't as tall as Fin, but she looked equally physically fit, in jeans and a purple sweater. Her accent struck me as more strongly local than Fin's, but not by much.

I shook her hand. 'Straightforward enough, thanks.'

I nearly said it was nice to see her again, but thought better of it. Helen knew who I was because she'd seen me fighting the shape-shifting lake monster. As far as I was concerned, she could have been any of the half-dozen swans who Fin had enlisted to help her when she'd agreed to lure the creature out of the water. I didn't think that counted as a proper hello.

Fin was filling the electric kettle at the sink beneath the back window. 'Tea or coffee, Dan?'

'Tea, please.'

'Seven o'clock all right for dinner?' Helen went to stir a cast-iron pot simmering on the cooker. 'I can hurry it up if you're hungry.'

'Seven's fine with me, thanks.' I looked at the clock on the chimney breast and was surprised to see it wasn't nearly as late as I thought. It had only taken us just over an hour to get here from Ely. The journey had felt a lot longer.

'Let me show you to your room then.' Helen headed for the plank door at the far end of the kitchen that led to the rest of the house.

As she lifted the black metal latch, I looked at Fin. She was busy with mugs and spoons. I picked up my bag and went after her mum. The door opened into a small hallway at the front of the house, where the main entrance was. From the boots and shoes piled up on the threshold, no one came or went out that way. Straight ahead, I could see a sitting room through a half-open door, and on my left, stairs headed up to the back of the house.

'Do mind your head,' Helen said with some concern as I followed her up.

She didn't just mean the sloping ceilings that showed how these upper rooms and windows had been fitted into the original house's roof space. A metal tie-beam cut across the landing at the top of the stairs. It was just the right height to smack into my forehead.

'I'll be careful.' And not just of the beams and ceilings. Subsidence hadn't only caused the need for a tie-beam to hold the back and front walls of the house together. The settling brickwork had shifted the joists underfoot and the boards sloped in all directions. I'm used to carrying marbles in my pocket when I'm laying floors, for a quick check that everything's level. If I dropped one here, it was anyone's guess which way it would roll.

Helen didn't seem to notice as she opened one of the doors to two rooms over the kitchen. 'Bathroom's in here. We're on a septic tank, but I guess you know about those?'

As I nodded, she pulled the light cord to give me a glimpse of the modern fittings before clicking it off and heading past me towards two rooms at the other end of the house, over whatever was beyond the sitting room. There were two more doors in between.

She opened the door to the end bedroom overlooking the back garden. 'I've put you in here. You should have everything you need. Let me know if I've forgotten anything.'

I heard a hint of tension in her voice. I wondered again why she'd asked me here. This wasn't the time for that conversation though.

'This looks fine, thanks.'

She smiled briefly. 'Come down when you're ready.'

I dumped my bag on the bed and looked around as she left. There was a small fireplace in the end wall that must be served by the same chimney breast as the room below. A vase of dried flowers in the grate made it clear that it was purely a decorative feature these days. That wouldn't be a problem, as a radiator under the window meant the room was comfortably warm. There was a double bed with folded towels at the foot, a narrow bookcase full of old and new paperbacks, a small wardrobe and a chest of drawers with a mirror. Everything I needed. More than I needed, to be honest. I didn't have this much furniture at home.

What there wasn't was any sign I'd be sharing that bed with Fin. I decided those arrangements were between her and her mother, and I'd just have to follow her lead. Never bringing girlfriends home cut both ways, I now realised. I'd never been taken home to meet anyone's parents. I didn't know the rules.

I did know I was thirsty. I dumped my bag on the small armchair by the radiator, went for a quick pee and headed back downstairs. As I came into the kitchen, I heard a car and saw lights in the yard. The back door opened and two women came in. More relatives. Mother and daughter, I guessed.

'My aunt Sylvia, and my cousin Laurel.' Fin handed me a mug of tea. 'This is Daniel Mackmain, as you've probably guessed.'

'Nice to see you again. Nice to meet you properly.' Sylvia grinned. 'Fin told us what happened after we left you by the lake, and we followed the court case in the papers.'

'Right.' I didn't know what else to say, so settled for a friendly smile.

'Good to know that's all over and done with. How's Blanche?' Laurel turned to Fin, who was getting more mugs out of a cupboard.

'She's fine. Sends her love.'

Fin shared an update on her sister's work and the Somerset river project generally. Laurel offered the latest news about other people who I guessed were relatives or friends. Sylvia accepted the change of subject with good grace, though it didn't stop her looking at me across the table with frank curiosity. I drank my tea and pretended to be interested in what Fin was saying, to avoid meeting her aunt's gaze.

I wondered if they had been invited to meet me, or if Sylvia had invited herself and Laurel had come along to keep an eye on her mother. I did notice the faint crease between Helen's eyebrows deepen as she added fish from the fridge to the pot of tomatoes and whatever else was simmering on the stove. Life without any relatives except my mum and dad really is much more simple.

We ate the fish casserole with rice and green beans. It was very tasty, with olives in it and herbs and garlic. Afterwards Laurel took her mother away before she could interrogate me any more about my work at Blithehurst. Over dinner, I kept expecting her to ask me about the dryads who live there, as a lead-in to asking about my mum. Every time I thought Sylvia was about to do that, Helen changed the subject. She asked me what I'd thought of Ely, and told me things about the cathedral's history. Apparently local rents had been paid in eels, by the thousand. She was looking tense again.

'That was great, thanks,' I said to her as Fin followed Laurel and Sylvia out to bolt the yard gates behind their car. 'Let me do the washing-up.'

'Most of it will go in the dishwasher.' She was already clearing the table. 'There are just the pans.'

I took those over to the sink and was filling the washing-up bowl with hot, soapy water when Fin came back in. Helen closed the loaded dishwasher and switched it on.

'I've got some work to finish, so if you'll excuse me.' She headed for the door to the stairs before I finished saying that was fine.

I looked at Fin. She shrugged.

'She'll tell us when she's ready.' But she was frowning now.

'What does she do, for work, I mean?' I rinsed the pan for the beans and put it on the draining board.

'Graphic designer, for a company in Peterborough. She goes into the office a couple of days a week. Shall I put the kettle on, or would you like a glass of wine?'

'I'm fine.' I scrubbed at the inside of the casserole pan where some sauce had stuck on the bottom. 'Do many of your family live around here?'

I glanced over my shoulder to see Fin sit down at the table. She shook off whatever was bothering her.

'Grandad died a couple of years ago, and yes, he knew what he was taking on and it didn't bother him. He was from an old Fen family and used to tell us all sorts of local folk stories, though I'm not sure half of them were true. Pubs round here used to hold contests to find the most entertaining liars. Gran lives in sheltered housing in King's Lynn now. She's still got her wits about her, thank heavens, but her arthritis is really bad, and her eyesight's going too, so she insisted. I think she missed Grandad too much to go on living here. Sylvia and Laurel are close enough to visit her most days. The rest of us are spread around, but not too far. Cambridge, Bury, Peterborough.'

'Apart from you and Blanche in Bristol.' I finished with the casserole and let the dirty water drain away.

'That's just the way things worked out. It's easy enough to keep in touch. One or other of us can always fly over to Slimbridge to catch up on the latest gossip.'

I looked around, startled. 'The wild fowl sanctuary?'

'Honestly, your face.' Fin grinned. 'You're too easy to tease. I'm kidding. We do have mobile phones and email. Though my aunt Stella, Will's mum, she has been known to stop by the winter feeding stations for the fenland bird life. If she's not happy with what's on offer, she rings up as an indignant birdwatcher.'

'Really?' I dried my hands.

'Really.' Fin came over and slid her hands around my waist. 'She got weighed and ringed in a survey once.'

I couldn't tell if she was teasing me again. That didn't matter. She tucked her head under my chin, rested against my chest and sighed. She sounded more content than concerned, for the moment at least.

I wrapped my arms around her and kissed her hair. 'Which one is your bedroom?'

'Next to the bathroom, but the floorboards creak.'

'I noticed that.' I can also take a hint, even if my cock had other ideas. I'd packed some condoms after all.

Fin laughed and pressed her hips against mine, before breaking free of our embrace. 'Maybe we can find a hotel for a night together when we head back. Once we know what's going on here.'

'That suits me.' And thinking about it, if we'd been in my childhood home, knowing that my dad was in a room across the landing wouldn't do much to put me in the mood for sex. 'How about that glass of wine?'

'Good idea, and there'll probably be something on the telly.'

We went through to the sitting room with two glasses and a two-thirds-full bottle of white out of the fridge. Fin opened the far door to show me a room with crammed bookcases from floor to ceiling on either side of another broad fireplace. That had once been big enough to heat the original hall of the house, before the space had been divided into two and the floor for bedrooms upstairs had been added. Now half of it housed an old-fashioned wood-burning stove and the rest was a cupboard where I heard a boiler firing up. There were two tall, old black oak cupboards as well as a couple of two-seater settees. A dusty gate-leg table underneath the window was piled high with all sorts.

'This was Grandad's lair. It comes in handy when everyone's home for some family gathering.'

'Where does your mum do her work?'

'She's turned the room next to yours into a studio.'

Fin closed the door and switched on the telly. I've no idea what channel it was on, but there was some programme halfway through where two idiots seemed to think customs officers were as stupid as they were, claiming a van load of cigarettes hidden in crates labelled something else entirely were for personal use. Fin seemed okay with watching it, so I was happy to go along with that.

She snuggled up beside me on the wide, sagging sofa. I was ready to put an arm around her, and maybe go a bit further than that, if she gave me some encouragement. Then those creaky floorboards warned me that Helen was coming downstairs. We heard her go into the kitchen and fill the kettle.

Fin swung her feet down to the faded rug that softened the herring-bone brick floor that must have been laid when the house was built. She leaned forward to top up our wine glasses on the blanket chest that served as a coffee table. 'Do you ever get any hassle, going through passport control?'

I shrugged. 'It's never come up.'

'You've never been abroad.' She halted mid-pour and looked around, surprised. 'Seriously?'

I shrugged again, but couldn't think what to say. It wasn't as if I'd ever had anyone to go with. Not really. A previous girlfriend had suggested a trip to Ibiza or Ayia Napa, but that really hadn't appealed.

Fin smiled, though she still looked as if she'd learned something unexpected and wasn't quite sure about it. 'Maybe we should think about a trip.' She nodded at the telly, where yet another advert was trying to persuade viewers to book their summer holidays in an airline's January sale.

'Maybe,' I agreed readily enough. I didn't think she'd suggest beaches and clubbing.

We watched the rest of the programme, and then one following traffic cops dealing with halfwits on motorways. When the announcer promised us a night shift in a hospital, Fin grimaced.

'I do think "fly on the wall" is an unfortunate turn of phrase for medical programmes. Not very hygienic.' She finished her wine and stood up. 'I should get you the Wi-Fi password. Then I think I'll have an early night.'

'Fair enough. I'll just use the bathroom.'

At least I got a long, lingering kiss when Fin knocked on my door and brought me a Post-it with the Wi-Fi code neatly written down. Her smile as she pulled away promised me more when the time was right. I could wait.

I woke up early. I always do after the first night in an unfamiliar place. I went along the landing as quietly as I could to the bathroom. Not going to lie, I was tempted to try slipping into Fin's bedroom, but her door was closed and the black metal latch would rattle. I settled for showering as quickly and quietly as I could, got dressed and went downstairs.

As I filled the kettle, I noticed the cold tap was dribbling. I'd seen that last night when I did the washing-up. I found the back door key on a hook and went out to the Land Rover. I don't keep all my tools in the back any more, now that I have a proper workshop at Blithehurst, but I still carry the essentials. A couple of hammers, screwdrivers – flat-head and Phillips – along with some adjustable wrenches and a set of Allen keys. You never know what you might need.

Those were in an old toolbox my dad had given me years ago, and there were all sorts of odds and sods in the top tray. I sorted through screws, nails, fuses and wall plugs and found I had remembered right. There were a couple of tap washers. Better still, one was the size I needed.

I found the stopcock under the sink. Shutting off the water, I got to work quickly, before anyone needed the taps upstairs. I was just putting everything back together when I heard someone coming downstairs. I expected it to be Fin, but Helen appeared.

All of a sudden, I felt awkward as I finished up and turned the water back on. I didn't want her to think I assumed she couldn't take care of things like that. 'Sorry, I should have asked. It's just that I noticed the tap—'

'Needed fixing.' Helen gave me an unfathomable look. 'So you fixed it. And before you made yourself anything to drink,' she observed as she walked over to find I'd filled the kettle but not switched it on. 'Tea or coffee?'

'Tea, please.' I put my tools away and stood the box against the wall beside the back door where no one could trip over it.

Helen put a couple of tea bags into a pot and then spooned coffee into a cafetière. 'You like to fix things. You like to help.'

Those weren't questions, but I answered her anyway. 'If I can.'

She waited for the kettle to boil, looking thoughtful, not looking at me. She made the coffee and the tea and brought them both over to the table. I took a seat as she fetched milk from the fridge and mugs from the dishwasher. She sat in the chair across the table and filled a mug for us both.

'Do you have hobs where you live?'

I didn't think she was talking about kitchen appliances, but I wasn't sure of much beyond that. 'By which you mean...?'

'Brownies, pixies, they have a lot of different names. Earth spirits inclined to take a fancy to human hearths and homes.' She took a sip of coffee. 'Around here they call themselves hobs.'

'I know what you mean,' I said cautiously, 'but I've never met one.'

'There have always been a few around here, and we've always been on good terms, but something's wrong.' Helen looked up as the door to the stairs opened and Fin came in. 'It's the hobs. They're really not happy.'

I wanted to ask how she knew, but that didn't seem polite.

'What's the problem?' Fin fetched a mug and poured herself some coffee.

'I've no idea,' Helen said, exasperated. 'I've seen them in the garden a couple of times, but they won't come close enough to talk to, let alone ask. If I walk towards them, they vanish. I don't want to press any harder and end up on their wrong side.'

Fin nodded with ready agreement, and I wouldn't argue. I remembered enough folk tales that suggested that would be a bad idea.

'Now the sylphs have vanished. Air spirits,' Helen explained, seeing I wasn't sure. 'Inclined to play silly games but harmless enough. I haven't seen one since before Christmas, and they usually love the decorations and the lights.'

'They're quite sweet, really.' Fin looked concerned. 'There's no reason you can think of?'

'None.' Helen looked at me.

I wished I could work out what she wanted. 'You think they'll talk to me?'

She smiled and looked more like Fin than ever. 'I was wondering if the Green Man could shed some light on whatever's going on. We've never had anything to do with him, but he's helped you out before now, hasn't he?'

I rubbed the back of my neck. 'It's more that he lets me know when there's a problem. He makes it clear he expects me to sort it out. He turns up when he wants to. I have no say in that.'

'Have you ever tried to ask him something?' Fin wanted to know.

'Not as such, not beyond just trying to get his attention. I'm not sure how I'd go about doing that around here, so far from old woodland.' I didn't want to sound unhelpful, but I didn't want to raise their hopes either.

'There's a Green Man on one of the pillars in St Peter's.' Fin looked at me, expectant.

So she'd remembered what I'd told her about glimpsing his presence in carvings at Blithehurst.

'I could show you,' she persisted.

'It couldn't hurt. I can't promise anything though.' I couldn't see what else to say.

Fin stood up.

'After breakfast,' Helen said firmly. 'Dan, can I interest you in beans on toast with an egg?'

'Absolutely.' That much at least was simple.

Chapter Three

We walked up to the village, leaving through a side gate rather than un-bolting the main ones. It wasn't far and the day was bright and clear. That meant it was cold enough for ice in the puddles, and there was a steady wind that I guessed was coming off the sea. I wasn't bothered, as I'd stuck my big coat in the back of the Landy just in case, and we both had gloves and hats.

When we reached the crossroads, Fin surprised me by turning towards the pub. It looked like a place worth visiting, well maintained and with a painted board listing recent awards for its food and beer. We walked through the car park to the back and found an open glass-panelled door leading to the bar.

Fin stood on the threshold and shouted, 'Neil!'

'Come on in!' a friendly voice invited. Now that was definitely a local accent.

Inside, a middle-aged, heavy-set man was wiping down tables and setting out beer mats. The dark wooden furniture was solid and well made and the floor was oak boards rather than carpet. It wasn't gloomy though. Colourful, old-fashioned prints were framed on the white-painted walls, and the wide windows let in plenty of light. I assessed the risks of banging my head on the low exposed beams. The garlands of dried flowers strung along them might soften the blow a bit, I supposed.

'Morning!' A woman around the same age was unplugging a hoover. She waved at Fin before carrying it away through a broad archway where an internal wall had been knocked through. We soon heard her switch it on.

'Who's this then?' The publican was shorter than both of us. He looked up at me with a cheerful smile. 'Brought Tom Hickathrift back to see us, have you?'

I had no idea who that was, but he clearly didn't mean any offence, so I smiled back. 'Dan Mackmain.'

'Neil Morrison. Pleasure.' He nodded rather than put down his spray bottle and cloth to offer a damp hand.

'Dan's here for a few days,' Fin said briskly. 'I thought I'd show him the church.'

'It'll be open.' From Neil's tone, that wasn't usual. 'Tom Kelly called for the key first thing.'

Fin looked surprised, and not in a good way. 'Tom? Not Mike?'

'Doctor Thomas Kelly,' Neil confirmed, before he glanced at me. 'And he'll thank you to remember that.'

'He must have set off early from Cambridge,' Fin observed. 'Keen to beat the traffic, I suppose.'

'No, he's staying here, in the house. Turned up one day at the end of October, demanding the keys.'

I heard an echo of irritation in the publican's voice. Whoever this Doctor Kelly was, he didn't seem very popular.

'In the middle of the term?' Fin was puzzled.

'On some sort of sabbatical, apparently.' Neil shrugged. 'I said I'd have to check with Mike, in case there were any bookings I didn't know about. It's a quiet time of year, but people looking for a big family get-together over Christmas have rented it before now. Tom didn't like that at all. Said he'd ring Mike himself. Took his phone out into the car park and it looked as if they were having an almighty row. But Mike rang me a few minutes later and told me it was fine. He didn't sound any too pleased, but it's none of my business. So I handed over the keys, and Doctor Tom's been there ever since. Goes out and about most days. Comes over here a couple of times a week, to eat and complain about the food or the beer or something else.'

That was clearly water off the proverbial duck's back as far as the publican was concerned.

'Do you two want a coffee?' he asked Fin. 'Wait for him to bring the key back?'

She hesitated, but shook her head. 'There's no telling how long he might be. We'll just ignore him.'

Given why we were going to the church, that might be easier said than done, but I trusted Fin to know what she was doing.

'See you later then.' Neil nodded at me, amiable. 'It's curry night tonight, if you're interested, and steak night tomorrow. As well as the usual menu.'

'Good to know,' I said, politely non-committal.

'Thanks.' Fin smiled.

He went back to his cleaning and we went out to the car park.

'So?' I asked as we headed for the road and waited for a tractor to rumble past, pulling a trailer loaded with what looked like giant mutant parsnips.

'Sugar beet.' Fin must have seen me looking curious. She waved at the substantial Georgian building overlooking the green. 'Talbot House. That's what we were talking about.'

If I hadn't known someone was living there, I'd have thought it was locked up and secured for the winter. I could see the long, white-painted shutters were closed inside all the windows, from the ground floor to the servants' rooms in the cellars.

'Where the Kellys live?'

She nodded. 'Kelley with a second "e", and Doctor Thomas will thank you not to forget that either.' Once she was satisfied a car wasn't going to come speeding up the rise, Fin crossed the road.

I followed. 'So he's some sort of academic?'

'Historian, I think, at one of the Cambridge colleges.' She glanced across at the shuttered house as we walked towards the church. 'The family have lived here for donkey's years, and used to own a lot of land. My grandad used to talk about "Mr Kelley the squire" when he was telling stories about fenland life when his parents were children, so that would have been before the First World War probably. Tom always thought he was too good for the village kids, my mum says, when they were growing up. Mike and Angela, the sister, were friendly enough, but they went off to boarding school, so they were only ever around in the summer.'

She pushed open the gate to the churchyard. 'The three of them inherited the house about twelve or thirteen years ago and everyone expected it would be sold. Or at least, it might have been, if the property market hadn't crashed. Mike and his family came up for holidays from London for a few years, but I think Angela lives in Scotland. Mum would know. Mostly, they rent it out for holiday lets. Neil looks after the keys and his wife Kate does the cleaning on changeover days. They do that for quite a few of the rental properties in the village, for families who've moved away, as well as the ones they own them-selves.'

'Are there a lot of rentals and second homes around here?' We reached the church's south door and I saw the notice in the porch inviting visitors to collect the key from Neil. He was a busy man. I also saw I'd misheard his surname. It was Moryinson, not Morrison. I bet he got a lot of misspelled letters in the post. I have enough trouble with Mackmain.

Fin opened the inner door. 'Quite a few. You wouldn't recognise the place in the summer with all the people here. It's better than seeing the properties left to rot though. This area always used to be too far out for people working in the bigger towns, so when houses came up for sale no one was really interested. That's changing though. London commuters are forcing up rents and prices in Cambridge and anywhere else on a railway line. So now the people who work there can't afford to live there, and they're moving further out, which means people who were born in the villages need to find somewhere cheaper, and the knock-on effect spreads wider.'

She lowered her voice as we went into the church, though there was no one in there that I could see. It was lighter inside than I expected, with a pleasantly airy feel. Plain windows let the sunlight flood in as the only stained glass was behind the altar. That stood in front of a fancy piece of panelling with a whole lot of gilded and painted figures that I guessed were saints. There were choir stalls and shallow steps down to the solid wooden pews on a floor patterned with red, black and yellow tiles. The font in front of us looked older than anything else in here, octagonal with little figures in carved niches worn into blurred anonymity. The tables by the end wall, holding hymn books, leaflets and other church stuff, could have come from any office furniture store last week.

I looked expectantly at Fin. She grinned and pointed to the carvings where the sturdy round pillars met the smooth, shallow arches that separated the main bit of the church with the pews from the sides with rows of rush-seated chairs below memorial plaques.

A band of leaves and fronds ringed the top of each pillar, with a small figure in the midst of each one, on the side facing the altar. Whoever these centuries-dead stone masons had been, they'd had a sense of humour as well as impressive skills. The closest was a little man twisted and grimacing with his hands raised above his shoulders so it looked as if he was holding the whole church roof up. The next one had his arms wrapped around an enormous fish in a net. They were both gasping and goggle-eyed. Next was a man, or maybe a woman, cutting wheat with a sickle, bending over with one hand pressed to the small of their back. There were five pillars on each side. We worked our way along towards the choir stalls. I saw a man in a pointed hat playing a tune on some sort of flute. On the last pillar, looking straight at the altar, I saw a Green Man.

These carvings come in a few different styles. I've been told I can be really boring about them, especially after a few drinks. Some people think it's a weird thing to be interested in. I can't exactly explain I've been catching glimpses of whatever ancient, powerful spirit these figures represent ever since I was a kid.

Back then he was mostly watching over me, warning me away from trouble or showing me some injured animal so I could fetch my dad. As I grew older, the Green Man turned up in my dreams, though not often. Usually when I needed to get my head out of my arse and make some decision I was trying to avoid. Recently, as I'd explained to Fin's mum, he seemed to expect me to sort out problems. Problems that needed someone able to see things that other people couldn't, and who could find a solution that the modern world would accept.

I looked up at the carving. This wasn't one of those creepy ones with leafy fronds growing out of its mouth, or worse, its eye sockets as well. This was a cheerful face, framed by what looked like hawthorn leaves at first glance, and like tousled hair when I looked again. There was more to it than just the face, which was unusual. This figure was carved down to its waist, wearing the same sort of pleated coat-type thing as the other people on the pillars. Its arms were raised and it was pulling its mouth wide with its fingers, sticking its tongue out at the altar. Somehow, I didn't think whoever had carved it had been the most devout church-goer.

I laughed. I couldn't help it. What I couldn't see, though, was any hint of eerie emerald light in its eyes. That's what tells me when the Green Man is looking back. Before I could say anything to Fin, a voice rang through the church.

'Excuse me.'

There are so many ways to say those two words. The man coming towards us from the far side of the church might just as well have shouted 'Oy, you!'

He was an inch or so under six feet, with long, wavy brown hair swept back off his face. He must have used some sort of gel or spray to hold it so firmly in place. He also had a goatee beard and moustache that must have needed stupid amounts of time to keep shaved so precisely. With his tweed jacket, checked shirt and corduroy trousers, he looked like someone out of a Sunday night telly drama set in the 1950s. The sort of tosser who gets murdered because nobody can stand him. So this was Doctor Thomas Kelley. There was no doubt about that.

'I don't know what you find so amusing, but this is a house of worship,' he said severely.

Whatever he was doing in here, he wasn't saying prayers. He held a black notebook open in one hand and a fancy fountain pen in the other.

'We didn't mean to disturb you,' Fin said, more politely than I would have done.

He came closer, putting his notebook and pen away inside his jacket. 'You're one of those Wicken girls, aren't you, from Fen End?'

Fin didn't like his disdainful tone any more than I did. 'I am.' Her gaze challenged him to make something of it.

He was more than ready to do it. 'You do realise your family have no moral right to Venturer's House? Or any of the property that goes with it?'

'Excuse me.' Fin's answer was easily understandable. Fuck you.

She turned away and took a pace, heading back down the church. He didn't like that. Outraged, he stepped forward and reached out to grab her arm.

I got in his way, and I made sure I stepped close enough to force him backwards. I try not to loom over people, but I can do it when I want to. I was also wearing the padded coat I'd picked up half-price in a skiing gear shop that makes me look even bigger. On the other hand, Fin and her family had to live here. I grew up in the countryside and know that keeping things civil is generally best.

I smiled, friendly enough. 'You live in that house across the green? Has anyone looked at those Leylandii lately?'

'Excuse me?' He had no idea what I was talking about.

'Those big fir trees along the side, between the house and the main road.' When I was driving across to Ely I'd seen a whole lot of the damn things out in the farmland, planted as windbreaks around exposed houses. That's all very well, but it was obvious that far too many had been left untended to grow dangerously tall. 'You really should get them cut back.'

Give the arsehole his due, he recovered his snotty attitude fast. 'You're offering to do that for me, are you?' he sneered. 'For twice the price anyone else would charge? When they'd probably say it wasn't even necessary.'

'I'm not in that line of work.' Perhaps that wasn't strictly speaking true any more. Eleanor Beauchene and I had been discussing setting up a Christmas tree plantation at Blithehurst, if we could get the dryads to agree. That's why I'd been reading up on evergreens.

I shrugged. 'Do what you like. Just bear in mind Leylandii have shallow roots and the ground's saturated this winter. If a storm brings a couple of them down, it'll be a lot more expensive mending your roof than getting a tree surgeon in now. Or you'll be dealing with the consequences if they block the road and cause an accident.'

'I hardly think that's likely.' He just couldn't help himself. He had to know better than anyone else, even when he knew sod all about a subject.

I shrugged again, and walked away to join Fin. She was waiting about halfway to the door.

'Did I tell you this church used to have a spire?' She tucked her arm through mine as we walked away. 'Until a storm brought it down in the 1700s.'

'I bet that brought down a good few trees as well,' I remarked.

'I think it did,' Fin agreed. 'They settled for rebuilding the tower and left it at that.'

We had our backs to Thomas Kelley, but we both spoke loudly enough to be sure that he heard. We didn't say anything else until we were outside in the churchyard again.

'No sign of our friend,' I said quietly. 'Sorry.'

'It was worth a try.' Fin looked at the house across the green. 'Just how dangerous are those trees?'

'Hard to say, but they definitely should be looked at.'

She glanced at me. 'Leylandii are an introduced species, aren't they? What do dryads make of them?'

'They dislike them, though not because they're new. Leylandii are a hybrid that would never happen in the wild, and the dryads seem to find that incredibly irritating.' That had come up when I was trying to persuade the Blithehurst dryads that growing Christmas trees was in everyone's interests. The manor house was a business that had to turn a profit, or they'd find themselves dealing with the National Trust sooner or later.

We crossed the road and headed down Fen End. Fin was looking thoughtful. 'I'll talk to Mum. If she mentions those trees to Kate, Neil can suggest getting someone in to Mike, and no one can say we're interfering.'

'So what's the stick up Tom Kelley's arse? What did he mean about your family and the house?' I wondered if he was making some sort of trouble, and if that was upsetting the hobs. If so, I couldn't see what I could do about it.

Fin stuck her hands in her pockets as we walked past the bungalows. 'Venturer is short for "Adventurer". They were the investors who set out to get rich when the draining of the fens really took off, after the English Civil War. Deals were done where the people who put the money in got grants of reclaimed land in return. The more money they put in, the more land they got. Once it was drained, fenland was prime farmland, and owning it brought in good rents. Some investors were London consortiums who just sat back and counted the cash. Others were locals like the Kelleys, who put together a scheme with a couple of other landowners around here. They built the house for the Dutchman they employed to do a survey, and to work out where the drains and sluices needed to go. Things didn't necessarily go to plan, not here anyway.' She chuckled.

'What's so funny?'

'Well, as you can imagine, the drainage schemes weren't popular with everyone. A lot of the Fen families reckoned they were happy enough with things as they were. They could make a living from fishing and fowling and cutting sedge and reed for sale. They lost rights that had been agreed and managed for centuries, and getting some of the drained land back as commons for grazing their own animals wasn't seen as a fair deal. There were protests, even riots from time to time. Dykes were blocked and banks were breached. Sluices and flood gates were smashed by gangs called fen tigers. Around here, Grandad said his grandad always swore that the hobs caused a lot of the mischief. They didn't want outsiders coming in.'

She shook her head as we walked past the water tower. 'Anyway, the Kelleys still made a fair amount of money, even if they never managed to drain the fen on their own doorstep. They built themselves that grand house on the green, and Venturer's House became the place where widows lived, or spare sons who didn't go into the church or the army. By the time the Crimean War came along, Eustace Kelley was living there. He studied botany at Cambridge, and then he settled here to be a gentleman naturalist, making lists of insects, birds and flowers in the fen, the dates the swans migrated, that sort of thing. A few years later, he met my great-great-great...'

She broke off and started counting on her fingers, before waving that away. 'I can never remember how many "greats" there should be. Let's just call her Great Aunt Dorothy, who was a respectable widow with a son and a daughter whose husband had died at Sevastopol. She came to keep house for her brother-in-law, who was the schoolmaster here. She seems to have done some illustrations for Eustace Kelley, drawing his specimens for a book. Anyway, they married not long after, and he adopted her children.'

'One thing led to another,' I observed.

'Hardly.' Fin smiled. 'He also wrote endless epic poems about Achilles and Patroclus, or heroes like Roland and Oliver. They're really not very good, and the subtext is pretty clear. There's an awful lot about manly breasts glistening with sweat and sun-bronzed corded thews.'

'He was gay?'

'We're pretty sure, not that anyone would ever say it, not back then. There's no way to know whether or not he ever did anything about it, which is a bit sad. Still, no one thought anything of wives and husbands having separate rooms in those days, so his secret was safe with Dorothy, and there's no reason to think he ever even knew hers. By all accounts they got on very well. When he died, he left the house to her children, along with the land that included the undrained fen, stipulating it should be preserved in perpetuity for the study of natural science.'

'Nice,' I commented.

'Useful,' Fin said as we reached the end of the tarmac where the road turned to gravel. 'It's been kept in the family ever since, come hell or high water, to give us a private place to learn how to cope with being who we are.'

'Very useful,' I agreed. Life as a dryad's son had its complications, but those hadn't included having to learn how to fly. 'But Tom Kelley objects?'

'Eustace's brothers objected at the time, but whatever else he might have been, Eustace wasn't stupid. His will was water-tight, along with some sort of trust for the fen that Cambridge University still has an interest in. We get students up here doing all sorts of projects. It's what got me interested in ecology.'

Fin paused outside the black yard gates. She looked around with that crease appearing between her eyebrows again. 'Do you want to see the fen? If there are any sylphs still around, that's where we'll find them.'

'Okay.' I didn't have any better ideas. It didn't look as if the Green Man was going to help us find out what was bothering the spirits who called this place home.

We carried on walking, and the differences on either side of the track soon became obvious. Down on our left, a farmer's field held grazing ewes round-bellied with imminent lambs. A ditch carried surplus water away, and temporary fencing stopped the sheep drowning themselves. If there's a way for a sheep to kill itself to cause maximum inconvenience, it will surely find it. On our right, a grassy meadow ran down to a mass of pale, dry, feathery grasses. These were substantial plants, taller than me as far as I could judge from here. The ceaseless wind set them whispering and rustling against each other. It would be easy to imagine voices on the edge of hearing. There wasn't a man-made sound to be heard. I found it a little eerie, and felt very exposed up here on the track.

'So this is all untouched, is it?'

Fin shook her head with a smile. 'Hardly. Left to its own devices, this would end up as woodland.' She waved a hand at the giant grasses as we walked along. 'Sedge moves in after reed beds have slowed a river down. The sedge gets thicker and the dead growth accumulates each year. That lowers the water level and the leaf litter rots down so other plants can start growing and setting seed. They help dry out the ground even more. Of course, it would still flood in the winter – that's what makes this a fen as opposed to marsh or a bog – but it's not long before trees that can stand wet feet get established, alder and the like. Once they've dried things out even more, the bigger trees move in.'

I wondered if this was somehow at the root of the antagonism between the woodland spirits like dryads and the naiads who claimed rivers and lakes for their own.

'So when Eustace said this should be preserved, how does that work?'

'We cut the reed every year, and the sedge every four years. That keeps things in check. This has been a managed landscape for thousands of years.' She paused to point at a broad, grassy path heading away between the waving sedge fronds. 'That's a drove, and it leads to a lode, which is a waterway cut to carry the sedge and reed, and whatever else used to be fished for and hunted here, out to the river. The Romans started digging those, and building the first banks to hold back the water, most likely. They weren't the first people to settle here though.'

She turned and gestured towards a clump of scrubby trees at the far end of the gravelly track. 'There's a small hillfort down there, from the Iron Age.'

'Hillfort?' I looked at her, surprised. 'Doesn't that need, you know, to be on a hill?'

She grinned. 'Around here that means anywhere high enough to stay dry in the winter.'

'Let's take a look then.' I couldn't see any oak trees, but the copse was the closest thing I could see to a wood around here.

Chapter Four

As we walked along the track, we left the village behind. The hillfort – and calling it that still sounded ridiculous to me – stood at the far end of a narrowing spur of higher ground that must have stretched out into the waters when the fen was flooded in winters gone by. There was a low bank surrounding the level ground that the trees had claimed. Beyond that, farmland on three sides showed the limits of Eustace Kelley's bequest. A series of water-filled pits scarred the tussocky land between the spindly birch and blackthorn trees and the waving sedge.

'Clay was dug out here, for those yellow bricks that built most of the village.' Fin stopped four or five metres short of the trees. 'There used to be kilns and workers' cottages where the water tower is now. Between that and gravel being taken out by local farmers, it was hard to say where the fort's outer earthworks ran. A group of archaeology students came out here a few years ago and worked out where the original ditches had been, using geophysics and stuff. They did some work to restore the rampart that had survived and dug some trenches. They didn't find much of anything, but Mum said they decided this site was most likely last used in pre-Roman days. She said the sylphs were fascinated. We could usually find them watching what was going on.'

She surprised us both with a brief laugh. 'I remember I was out here last summer, and there was a couple with cameras, tripods, special lenses, all the kit. There's a public footpath runs as far as here before it cuts back across the fields to the village, so we often get birdwatchers and hikers. Anyway, this bloke had his heart set on photographing some particular flower. Every time he was ready to take his shot, one of the sylphs blew on it, moving it just enough to stop him. Just for fun, I think. Maybe to see how long he'd persevere.'

'Who won?'

'The sylph got bored first, if that counts.' She looked around. That crease reappeared between her eyebrows. 'It really is odd, not to see any sign of them at all. I mean, they're not always interested in talking, but they let you know that by turning up and vanishing as soon as they know they've got your attention.'

She began walking towards the trees. 'We used to play out here when we were kids. After we'd learned about Boudica at school...'

Something rolled under my foot, throwing me off balance. I looked down as I stumbled, and saw a dark lump of flint with a scalloped edge. Curious, I bent and picked it up. As I turned it, I realised how neatly it fitted into my hand. All at once, I saw this was a knife. It was a tool made by a craftsman, for someone like me, for ordinary, everyday use.

Then a whole lot of things happened at once. The sky darkened, or maybe my sight dimmed. Either way, I was surrounded by shadowy people wrapped in shapeless cloaks and tunics. They were driving mottled, leggy sheep towards the hillfort where I could see three rings of earthworks now. The outer ditches were flooded, making them harder to cross. A solid wooden palisade ran around the innermost bank and tall, reinforced gates defended the entrance. Since they were standing open, I could see over the hurrying crowd's heads into the fort. Sizeable round houses with mud-coloured walls had conical roofs that were thatched with what I guessed must be reeds from the wetlands on all sides.

As soon as I registered what I was seeing, and wondered where they could have got that much timber, everything changed. The track was full of men, women and even children, dragging heavy baskets and wrestling handcarts. They were wearing clothes like the carved figures in the church, and there was a strong smell of fish. My ears told me I should understand what they were shouting, but my brain made no sense of the words at all.

Everything changed again. A shot rang out, not close by. It was a deeper, more menacing sound somehow than a shotgun fired at pheasants. Over on the far side of the fen, immense flocks of waterfowl soared into the air. I couldn't tell one species from another; there were too many of them. Black against the clouds that were dappling the dawn sky, the birds clamoured with alarm and distress. More shots rang out. A dog barked and another answered it eagerly. Someone, somewhere, laughed.

Once, when I was a kid, I did have a cold, or maybe flu, that was bad enough for Dad to take me to the doctor. What convinced us both I needed to see her was the fact I couldn't stand up without getting so dizzy I started retching. Labyrinthitis, the doctor called it, and I had to stay in bed for a week till it went away. This felt the same, though thankfully without the heaving.

I found myself on my hands and knees on the stony ground, squinting and blinking, trying not to shake my head. I wondered where Fin had got to. Had she been caught up in the same thing as me? Could she tell me what had happened? Now the first shock was receding, I realised this felt a little like being swept along by a dryad's power, or a naiad's. Like it, but far more brutal.

Looking up, I found myself face to face with a squatting figure. It was startlingly ugly, with misshapen features that reminded me of one of those bog bodies that turn up in peat. Its skin was about the same colour, tanned dark brown, and so were its ragged trousers and a coat that looked like one of the carvings in the church. It was hard to tell where its skin ended and clothing began, and there seemed to be twigs in its matted black hair. Its feet were bare, with crooked toes and yellowed nails that looked more like claws. Its fingernails looked like talons as its cupped hands reached for my face.

42

I would have recoiled, but in that same instant, I met its gaze. That was a mistake. I couldn't move. All I could do was stare helplessly at the creature. Its eyes were vivid gold, without pupil or iris. You might think that would make it hard to work out where a supernatural creature is looking. You'd be wrong. It was looking straight at me, and that gaze was merciless, as its thin lips curved in a satisfied smile. Not a friendly smile, by any stretch of the imagination. Its uneven teeth looked scarily sharp and its tongue was a deep, disconcerting red.

Its grin widened as it withdrew its hands. Now it raised a swollen-knuckled finger to its lips. Its meaning was clear. Hush. Don't say a word. It was equally clear this wasn't a game. This was a warning. If I spoke out, there would be consequences. Those blazing eyes conveyed that message loud and clear, unblinking.

'... an Iceni camp.' Fin's voice sounded an unimaginable distance away.

The creature vanished.

All this had happened in less time than Fin took to finish her sentence. The sun was bright and the air was clear and cold. I could hear birds singing, and further away, those pregnant ewes were bleating. I could feel stones under my gloved hands, and more painfully, under the knees of my jeans.

'Dan, are you okay?'

'Yes, fine.' I forced the words out as I got to my feet. I'm a lousy liar. That's something else that goes with dryad blood. They don't lie, and they can always hear a falsehood. But that doesn't mean always telling the whole truth, and that was something the Blithehurst dryads excelled at. I was trying to get better at doing it myself. 'I tripped on a loose stone.'

I looked for the flint knife, but that had gone. I shouldn't have been surprised. I clapped my hands to knock the mud off my gloves and resisted the temptation to brush my knees. That would only smear the mud. Let it dry and it would sponge off easily enough.

'I'm fine. It just caught me by surprise. I should have been looking where I was going.' I hoped Fin would put anything odd in my voice down to embarrassment. I certainly felt stupid, to be caught like that. I started walking towards her.

'Let's look at this fort then.'

'Okay.'

Fin seemed perfectly happy, so I breathed more easily.

To be honest, there wasn't much to see. The birch and thorn trees had claimed most of the ground surrounded by the low earthen bank that had somehow survived through the centuries. There was nothing to show where the ditches and other earthworks had been outside that. I reckoned you'd need an archaeologist's latest hi-tech gear to tell what this place had once been. Either that, or have a hob show you what it had looked like a couple of thousand years ago. I wouldn't recommend that. My heart was still racing.

Fin was looking around, her concern warring with exasperation. 'Where have they got to?'

She wasn't asking me. I looked around in case a hob decided to answer her. There was nothing else that creature could have been. Nothing appeared. I wasn't sure if I should be relieved, or apprehensive that it seemed more interested in me.

Fin sighed as we circled the mound without seeing anything but a fieldfare plucking a few late berries from a sturdy creeper on a low bush. Translucent, they shone vivid red in the sunlight.

'Let's get back.'

Once we arrived at the house, we both took off our boots. Fin went through to the hall to shout up the stairs to her mum.

'We're back! Kettle's on!'

I took the hint and filled it at the sink. When I turned round after putting it on its base and hitting the switch, I realised Fin was looking at my socks.

'I should have told you to bring some slippers.' She was wearing a sheepskin pair that must have been out by the front door. They would definitely be proof against the chill of these tiles and those old brick floors.

I grinned. 'Don't have any. They're not easy to find in a size fourteen.'

Helen appeared through the door from the stairs, and looked from Fin to me. 'How did you get on?'

I thrust away an unbidden memory of the hob confronting me. I chose my words carefully in case something unseen was listening. 'That's an unusual Green Man carving in your church. I haven't seen one like it anywhere else. I'm afraid I didn't see any sign of his presence though. Still, maybe he'll realise we were looking for him. That's happened before now.'

'Thomas Kelley was in the church.' Fin was scowling as she got a cafetière out of a cupboard. 'Did you know he was staying in the big house?'

'Kate told me.' Taking a seat at the table, Helen seemed surprised that Fin thought it was worth mentioning. 'He's writing some sort of family history, I think she said. I suppose he was looking at the family tombs.'

'He told me we have no moral right to this house.' Fin was sarcastic as well as annoyed. She looked at me. 'Tea, Dan?'

'Coffee's fine, thanks.' I sat opposite Helen. 'Is he generally so obnoxious or is this something new?'

She was still looking surprised. 'He's never been the easiest man to get on with. I'm sure you've met the type. Things are never going his way, even when he's got nothing to complain about, not really, not compared to some. Not compared to a lot of people these days. And of course, that's always because someone else has done him down, or they were handed a favour they didn't deserve.'

She frowned as she obviously remembered something. 'He had a go at Stella, when we were teenagers. He'd been pestering her to go out with him one summer, but she wasn't interested. Everyone could see he was just after his first shag. She called him a whiny loser when he wouldn't take no for an answer. He said we had no right to this house and we only lived here because we were a family of sluts. Stella told him to piss off, and Mike threatened to tell their dad. Mr Kelley would have hit the roof if he had, so we heard no more about it. We didn't see much of Tom for the rest of the holiday, come to think of it.'

'Was there ever any sign, when you were kids, that Thomas could see the hobs—' I coughed to cover a catch in my voice '—or the sylphs? Anything out of the ordinary?'

Fin brought over the coffee and mugs. She fetched milk from the fridge and a storage jar of sugar before sitting down. 'Could his brother and sister?'

'No.' Helen had no doubt about that. 'The sylphs used to hang around the school playground when we were little, and it was easy to tell who could see them and who couldn't, when we were supposedly playing with our imaginary friends. Once, when Mike and Stella went looking for a little privacy—' She laughed and drank some coffee. 'Let's just say a sylph watching and pulling faces can really put a girl off her stroke. But Mike didn't notice a thing. The hobs keep their distance, but my grandmother Edith, she worked as a housekeeper up at the house, and there was one she had dealings with from time to time. There was never a Kelley who could see her, the hob I mean. '

'Have you any idea what their family history might turn up?' I looked across the table and saw that Fin was thinking the same as me. Last year, we'd had to deal with the consequences of previous generations getting involved with the supernatural. People who'd had no idea what they were dealing with until someone ended up dead.

'I wonder if Tom thinks he's found a way to get round Great Uncle Eustace's bequest.' That was clearly still irritating Fin.

'I'd be very surprised, if his family couldn't overturn the will at the time, and they certainly tried. Besides, how would a hob know about that, enough to get worked up about it?' Helen stood up, coffee in hand. 'Sorry, I'm on a deadline. Is there anything else we can try, do you think, to attract the sylphs or get a hob's attention?'

I swallowed the urge to tell her I'd already done that. I also resisted the temptation to suggest Fin and I go back to the hillfort and see if a few passionate kisses drew the sylphs out from wherever they were hiding.

'The Green Man could well turn up in a day or so,' I said instead. 'This is a nice place to visit while we wait and see.'

Helen managed a smile. 'You're very welcome.'

Fin was looking thoughtful. 'We could go over to Sedgeport.'

That clearly meant something to her mother. 'Good idea. Have lunch out and I won't need to cook this evening.'

'What's in Sedgeport?' I asked.

Fin grinned. 'Wait and see.'

Helen went back to her studio and we finished our coffee.

'Shall we take my car?' Fin kicked off her slippers.

'If I fit in it.' I put my boots back on.

Actually, the Toyota wasn't as cramped as I feared, and it wasn't far. We turned right at the crossroads and went down the slope past what had once been the village school. Whoever had converted it into two houses had done a nice job retaining the original features. Seeing the words carved on the stone lintels, I wondered if the postman delivered letters addressed to "Infants" to one door and to "Juniors" through the other.

'I meant to ask,' I said a bit further on, 'what did your mum mean about the hobs being unhappy? How does she know if they won't talk to her?'

'The usual things. Open some milk at breakfast and it'll be sour by lunch, even though it's been in the fridge. Bread won't rise. The boiler won't stay lit. When Gran kept hens they'd go off lay. These days, eggs will break in your hand as soon as you pick them out of a carton.'

Fin slowed to drive through a puddle that stretched across the road. As she accelerated, she shot me a smile. 'That's stopped, so they must be happy you're here.'

I thought about the ways the Blithehurst dryads could mess with electrics. I decided not to mention that around the house, in case the hob overheard me.

The road crossed a broad stretch of farmland cut into rectangles by drainage ditches. We passed a couple of turnings into lanes leading to isolated farm buildings. I couldn't see people or vehicles at work. There was nothing moving that wasn't being stirred by the wind.

Fin took another right. A bit further on, and we were driving alongside a river that broadened into a shallow estuary. The sky seemed higher and wider than ever. We reached a village where round-shouldered cottages and later terraces with straighter lines had all been built of the local pale yellow brick. Fin pulled up in the cobbled square overlooking the water where a handful of cars were parked.

I stared through the windscreen. 'Bloody hell.'

'Welcome to Sedgeport.' Fin's laughing tone echoed the cheesy holiday adverts we'd seen on the telly last night. 'It was going to be the next big thing, as soon as the railway arrived. A rival to Boston and King's Lynn, and a hub for trade across the North Sea. So they built a town hall, a hotel and those Assembly Rooms. Plots of land were put up for sale on both sides of the river, and they waited for the cash to roll in.'

I looked at the impressive neoclassical buildings ahead of us, and wondered where that amount of building stone had come from. Nowhere around here, that was certain. 'They?'

'The same sort of people who'd got rich draining the fens. They didn't get rich here,' Fin said with mild satisfaction. 'The railway never arrived, and while the river was okay for shallow boats bringing reed and sedge out from the fens, it was never any good for bigger ships.'

'People including the Kelleys?' I could see that the building on the right, which had once been the Assembly Rooms, was now the Sedgeport and District Museum.

Fin's smile told me I'd guessed right. 'That's where their family papers are kept. Come on. It's quite a place.'

We got out of the Toyota. The wind from the sea was stronger and colder than it had been inland. Fin huddled into her coat and we hurried across the uneven cobbles. I saw that the hotel, now more of a pub and called The Maid's Eye, had several warped windows that hinted at subsidence. It looked a decent bet for lunch though. The town hall had been turned into some sort of local enterprise business centre. Maybe the Internet and remote working were bringing jobs back to places like this. That and yachting. I could see thickets of aluminium masts a short distance further down the estuary.

We walked up the broad steps to the Assembly Rooms entrance. I noted the flood levels and dates engraved on the side of the building. The water had never quite reached the threshold, but it had come close.

Tall double doors of white-painted wood stood wide open. One half of the glass inner doors opened into a sizeable pillared hall with a floor-to-ceiling window at the back. Tables and chairs and an empty counter showed this was a cafe during the tourist season. There were rooms just as big, or bigger, on either side, with doors at the front of the building and the rear. Those were both open on our left, and I could see old-fashioned glass display cases. The doors to our right were both closed. There was a welcome desk, with a till and books and souvenirs for sale, in front of the one closest, tucked in between the pillars.

The man in a thick blue jumper sitting there was absorbed in making notes from a book. There was a stack of others waiting. He quickly finished his sentence and looked up as I closed the door. 'Welcome to Sedgeport— Oh, hello.' He smiled as he recognised Fin, and ran a hand over his untidy dark hair.

'Hi.' She smiled back as she gestured at me. 'This is Dan, he's visiting for a few days. Dan, this is Chris. Don't ask about his thesis.'

'I won't.' I wouldn't know what to say.

Chris picked up his pen and gestured at the open doors across the hall. 'Go ahead. You don't need me to give you the spiel.' He had the remnants of a Welsh accent, long since smoothed out by moving away.

'But you do it so well,' Fin protested. 'Seriously. I'll forget something.'

He narrowed his eyes at her, but put down his pen and stood up readily enough. 'She told you about the land speculation scheme here?' he asked me.

I nodded as he walked around the desk.

'Okay. Well, when it was clear the railway was never coming here, the Sedgeport Scientific and Historical Society took over this building. That was an association of local gentlemen who were interested in history, obviously, as well as geography, geology, botany, beasts, birds, butterflies, moths and beetles, you name it. Those are their portraits, including Eustace Kelley.' He nodded at Fin as he waved a hand at the pictures hung around the hall. So he knew about that link with her family.

'These days we'd call them amateurs, and they certainly assembled an eccentric collection of specimens and curios, but they were very dedicated and one or two of them made some significant discoveries. They held regular meetings to share papers that they'd written, as well as bringing guest speakers from Cambridge and London. Those meetings were open to all, and there were classes here for the fen families and their children, teaching mathematics and reading and writing. The founders also bequeathed their personal libraries to the Society's Reading Room—' he gestured at the closed doors behind him '—as well as money to endow the trust that became the charity that keeps us open today. The Society is still going, supported by various local and national grants. Entrance is free, though of course all donations are very gratefully received.'

His speech was well rehearsed but no less sincere for that. I reached for my wallet. He raised a hand.

'Do that on your way out. Take as long as you like. We have some unique exhibits here as well as paintings and early photographs of life in the Fens in days gone by. There's also a display showing the different uses this building's been put to, serving the local community through the decades. There were dances and film shows here in World War Two, when airfields brought thousands of servicemen to the area. Don't hesitate to ask if you have any questions.'

He looked at Fin. 'How was that?'

'Wonderful, thanks.' She turned to head for the open doors, before turning back as if she'd just thought of something.

'Did you know Thomas Kelley is staying in Saw Edge, Chris? My mum says he's on a sabbatical, doing some sort of family history project.'

He nodded, tight-lipped. 'He's been over here. He is a member of the Society after all.'

'What's he done?' Fin could see there was something more to be said, the same as me. A lot more, by the look of it.

'I only met him to say hello,' I observed, 'but he seemed like an arrogant sod.'

'He said something very odd, about us having no right to our own house. We're worried he might be trying to find a loophole in Eustace Kelley's will,' Fin said bluntly.

Chris's face cleared a little. 'If he is, he hasn't been looking here. He's been going through the early family archive, from the 1600s. The astrology and alchemy stuff. God knows what he expects to find. It's complete gibberish. Though I suppose—' He broke off, looking self-conscious.

'What?' Fin persisted. 'Come on, tell us.'

Chris glanced at the glass doors, but there was no one coming up the steps, and there was no one else in the building. He went back to sit behind the desk.

'You didn't hear it from me, but he's not on any sabbatical. He's been suspended, sent on gardening leave, whatever you want to call it. I got a phone call from Professor— Well, never mind who it was. The Society has been advised not to let him have unsupervised access to its library here until some irregularities have been sorted out. You can imagine how well that went down, when I said I'd have to be in the Reading Room with him, as long as I could get Trish from the pub to cover the desk.'

He leaned forward, fiddling with his pen. Neither of us needed to ask what irregularities he was talking about.

'Things have gone missing from one of the university's special collections, and he's one of only a handful of people who've been anywhere near those particular papers for years. The collection included a Kelley family bequest, apparently, and Thomas has been known to say those particular papers should never have been handed over in the first place. So of course, when another researcher couldn't find what they were looking for, all eyes turned to him. There's no proof that he's done anything, of course. It wasn't actually the Kelley family papers that vanished. Nothing's come up for sale, and that's usually the smoking gun in cases like this, once a provenance is examined.'

'Couldn't whatever it was just have been put in the wrong place?' I wondered.

'That's the obvious answer, and believe me, they'll have looked,' Chris agreed. 'The thing is though, these individual documents were recorded in a good old-fashioned card index catalogue, and someone's taken those record cards as well. That can't be an accident.'

Fin frowned. 'If the papers and the record cards are gone, how do they know some of the collection is missing?'

'The cards were put on microfiche ages ago. That's what this other researcher was working from, to find sources for their thesis. The thing is, Thomas Kelley didn't know that had been done. That's what I heard anyway.'

'What was this other researcher working on?' I asked.

'Something mid-Victorian?' Fin looked apprehensive.

'No idea. Not my period. Something Tudor, I think.' Chris shrugged. 'Nothing that need concern the likes of me, the same as whatever Thomas Kelley came to do some work on here.'

I heard the echo of the arrogant man's dismissal. Whatever he had said had left Chris with a grievance that he was ready to share. Serve Kelley right.

'If you ever want to know anything about the social impact of the Napoleonic wars on the Fens, Chris is the man to ask,' Fin assured me.

'Good to know,' I said politely.

'I'll wait for your call.' Chris wasn't serious, or in the least offended.

'We'll let you get on. Thanks.'

Fin headed for the open door leading to the museum's collection. I followed as Chris went back to his books.

He was right. The museum was an eccentric mishmash of all sorts of things. The centre of the room was given over to chests holding drawer after drawer of neatly pinned insects, each one identified by its Latin name written on a card in spidery writing. Cases on top of the chests held corals and shells. Around the walls, behind old, wavy glass, there were a lot of old tools and household goods from the days when everything in the fens had been done by hand. Cutting reed and sedge, digging peat and catching fish, eels and waterfowl had supported thriving communities, judging from the old pictures. Well, the people who didn't catch malaria thrived. Though the ones who caught it probably weren't too bothered. I was startled to read about the quantities of opium and laudanum that had been sold to treat marsh ague.

Fin came to see what I was looking at. 'No one took much notice of fanciful stories of fairies out in the sedge when the people who saw them were doped to the eyeballs,' she remarked quietly. 'Not outsiders, anyway.'

And who would believe stories about people who could turn into swans, I thought.

Cast-iron spiral staircases at the front of the room led up to a balcony that ran around three sides of it with an ornate cast-iron balustrade. More display cases on the walls held rocks and fossils, memorabilia from local regiments and a collection of carvings and basket work from West Africa and Malaya. It turned out that several members of the Society had been important colonial administrators.

'Seen enough?' Fin asked when I finished reading about that.

'Yes.' I had no great interest in the fossils that were next along.

We went out to say goodbye to Chris. I donated a tenner and filled out a Gift Aid form. We went to The Maid's Eye and had a meal. The lunch menu was limited given the time of year, but the food was very good. I took the opportunity to have a bacon cheese burger, since Fin's family didn't seem to eat meat.

We went back to Venturer's House and took another walk out to the hillfort, but nothing happened. Not even when Fin drew me into a kiss that told me she'd had the same idea as I had earlier. That evening, she thrashed me at backgammon, and I thrashed her and Helen at dominoes, playing threes and fives. Helen had put on the bread maker while we were out, and her bread had risen fine. So that was supper with cheese and pickles. We watched some American cop show on telly, and then we went to bed.

As I switched off the light, I wondered if I was going to see the Green Man in my dreams. I needed some sort of clue if I was going to be any use here at all.

Chapter Five

I didn't dream about the Green Man. I slept until I was suddenly wide awake at who-knows-what o'clock. I didn't need to put the bedside lamp on to find my phone to look at the time. The hob was sitting cross-legged on the little armchair by the window. Coppery light rose from a bowl beside him. He dipped a white cloth in it and wiped the knees of my jeans, which he had draped over his thigh.

'Hello,' I said cautiously.

'Hello yourself, son of the greenwood. You sleep sound,' he observed.

'Like a log.' That got no response at all. Did hobs have a sense of humour? I chose my next words with care. 'May I ask, what should I call you?'

'Master Hob.' He glanced up with a warning flash of those golden eyes, before returning to his task. 'So I see you can keep a secret. You said not a word to the swan's daughters. Well done.'

If he knew that, he'd been watching us somehow. 'Thank you.'

'You are welcome.' He tossed the jeans over to the bed with disconcerting ease. 'Now, one good turn warrants a favour in return.'

Shit. I hadn't been thanking him for cleaning off that mud, and the hob sodding well knew it. He'd never admit it though, not when he could claim I'd acknowledged an obligation to him. I really needed to watch what I said, and to be aware that I was being watched.

'Did the Green Man send you?'

He laughed, coldly amused at my expense. 'I owe your master no allegiance, greenwood. I look to the Master of Fords and Ferries.'

I hoped Fin had some idea who that might be.

'By mine own choice, freely made,' he added sharply.

The light striking up from the bowl made his face an eerie mask of coppery glints and shadows. There's a reason horror movies use that sort of effect. The bedroom was still warm enough, even if the heating had gone off hours ago. I felt goose pimples rise on my arms regardless.

'That's good to know. What sort of favour might I do for you?' I really hoped that question was sufficiently non-committal to keep me out of trouble and still get me some answers.

The hob dropped the cloth in the bowl. The light didn't even flicker. 'There are those who would compel the service of our kind. Those who would have us do wrong.'

He looked over to see how I took that. I shook my head with a disapproving frown, and waited for more.

'We keep well out of sight, me and mine,' he went on grudgingly, 'but there are those with no more sense than a mayfly. We have scared them away for the present, but they will return. As soon as he sees them, they will be caught. He will force them to do his will, whatever that might be.'

'The sylphs?' That seemed a safe guess.

He nodded. 'That is one name for them.'

So that was one answer. The next question was obvious. I asked it reluctantly all the same. I'd much rather just be here on holiday.

'Who will catch them?'

'The stargazer's son.' His scorn implied I was a complete idiot.

For a moment, I had no idea who he meant. Then I remembered what Chris at the museum had said. Alchemy and astrology.

'Thomas Kelley?'

'So free with your names, you mortals,' he hissed with contempt.

I decided to take that as a yes. 'I was told he can't see your kind.'

'Which is why he seeks the sorcerers' crystal.' The hob seemed to think he was talking to an utter moron. 'To show him where they are. To see me and mine, if we were fool enough to let him.'

I tried not to let his contempt annoy me. 'Do you know where this crystal is?'

'If I did, do you think I would let it be found? Are you as dense as your mother's trees?'

'Then what do you want me to do?'

'Stop him!' The hob sprang to his feet in a single fluid motion. 'Now!'

He crouched on the seat, waving frustrated hands. The bowl toppled over and fell off the chair. Nothing spilled out, and the bowl vanished before it hit the floor. The light was still coming from somewhere, but I had no idea how. My fists tightened on handfuls of duvet. The hob might be barely half my height, but I really wouldn't want to have to fight him.

Then I realised the creature wasn't just gesturing wildly. He was pointing along the landing. Since I didn't think there was anything mystical hidden in the bathroom, I realised he must mean the most significant thing outside the house in that direction.

'The hillfort? He's there? Now?'

'On the long isle, yes!' The hob threw up his arms as if to say 'Finally!'

I was already getting out of bed. 'Wake the others.'

'No.' The hob was adamant. 'You go alone.'

'This is their house. Their land,' I protested.

'Not if I drive them out.' The hob left me in no doubt that he could do that if he wanted to.

'Why would you?' I demanded as I dragged the pristine jeans over my pyjama shorts.

'If he finds what he seeks? If they take it for themselves?'

The hob's growl sent a shiver down my spine. I was still angry on Fin's behalf though, and Helen's.

'You're not worried I might take it?'

The hob stood motionless and his eyes glowed brighter. 'That would be most unwise, greenwood.'

I was reminded of someone in a pub calling someone else 'mate' just before throwing a punch.

'I won't, I promise you that,' I said quickly as I found socks and a sweatshirt.

'Then do as I say.' The hob vanished.

I gave serious thought to waking Fin up regardless as I walked towards the stairs. Then I realised the floorboards were silent underfoot. I might not be able to see the hob at the moment, but that didn't mean he wasn't still there.

There was also no saying I'd be able to wake her, I thought uneasily as I made my way downstairs. There was no sign that Helen had heard me talking to the hob, and he had been shouting at me. These walls were only lath and plaster, but she hadn't been disturbed.

I got my boots and coat on in the dark kitchen, lit only by the microwave's clock. Thanks to the keen night sight that comes with dryad blood, I could see what I was doing, and I already knew where to find the back door key. After a moment's hesitation, I left it in the unlocked door. I really didn't like leaving the house unsecured, but I didn't want to risk losing the key.

'Master Hob?' I said quietly as I pulled the door closed behind me. 'If anything happens to these women, you and yours will have a serious problem with me and mine.'

I put all the conviction I could into those words. That wasn't hard. I wasn't lying. The Blithehurst dryads knew Fin and they liked her. I'd bet good money they would know some way to strike back at a hob. Debts aren't always owed for favours. My mum can hold a grudge for decades until she gets satisfaction.

Nothing. No response.

Fuck it. The sooner I went, the sooner I would be back. Add to that, it was sodding freezing outside, so the faster I ran, the warmer I would be. I unbolted the side gate and made sure it was latched securely. I took a quick look around as I found my gloves in my coat pocket, but there was no sign of life anywhere. No one to see me leaving and think about trying their luck through the unlocked gate. I fervently hoped so anyway.

I began jogging along the track. There was enough moonlight for me to see my way clearly enough. About halfway to the hillfort, though, I realised my boots were loud enough on the gravel to stir nosy bleats from those bloody sheep down in the darkness away in that field. I slowed, trying to find the sweet spot between making good time and not letting Thomas Kelley know I was coming.

I needn't have worried. As I got closer to the hillfort, I saw a torch's glow in the middle of the trees. That was enough to show me Thomas Kelley was wearing headphones, big over-the-ear ones. He was using a metal detector. I stopped and got out my phone and took a few moments of video of him sweeping it to and fro. The beam of the torch in his other hand was following the metal ring across the uneven ground.

He froze. Not because he'd seen me. He must have heard a bleep indicating there was something buried there. Setting the detector down, he fumbled in a pocket of the long waxed-cotton coat he was wearing. I'd bet he had green wellies on as well. As he crouched down, the torch beam showed me a trowel in his other hand. Kelley started digging, still wearing his headphones.

Once I was off the gravel, I could move silently on the dry grass and dead leaves. I circled around so I could come up behind him unseen. I slapped a hand down hard on his shoulder.

'What the fuck do you think you're doing?'

I said it as loudly as I could without shouting, but I still don't think he heard me. He fell forward onto his hands and knees with a squeal like a startled piglet. Scrambling away, he tripped as he tried to stand up. He made it to his feet the second time and pulled the headphones off. As he gripped them, his hands were shaking as much as his voice.

'What— what—'

'I said,' I repeated with deliberate menace, 'what the fuck do you think you're doing?'

'Nothing that need concern you.' His defiance was a feeble effort, compared to his arrogance in the church this morning. No, that had been yesterday morning, I realised.

'At four fucking thirty a.m.?' I took a step closer.

He took a step back, and found himself pressed against a birch tree. 'Do you have to swear?' he demanded. His voice was high and tight and his hair stuck up at ridiculous angles.

'Yes, I think I fucking do.' Since he obviously didn't like it. The more I kept him off balance, the better. 'So, for the third time, and believe me, I'm getting fucking tired of asking, what the fuck do you think you're doing?'

He drew a shuddering breath and squared his shoulders. He smoothed his hair with an unsteady hand. 'A preliminary survey. Nothing to concern you.'

'Without the landowner's permission, and at half-four in the fucking morning?'

'The Wicken family don't own this land,' he insisted instantly. 'As for the time, well, I thought it best to pick a quiet time, to avoid walkers and their dogs. Ignorant curiosity—'

'Oh, fuck off. You're talking bollocks. Even if the county archaeologist or someone like that gave you permission, they'd have let the Wickens know. Got the paperwork with you? No, you fucking haven't. You're breaking the law, arsehole.' Blithehurst had hosted a couple of weekend events for detectorists, so I knew that much about the legalities.

Kelley's beard twitched. Whatever game he was playing here, he really didn't have a face for poker. He was defiant now though, stooping to gather up his metal detector, shoving the trowel into a pocket.

'You can't prove a thing. Any animal could have been digging here. It's your word against mine.' His tone made it plain who he expected the police to believe.

I smiled. 'Your word against the photos I took when I saw what you were doing. Before you knew I was here.'

Of course, I had no idea how clear any evidence might be until I downloaded the video, but that wasn't the point.

'What?' His eyes narrowed. 'You're lying. Show me,' he challenged.

I laughed, short and mocking. 'So you can try knocking the phone out of my hand, to smash it? Fuck off.'

His beard twitched again, telling me I was right about what he'd hoped to do. He glared at me anyway. 'I am going to leave now. If you try to stop me, that will be common assault.'

'So you do know some law. Go on, piss off.'

He flinched as I waved my hand towards the track. What he didn't know was I wasn't about to touch him. I've had some run-ins with the police in the past, and in my experience, the likes of me don't get the benefit of much doubt. Not compared to a Cambridge professor or whatever Kelley was, for the moment at least.

He stumbled over tree roots as he made his way towards the gap in the earth bank where those great gates had stood. I followed, and once we were on the track, I used my longer stride to keep him walking faster than he liked. He liked the idea of me catching him up even less and hurried along. He was wearing green wellies, and they were at least a size too large, flapping and slipping. I reminded myself not to underestimate him just because he looked like a prat.

When we reached Venturer's House, I stopped by the gates and watched him go on down the lane. Once he reached the tarmac where the street lights began, he snatched a backward glance. I waved my phone at him, now that he was too far away to do anything about it. He scurried away faster than ever, even without me pursuing him. I stood there until I lost sight of him in the shadows by the houses around the water tower. Then I went through the side gate and bolted it behind me.

The hob was sitting cross-legged outside the back door. 'Well?' he demanded.

'Whatever he's looking for, he hasn't found it.'

The hob's golden eyes narrowed with suspicion.

'Neither have I. Now, let me pass.'

He stood up, but stayed in front of the door. 'You must learn what he knows. Since I kept the swan's daughters safe for you—'

'I didn't ask you to do that.' Not in so many words. I'm not some fairy tale woodcutter's dumb son. Not once I've woken up, anyway.

The hob tried a different approach. 'He threatens them.'

'He does,' I agreed, 'but that's between me and him and them.'

The hob glowered. He didn't seem to realise that I was just as keen to find out what Kelley was up to.

'If I were to share what I learn with you, that would be a debt you owed me,' I said firmly.

'That would be so,' the hob said grudgingly.

He was agreeing, but making it clear that didn't mean we had an agreement. That suited me for now.

'Let me in. I need to tell... the swan's daughters what's just happened.' If he wasn't using real names, neither would I.

'No,' the hob said instantly. 'You may enter, but you tell them nothing.'

'You have no right to give me orders.' I was suddenly tired of this. 'They asked me to come here because they were worried about you and yours, and the sylphs. They had no idea what was wrong. They hoped I could help them find out.' I decided not to mention they'd hoped to enlist the Green Man. There didn't seem much point. I didn't think he was going to show himself any time soon.

The hob was scowling. 'They wish to put me in their debt.'

'No, they don't.' I managed not to ask why he was quite so paranoid, or to point out that he was the one who'd started this with sour milk and broken eggs. Always assuming he was the hob who had done those things. I realised I didn't actually know that, and Helen had talked about hobs plural.

I didn't ask. He doubtless had his reasons for being wary, and I certainly didn't trust Thomas Kelley, so why should he? Besides, this unexpected visitor was the only hob who was talking to us. I didn't want to get on his bad side and lose whatever information he could give us.

I reached over his head to the door handle. 'They want to help because it's the right thing to do.'

He moved aside reluctantly. 'So say many who serve their own interests.'

I couldn't argue with that. 'How can I let you know if I have something to tell you?'

'I would consider food and drink an invitation.' There was unexpected longing in his voice.

'I'll remember that.'

He was gone before I finished speaking. I went on into the house, locked the door behind me and hung the key on its hook. As I sat down to take off my boots, the stairs creaked.

'Fin?' I called out quietly, to let her know I wasn't a burglar.

Helen looked around the door to the entrance hall. She was wrapped in a thick dressing gown. 'What are you doing up?' she whispered, incredulous. She squinted at the microwave clock. 'It's not even half past five.'

'I had a visit from your hob. Well, a hob anyway.'

'Mum?' Fin was somewhere on the stairs or the landing.

Helen ducked back through the door to speak to her. 'Dan's seen a hob.'

I heard Fin coming down the stairs as well and went to fill the kettle. Helen switched the lights on. I winced, blinked and managed not to say 'shit' too loudly.

Helen made tea and coffee and we sat at the table. I told my story, including the deliberate misunderstanding about the jeans. They needed to know to watch what they said to the hob. If he ever decided to trust them.

'A sorcerer's crystal? That's what Tom Kelley is looking for? Let's see if we can find it.' Fin looked at the window, but there was no sign of dawn approaching.

'It's just as illegal for us to go digging around up there,' Helen pointed out. 'The hillfort's a scheduled ancient monument, and that means no one does a thing on the site without permission from Historic England. Besides, the archaeologists did all sorts of surveys when they were here, as well as digging their trenches. Geophysics and magnetic resistance and stuff like that. I can't think there's anything buried up there. Not that a metal detector will find.'

'Dan said Tom found something,' Fin said stubbornly.

'That could be anything. An old drink can.' Helen yawned. 'The archaeology students filled a bin bag with rubbish like that.'

'We can take a look without doing any more digging.' I didn't want to get in the middle of an argument. 'It would help if we had some idea what we were looking for though. How big is this thing? How does it work? The hob didn't say.'

'Do you think he could tell us?' Fin wondered.

'Not unless we have something to trade.' I was pretty sure about that.

'I'd better get some pork pies and beer in,' said Helen. 'Very popular with hobs,' she explained.

I couldn't argue with that, but I still reckoned we needed something meatier, so to speak. 'The hob says Kelley wants the sylphs to do something, something wrong, but he didn't say what.'

'That doesn't mean he doesn't know,' Fin observed. 'Same as the crystal.'

'True,' I acknowledged, 'but asking him things will put us in his debt. If we can find out for ourselves what the pointy-bearded bastard is up to, and better yet, work out some way to stop him, then the hob will owe us. That's got to be safer, hasn't it?'

'Definitely,' Helen said with feeling.

'Could there be some clues in the Kelley papers at Sedgeport?' Fin wondered.

'Maybe, if we can find some excuse to look.' I remembered what Chris had said about that bit of the archive being gibberish, but I didn't have any better ideas.

'You said he was in St Peter's making notes.' Helen looked thoughtful. 'There are brasses on the oldest Kelley graves in there, with engravings that no one's ever made much sense of, beyond saying they're astrological.'

'Could there be something *in* a family grave?' Fin didn't look keen on that idea.

Nor was I. 'Any hint of him digging up bodies and we go straight to the police.' The cops do have their uses.

'Talking of which...' Helen looked at me. 'Couldn't we put a stop to all this by taking the film of him metal-detecting to the authorities?'

'Let's see what you got.' Fin went to get her laptop.

Helen made some toast and got out butter and jam while we were downloading the video. I was relieved to find it was clear enough to show who Tom Kelley was and what he was doing. That was something worth having, though not as much as it could be.

'I did stop him before he dug anything up,' I said, apologetic. 'I didn't want to risk him finding whatever he was looking for. I'm pretty sure that means he'd only be fined a few hundred quid, and I don't think that's going to stop him. It's the people who find a stash of gold coins and don't declare them who get locked up.'

Much to the vengeful satisfaction of the law-abiding detectorists at Blithehurst, as I recalled. I ate some toast.

Fin grimaced. 'Meantime, going to the police or whoever tells him we're on to him.'

'I think he knows that already. I did my best to scare him off.' A yawn interrupted me.

'Going to the police does escalate things.' Fin drummed her fingers on the table. 'We might be better off leaving him wondering.'

Helen had other concerns. 'How much trouble could we get into, if we find this thing and don't report it? If Tom realises we've got it and calls the police about us?'

'That depends what it is, doesn't it? A crystal you could wear as a pendant or something the size of that?' I nodded at the laptop and yawned again.

'We're going round in circles.' Helen gathered up hers and Fin's plates. 'Dan, finish your toast and go back to bed. Let's all get a bit more sleep. The museum doesn't open till ten. I think you're right. That is the best place to start.'

'Yes, Mum,' Fin said with an affectionate grin.

I didn't say anything. I just did as I was told. As my head hit the pillow, I barely had time to wonder if I was going to dream about anything useful this time.

Chapter Six

Fin woke me up, tapping on the bedroom door and coming in with a cup of tea. 'Rise and shine, Sleeping Beauty.'

'I feel more like Red Riding Hood's gran.' I sat up and reached for the mug. 'I hate broken nights.'

'My, what big—' she looked me up and down with a teasing smile '—arms you have.'

'All the better to cuddle you with.' Not that there was much chance of that. She was fully dressed.

She held out her hand for the mug as soon as I'd drunk the tea. 'It's just gone nine. Let's get over to Sedgeport.'

We took her Toyota again. She knew the roads, after all. The morning was still and cold, and mist hung in the air, thicker over the river. There were the same few cars in the marketplace, but no other signs of life. The museum's doors were open though.

'So how are we going to handle this?' I asked as we got out of the car.

Fin wrinkled her nose. 'Play it by ear, I suppose. Follow my lead.'

We caught Chris taking a kettle out of a cupboard behind the cafe counter. He had a mug and a jar of instant coffee waiting.

'Hello,' he said, surprised.

'Hi.' Fin smiled at him.

'What brings you back so soon?'

He glanced from her to me. I looked at Fin.

'You remember we said we thought Thomas Kelley was up to something?' Fin spread her hands. 'We caught him metal-detecting up on the hillfort in the middle of the night.'

'What the—?' Chris stared, incredulous, for a moment. Then he put down the kettle and went straight to a phone on the wall. 'That's a scheduled ancient monument.'

'And he'll just deny it,' Fin said quickly. 'It'll be his word against ours.'

I was glad Chris had his back to us, so he didn't see me looking at Fin, surprised. She narrowed her eyes at me as Chris reluctantly hung up the phone and turned around.

'I suppose so. Did he do any damage? Did he take anything away?'

'Not that we saw.' I wasn't lying about that, strictly speaking.

'Even so, just metal-detecting on the site is a punishable offence.' Chris looked at Fin, bemused and not particularly happy about any of this. 'Why tell me, if you're not going to report him?'

'We thought if we took a look at the Kelley archive here, we might get some idea what he's up to,' she said, hopeful. 'Whether he really is out to make trouble for my family, or if he's after something else.'

Chris looked dubious. 'The Reading Room's not open to the public, not as such, and you're not members of the Society. You could write to the trustees—'

'How long will that take? Who's to know if we just take a quick look this morning? Please, Chris, you know you can trust us, and if Thomas Kelley has been stealing papers in Cambridge, that's more than can be said for him.'

Fin smiled at him, appealing in every sense of the word. I wasn't at all sure I liked seeing her use her allure to get her own way like this. The thing was, though, I wasn't at all sure she was doing it deliberately.

'If we can work out what he's after, that might strengthen the university's case against him,' she added. 'Or give them some idea what he might try to steal next. Or where he might go digging without permission, when there's no one to see him and stop him. Who knows what damage he could do?'

Whether it was Fin's unfair charm or her arguments that won him over, I couldn't say, but Chris nodded slowly.

'I suppose so. But you need to let me know whatever you find out. If you come across anything that could be relevant,' he added, still doubtful. 'And I can't let you take photos or take anything away. You'll have to apply to the trustees if you want copies of anything.'

'Of course,' Fin agreed. 'But you can sell me a notebook and pen.'

'I can sell you a notebook and pencil. No ink allowed in the Reading Room, or matches or lighters, but you're not a smoker, are you? Got a vape?' Chris glanced at me as he walked across the pillared hall to the welcome desk.

I shook my head as he took a bunch of keys out of a drawer.

'I should make you leave your coats with me, but the heating's off in there so it's going to be cold,' he said reluctantly. 'If you want a coffee to thaw out, you'll have to drink it out here. No food or drink allowed either.'

'Thanks, we really appreciate this,' Fin assured him.

I took two pencils from the souvenir display and two little notebooks with a drawing of the museum on the front. I left a tenner on the desk. 'Put the change in the donations box.'

'Thanks.' Chris unlocked the Reading Room door and switched on the lights.

I followed him and Fin. It was like walking into a fridge, if a fridge was full of shelves holding leather-bound and gold-embossed books, in every shade of brown, black and red. They lined the walls, and more bookcases divided most of the space opposite into bays with tables and chairs, lit by long windows overlooking the reeds along the river. The wall where the doors came in had display cases though, over polished mahogany cupboards.

'They do open this room up on Saturdays in the summer, for visitors.' Fin saw me looking at the old books behind the glass. They were propped on stands, and open to pages of impossibly neat handwriting or old-fashioned illustrations of plants and insects that were works of art in themselves.

Chris was heading up a spiral staircase to get to the balcony that ran around the upper half of the room, the same as over in the one displaying the collections. The shelves up there held what looked like black box files. 'So what exactly do you want to look at?' he called down.

'Whatever Tom Kelley was interested in?' I suggested, just as Fin called out to answer him.

'We might as well start at the beginning.'

There was a pause as we heard Chris moving stuff around. Then he came carefully down the stairs carrying two sizeable black boxes. 'Then you're in luck, because that's the same thing. Not that there's a huge amount here. The archive starts with the first Thomas Kelley buying a house over in Saw Edge St James in 1598.'

'Where did he come from?' I asked.

'That's not really clear.' Chris put the boxes on the closest table. 'He seemed to have come from London with his wife and children, according to the financial records anyway. Then there are bills with notes that relate to visits to his wife's family over the next few years. He seems to have owned property there. But there's a letter from 1609 where he claims to be from Worcester. He explicitly states that he's never lived in London. Of course, that might be because whoever he was writing to was after him, trying to recover some books he'd supposedly got from John Dee's library. Thomas Kelley denies ever having any such thing, and insists that the Edward Kelley who was Dee's colleague is nothing to do with him. The matter seems to have been dropped. When Matthew Hopkins came along hunting witches in the 1640s, the story changes again, saying they came here from Ireland. They're very vague on detail, apart from insisting once again that the family never had any dealings with Dee.'

'You're very well informed,' Fin said, admiring.

Chris looked a little self-conscious. 'I took a look myself, after the latest Thomas Kelley had been in here being such a pain in the arse.'

He laughed. 'When the family books were turned over to the Society a cou-ple of hundred years later, several turned out to have had John Dee's name in them, before the ink had been bleached out and over-written. By then the sto-ry was that the first Thomas Kelley had somehow got his hands on a few books after Dee's library was ransacked. Most likely he claimed to be one of those Kelleys who had worked with Dee to get a better price selling the books on. He might even have changed his name from something else. Then Dee fell out of favour and that association was getting dangerous, so these Kelleys dropped their pretence. But if Doctor Thomas Kelley thinks he can get his hands on those books now, he's in for a disappointment. They were sold decades ago to pay for work here to deal with some subsidence.'

'Did you tell him that?' Fin wanted to know.

'I haven't seen him to tell him, and it's not like he left me his email or phone number.' Chris looked a little defensive. 'Besides, he made it very clear my assistance or opinions were neither sought nor wanted.'

That sounded like an echo of something the prick would say.

'Doctor Dee?' I asked. 'The one who cast horoscopes and stuff? Shake-speare's inspiration for Prospero?'

Fin was caught unawares. 'How do you know that?'

'You don't think a man who works with his hands can be interested in Shakespeare?' I challenged her.

Chris looked aghast, and Fin bit her lip. She wasn't sure I was serious, but she was uncertain enough to be just a little concerned.

'You should see your face. Too easy.' I grinned. 'I grew up less than twenty miles from Stratford-upon-Avon. How many school trips do you think I went on there?'

That was thanks to our English teacher, Mrs Roberts, who firmly believed that kids should see Shakespeare on the stage before they read it on the page. It also didn't hurt that the first production I saw was *A Midsummer Night's Dream*. That play made perfect sense to me, though I knew better than to say why to anyone at school. I'd enjoyed plenty of others since. I got a grade A for my essay discussing the Forest of Arden as a place of refuge in *As You Like It*, after reading the play with my mum.

Fin laughed. 'Fair enough, I deserved that.'

'We're friends again then?' Chris had no idea what was going on. He was just relieved it seemed to be over. 'Right, I'll let you get on. You'll have to leave by twelve-thirty though. That's when Trish comes over to cover the desk at lunch time.'

I held up a hand as he turned to go. 'Do you have any books here about John Dee?'

He thought for a moment. 'I think there's something on that bottom shelf over there.'

He pointed to one of the bookcases making up the bays. I saw they held an assortment of more modern books.

'Thanks.'

He didn't close the door behind him, so Fin and I kept our voices low as we sat at the table and opened the boxes. She began taking out folded-up sheets of beige paper with faded ribbon tied around them. Mine held collections of letters and accounts that someone sometime or other had sorted into folders that were now dog-eared and creased.

Fin smoothed out a piece of paper divided with diagonal lines drawn from the centre of each side. There was a square with what looked like a date in it in the middle of the central diamond. 1590 or something like that was all I could see from this angle. The triangles at each corner were full of tiny writing and squiggly numbers.

'Why are you so interested in John Dee?' she asked quietly.

'Have you ever seen *The Tempest*? Prospero is a magician who has enslaved a spirit of the air called Ariel, as well as another half-human-looking monster called Caliban. He forces them to do what he wants, even though Caliban and Ariel have magic of their own.'

Fin stared at me, and I saw realisation dawn in her eyes. She was remembering what the hob had said to me. 'How about you find that book on Doctor Dee while I see if there's anything useful in here?'

'Are you sure? That stuff doesn't exactly look easy to read.'

'It's not too bad once you get your eye in.' She grinned. 'I'm guessing I've done archive research more often than you.'

'That's a safe bet, because I've never done anything like this.' I got up and went to the shelf Chris had pointed out. After a bit of searching, I found a book on the life and times of John Dee. Since it had an index, the first thing I looked up was 'Kelley'. Since there were three of them and a full column of references, I turned to the first page listed and began reading.

For the next long while, the only sounds were Fin shuffling papers and making notes and Chris occasionally moving about in the entrance hall. I looked towards the door when I heard him put the kettle on. I was less interested in drinking a coffee than just having a warm mug to hold for a bit.

I glanced across the table and met Fin's eyes. I wondered if she was as tempted as me to take a few photos on her phone. It wasn't as if Chris could see us, and my hands were so cold by now that my fingers were stiff when I tried to use my pencil. My own notes looked as indecipherable as the faded handwriting she was trying to read. Better not, I decided reluctantly. If Chris walked in and caught me, we'd lose a valuable ally.

Fin tapped her watch. 'We should press on,' she said in a low tone. 'We've only got till half-twelve, if that.'

Maybe she had been deliberately turning her charm on Chris. She certainly seemed to know when it would wear off. A clock somewhere in the building had barely struck midday when he came into the Reading Room.

'Look, you're going to have to go. I shouldn't really have let you in here.' He was very apologetic, but he clearly regretted doing Fin this favour.

'That's fine. We understand.' She began putting the papers back in their boxes. She'd been retying the ribbons and stacking the creased folders neatly as she went through them.

'We really appreciate this.' I got up to take the book on John Dee back to its place on the shelf.

'Let me do that.' Chris took over sorting out the papers. 'Did you find anything useful?'

'Hard to say,' Fin said frankly, 'since we don't actually know what he's up to. As you say, he might think he's got some claim on some family books, in which case it's nothing to do with us. Or he might be trying to cause trouble over something to do with the original leases and agreements with the other investors when Venturer's House was built. There are a lot of amendments and alterations, and frankly, I can't make any sense of it.' She shrugged. 'We won't know until Kelley shows his hand. If he does, we'll write to the trustees, so someone who understands the legal side can come here and go through these records officially,' she assured Chris.

'Fair enough,' he said, relieved.

'We'll get out of your hair. Thanks again.'

Fin headed out of the Reading Room and I followed. As we headed through the outer door, a middle-aged woman well wrapped up against the cold came up the steps. She smiled and nodded as she passed us.

'You'd think he could just put up a closed sign for an hour,' I remarked after she went in.

'Not according to the terms of the trust.' Fin got her car keys out of a pocket and weighed them in her hand. She nodded towards the pub. 'Do you want to get something to eat, or a coffee?'

It didn't sound as if she wanted to.

'How about we head back?' I suggested. 'We won't need to say everything twice if your mum's there when we swap notes.'

'Good thinking.' Fin headed for the Toyota.

We drove back in silence. There wasn't any point in talking until we could have a proper conversation. So I sat and enjoyed the warmth as Fin whacked the heater up to maximum. It was good to feel my toes again.

We soon reached the house and I got out to open the gates. As Fin parked the Toyota beside my Land Rover, Helen opened the kitchen door.

'Well? How did you get on?'

'Let's get inside first.' Fin locked the car with her remote.

The kitchen was warm and a pot of something on the stove gave off a tempting scent. Helen went over to give it a stir. 'I got some soup out of the freezer and made another loaf.'

We were soon sitting at the table. Over lunch, Fin explained to her mum what Chris had told us about the Kelley family's history, and what we thought it might mean for the hobs and the sylphs if I was right about *The Tempest*. Then she said what she'd said to him about the changes made to the original agreements to build this house.

'Though I can't imagine Doctor Tom could have found anything that Eustace's brothers overlooked when they were trying to contest his will and break the trust.' She spooned up the last of her soup. 'I think he was after the alchemy and astrology stuff. As well as diagrams and tables that I couldn't make head or tail of, there were a couple of letters that definitely mentioned a crystal, as well as referring to the prayers, preparations and rituals needed to use it to see spirits.'

'That ties up with what Edward Kelley was doing with Doctor Dee.' I wiped out my soup bowl with a crust of bread. 'He used a crystal ball, most likely more than one, to summon angels who promised all sorts of revelations. When ugly demons didn't turn up to disrupt things.'

I got my notebook out of my pocket and opened it to a drawing I'd made. 'There was a sketch of one of the balls. It was set in a framework to lift it up off the table.'

As far as I could make out, there was a broad ring for a base with four arched arms rising up to meet in the centre. That's where the crystal ball sat, held secure in another metal ring topped off with a little cross. The whole thing looked a bit like one of those crowns the Queen wears to open parliament, without all the extra diamonds and fancy bits. Though if this had been a crown, the crystal in the middle would have been about the size of a grapefruit.

'There are no dimensions, or any note of what the frame was made of. Though there are other references that might mean it was gold.'

'Is that what Doctor Tom was looking for last night?' Fin looked across the table, wide-eyed.

'I can't imagine the archaeological survey would miss something like that,' Helen objected.

'What if it was hidden? By someone or something? By one of these rituals?' Fin tapped a finger on her own notebook lying on the table.

Could supernatural influences or magic spells foil ground-penetrating radar and whatever else the archaeologists had used? I had no clue who we could ask about that without sounding completely mad.

Helen looked at me. 'What happened to this Edward Kelley? Does he have any ties to this area?'

'John Dee did. He was a student and then a reader, whatever that means, at Cambridge University.' I checked the timeline I had scribbled down. 'Kelley first turned up in 1582, when Dee was living in London, though. That's when he convinced Dee he could see these visions of angels. After that, he spent a lot of time in and around Germany, Poland and Prague, setting himself up as an alchemist and scholar, getting paid by various rich nobles. He may or may not have been a spy, and he may or may not have been blackmailed into doing that. John Dee went with him to Europe, but Dee came back to England with his family after five years, in 1589. Dee was told Kelley was dead in 1595, but there were other reports of him being alive until 1598. As far as anyone knows, he disappeared in Germany or maybe Russia sometime after that.'

I turned to the next page. 'When he first turned up, he used Talbot as an alias, and was thought to come from Ireland. On the other hand, there are records of Edward Kelley, Thomas Kelley and Elizabeth Kelley being baptised in Worcester. Later on, Thomas and Edward may or may not have been mixed up in Catholic plots against Queen Elizabeth.'

Helen got up to clear the table, shaking her head. 'Which may or may not tie up with what we know about the Kelleys who turned up here. What we don't know is, was this Thomas Kelley telling the truth at first, and then the family started lying to avoid accusations of treason or witchcraft? Or was he trying to con people until that got too dangerous, so they came clean? How are we ever going to find out?'

'Do we need to?' I said mildly as I began washing up the soup pan. 'Surely what matters is what Doctor Tom believes, and whatever he was out there looking for last night?'

'The hob is convinced he's after something that will give him control over the sylphs,' Fin pointed out. 'We need to do something to convince him Doctor Tom won't get hold of it, if we don't want the freezer defrosting again.'

Helen looked at the two of us as she closed the dishwasher. 'So we had better go and see what Tom was doing up at the hillfort, I suppose.'

'I hope he didn't come back this morning, while we were out.' I was suddenly uneasy. 'He might have seen us drive away.'

Fin raised her eyebrows. 'Wouldn't the hob have alerted Mum?'

'My study window overlooks the lane. I didn't see him,' said Helen. 'He could have come around by the footpath, I suppose, but I doubt he'd have the balls to try again in broad daylight. Come on then. Let me find my boots.'

'How's your deadline?' Fin grinned as her mum hesitated. 'You get back to work. We'll report whatever we find.'

Helen smiled, looking more like her daughter than ever. 'Okay. I want to hear every detail, mind you.'

Chapter Seven

There was still mist blurring the leafless trees in the distance as we walked along the track to the hillfort. The sheep were huddled on the far side of their field and there was barely a breath of wind to stir the sedge. The silence felt expectant, somehow.

I remembered something I'd meant to ask Fin. 'What are we going to do with that video of Doctor Tom illegally metal-detecting? I realise why you didn't tell Chris about it,' I added. I'd been thinking about that on the drive back.

Fin nodded. 'He'd have had someone from the local Historic Environment Team knocking on Mum's door before we got back. We'd never get a chance to have a look around for ourselves.'

We walked a little further before she spoke again.

'I say we keep that video in reserve, in case we need something to use against Doctor Tom. We can tell him we'll take it to the authorities unless he backs off, or whatever else we might need him to do.'

I could hear the distaste in her voice, and I shared it. Blackmail wasn't an appealing prospect. That didn't mean she was wrong, although I could see other potential problems.

'What if he calls our bluff? I have no idea what penalties we might face for failing to report a crime when we've got evidence.'

'I was wondering that, and I don't know,' Fin admitted. 'But he's got more to lose than we have, hasn't he? He's already under suspicion for stealing documents from the university.'

'True,' I agreed. 'I wonder what he took. Chris said whoever blew the whistle was studying something Tudor. Could it have been something to do with John Dee?'

'I can't see us talking our way in to whoever's in charge of those special collections to find out.' Fin managed a rueful smile. 'If I had to put money on it? I'd say so.'

'I agree.'

We walked on to the clump of trees. It was easy enough to find the shallow scrape Kelley had made last night.

'It doesn't look as if he's been back.' I looked at Fin. 'So are we going to commit whatever offence it is to do some digging here?'

She took a trowel out of her pocket and crouched down. 'Keep a look out for dog walkers.'

I did as she asked. There wasn't any movement to be seen.

A few minutes later, she stood up with something small between her gloved fingertips. 'Do you suppose this is what gave him a signal?'

It took me a moment to recognise a corned beef tin's key. 'How did that get up here?'

'Someone's picnic?' Fin stooped down again and shoved it back into the disturbed earth, as deep as she could. 'There had better be something to find if we do end up setting the authorities on Kelley.'

She stood up and brushed soil off her gloves. 'So what now?'

I looked around. There still wasn't anyone in sight. 'Master Hob!' I called out. 'Are you there?'

No response. Nothing. Even the birdsong had stopped.

Fin sighed, frustrated. I knew how she felt.

'Shall we walk up to the church?' she suggested.

'Take a look at the Kelley family tombs?' I nodded. 'We might as well.'

As we reached the crossroads, I glanced over at the big house. The windows were still shuttered and I reminded myself that meant Tom Kelley couldn't see out as well as stopping other people looking in. Hopefully he hadn't seen me and Fin heading for Sedgeport this morning.

'We could book a table here for dinner tonight,' I suggested as we went around to the back of the pub. 'For the three of us. My treat, to say thanks to your mum?'

'Could do,' Fin said agreeably. 'I don't think we need to stand vigil over the hillfort, do you?'

I shook my head. 'If he tries again, it'll be in the dead of night, and I don't think he knows about the hob early-warning alarm system.'

She pushed open the door and went in. A few tables were occupied. A teenager approached us with a hopeful smile and a couple of menus.

Fin raised a hand, apologetic. 'We just came to get the key to the church.'

'Oh.' The lad looked uncertain. 'Neil's through there.'

He half turned, and we all looked over the bar to see the landlord standing in a tiled hallway. He was on a mobile phone. I could just make out what he was saying, with the clipped words of a man trying very hard to keep his temper.

'If you could ring me, please, as soon as you get this message. If I don't hear from you by six this evening, I'm sorry but I will have to ring Mike.'

He lowered the phone and stabbed at the screen so hard I thought he might break it.

'Neil?' Fin waved to get his attention. 'Could we have the keys to the church? Tom Kelley was quite unpleasant yesterday, so we didn't stay long. There's more I'd like to show Dan.'

The landlord stared at her, appalled. 'The church? God help us.'

He was angry, not praying. We stood there, waiting.

'Is something wrong?' Fin asked.

Neil made a sudden decision. 'I'll have to come over there with you. Jacob, tell Kate I won't be long.'

As he spoke, he was taking a coat off a hook. He opened a metal box on the wall and took out a couple of keys on a ring. Coming through the hinged flap in the bar, he led us out of the pub. He was a man in a hurry.

The church had two locks. One was black iron that looked a hundred and fifty years old, with a heavy key to match. The other was a modern Yale that was probably a hundred times more secure. Neil shoved the keys back in his pocket, pushed the door open and went straight to switch on the lights. The daylight was fading, and it was too dim to see much inside the church even with its tall, clear windows.

Neil went straight across to the far side. That's where Tom Kelley had been lurking when we'd been in here before. Fin and I followed. We shared a glance of agreement to wait and see what the landlord had to say.

There was one of those old stone tombs by the wall, with two flat brass figures on the top, surrounded by arches that looked like the church windows. The man and woman were in what looked like Shakespearean costumes to me. There were also carved slabs in the floor and ornate plaques below the windows. A whole lot of Kelleys were buried here.

Neil was stooping over the brass couple. Then he leaned down further and examined the sides of the tomb. There were little figures carved into the stone. I really wanted to see what they were doing, but that would mean disturbing Neil. I didn't want to do that just yet.

'Nothing to see here. That's something at least.' He was talking more to himself than to us. Straightening up, he looked around the church. He seemed uncertain what to do next.

'What's wrong, Neil?'

He looked at Fin. I could see her talent for encouraging people to share things with her was having an effect.

'Help me check for any signs of damage, anywhere at all.'

'Okay. We'll start by the altar. You start by the font,' Fin suggested.

We made a thorough survey. Thankfully, everything looked the same as it had done before. There was no sign of any attempt to get into any of the cupboards in the panelling around the little organ. A door leading to a side room that I guessed was for priests was locked and looked untouched.

I took a moment to give the Green Man on the pillar a hard stare, but I saw no sign of any response. It was hard to feel the little figure sticking its tongue out at me wasn't taking the piss.

We met Neil in the middle of the church. Now he was looking apologetic. 'Sorry about that. It's just if there had been any damage, and you'd been the last ones in here, I'd hate to see you blamed.'

'Why would there be damage?' Fin asked, concerned.

'The last person in here was Thomas Kelley, wasn't it?' I added.

That was enough to tip Neil into venting his anger.

'He was, and I want words with him,' he said savagely. 'Do you know what Kate found in the big house, when she popped in to run a hoover around the place, seeing as he'd gone out? He expects her to come in and clean once a week, but he won't have her do it when he's working, oh no. Not that he'll arrange to be out any time regular that suits us. So she hasn't got in there for ten days now. Anyway, he's ripped out the window seats, in every bloody room. Left the place in a hell of a mess besides, but we were expecting that. Not that sort of damage though. It must have been him. There's no one else been in there. I don't know what he'll have to say for himself, but I'll have to ring Mike this evening.' He clearly wasn't looking forward to that conversation.

'I could take a look if you like,' I offered. 'I'm here for a few days' break, but I am a carpenter by trade. Not to do the work – I'm sure you've got someone local for that. But I could give you an idea of the time it'll take and the cost to put things right. I'm used to working on old houses.'

Neil stared at me. I couldn't blame him for being taken aback.

'I can let you have some references, if that would help?' I suggested. 'Or we can just forget about it. I'm fine, either way.'

'I might take you up on that,' Neil said slowly. 'I'll have to talk to Mike Kelley first though.'

I nodded. 'Understood.'

'You've got our number, up at the house.' Fin slid her arm through mine. 'Look, we'll head back, and you can lock up here. You've got enough on your plate at the moment.'

'I certainly have,' he said with feeling as we all walked towards the church door.

'Could it have been a break-in, over at the big house?' I didn't think so, but I wanted to keep Neil talking.

He shook his head. 'Whoever it was got in with a key, clear enough. There's no sign of damage to any of the doors or windows. Nothing's been stolen that I could see. Not that there's much to take, what with it being a rental. Most folk are honest enough, but there's no need to take chances with the ones that aren't.'

I guessed that's why no one had mentioned the house being alarmed. We went out into the porch. Neil closed the heavy door and then pushed it, to be sure the Yale was secure. He turned the big key in the black iron lock and then clenched his fist around it.

'Anyway,' he said with sudden venom, 'if someone broke in, why didn't Tom do something about it? Ring 999 or run over to the pub? He stood there and watched while they wrecked the place, did he? Because that wasn't a five-minute job.'

He broke off, breathing heavily. 'Well, I'll say good night. I'll let you know what Mike Kelley says, if he wants you to take a look.'

We let him stomp off down the path through the churchyard ahead of us. Then we went back to Venturer's House. Helen came down from her studio to the kitchen when she heard us come in.

I remembered something I'd been meaning to ask. 'Helen, what would you have done the other night, if I had been a burglar?'

'Seen how you felt about facing an angry swan.' She looked perfectly serious. 'Haven't you heard we can break a man's arm with a single blow from a wing?'

Fin laughed. Helen grinned. I realised this was an established family joke. She wasn't kidding about the burglar though.

'So how did you get on?' she asked.

We told her what had happened. She was as astonished as both of us, and shared Neil from the pub's concerns.

'There's no sign of Tom at all? And he's not answering his phone? Is Neil going to ring the police?'

'Not yet, not till he's spoken to Mike. Tom went out just after breakfast, in his car and heading off towards St James.' The jerk of Fin's head indicated the fourth road that arrived in the village beside the green, the left turn out of Fen End. 'That's when Kate went over to tidy up.'

'That was quick thinking, Dan, offering to assess the damage for Neil.' Helen looked at me, approving. 'We might learn something if you can get in for a look around.'

'Possibly, but it's not just that,' I admitted. 'I can't help wondering if I'm part of the reason this happened. I threw a real scare into him last night, and I did it on purpose. Maybe he panicked and this is the result.'

'We still don't know what he's up to.' Fin scowled, frustrated. 'Who can we ask, who might know something?'

She spoke at the same time as Helen, who was still looking at me.

'Can you give me your boss's information? I can email Neil, to let him know you really do know which end of a hammer to use. Before he talks to Mike. That might help get you through the door.'

'I'll get my laptop.' As soon as I had that set up at the kitchen table, I sent her a link to the Blithehurst website, and also to the firm of architects where Eleanor Beauchene's brother works. I'd managed a major house renovation project for one of their clients, as well as solving a problem none of them knew they had. That had been the monster in the lake that Fin had helped me kill. 'I'll give Eleanor a ring, to let her know she might be getting a call.'

'I'll email Neil now.'

Helen headed upstairs and Fin started getting pans and things out of cupboards.

'Pasta okay for dinner?

'Great, thanks.'

I rang Eleanor Beauchene. She was surprised to hear from me, and even more astonished when she heard what was happening.

'So much for a quiet holiday. Can't you go anywhere without getting mixed up in something odd?'

Odd was an understatement, but as a dryad's descendant, Eleanor has seen far more frightening things than a hob. That's why she'd needed my help at Blithehurst, when I found myself sent there by an unexpected chain of events.

'Who knows?' I said. 'If the Green Man had a hand in getting me here, he's certainly not saying. Where are you at the moment?'

'Still at Blithehurst.'

That was good news. Eleanor spends most of her time in Durham, where she's doing a PhD in medieval history. Now that the resident dryads have agreed to let her leave without giving her grief, on condition that I'm there to give them a contact with the mundane world.

'Can you talk to Asca and Frai for me? Ask them if they know anything that might help us here? If they have any idea what Kelley might be up to? I know it's a long shot, but we'll try anything just at the moment.'

'I can ask.' Eleanor sounded dubious. 'You know you'll owe them for any-thing they tell me.'

'If they know something useful, it'll be worth it.' I certainly hoped so, any-way.

'Okay, I'll talk to them tomorrow and let you know how I get on. Anything else?'

'No, that's it. Thanks.'

We said goodbye and I ended the call.

Fin was chopping onions. She grinned at me. 'Make yourself useful and do those mushrooms.'

I held up my phone. 'Okay if I just ring my dad?'

She nodded. 'Go ahead.'

I could picture him in his chair by the fire at home as he answered my call. I guessed Mum would be out with the trees. Since I'd left school and then left home, she needed to spend less and less time pretending to be a human wom-an.

'How's life in the Fens?' he asked. 'Enjoying the peace and quiet?'

I laughed, and then explained why that wasn't actually so amusing. 'Can you ask Mum what she knows about hobs for me? And sylphs. Anything might turn out to be relevant. And anything she knows about mortals finding ways to control them against their will.'

Dad laughed. 'Ask her yourself.'

'Hello, Dan.' Mum joined the call. Not using a phone, but somehow tapping into the signal that was carrying our voices. She can listen to the radio too. Don't ask me how she does it. I asked once, and got thoroughly confused as she started talking about pigeons and magnetic fields.

'Hobs are of the earth, and sylphs are of the air,' she said thoughtfully. 'We seldom see them out in these woods, and only ever passing through. Sylphs prefer open country where the winds can blow unfettered. They ride the breezes for miles. Hobs stay close to home. They became fascinated by hu-mans, time out of mind ago. They learned to trade their labour and favour for warmth, food and shelter. There used to be a couple in the village here, but I haven't seen them since before you were born.'

Mum sounded disapproving, which I thought was a bit unfair. Dryads had come to realise how coppicing and other human forestry techniques could benefit their woodlands. They also started seducing human men, enjoying sen-sual pleasure freely given and received. That went back to the ancient Greeks and beyond. I wondered how long ago a dryad considered beyond the bounds of memory. Mum mentions the English Civil War as if it was only last week, and her grandmother remembered the Romans arriving.

She was still talking. 'Sylphs were lured ever closer to humanity's hearths, built for cooking and as they worked clay and ore. They delight in the ways that fire stirs the air. The more uses mortals made of such things, the more the sylphs revealed themselves. Like the hobs, they grew closer to the people they favoured, sharing knowledge of themselves and their talents, until they learned their mistake. Too often they learned too little and too late. Those of us born of wood and water heard enough tales of woe to be very glad we had kept our distance. Too many mortals proved greedy or ungrateful, obsessed with their own short-lived concerns. Worse, some knew enough of a hob's nature, and a sylph's, to bind them to their will through arcane ritual.'

So the hob who lived here wasn't making that up. 'Do you know how they did that? Do you know how to break that hold?'

'I'm sorry, I don't.' She regretted not being able to help me, but she still wasn't exactly sympathetic to the hobs or the sylphs. 'We of wood and water grew ever more cautious in our dealings with humanity, as they should have been from the start.'

So much for supernatural solidarity. There was a pause as I wasn't sure what to say.

Dad realised Mum had said everything she was going to, for the moment at least. 'Well, watch your step, Dan. Let us know how everything goes.'

'I will.' I could tell he was worried. He wasn't alone.

'When you've got it sorted out, maybe you could bring Finele to see us here?' he suggested. 'I know your mum would love to meet her.'

So Mum had disappeared before she could be asked anything more about hobs or sylphs. I looked across the table at Fin. She had a pan of pasta sauce simmering, and was leaning against the units, watching me make my call.

'I'll ask her. See you soon, Dad.'

He said goodbye and so did I.

'Ask me what?' Fin asked as I put down the phone.

'Do you fancy a visit to meet my parents?' I tried not to let her see how very odd I found saying that.

'Oh.' Whatever she'd expected, that wasn't it. 'Okay, we could stop off there. It's not that far out of my way, heading back to Bristol. What else did he have to say?'

I was as glad as she was to change the subject. I explained what my mum had told me. 'So I don't think we can expect much help from the Blithehurst dryads.'

'It does look as if we're on our own,' Fin agreed. 'Well, I'll get the pasta on. You can wash up since you didn't help with the cooking.'

She grinned, and I could see she was far less concerned by our lack of outside help than I was. I supposed her family had always had to be self-reliant. They'd always had each other to depend on as well.

We ate dinner, I washed up, and Helen went to watch the latest episode of some drama she was following on the telly. Fin and I stayed in the kitchen, each of us with our own laptop. We spent the evening seeing what we could find on the Internet about John Dee, Edward Kelley, sylphs and hobs. We found ourselves clicking through links to some increasingly odd websites, but what we found didn't really amount to much more than we already knew.

I went to bed, wondering what the night might bring. I hoped it wasn't a hob with a problem we had no way to solve.

Chapter Eight

Nothing woke me up. I wasn't sure if I should be sorry about that, or worried, or simply relieved. A text from Eleanor Beauchene as I was getting dressed was much more straightforward. Michael Kelley had rung her bright and early, to follow up on the email from Helen that Neil had forwarded to him.

The landline in the sitting room rang as Fin and I were finishing breakfast. I got up to answer it without thinking.

Fin waved a hand. 'Leave it. Mum's got an extension upstairs.'

Helen came down a few minutes later. 'That was Neil, asking if you could meet him at Talbot House at ten. I said that would be fine.'

'Great, thanks.'

'Just Dan or both of us?' Fin looked at her mum.

'He didn't say.' Helen shrugged.

'Then I'll come too. Carry your tools or something.'

'I'm only going to assess the damage,' I reminded her. That was a good thing too, since I had so few tools with me. 'But that does give us an excuse to take plenty of photos.'

'Let's hope we see something useful,' Fin agreed.

I went to the Land Rover to get a steel tape measure, and stuck the notepad and pencil from Sedgeport in another pocket. As we walked past the bungalows behind the pub and Talbot House came into view, we saw Neil Moryinson was already waiting by the front door. We crossed the main road to join him, careful not to be flattened by a speeding HGV.

'I do appreciate this.' He offered me his hand. He still looked as stressed as he had done last night.

'No trouble,' I assured him as we shook.

'Have you heard from Tom? Has Mike called the police?' Fin looked at Neil, expectant.

The landlord was torn between not wanting to gossip and not wanting to be rude. 'No one's heard from Tom,' he said after a moment. 'Mike's still deciding what to do. He doesn't want anything touched,' he warned us, 'in case it does end up as an insurance job. Can you still do what you need to, just to give us an estimate?'

'Let's see.' I couldn't see a claim going through for this sort of wilful damage by a house's part-owner.

Neil unlocked the porch. The inner door opened into a tiled hall with elegant stairs at the rear and a big window above the half landing letting in plenty of daylight. Doors on either side stood ajar. The wooden shutters on these windows were still closed, so Neil started switching on lights to show us two sizeable sitting rooms, one with a TV and one without. As a high-end holiday let, both rooms were comfortably furnished with carpet, modern sofas and side tables, but they lacked the personal clutter of a house where people actually lived.

Somehow that made the damage more shocking. There were three sash windows to the front of the house and two to the side. Window seat cushions matching the sofas had been made for the deep, low sills. Those had been tossed on the floor, and Doctor Tom had ripped out the white-painted wood. Some bits had been thrown after the cushions. Other lumps stuck up at odd angles, bristling with vicious splinters. He must have used something like a crowbar, and he hadn't used it with any skill or care. The wood had been broken from the middle. He had forced the sharp chisel edge between the planks, rather than lever them up from the ends with the claw end. Mind you, that meant the shutters were undamaged, which was a plus for the other Kelleys, because those looked original to me.

I walked over for a better look, careful to avoid treading bits of wood and chips of paint into the brown carpet. There was no sign that there had been any storage space originally built in beneath the windows. These walls were built of solid stone, brought here by Kelley money from somewhere outside the fens.

'God knows what he thought he was doing,' Neil muttered savagely. 'It's as bad in every room.'

He led us past a narrow hallway leading to a side entrance. There were two more doors at the foot of the stairs. The one on the right opened into a big dining room, where the chairs around the table were shoved askew. The other door went into the kitchen, where a pine table was piled high with dirty pans and crockery. Cupboards ran around the inner walls and the work surfaces were cluttered with lidless jars, open packets of cereal and empty bags for sliced bread. The cooker, a big double-fronted fridge and the sink unit stood between the windows. Like the front rooms, there were two windows in the side wall and three overlooking the back garden. They had all had their sills ripped out.

'There are six bedrooms upstairs, and the bathrooms. He's done the same up there.' Neil was as baffled as he was angry.

'What about the top floor?' I asked.

'He left that alone, as far as I can tell.' Neil didn't seem to feel that was much consolation. 'No window seats up there.'

I thought fast. 'Are those floors carpet or wood?' I waved a hand at the destruction. 'If I had to guess, I'd say he was searching for something, wouldn't you? If he did this in every room, it doesn't look as if he found it. Would he stop looking?'

'It is all wood up there, but I wasn't checking the floorboards,' Neil admitted.

'You may as well see if there's any damage, Dan.' Fin slipped past me into the dining room.

I turned to Neil. 'We might as well be sure.'

I'd seen what she'd seen, and I was just as curious about that, but we needed the landlord out of the way. I wished I knew how to use my greenwood blood to encourage him to do what we wanted.

'I suppose so.' Focused on this new and unwelcome possibility, Neil headed into the kitchen. 'The back stairs are through here.'

I followed him through to a utility room that must have once been a scullery. Beyond that, there was a back hall where another door led out to the garden. The servants' stairs were narrow and uncarpeted, and there was no sign that the cupboards underneath them had been touched. The four attic rooms looked perfectly fine as well. I still took my time checking under the beds and chests of drawers, as well as moving the sofa bed in what could either be another sitting room or somewhere for more people to sleep.

I pushed it back against the wall. 'If he was up here, he didn't try lifting these floors.'

'Good,' Neil said curtly.

He headed back down the stairs, and I followed. We found Fin in the hallway. She held up her phone.

'I've taken some photos, so you have a record.'

'Thanks. I meant to do that myself. It's just – this is all so...' Neil hesitated, uncertain what to do next.

I took the tape measure out of my pocket. 'Let me go round and measure up. Then I can write you an estimate. I'll email it, and you and Mr Kelley can decide what to do. You'll know who's the best person to do the work locally.' I took the pencil and notebook out of my other coat pocket. 'You okay taking notes for me, Fin?'

'No problem.' She looked at Neil. 'You must have things to do. How about we get on here and I ring you when we're finished? You or Kate can come over and lock up.'

Neil rubbed a hand around the back of his neck. That clearly appealed. 'What if Tom comes back while you're here on your own?'

'Then we say we're here with his brother's permission, and we leave. No fuss, no discussion. I'm not interested in getting into any sort of argument,' I assured him.

'And I'll ring you straight away,' Fin added emphatically.

'Then he can take up any problem he's got with his brother.' I pulled a few inches out of my tape measure and let it spring back with a snap. 'Okay?'

Maybe it was both me and Fin trying to persuade him. Maybe it was remembering everything he had to do waiting for him at the pub. Either way, Neil nodded. 'Fair enough.'

He headed for the front door. As he closed it, I turned to Fin. 'Well?'

'Come and see.'

I followed her into the dining room. I'd noticed the scraps of torn paper on the carpet the same as she had, and the pencil shavings smeared across the polished table. As we walked around straightening the chairs, I saw the marble fireplace was full of burned paper. Thoroughly burned and stirred with the poker that had been left lying in the ash spilling into the fender.

'Anything?'

'No.' She shook her head, frustrated. 'Whatever else he is, Doctor Tom's not stupid.'

I bit down on my own disappointment. 'Let's see if we can find any clues anywhere else then. We may as well start in here.'

I started with the window that was in the middle of the house in each room. I measured and read out numbers to Fin. She made a list, giving each room a separate page in the Sedgeport notebook. There was nothing unusual anywhere that we could see. What there would be was a hefty bill for Doctor Thomas Kelley when his brother and sister got hold of him, if they had any sense. If they got hold of him any time soon.

When we moved upstairs to the bedrooms, it was obvious where Doctor Tom had been sleeping, from the unmade bed and overflowing waste basket. There were what looked like tea or coffee stains on the carpet by the door and empty mugs waiting for Kate from the pub to tidy up after him.

'No clothes, clean or dirty,' I observed. 'No suitcase or anything like that.'

We moved on to the bathroom next door. The sink was filthy with shaving foam scum, bristles and toothpaste. There were swirls of matted hair in the shower tray. I could picture the lazy bastard sweeping a clog out of the drain with his foot but not bothering to do anything more about it.

82

'No razor or toothbrush. No shower gel. I don't think he's coming back,' Fin said.

'Not any time soon,' I agreed.

We did find something else, under the corner side window over the dining room. The discovery didn't get us any further though.

Fin stared into the dark hollow beneath the torn white-painted wood. 'So what the hell was in there?'

It looked like a cavity in a rotten tooth to me. I knelt down and reached in, careful not to catch myself on anything sharp. I searched the empty space with my fingertips. It wasn't huge, about two hundred mil by three hundred, or more likely eight inches by twelve to whoever originally made it. All I could feel was smooth stone.

'I don't think this was chiselled out later. It was designed as a hiding place when this house was being built.'

'Do I make a note of it?' Fin's pencil hovered.

'I don't think so. We don't want to give anyone the idea that we're taking any special interest, do we?' I got to my feet. 'Let's see if there are any others.'

There weren't. We headed back downstairs.

Fin growled with wordless irritation as we reached the hall. 'So why did he rip up the rest of the window sills if he'd found what he was looking for? That can't have been the last place he looked.'

'Maybe he thought there might be more hidey-holes. No, wait.' I held up a hand as Fin got her phone out. 'Don't ring Neil just yet.'

I checked the time on my own phone. It was already nearly midday, but I reckoned we could stay a little longer before Neil wondered what we were doing over here.

She followed me into the dining room. 'What is it?'

I looked around. 'You know those TV shows where the story starts in the middle, so you have to try to work out what the hell's going on? Then you get "twenty-four hours earlier" on the screen after the ad break, and see if you guessed right?'

'Okay.' She had no idea where I was going with this, and I couldn't blame her.

'I told you the hob showed me glimpses of the past when I first saw him on the path to the hillfort,' I said slowly. 'Do you suppose there's any chance he could show us what happened in here over the past few days? So we could get some clue what Tom Kelley was up to. Or does that sound completely mad?'

I really couldn't decide if this was a good idea or not, but I couldn't shake it either. The possibility had occurred to me as we checked the first window upstairs. I'd been about to dismiss it as too unlikely or too risky, if it was even possible. Then we'd found the hiding place. The empty hiding place.

Fin stared at the black scraps in the fireplace for a long moment. She heaved a sigh. 'It sounds mad, but it's got to be worth a try. We're out of other options, aren't we? Though I don't think a few pork pies and some beer will cover it. I reckon the hob will want you to owe him some massive favour in return for something like that. You need to be very, very careful to agree terms with him first. Then we'd have to find some excuse to get back in here. That won't be easy.'

'Easier'n you think, if I choose to help you.'

Fin yelped. I swore. 'Shit!'

We both spun around to see who had just spoken up behind us.

A small figure stood just inside the dining room door. It was a hob, but not the one I had met before. She wore a long dress, baggy-sleeved and belted at the waist with a knotted cord. The garment was so plain it could have come from any century. Some sort of scarf was tied around her head. All the cloth was so dark brown that it looked almost black. Except I knew it wasn't black, and no, that made no sense to me either.

She was as ugly as the first hob. No, ugly wasn't really the right word, I now realised. It's more that there was something about their features that was so not-human that instincts I didn't even know I had warned me this was a potentially dangerous encounter. Those were instincts I must have got from my father's mortal blood, while it was my mother's heritage that gave me the ability to see such things.

She folded her arms. 'Good day to you, Master Greenwood, Mistress Swan.'

'Good day, Mistress Hob,' I said cautiously. Talking like some extra in a historical drama felt like the safest thing to do.

Fin clearly thought the same. 'Good day, Mistress Hob. Please excuse us. We didn't mean to trespass. We—'

'I know what you been doing.'

It was impossible to tell if the hob approved or disapproved. Still, why would she have shown herself if she wasn't at least prepared to discuss helping us? The next question was, how much could she do? Was she only offering to let us back into the house if we talked the hob from the fen into showing us what Tom Kelley had been doing here? Or could she do what we wanted herself?

Fin had worked that out too. 'I wonder, might you have seen what... what the stargazer's son was doing in here, over these past few days?'

'I might at that.' The hob's sly smile said she appreciated Fin's carefully chosen words. It also told us she wasn't going to tell us anything for free.

Okay, but I wanted to find out as much as I could about what we were buying, before we agreed a price. 'Might you have seen what he found in that hiding place upstairs?'

The hob scowled. 'If I was fool enough to stand there where I might be seen, when he got his hands on the treasure he sought.'

After giving it a moment's thought, I was pretty sure that was a no. It also sounded as if Doctor Tom had found what he was looking for. The hob had said 'when', not 'if'. Did that mean she'd known what it was, and where, all along? The hob in the fen hadn't had any idea. I wondered how much these two shared with each other, or if they even spoke.

I glanced at Fin. 'We know he seeks a crystal to show him what he can't usually see. We believe he has some of the stargazer's writings that will tell him how to use it to do that.'

She nodded. 'We know he means nothing good for those he might catch sight of through it.'

'They would be wise to avoid that happening, don't you think?'

'Very wise,' Fin agreed.

This was starting to sound like a computer-generated conversation in some fantasy game. I wondered how to move things on.

'If we could find him, we could put a stop to what he's doing.' How we might do that was a whole different conversation. One I wanted to have without a hob eavesdropping.

'To do that, we'd need to know where he's gone.' Fin was looking at me, but I'd bet any money she was fighting the same urge as me: to look at the hob and see how she was taking this.

'If we could see what he had been doing, we might know where to look.'

The hob laughed. 'And so you come full circle, Master Greenwood.'

Fin and I both looked at her. We waited.

The hob smiled briefly. Then she looked at us, intent. 'I can show you what occurred here.'

That was a direct answer to our question, but it wasn't an offer as such. We both waited for more, without any need to discuss it.

The hob put her hands on her hips. 'I will do this thing for you if you do me some service of equal value. I will deal with you more fairly than the hob of the long isle will,' she warned.

'I would think,' I said carefully, 'that us putting an end to whatever the star-gazer's son is up to would be doing you a great service.'

The hob drew a long breath, and then nodded. 'That would be so. I am willing to do what you ask and trust that you will do what you promise. If you do not put an end to his schemes, we will discuss what you owe me then.'

That sounded ominously like a threat, but I reckoned it was the best deal we would get. I looked at Fin. 'Agreed?'

'Agreed,' she said firmly.

'So—'

Before I could say anything else, I felt the familiar and unpleasant sensation of being swept up in a supernatural being's power. The closest I can describe it is that way you think the room is spinning when you fall into bed stupidly drunk.

Chapter Nine

When I'd been carried away by a dryad, and by a naiad on previous occasions, I'd closed my eyes and tried not to throw up. This time I forced myself to keep my eyes open and did my best not to think about having to explain a puddle of vomit to Neil. Mercifully, the dizzying sensation faded. Not entirely, but enough for me to unclench my jaw.

We were in the dining room, me, Fin and the hob, standing exactly where we had been. The shutters were closed and the bright light overhead was switched on. There was a fancy silver clock on the mantelpiece and I could just make out the hands. It was ten past seven, and I could see pale daylight outlining the shutters, so this must be yesterday morning, after the confrontation at the hillfort.

We weren't alone, but there was no indication Tom Kelley could see us. He was sitting at the head of the table, in front of the smouldering fire in the hearth. His tweed jacket was draped over the back of a chair and he was wearing a waistcoat, but apart from that he looked the same as he had when we met him.

Leaning forward, he was peering at a handwritten book through a magnifying glass. That had a plastic handle, and I could see it was nothing special, something you can buy in any high street. He wasn't doing anything that might be useful for us, like talking to himself. As he concentrated, the only sounds in the room came from a few early cars or lorries going past outside the house.

The rest of the table was covered with paper. There was an untidy stack of old, creased documents that looked very like the records Fin had gone through in the Sedgeport Museum archive. I wondered if those were the papers he'd stolen in Cambridge. Modern photocopies of more of the same were starkly black and white beside them. Some of the pages, old and new, were covered in dense handwriting. Others had tables and diagrams. Circles and many-pointed stars were marked up with weird symbols as well as the ordinary alphabet. This collection looked very similar to the illustrations I'd seen in that book on John Dee.

Tom Kelley had been trying to decipher something, as far as I could make out. Ruled pages torn from an A4 notepad were covered with pencil notes, crossings out and arrows leading from one section to another. Other bits were circled or marked with asterisks. What I couldn't see was what any of it meant. Fin was closer. I hoped she had a better view.

Then I had an idea. I reached for my phone. I might as well try to take a photograph, even if I had no way to know if that would work. If it did, we might see something if we zoomed in on whatever I got.

It was a bad idea. As soon as my fingertips touched it, my whole hand went into spasm. It was worse than the worst cramp I'd ever had. I honestly thought my bones or tendons might snap. The pain was so intense I felt light-headed.

It took all my strength to drag my hand away before I passed out. I tucked my aching fingers under my other armpit, trying to ease the lingering ache. I saw the hob looking at me. She was silently laughing, and she didn't care that I saw it.

I concentrated on the table. As well as everything else, there were a lot of maps. Some were hand-drawn, old and new. Others looked like the reprints you see framed and hung on walls, from every era from Tudor to Victorian. There were three Ordnance Survey maps spread out, and a couple more still folded up, half covered up by other papers. From the shape of the coastline, the maps I could see covered the whole of the Fens on either side of the Wash. There were marks here and there, in red and green marker pen.

I tried to take a step closer, to get a better look. I couldn't move. My feet were fixed to the floor. I saw the hob laughing at me again. At least someone was getting some amusement out of this.

Tom Kelley sprang up, shoving his chair back so hard it nearly fell over. I jumped, startled. So did Fin. We couldn't help it. I didn't look at the hob, who must have been splitting her sides by now.

Doctor Tom started gathering up his papers. He took a battered brown leather briefcase off a chair. It was one of those big, old-fashioned upright ones that open at the top, rather than a flat one for a few file folders. He stowed the oldest documents inside it. Closing the handwritten book he'd been reading, he unearthed four more from under the scattered papers. The notebooks were identical, with stiff black covers, and they went in the briefcase as well. I guessed they were journals of some kind. Sorting through the photocopies, he tore some pages into halves and quarters. The rest went into the briefcase. He did the same with his handwritten notes. Then he put his pencils and marker pens in a wooden box with a sliding top and tossed that in as well.

Turning to the fire, he shovelled some more coal from a scuttle onto the embers. While that was catching alight, he went to the far end of the table to fold up his maps. He was taking all of those.

As soon as the fire was blazing again, he went back to the hearth and dumped the torn pages on the flames. Satisfied they were well alight, he left the room. Bastard. There was no way we could follow him. Of course, we hadn't known that when we'd come up with this plan. Naturally the hob wasn't going to tell us, was she?

At least we could hear what was going on. That was pretty obvious. A door opened and slammed, somewhere beyond the kitchen. The sound was too light to be him going into a room. It must be a cupboard. That's where he found the crowbar, I guessed. We heard wood splintering as he began his search in the kitchen.

He was methodical, I had to give the prick that much. Fin and I stood and watched as he came back to the dining room and ripped up the window sills around us. He left, and we could hear the destruction in the sitting rooms. There was a pause as he went up the stairs. Then we heard him smashing through the painted wood in the bedrooms.

Since we were right underneath the hidey-hole, we heard his triumphant exclamation as he found whatever he'd been looking for. Then there was a long pause before we heard splintering wood again. Was he looking for something else or just leaving nothing to chance? I saw my frustration mirrored in Fin's eyes.

Movement caught my eye, and I looked at the hob. She was smiling, but not at my expense this time. She raised a yellow-taloned hand. Her meaning was clear. Wait and see. Of course, I realised as we heard Kelley coming down the stairs. He'd left his briefcase and jacket in here.

He was carrying something cupped in both hands. It was wrapped in what looked like wash leather. He put it carefully down on the table and went to use the poker to satisfy himself that everything he had thrown on the fire was thoroughly burned. His prize rolled a little and the leather flopped down to show us what looked like black silk inside. It was wrapped around a sphere, there was no doubt about that. I reckoned it was about six inches in diameter. So the stargazer's crystal really was a crystal ball.

Tom Kelley put it in the briefcase. At least, he tried to. He had to have several goes, taking out the maps and journals to rearrange them. Finally, he was satisfied, even if he couldn't close the case. He put on his jacket and carried the case out of the room with his arms wrapped around it.

We heard him go back upstairs. He was moving around doing something. Packing up, I realised as I heard him come back down the stairs, more slowly, with a heavier tread.

I heard a door open, and it was definitely a door this time. The sound of a passing vehicle was suddenly, briefly louder, and I realised he'd gone outside. There was a pause where I guessed he was carrying things out. Then the door out to the garden closed with a solid thud and we heard his key in the lock. A car started, somewhere behind the house.

The hob clapped her hands. The engine sound cut off abruptly and I realised we were back where we'd started, so to speak. When was another question. I reached for my phone to check the time. As I did so, memory of the pain I'd just felt made me hesitate.

The hob cackled. There's no other word for it. 'Now you know how cold iron feels to us, Master Greenwood.'

There was nothing I could say to that, so I said nothing at all. I looked at my phone and saw that barely twenty minutes had passed since I'd last looked at the screen. It still felt as if we'd been standing here for well over an hour.

'Where did he go?' Fin looked at me.

'Your guess is as good as mine.'

'I can't help you with that. You had better find them as can be of use to you, and quickly.' As the hob looked from Fin to me, her tone made it clear we'd be in trouble if we didn't.

'We will do all we can. Thank you, Mistress Hob, for your help.' I acknowledged her with a nod that came ridiculously close to a bow before I realised what I was doing.

The hob liked it. 'So your lady mother taught you some manners, Master Greenwood. My compliments to her.'

I didn't dare look at Fin. 'We should leave, if we're to start looking for Tom Kelley.'

'Then go.' The hob flapped her hands to dismiss us and walked into the wall behind her. By which I mean, she disappeared into it like someone walking through a curtain. I realised that hobs looked the same when they were ethereal and when they were solidly present in the human world.

We went out through the front door. Fin rang the pub, and Neil came over to lock up.

'What sort of car does Tom Kelley drive?' I asked him as casually as I could. 'Just out of interest.'

'I was thinking of showing Dan some more of the area,' Fin explained. 'Wisbech, King's Lynn. You never know, we might see him.'

Neil's grimace as he shoved the keys in his pocket said he thought that was unlikely. 'A red Jag. Not one of the brand-new ones, but it's pretty flash.'

'Fair enough. Okay,' I said briskly, 'I'll get this written up this afternoon. One other thing, can you book us a table for this evening? For three, at seven-thirty?'

Neil nodded. 'No problem.'

We crossed the green and the road together, and went our separate ways.

'Do you think they'll have anything new to tell us by this evening?' Fin clearly had her doubts as we passed the bungalows.

'Only one way to find out, and besides, I owe your mum a thank you for having me here.' I looked around and wondered if we were being watched, and if so, by what.

I abandoned any regrets about never seeing those hobs back home that Mum had mentioned. The idea of being under observation, without ever knowing such creatures were hiding in the walls, was giving me the creeps. It was worse than those Internet-connected speaker assistant things. At least you can see where those are, and it's your choice to have one in the first place.

Fin's thoughts were elsewhere. 'So how do we track Tom Kelley down?'

'It would be so much sodding easier if this was TV, wouldn't it? If we were cops.' It was easy to remember the jargon. 'Put out a BOLO. Get the tech unit to ping the GPS on his phone. Flag his car registration for ANPR alerts.'

'Have we got any idea where he's going? That might give us a lead.' Fin's frustration was growing.

'Maybe. Sort of. Can I have that notebook a minute?' I held out my hand.

She passed it over. 'What is it?'

I flipped back the pages to the notes I'd made in the Sedgeport Museum Reading Room. 'I was wondering what Doctor Tom was doing with all those maps. Then I remembered something in that book about John Dee. He applied to William Cecil for an official licence to go looking for buried treasure. He talked about hearing reports of people seeing visions of hoards being buried, or dreaming about them. He was ready to take these tales seriously.'

'That's not such a stretch,' Fin allowed, 'if Edward Kelley was finding sylphs and hobs with that crystal ball and forcing them to tell him what he wanted to know. That would convince Dee there were more things in heaven and earth and suchlike.'

'Dee was interested in treasure hunting well before they met, but fairly early on, Kelley produced some sort of map with clues that were written in code. Supposedly it showed where Danish warrior kings had buried their valuables in places across southern England. There are supposed to still be copies around, according to the Internet anyway, but there's no way to know if they're accurate. Dee's papers and books were stolen and scattered, like Chris said. No one's ever been able to make any sense of these so-called maps anyway.'

'Seriously?' Fin stared at me. 'Tom Kelley's treasure hunting?'

'He could be, couldn't he? If he's found the original map and he has some way to decipher it. If Edward Kelley was forcing sylphs to pretend to be angels dictating mystical scrolls to John Dee, maybe Doctor Tom can use the crystal to see them and somehow make them explain what those clues really mean. Maybe he has some way to force the local hobs to show him things happening in the past, so he knows exactly where to dig. How much was that Viking hoard worth, the one those metal detectorists were jailed for not declaring and selling off bit by bit on the quiet? Three million quid, wasn't it?'

'Or maybe he will declare what he finds,' Fin said slowly. 'Show the world that he's the genius who solved the riddles of John Dee's treasure map. Be the historian who found a treasure to rival the Sutton Hoo burial, if there's one to be found. He'd be famous. That would show everyone he wants to get even with, personally and professionally.'

'There's no way to be sure, but it's the best I can come up with.' I shook my head. 'Not that it's much use if we've no idea where he is.'

'We may not be able to put out an all-points bulletin,' Fin said thoughtfully, 'but I can see if the family grapevine can help. I have a fair few relatives, on both sides of my family, and they know a lot of people. It's not as if Tom Kelley's some anonymous bloke in jeans and a sweatshirt. He's pretty recognisable.'

'What will you say?'

'I'll tell my mum's family the truth. That he's threatening the hobs and the sylphs here,' she clarified. 'They can tell other people he's gone off without a word, leaving Talbot House in a hell of a state, and his brother and sister are worried. That's what I'll tell my dad.'

She took out her phone. 'I'll give my cousin Will a ring now, and tell him to look out for a red Jag. He's out and about a lot.'

'What does he do?'

'Photography. Trade stuff mostly, and he has clients all over. He has a sideline in his own work too, selling cards and prints, landscapes and wildlife for the tourists. One way and another, he covers a lot of miles.' She smiled briefly. 'It's the best I can come up with at the moment.'

She made her phone call as we walked back to Venturer's House. I was flicking through the notebook and making a few rough calculations for the repairs.

We brought Helen up to date over lunch. Then I got my laptop out and drew up Neil's estimate. Fin sat across the kitchen table and emailed her relatives. When we were both done, we walked along the track to the hillfort. There was no sign of the hob or anything else that any ordinary person wouldn't be able to see.

After Helen finished work for the day, we went out to dinner at The Wheat Sheaf. I had a steak, and the food was as good as I'd hoped. There was no more news of Tom Kelley. Helen took Kate aside to see if she could learn anything else, but all she got was more detail than anyone needed about his unpleasant personal habits.

When we got back, Fin checked her email. No one had seen or heard anything that might help us find him, though they promised to do what they could. We had to be satisfied with that, for the moment at least. I wondered how far Tom Kelley could have got with two days' travelling time. Maybe we hadn't seen him because he was already on the other side of the country.

As I switched out my bedside light, I had another idea. My mum had said sylphs liked open country, and they could ride the breezes for miles. Was there any way we could ask them to help us look for Tom Kelley, searching as far afield as they could go?

The hob had said he'd scared them off though. If we needed his help to get them back here, so we could talk, that meant striking a bargain. We'd need to be very careful. Then there was the question of what we could offer in return for the sylphs' help. I'd have to talk to Fin and Helen about it all in the morning.

I should have stayed awake and thought a lot more seriously about sylphs.

Chapter Ten

A crash somewhere downstairs woke me up. It took me a moment to re-member where I was. Then I took another moment to work out the noise was coming from downstairs. It was right below where I was sleeping. It wasn't stopping either, even if it wasn't as loud.

'Mum?' Fin called out, concerned. She was coming along the landing.

'I'm fine. What *was* that?' Helen's door opened as she answered. 'Dan?'

'There's something going on downstairs.' I was already dragging my clothes on.

Helen and Fin were in dressing gowns as I followed them down to the sitting room. The curtains were drawn, but there was enough daylight filtering through to see that everything looked the same as we'd left it last night. The door to the end room was closed though, and that's where the noise was com-ing from.

Bugger. That's where the original hall's fireplace was, and the one in the kitchen was full of a cooker and the Aga. There were no fire irons to be had in here or in there.

'What are you looking for?' Helen had seen me searching the room.

'Ideally, a poker. Something heavy, made of iron.' I didn't bother lowering my voice.

In the unlikely event there was a burglar in the end room, hearing that might make him think again and climb out of whatever window he had bro-ken. I expected to find something else, though, something that iron could really hurt. Whatever it was, it needed to know we weren't people to be messed with.

The noise behind the closed door stopped. Fin ducked out of the sitting room and came back from the kitchen with a hefty cast-iron frying pan, big enough for six rashers of bacon.

'Sorry about the cliché.' She handed it over.

No wonder I hadn't seen Helen using this. The thing weighed a tonne. Good. I hefted it in one hand and pulled open the door.

These curtains were open, so I could see the room was filled with a blizzard of flying paper. As I stepped across the threshold, the torn pages stopped swirl-ing and swooping. They darted straight at me instead.

'Ow!'

The papers didn't flap around me, trying to block my view of whatever was in there. The pages zipped straight at me, horizontal. At the last instant, they veered away. That didn't mean they missed me. Each sheet hit me, edge-on, one after the other, too fast to count.

I'd got as far as jeans and a T-shirt, getting dressed. Within seconds, my bare arms were red with hairline paper cuts that stung like a son of a bitch. The tornado of pages rose higher. Now they were swirling around my head. I felt one brush my face. If one cut my eye, then I would be blinded for real.

I began sweeping the flying paper out of the air with violent swings of the frying pan. It must have looked ridiculous, but I wasn't thinking about that. I'd seen a figure on the far side of the room. It was about Fin's height, over by the emptied bookshelves.

I'd never seen a sylph, but that's what it must be. Male? Female? I couldn't tell. Since I wasn't trying to get it into bed, that really didn't matter. A dryad in her ethereal state is green. A naiad is slate blue. This slender figure was pale cream, like summer sunrise clouds, wearing what could be a long tunic or a short dress. The face looking at me was strikingly beautiful, with ice-cold, bright blue eyes. Beautiful, but not at all friendly. Unfriendly, and unnervingly intelligent.

The sylph raised a hand and the flying paper fell to the floor. I took a long stride towards the bookshelves. I nearly did the sodding splits. Whatever I had just stepped on was ripped out from under my foot. I didn't just slip. As my weight landed, my footing was deliberately pulled away. Agony ripped through my thigh and groin.

I had other things to worry about as I tried to force my way closer. Books flung themselves at my head. I batted them away with a two-handed grip on the pan. Magazines surged towards me, rolling themselves into tight cylinders. Paper's made of wood, and these might as well have been sticks as they stabbed me in the ribs and kidneys every time I raised my arms. When I flinched, instinctively dropping my elbows, another paperback smacked me round the face.

The sylph moved and the storm abated for a few seconds. I saw the pale figure glance at the windows at the front and the back of the house. So that's how they got in. Those old panes were leaded. A naiad had once dragged me through an old lead mine, so encountering that metal clearly wasn't a problem for such beings. The fireplace, on the other hand, was filled with the ancient iron wood-burning stove, as well as whatever flue arrangements vented the oil-fired boiler in the cupboard. So they weren't leaving that way.

The sylph took a step towards the back of the house. Too slow. Bright light flashed. A swan swept past me to land on the gate-leg table. She spread her great white wings, stirring up her own storm of flying paper. Head weaving on her long neck, she hissed with chilling menace. The sylph turned for the other window. The other swan was already there, flapping on the little settee.

In the sylph's moment of indecision, I took two long strides. I swept the pan around with all my strength behind it. The sylph was more solid than I expected. They staggered all the same, and recoiled as I raised the pan for the backhand stroke. That was a mistake. Stepping into the arch of the great fireplace meant coming up hard against the wood stove. The sylph cried out with a high-pitched wail that could have been a child's voice or a bird's.

I didn't care. I had the pale figure trapped in the fireplace now. With my reach, there was no getting past me without getting a smack on the face from the frying pan. That would hurt. I could see that the mark where my first blow had landed was spreading up the sylph's arm and shoulder. It was the dusky blue of a storm cloud, or the worst bruise you've ever had.

I had no sympathy at all. Burning pain in my groin had me seriously worried. I'd torn a muscle, or done something even worse. I shifted my weight from foot to foot, trying to ease the vicious discomfort.

Light flashed behind me again. A moment later, Fin was at my side, looking a little tousled and retying her dressing gown's belt. She stooped for the poker in the set of fire irons. As Helen appeared at my other shoulder, Fin tossed her mother the log tongs. This sylph was going nowhere.

'Is this someone you know?' I asked the Wicken women. I didn't take my eyes off the sylph.

'No,' Helen said thoughtfully. 'I don't think I've seen you here before, have I?'

'Why are you here?' Fin demanded. 'What are you doing?'

'Who are you doing it for?' I raised the frying pan. 'You're going nowhere till we get some answers. That's the price you pay to leave.'

'Do your worst.' The sylph's blue stare challenged me. 'It cannot equal what I will suffer if he who sent me learns he is betrayed.'

'Who's that?'

I can't explain how eyes with no pupil or iris can look sardonic, but the sylph managed it. 'I am forbidden to speak his name.'

'The stargazer's son?' Fin said quickly.

'Some have called him that,' the sylph agreed. 'Excuse me. Doctor Stargazer's Son.'

So this was Tom Kelley's doing. That was no great surprise, though I had a lot more questions to ask. First I needed to get the measure of this sylph. I'd made a bad mistake, I realised.

Fin and her mum had called sylphs sweet and harmless, and said they were inclined to play silly games. The hob of the long isle had talked about them having the attention span of mayflies and boasted of scaring them off. Without realising, I'd been thinking of them as like the sprites I was used to seeing back home. Little creatures that delight in sunlight and flowers, shyly curious around the likes of me but never really getting involved in anyone wholly human's business. I should have been rereading *The Tempest* instead.

'Why are you here?' I asked.

The sylph smiled without humour. 'I am forbidden—'

'To tell us. Okay.' I tried to think of a way around that.

The sylph turned to Helen. 'We have never met, but I was acquainted with your father. Not that he knew my nature when we passed the time of day on his walks. He was something of a scholar when it came to local lore.'

We all looked around the room, at the devastation the sylph had made of Fin's grandad's books and magazines.

'Does Tom Kelley know anything of our family's nature?' Helen demanded, her voice sharp. 'Are you going to tell him?'

'He knows nothing of the swan folk. He has no idea you've enlisted a son of the greenwood to help you. It's not my place to tell him any of this. If he were to ask me though?' The sylph shrugged. 'I am compelled to answer.'

A flash came and went in those blue eyes, as swift and as dangerous as lightning. So the sylph – or sylphs – might be forced to follow Tom Kelley's orders, but they really weren't happy about it. I wondered if the bastard realised just how determinedly they and the hobs would look for loopholes in whatever instructions he gave them. Was he arrogant enough to believe they would simply do as they were told? For the moment, that was the best we could hope for. It would only get us so far.

'Can you tell us where he is?' Fin asked without much expectation.

The sylph glanced at her, pitying. 'No.'

'What will you tell him about what you did here? What might you tell him?' I corrected myself, in case talking hypotheticals got us any further.

The sylph gave me a look that said 'nice try'. 'I will say I have done all that he asked of me.'

'If he asks you to do something else here, you wouldn't be able to warn us, would you?' Fin said slowly.

The sylph answered with a shrug.

'But if the hob of the long isle were to see you first, he could warn us that you were here, couldn't he?' she went on.

The sylph answered with a shrug and a smile.

'Have you anything else to say?' Fin asked.

The sylph just smiled.

'Will you tell us your name?' I challenged.

'No.' The sylph's eyes flashed again.

'Then I think you might as well leave.' Helen took a step back, lowering the log tongs.

It was her house, so that was her decision, but I had one last question. 'Are you alone here, now, in this room?'

'Yes.'

Fin and I both stepped back, with our hands and weapons at our sides.

The sylph turned translucent, and then transparent, springing into the air as gracefully as a medallist jumping off a diving board. The last trace of a foot passing through the leaded window was as insubstantial as steam, though steam doesn't usually glitter like that.

'Put that on the window sill.' I nodded at the poker Fin was still holding.

Helen was already leaning over the gate-leg table to put the log tongs on the sill overlooking the garden. 'I'm not sure this will keep them out. Do you think we need something else?'

'It should give them pause for thought, if a horseshoe over the door used to be enough.' I was trying to think what else we could do.

'Bars on the windows?' Fin didn't like that idea.

Helen shook her head. 'Not on a listed building. Not and give Tom Kelley an excuse to make trouble.'

'Not and give him any reason to suspect we know what he's up to,' Fin pointed out, 'and start him wondering how we know.'

Helen nodded. She looked around at the chaos. 'I suppose we'd better tidy up.'

'Chains,' I said suddenly. 'There must be a garden centre around here that sells iron chain. We can hang lengths of it from the curtain poles. That's not permanent, and no one will be able to see what we've done from outside the house.'

'Good idea.' Helen approved. 'You two have some breakfast, then go and sort that out. I'll tidy up here.'

'Not on your own,' Fin objected.

'If we do it together, hopefully we'll find whatever the sylph wanted to destroy that much faster.' I gestured at the ripped-up books and torn pages of magazines. I corrected myself. 'Or what Tom Kelley wanted destroyed.'

Helen looked around at the devastation again, baffled. 'What did he imagine we'd think waking up to all this, if he thinks we know nothing about sylphs? That we'd had a small, very localised tornado?'

'Or a poltergeist?' Fin suggested. 'Maybe he wants to scare us away.'

'Fat chance.' Helen dismissed that with a gesture. 'I'm going to get dressed and put the kettle on.'

As she left, I moved cautiously and bent down to pick up a hardback book with its front cover missing. 'Fucking vandal.'

'Are you okay?' Fin was concerned.

'I've pulled... something,' I admitted. 'Upper thigh.'

'How bad is it?'

'Not sure. Hopefully not too bad, and I do heal quickly.' I wasn't about to undo my jeans and see what damage I could feel around my cock and balls with the risk of Helen walking back in.

'Sit down, at least.' Fin swept debris off the closest settee. 'And we should do something about your arms.'

'When everyone's out of the bathroom.' I lowered myself carefully down beside the gate-leg table. 'Pass me some stuff to sort out. No, wait!' I stiffened. 'Can you smell gas?'

'We're not on the mains here. The boiler's oil-fired.' She stared at me, puzzled. Then she caught her breath, alarmed. 'Hang on.'

She dropped to her knees and lifted up the flap of the gate-leg table. Tucked underneath, well out of sight, I saw an old metal heater, the sort that runs on bottled gas. She dragged it out and turned it around. The back panel was long gone. I could see that the plastic switch on the connector was at an angle. It wasn't all the way open, but that was enough to let the gas leak out. There was no hissing, so it must be empty by now.

'How much was in there?'

'I've no idea.' Fin looked around the room. 'How much do you think is in here?'

'Hard to say. The sylph might have done something to stop us smelling it.' I wasn't about to take any chances.

Fin agreed. 'It's not paranoia if they're really out to get you.'

Helen came through the door. 'There's no hot water. The pilot light must have gone out.'

She opened the boiler cupboard.

'No!' Fin and I shouted together. Helen looked at us, surprised.

'Grandad's old heater was leaking gas.' Fin got up and opened both windows.

'Grandad's old heater was turned on, so the gas leaked out. The sylph must have done it.' I leaned over and disconnected the gas bottle. 'Remember what my mum said about hearths and fireplaces fascinating them? I'd say that one we just met knows the way around a central heating system, and enough about propane to know that it's dangerous.'

'Tom Kelley wanted to blow the house up?' Helen was appalled.

'Has he ever been in here, to know about Grandad's heater?' As Helen shook her head, Fin did the same. 'Then how would he tell the sylph what to do?'

Neither of them had an answer for that.

'I think whatever he said, that sylph got creative.' I wished my mum had told me more that might be useful. 'I don't think we can trust them, whatever they say. Just because they hate Tom Kelley, that doesn't mean they're our friends.'

Helen looked at the chaos around the room. 'So there may be nothing in here that we need to know? This could all be misdirection?'

'Or fuel for a fire the sylph hoped to start,' Fin suggested. 'We know Tom Kelley wants us gone, even if we don't know why.'

'All he knows is I caught him metal-detecting up at the hillfort. Maybe he just wants us too busy with our own problems to think about reporting him.'

'Or there's still something up there that he wants.' Helen shuddered, or maybe she was just shivering in the cold breeze coming through the open windows. 'I think we'd better string up those chains as soon as possible.'

'Agreed.' I levered myself off the settee with some difficulty. 'Pulled a muscle,' I explained as I saw Helen's concern.

Fin followed as I made my way carefully upstairs. She came after me into the bathroom as well, and opened a cupboard. 'Cotton wool, Savlon, ibuprofen.'

'Thanks.' At least the paper cuts on my arms had stopped bleeding, so I could clean myself up. I still looked as if I'd fought a house full of cats and lost. Now I had some privacy, I checked for other damage. I had torn a muscle, high inside my right thigh. I took some painkillers and hoped that would take the edge off.

By the time I'd found a clean T-shirt and a sweatshirt, Fin was dressed and ready to go out.

'Shall we grab a coffee and something to eat while we're out?'

'Fine by me.' I followed her out to the Toyota. There was no debate about who was going to drive.

This time we turned left out of Fen End and took the road Thomas Kelley had disappeared down. There was no sign of any red Jaguar.

Fin surprised me by turning off into a small retail park just before we reached Saw Edge St James. She took a cotton shopping bag out of the door pocket. 'I'll be as quick as I can.'

She was still longer than I expected, but that was explained when she got back. She had a cardboard tray with two coffee cups and a paper bag in one hand, and the cotton bag in the other. Putting breakfast on the roof, she opened the door and swung the cotton bag into my lap.

'An ice pack for when we get back, some strapping and the strongest anti-inflammatories the pharmacist would sell me.'

'Thanks.' I waited for her to get into her seat and accepted a coffee. 'I've been thinking.'

'Go on.' She offered me the paper bag and I took a blueberry muffin.

'For a start, when we don't want to be overheard, we should sit in a car to talk.' I gestured at the metal surrounding us. 'Drive out here, or somewhere like it, if we want to be absolutely certain.'

Fin nodded as she sipped her coffee. 'Agreed. What else?'

'Last night, I was wondering if we could ask some sylphs to help us find Doctor Tom, but this morning's encounter blows that idea out of the water. We still need to find him though. I reckon we should try to find a nereid to talk to.' I took a bite of muffin and gestured to the side of the car park where a fence had a life belt and signs warning about deep water. I swallowed.

'You said these ditches and lodes and the rivers are all connected. If we could persuade a nereid to help us, hopefully more than one, couldn't they search for Tom Kelley pretty effectively? They might even have some idea where to start looking for him. It'll be somewhere off the beaten track, don't you think? He won't be digging for buried treasure somewhere like this.'

'They're called dykes around here, not ditches. No, he won't be doing whatever he's up to where anyone could see him.' Fin gazed through the windscreen at the passing shoppers. They had no idea that the creatures that threatened us really existed. They were in danger too, though they'd never know it. 'But how do we persuade a nereid to risk taking on Doctor Tom?'

'I'm not so sure it is such a risk. Remember what my mum said about sylphs and hobs getting into trouble because they got too close to humans? That's why people found ways to control them. That's why they're so paranoid about us knowing their names, don't you think? Dryads and naiads aren't bothered

THE GREEN MAN'S SILENCE

about that. They kept their distance from the likes of Doctor Dee, and my mum said they can't be controlled in the same way. I reckon nereids will be the same.'

'It can't hurt to ask,' Fin conceded. 'So how do we find one to ask?'

'That's where things get tricky.' I drank more coffee. 'The only person I can think of who might help us is the hob. The hob of the long isle,' I clarified. 'He said he answers to the Master of Fords and Ferries. That's got to be some powerful being associated with the waters around here.'

'You want to go right to the top? Or the deep?' Fin looked sideways at me. 'What's that going to cost us, by way of a bargain with the hob?'

'I have no idea,' I admitted, 'but it can't hurt to ask.'

'True enough.' Fin finished her breakfast. 'We can try that when we get back.'

I grimaced. 'I'm not really up for a hike to the hillfort.'

'That's okay.' She turned the ignition key. 'I have a better idea.'

We drove to the garden centre and bought enough cast-iron chain to hang in all the Venturer's House windows. We decided two chains for the bedrooms would do, with three lengths for each window downstairs. It wasn't cheap, but I remembered what I'd said to Tom Kelley. It would work out a lot more expensive if some creature under his spell managed to destroy the house. We got it cut to length to save time. I have no idea what the lad who served us thought we wanted it for, but my expression successfully convinced him that he really didn't want to ask.

I also got Fin to stop at the retail park again. Limping into a DIY store, I bought some packets of cup hooks and wall plugs rather than rely on whoever had fixed those curtain rails. I didn't want to get halfway through the job and find I had unexpected repairs to make without the tools I needed. At least Fin could assure me they did own a drill. I bought some drill bits, just in case.

We got back to find Helen had shut the windows and switched the boiler back on without an explosion. I'd much rather she had waited, but what was done was done, and it was a painfully cold day to have the windows open. She found me the drill, in a box well supplied with drill bits for wood and brick as well as wall plugs. I started fixing cup hooks. I was relieved to find the old brick was solid enough to take the weight of the chain.

Fin took her mum outside to sit in the Toyota, and told her what we'd discussed.

'That all makes sense,' Helen said to me as they came back into the kitchen. 'As well as this spy novel stuff in case anyone's listening in.'

Fin helped me fix the rest of the chains in the windows. By the time we had finished, my torn thigh muscle was hurting like a bastard, even with the strapping I'd put on it when we got in. I'd put the ice pack in the freezer in the utility room as well. I didn't argue when Helen handed it over, wrapped in a tea towel, and told me to sit on the settee under the window in the end room. I could see what I could find that might be of use in the old magazines that she had gathered up.

She and Fin were putting the books back on the shelves as best they could. The damage wasn't as bad as I'd feared. A lot of the flying paper had been newspaper cuttings that Fin's grandad had kept in old envelopes for whatever reason. They still put a growing stack of books aside, missing pages or covers. I began sorting through the loose pages and other debris, trying to find the missing pieces.

Helen did her best to hide it, but she was upset. Saying the room had needed a good tidy and polish for a long time didn't fool me or Fin. The second time she took far longer than necessary to fetch clean dusters from the utility room, Fin went to find her.

She came back looking damp-eyed herself. 'Mum's remembered some emails she needs to deal with.'

I heard Helen heading upstairs, as well as the half-truth in Fin's words. This was one more score we had to settle with Doctor Thomas Kelley, I decided.

I stretched out my arm. 'Can you spare five minutes for a break?'

Fin dropped onto the settee beside me. That brief cuddle was the best bit of the whole sodding day. Then she got up, made some tea, and we carried on.

I learned the reason that fenland roads and even the rivers are raised up above the farmland is that centuries of drainage have seen the peat dry out, and that means the land has steadily sunk. There are cast-iron posts at a place called Holme Fen that show four metres of shrinkage since the 1850s. I wondered if there was any other reason for using iron way out there.

I found out that Tom Hickathrift was a legendary fenman of far more than ordinary height and strength. He fought a local giant and found his hoard of treasure, which made him very popular. That brought him to the King's attention, and Tom was sent to the Isle of Thanet to kill another giant and the dragon he rode in on. He did that and came back home to live peacefully in the Fens. I couldn't help wondering if Neil at the pub had been closer to the truth than he knew when he'd joked with Fin about my height. The stories said Tom Hickathrift lived with his mum, so she was probably human, but I'd bet his father hadn't been.

I also learned that images of water fowl, especially swans, can often be found in early Celtic metalwork, sometimes cunningly hidden in abstract designs. Apparently that might well mean the birds were seen as messengers to the otherworld which could be glimpsed in the reflections on rivers and standing water. According to the little book I was reading, springs, marshes, fens and the like are considered liminal places, where the boundaries between different realms are thinner. I didn't know about that, but there was no denying Fin and her relatives can see a lot that ordinary people can't. I wondered just how long her family had been living here, if these legends went that far back.

What I didn't find was anything that could help us find Tom Kelley, or an ally against him. By the time the daylight was fading, I was getting thoroughly discouraged. If there was something potentially useful mixed up with these local legends, ancient scandals and old wives' tales, I didn't know enough to recognise it.

So it was a surprise to look up and see Helen come into the room with a newly determined smile. She had a coat and shoes on.

'Come on, Dan. Let's show you what's at the bottom of the garden.'

Chapter Eleven

I hadn't paid much attention to the back garden. There was a patio laid across the back of the house, and then a lawn flanked with flowerbeds. There wasn't anything much growing there at this time of year. Further on there were fruit trees and what looked like raspberry canes. Beyond that, there was a greenhouse and a vegetable patch, dug over and left empty for the winter.

I followed Helen down the garden path. Fin locked the kitchen door and came after us. The path curved around behind the old outbuildings that had been converted into a long, low garage and a wood store. There was a firepit there, dug into the ground and lined with old red bricks, presumably from an outbuilding that couldn't be salvaged. That explained the small stack of weathered bricks I had seen in the yard as well.

This fire wasn't for burning rubbish. The hearth was in the centre, with a circle of brick paving around it and a gravel soakaway for drainage. Then the pit had been dug out with a wider second level. That made a ring of bench seats, also lined and backed with brick. Ground level was at shoulder height, so people could sit in comfort. This was a place to relax and chat and drink an evening away with the fire to keep you warm, or even to cook on.

Helen had already lit a stack of logs, and there were cushions. There was also a tray with bottles of beer, plates, bread, cheese, pickles and pork pies. 'Can I offer you a drink, Dan?'

'Thanks.' I made my way cautiously down the steps and took a seat. I was glad I was wearing my coat, but once the fire really got going, this would be a comfortably warm and sheltered hollow. 'An IPA, thanks.'

As Helen handed me the bottle, Fin looked around the twilit garden. 'If the hob of the long isle would care to join us, he will be most welcome.'

Her voice carried through the clear, cold air. For the moment only the distant chatter of birds settling to roost for the night answered her.

'There'll be a proper dinner later, but I thought we should eat something. I've just realised we didn't stop for lunch.' Helen looked a bit embarrassed.

I had realised, but I hadn't liked to say, so I was starving. 'This is great, thanks.'

She handed me a plate with a slice of bread, some cheese and a pie. 'Rhubarb chutney?'

'My dad built this.' Fin came down the steps. 'The hobs loved it. When I was a kid, visiting Gran and Grandad, they'd settle down in here to enjoy the last of the fire once we'd gone back up to the house.'

'Hobs plural? More than the one I met?'

'Two or three, though I'm not sure it was always the same two or three. They weren't ever inclined to talk to us.' Helen laughed. 'We'd see them in the shadows sometimes, waiting for us to leave. If my mum left food out here, she'd find the weeding done for her the next morning, things like that. We've never had any trouble with slugs or snails in the garden either.'

I wondered if the hobs ate them. If they did, no wonder they preferred pork pie.

Fin helped herself to some food. 'We don't do this very often now, but we thought it was worth a try.'

'Good idea.' I resisted the temptation to look around to see if it had worked.

'Good even to you, mistress of the house.'

I managed not to knock out a tooth with my beer bottle when the hob appeared on the far side of the fire.

'Good evening, Master Hob.' Helen cleared her throat, a little nervously. 'May I offer you something to eat and drink? Freely given, without obligation.'

'You are our guest here tonight,' Fin added.

I guessed they had spent some time earlier discussing how best to win the hob over. He didn't look impressed at the moment. I wished I'd been part of that conversation. If this hob really could scare off sylphs like the one we had met, we had better not underestimate him. That reminded me of something I had to ask.

'Excuse me. Are you alone? Can you tell us if there are any sylphs here, ones we can't see?'

'There are none here that I know of. I told you I drove them all away.' He squinted at me suspiciously across the rising flames. 'Why do you ask me that?'

'What can I offer you to eat?' Fin said quickly.

The hob's eyes gleamed and his face momentarily betrayed his longing. 'Bread and meat and beer, if you please. Butter on the bread,' he added.

Fin opened a bottle and put the food on a plate. When he made no move to come and get it, she walked around the fire to put the plate and bottle down on the brick seat about halfway between us and the hob. He didn't move until she came back to sit beside me again. Then he walked along the bench. I expected him to take the food back to where he'd appeared, to keep the fire between him and us. Instead he sat cross-legged and took a long drink of beer.

He wiped the back of his mouth with a hand and bared his teeth. 'Time was we could serve ourselves, when bottles came corked and barrels were tapped with wood.'

106

I realised with a shock that was actually a smile. The hob was making what passed for conversation, maybe even a joke. Then he scowled at me.

'Don't think I don't know you want something from me.'

'We would value your counsel,' Fin said carefully. 'So that we might help you and yours by stopping the stargazer's son's schemes.'

The hob looked at her, scornful. 'You have already made that bargain with the hob of the house at the crossroads.'

So they did talk to each other. I wished they called each other by shorter names. 'Then you know he's found the crystal he was seeking, to see what would otherwise be beyond his gaze. The hob of the house at the crossroads must have told you that.'

The hob glowered as he crammed buttered bread into his mouth, but he didn't contradict me.

'We know he also has the means to compel you and yours to do what he demands. He sent an unwilling sylph here today.' I knew the hob could tell I was telling the truth, but I deliberately didn't go into details. If he wanted to know what had happened, then he'd have to give us something.

'He cannot compel us to do anything.' Fin's gesture included me and her mum. 'We can take away whatever gives him that power over you and any others.'

'Isn't that a service that will repay whatever help you might give us,' I demanded, 'as well as the hob of the house at the crossroads?'

'*If* you can do such a thing.' The hob challenged me. 'When you hazard so little of yourselves. How can I be sure you will stay the course?'

Helen spoke up, putting her own plate aside. 'If we help you, we help ourselves. The stargazer's son tried to hurt us today. We owe him payback for that.'

'Then my debt would not be so great,' the hob said swiftly.

The three of us exchanged a glance. We waited. The hob finished eating. He took his time and avoided our gaze.

Finally he looked up. 'If I knew what you sought, I might consider it. I will take more food and drink as I do so, mistress.' He nodded to Helen. Then he snapped his fingers at Fin and pointed at his plate.

She didn't move. The hob grinned again. 'If you please, Mistress Swan.'

He was seeing what he could get away with. But he'd still come here in the first place, and he was staying to hear us out. It looked as if we were right to hope that he realised he needed us as much as we needed him.

I took the cap off another bottle of beer and handed it to Fin. 'If we're going to stop him, we need to know where he is.'

She walked round to the hob. 'We wouldn't ask you or yours to risk your-selves, nor the sylphs, but there must be those who could search for him.'

He didn't take the bottle from her, but he didn't move away. As soon as she put the beer down, he snatched it up. Fin took his plate back to Helen.

'We would like to speak to a nereid.' As I said it, I realised he might have no idea what I meant. 'Nereid' is a word from Greek myth, after all. My mum's people and the river spirits had adopted such terms long ago, in their dealings with humans, but who knew if the hobs had done the same? 'One of those who live where the rivers meet the sea? Born of fresh water and salt?'

The hob waited for Fin to bring him more food.

'They could use the waterways to look for him, couldn't they?' She waited a moment before putting down the plate. 'Get some idea of what he's doing? Without risking themselves?'

'The daughters of the tide would be safe from his malice,' the hob con-firmed grudgingly.

That was a relief. 'If you think that the Master of Ferries and Fords would have no objection.'

I knew I was taking a risk. I'd just handed the hob a get-out-of-jail-free card, and I couldn't complain if he used it. On the other hand, I really didn't want to get on the wrong side of a majorly powerful spirit, especially since I was here without the Green Man to back me. I'd crossed paths with the Horned Hunter last year, and I'd seen what he could do to humans who pissed him off.

It all depended how badly the hob wanted our help, however hard he tried to pretend he was the one doing us a favour.

We waited while he ate his second plate of food.

'I could ask such a one if she would be willing,' he said eventually. 'Provided her master approved.'

'Thank you.' Helen got to her feet. 'Would you like some more wood on the fire?'

'That would be welcome,' the hob said graciously. 'And you may leave the bread, meat and beer.'

I glanced at the others, and saw that they agreed we might as well accept this dismissal. Helen sliced and buttered the rest of the loaf and left the last pie and the cheese on the bread board. I built up the fire while Fin took the tops off the last two beers.

Helen picked up the tray and we walked back up the garden. Fin set a pace that was faster than comfortable for my strained thigh. I didn't say anything though. Once we were away from the fire pit, the evening was turning bitterly cold. I looked up and saw there wasn't a cloud in the sky. Even with the faint glow of the street lights on the far side of the house, the stars were spectacular.

'Do you suppose any more hobs will join him?' Fin wondered as she unlocked the back door.

'I don't think we'd be very welcome if we went back to see.' Helen put the tray on the table and went to stir a pot simmering on the cooker.

I started putting plates in the dishwasher. 'Let's hope so. The more help we have on our side, the better.'

We had dinner, watched some telly and went to bed. Dinner was some sort of lentil and bean cottage pie that was very tasty but made me glad I was sleeping alone. A relationship needs to be well established before farting in bed is no big deal.

Chapter Twelve

We woke up to thick fog. I made my way carefully downstairs and found Fin in the kitchen staring out of the back window. I joined her. We couldn't see to the edge of the patio.

'Do you think this is something that sylph has done?' she wondered, dubious.

'Fog was on last night's weather forecast.' Then I realised there was no sign of Helen even though I'd heard her go downstairs before I got in the shower. Despite what I'd just said, I felt uneasy. 'Your mum hasn't gone out to the fire pit alone, has she?'

'No, she's got meetings in Peterborough today.' Fin turned to me. 'How's the leg?'

'Much better,' I said, relieved. 'I do heal fast.'

'I can see that from your arms.' Fin slid her hands around my waist. 'Mum left me a list for a supermarket run, but that won't take us long. If we've got the house to ourselves—'

Movement in the fog on the lawn snagged my eye through the window. Something hit the back door with a sharp crack. Mist swirled as a small, familiar figure stepped forward and threw another stone at the house. It was the hob.

'All right. Hang on.' Fin unlocked the back door. She opened it and we both shivered in the cold, clammy air.

The hob made no move to enter the house. He was furious. 'You seek my help, and yet you bar your windows to me and mine?'

'I'm sorry,' I said quickly, though I wasn't sorry to know those chains were so effective. 'We have to keep out the sylph who tried to start a fire in here yesterday.'

'Forced by the stargazer's son,' Fin added.

The hob didn't hear, or he didn't care. 'I did what you asked of me. It's your fault I couldn't tell you. The child of the tide may still be waiting, or she may have gone. Either way, you owe me this debt,' he growled.

'What?' My brain caught up with my ears. He'd found a nereid to talk to us. 'Where is she waiting for us?'

'Out by the Sedge Lode,' the hob hissed, as though that should be obvious.

Before I could ask anything else, he vanished.

Fin was already fetching our boots and coats from the front hall. 'Do you think we can teach him how to use a doorbell?'

'Or a wooden whistle. Do you know where he means?'

'I think so.' Fin wrapped a scarf around her neck and put on her woolly hat.

'Let's hope so.' I found my gloves. 'Hang on, when did your mum leave for Peterborough?'

'About half an hour ago.'

'Then why didn't the hob tell her? He can't have been waiting out there for too long.'

'That's a good point.' Fin nodded. 'He wants to keep us on the back foot, doesn't he? Thinking we owe him more than we do.'

'Whenever possible,' I agreed.

All the same, we didn't hang about as we headed out along the track to the hillfort. It was pretty creepy in the fog. We couldn't see if those sheep were still in their field, because we couldn't see the field. The ditch – sorry, the dyke – was a black line below the grey. On the other side, the sedge was the faintest shadow in the mist beyond the rough grass. There was no movement in the air and not a sound to be heard. No birdsong. No rustle of leaves. Nothing. Looking ahead, I couldn't see the trees on the hillfort. Looking back, I'd lost sight of the house completely.

'It's this way.' Fin made her way slowly down to the grass.

I followed, even slower. I tested my footing with every step. This fog had swept in overnight and kept the frost off, but that meant the long, limp grass was slick and wet. My pulled muscle might be healing, but it wouldn't take much of a slip to knacker myself again. I breathed a sigh of relief when I got safely down the slope.

Fin was waiting. She slipped her arm through mine as we followed the broad, grassy track that I'd seen before as it cut a way through the sedge. The pale, feathery fronds were taller than me, and that was an unfamiliar, unwelcome sensation. Nothing was moving, and the silence felt increasingly oppressive. The scent of still water grew stronger. I could see the sedge stems were standing in the dark glimmer of flooding. It wasn't stagnant water. This was a clean smell.

It just wasn't the scent I knew, the warm aroma of the greenwood. That is leaf mould, and the sweetness of rising sap undercut with the sharpness of bark. There's maybe a hint of blossom or fruit, depending on the season. That's the smell that tells me I'm home and I'm safe. This cool blend of water and earth, of weed and reed, made me feel that I had no place here. I didn't know how to navigate the fen. Keep to this grassy path and I would be safe. If I strayed off it, there were no guarantees.

As I realised this, Fin took a deep, happy breath. She hugged my arm to her side, and as I looked down, she smiled up at me. This place was in her blood, I realised, in the same way that the wildwood was in mine. The sedge surrounding us was home and shelter and safety to her. What did that mean for the two of us?

Some way further on, the sedge gave way to darker, sharper reed beds. A channel had been cut through them to reach a sturdy wooden stage jutting out into the waterway. A bright orange fibreglass kayak was tied up beside it, and a muscular figure with short dark hair was standing on the planks. They had their back to us as they gazed out into the mist beyond the slowly moving lode.

They wore a sleeveless jacket and life vest over what looked like a dry suit. Crap. Some mad water sports enthusiast. Who the hell went out in this sort of weather? Never mind that, we'd need to get rid of them. I only hoped they hadn't scared off the nereid.

Then she turned around and raised a hand. First, I noticed she wasn't wearing gloves, and thought her hands must be absolutely freezing. Then she spread her fingers, and I saw translucent webbing, just a centimetre or so of it, stretched between the lowest joints. Okay, that would make wearing gloves awkward.

'Morning,' she said cheerfully. 'I'm Witta. The hob said you wanted to speak to me.'

Her grey-green eyes looked human until she blinked. Then I glimpsed the lack of pupil and iris that showed humans like me and Fin her true nature.

'Thank fuck for that,' I said under my breath. 'Someone who gets to the point.'

Fin laughed, and let go of my arm. 'Hello, and thanks for coming. I'm Fin and this is Dan. What exactly did the hob tell you?'

The nereid grinned. 'Close to damn all, but that's hobs for you. You need someone or something found?'

'If you're willing to help, we really would appreciate it. We...' Fin hesitated.

The nereid raised her hand again. 'I don't barter and bargain like a hob. To be honest, there's nothing you can offer me that I need. Tell me what's going on. If I think it's important, I'll help you. If I don't, I won't. If I think what you're doing will do harm, we can discuss that, or I will stop you. Your choice.'

Her voice was still friendly but her face was uncompromising. I'd encountered naiads and so had Fin. We both knew river spirits weren't to be messed with. It looked like their daughters were just as strong-minded. Maybe even more forceful. I wondered if that came from their fathers' bonds with the sea.

112

'Have you ever heard of Doctor Thomas Kelley?' Fin didn't wait for Witta to shake her head. She explained what was going on, what we knew and what we suspected. She kept it as short and sweet as she could, but my feet were freezing by the time she was done. This really wasn't weather for standing around. Fin was shivering. I put my arm around her and she leaned against me.

'It's easy to be wise after the event,' Witta remarked. 'My people – and your mother's—' she nodded at me '—we didn't keep our distance from humanity because we had any idea what might happen when the hobs and the sylphs got too close. These days, we enjoy advantages we never earned, now that people come and go and human lives are full of strangers. We can hide in plain sight, and shape ourselves as we see fit, to fit in. More or less, anyway. When we get bored, we can let the waters carry us away, just as your mother and her sisters can vanish into their trees. Hobs have no such choices, as sons and daughters of the enduring earth. All they can do is evade mortal eyes by passing through wood and soil and stone.'

I'd been wondering about that. So it seemed hobs were stuck with the shape they were born with. No wonder they hide from the modern world.

'What about sylphs?' Fin asked.

'They can masquerade as human, though few ever do, unless they want to seduce a mortal for some passing amusement. Then they become a man or a woman, depending on what the object of their affection desires. They can't sustain that pretence for long though, even if they might want to, and that's rare enough to count as never. Don't expect any alliances they make with you to last. There's a reason people talk about fickle breezes.' Witta shoved her hands in her pockets, though she didn't seem to be feeling the cold. 'But no one deserves to be forced to serve another, especially not by a thief and a bully. I would very much like to know what he's up to, but first, you're right, we need to find him. I'll see what we can do.'

She grinned. 'That's one thing about water. It gets everywhere. Right, when I have news, I'll come up to the house. See you soon, I hope.'

'Thanks.'

'We really appreciate this.'

As I echoed Fin, Witta shook her head. 'You can thank me when I have something for you.'

She got into her kayak more quickly and gracefully than I reckoned any human could, and paddled away with strong, swift strokes. Within minutes, she vanished into the fog.

'That was not what I expected,' Fin said with feeling.

'Me neither.' I felt considerably more optimistic about finding Tom Kelley now. Also, it felt as if my feet were frozen solid. 'Can we get some breakfast now, and a hot drink?'

'Oh hell, yes.' Fin led the way back to the house.

Before we went in, we collected the bread board and the empty beer bottles from the fire pit. While I was scrambling eggs and making toast, Fin emptied a packet of biscuits into a plastic box and went out to leave it there as a thank you for the hob.

After we'd eaten, we went out to the supermarket to do the shopping on Helen's list. It felt strange to be surrounded by so many noisy, busy people as we discussed brands of tea bags and preferences in pasta. It was a world away from our encounter out by the lode.

I got Fin to stop at the garden centre again. When Helen arrived back from Peterborough, she was the proud owner of a set of bamboo wind chimes on a new bracket fixed to the wall by the kitchen door. She wasn't thrilled. We explained the problem we'd created for the hob by hanging iron chains in the windows. Even so, she wasn't convinced.

'Are we supposed to rush out here every time there's a stiff breeze?'

'Give me a minute.' I'd bought a big ball of sturdy twine as well. I threaded long strands through each hollow length of bamboo. Knotting those about twenty centimetres below the chimes, I plaited the strings together. 'Can you fetch me one of those spare bricks from beside the garage?'

When Fin brought that over, I tied the bottom of the plaited cord around it. I'd been working by eye rather than measuring everything, but my skills hadn't let me down. The brick rested on the ground, and its weight held the chimes still and silent. Pick the brick up, and there was enough slack to rattle the bamboo.

Helen pursed her lips as I demonstrated. 'I suppose so. As long as the hob can work that out.'

'If he can't, he can throw stones at the door again. Just as long as he doesn't put a brick through a window.'

She hadn't considered that. 'Good point.'

Helen had more work to do after her meetings, though she found five minutes to ring Kate at The Wheat Sheaf. There was no news of Tom Kelley, and apparently his family weren't ready to report him as a missing person just yet. They didn't think the police would consider him a priority case, for one thing. That suited me. The last thing I wanted was the cops involved.

Fin and I carried on reading through her grandad's accumulated local lore. She checked her email several times, but none of her friends or family had contacted her with any sighting of Doctor Tom or his car.

She looked over her laptop screen and sighed. 'I haven't heard the wind chimes rattle. Have you?'

'No.' I put down a booklet about the Littleport Riots. 'Or any noise from the chains in the windows. With luck that means there aren't any sylphs trying to get into the house to screw with us again.'

'True.' Fin was still exasperated.

I shared her frustration. All we could do was wait.

Chapter Thirteen

The nereid knocked on the kitchen door just after lunch the next day. Fin and I hadn't been back for long. We'd driven over to King's Lynn to see the so-called Seahenge in the town's museum. Helen had promised to ring Fin if there was any news.

I found the Seahenge display and the whole idea as enigmatic as it was fascinating. Had the Green Man had any sort of hand in these long-ago people erecting a circle of split oak around the massive, inverted stump of what had once been a magnificent tree? If he had, he didn't show himself to let me know what had been going on there, or to tell me anything else. That was disappointing, because it was at least half the reason we'd made that journey. The other reason was we'd both had more than enough of sitting in Venturer's House sifting through Grandad's eccentric archive.

Witta was dressed for hiking today. As she walked through the door, the rain beading her dark hair and jacket disappeared.

'Please, sit down.' Fin pulled out a chair and went to call Helen down from her studio.

I joined the nereid at the table. 'I feel I should offer you a tea or a coffee or something.'

'I drink green tea when it suits me to be sociable.' She grinned. 'I told you we're good at fitting in.'

At least I'd had the experience of growing up with a dryad for a mum who routinely masqueraded as a human woman. Helen was used to seeing hobs and sylphs that no one else could see, and when they were in their natural forms. She couldn't help staring as she came into the kitchen.

Either Witta didn't notice or she was too tactful to comment. She was also all business. 'Right, we've found him. He's staying at a hotel called The Ring of Bells in Reedmere Bridge.'

Fin had fetched her laptop as well as her mum. She soon found the place online. 'That's not far,' she said, surprised.

'Far enough not to have to deal with his brother and sister, after wrecking their house. As long as he doesn't answer his phone, they can't get hold of him.' I stood behind Fin to look at the hotel website. I guessed the sizeable property had been someone's summer home built between the world wars. It had found a new lease of life in the tourist trade, offering boutique bed and breakfast and an unexpectedly pricey restaurant.

'Maybe it's closer to whatever he's looking to dig up?' Helen suggested.

116

'Quite probably,' I agreed.

'Hopefully.' Fin looked at Witta. 'I don't suppose you've seen anything that might give us a clue what he's up to?'

The nereid shook her head. 'You didn't ask me to do that.'

That didn't mean she didn't know, or at the very least have some suspicions. I reminded myself that however human she looked, Witta was far closer to naiads and dryads than she was to me or the Wickens. She would have her own priorities and concerns.

I laid my hands on Fin's shoulders. 'Let's go and take a look.'

'He'll recognise you,' Helen objected. 'No offence, Dan, but you are hard to miss.'

'We'll be careful not to let him see us,' I promised.

Fin closed her laptop and stood up. 'I don't suppose he can tell one swan from another.'

Witta laughed as she got to her feet. Then she looked at the three of us, serious again. 'It will be far better if you can remove this threat to the hobs and the sylphs by yourselves. Do it as quickly as you can, before Kelley starts digging where he has no business and stirs up trouble for all of us. Some of my kindred are none too fond of mankind. If they feel a need to resolve this, their methods won't discriminate between the truly guilty and bystanders.'

Not innocent bystanders, I noted. Did that mean her kin considered humans were all more or less to blame for – well, I could imagine nature spirits had plenty of grievances. I wanted to ask what she meant about Kelley stirring up trouble, but I was pretty sure she wouldn't tell me, and we didn't want to annoy her.

'We'll just see what there is to see, to start with.' I glanced at Helen. 'We'll take the Land Rover, so there's no risk of him recognising Fin's car.'

'We will be careful,' Fin assured her.

'Then I may as well get back to work.' Helen stood up too. 'Are we saying anything to Neil or Mike Kelley just yet?'

'I don't think so. We don't want to spook him. If he leaves this hotel, we're back at square one.' I was relieved to see Fin's nod.

'Let's save that for when we do want to knock him off balance.' She sounded as if she would enjoy that.

Helen agreed. 'That's pretty much what I was thinking.'

I looked at Witta. 'Do you want to know how we get on? How would you like us to contact you?'

'Well, I don't have a mobile number. I'll check in when I'm passing this way.' She looked at Fin. 'Would you please open the door for me?'

'Of course.' Fin hurried to lift the black iron latch.

'So she trusts us,' Helen remarked once the nereid had left and Fin had closed the door behind her. 'To come in here and sit down with us, with the door shut.'

'Or she was testing us,' Fin said wryly. 'I get the distinct impression she could force her way out of anywhere she didn't want to be.'

'I'd say that's the safest assumption.' I headed for the stairs. 'I'll get my keys and we can go.'

Helen took care of the yard gates for us, and Fin put Reedmere Bridge into my satnav. She'd also brought an OS map from Grandad's collection. She nodded at the dashboard. 'In case that tries to take us somewhere stupid.'

'Fair enough.'

As it happened, the satnav didn't play silly buggers, and it wasn't awkwardly far. The hotel was out in the depths of the fens though, on roads that made driving in fog no fun at all. Reedmere Bridge was a tiny place that made Saw Edge St Peter look like a centre of civilisation. We parked on the forecourt of a boarded-up village shop. At least there were enough four-wheel drives around that no one should give the Land Rover a second look. Not for a little while anyway.

'What do we do now?' Fin looked across the road at the hotel.

'Unfold that map, so it looks like we pulled up because we're lost.'

Fin did that. 'The first thing we need to know is if his car's in the car park. I'd better take a look.' She hid her blonde hair with her baggy hat. 'I'll be quick.'

She was, though that didn't stop my stomach churning as I watched her cross the road and head around the side of the white-painted building. I told myself not to be so stupid. Tom Kelley had no reason to think anyone in particular was looking for him, even if he was avoiding his family. He was hardly going to do anything to Fin, even if he recognised her. Not in broad daylight, or as close to daylight as we had in this fog. Not with witnesses around. That didn't reassure me. We had no idea what that sodding sylph might have told him.

Fin ran back across the road. 'The car's there,' she said breathlessly as she got back into the Landy.

'So is he in his room or is there a hotel lounge?' The front of the building gave me no answers. Net curtains masked the wide windows on either side of the front door. 'What is his room number, and how do we get in there, to look for – what exactly?'

'Clues?' Fin wrinkled her nose. 'How are your lock-picking skills?'

'Non-existent. You?'

'Same.'

'I could probably kick his door in, or try breaking in with a screwdriver, but someone's bound to notice. We haven't got any sort of excuse that the police would accept, even if they were willing to listen.' Which they wouldn't be, I could guarantee that.

Fin nodded. 'And whatever we do, he mustn't suspect we're after him.'

'Can you think of an excuse to ask for his room number that won't have the receptionist ask him first? Because I can't.'

We sat there in frustrated silence. The day was growing gloomier.

Fin stirred. 'We should move before someone rings the police, on the off-chance they can spare a car to come out this far.'

'In a minute.' I was watching a lad slouching along the pavement on the other side of the road. He was wearing jeans and a battered jacket over a hoodie. Late teens, maybe early twenties, and he was dragging on a cigarette as if his life depended on it. He stopped at the entrance to the hotel car park to finish his ciggie. We were too far away to see his face, but his rounded shoulders as he stared at his feet didn't make me think he was enjoying life.

He chucked his dog end away, making no effort to cross over to the bin by the bus stop, or even to drop it into the tub with an ornamental tree just inside the car park. He headed towards the back of the hotel.

'Where's the nearest ATM?' I started the engine. 'Can you look that up online?'

Fin got out her phone and swiped the screen. 'You'll have to drive somewhere first. I've got a few bars of signal but no data. Why do you ask?'

I explained as I pulled out and drove across the bridge that gave this place its reason for existing. Fin wasn't convinced, but she had to admit she couldn't come up with any better plan. So we found a cash machine in the closest village big enough to still have a village shop that doubled as a Post Office. We also found a garage there, and that was good because I realised I needed to get fuel. Fin insisted on paying for the diesel and I didn't object. It wasn't as if we could send an expenses claim anywhere.

She came out of the forecourt shop and surprised me with a grin as she got into the passenger seat. 'Look what I got.' She showed me a pair of cheap compact binoculars.

'Those could come in useful.' I turned the Landy back towards Reedmere Bridge.

We drove through the village and parked in a field gateway just beyond the last house. Given the size of the place, it wasn't a long walk back to the hotel. I was even more glad we hadn't brought Fin's car. People might worry a vehicle like that had broken down, and the last thing we needed was a Good Samaritan. A Land Rover could have all sorts of reasons to be stopped on a country verge.

Fin reached for the passenger door handle.

'Hang on.' I stretched out a hand. 'This was my idea.'

She looked at me, eyebrows raised. 'You don't think I've got more chance of talking him into it?'

'You don't think there's less chance of him trying something on with me?' I countered. 'Or turning nasty?'

'What will you do if he does? Make a run for it on your dodgy leg?' She wasn't about to back down.

We sat there looking at each other. After a long moment, I reached for the stash of coins I keep for car parks. 'Toss you for it?'

Fin narrowed her eyes at me, but she nodded. 'I suppose so. Tails.'

'Heads.' I won. 'I'll text you to let you know how I get on.'

'I'll be ready for us to make a quick getaway.'

'Have you ever driven a Land Rover?'

'My dad's, on the farm. Go on, if we're going to do this.'

Trying not to look too relieved, I got out of the Landy. Fin slid over into the driving seat and started adjusting it for someone her height.

As I walked back through the village, I turned my phone to vibrate and put it in my front pocket to make sure I wouldn't miss a message or a call from Fin. Thankfully we both had plenty of battery. There was still no one about, and in any case, anyone can go into a hotel. If anyone asked, I planned to say I was interested in making a booking. No one asked me anything.

I discovered a sizeable, more modern extension around the back. I found the back door to the kitchen and looked around for cigarette butts. After a few minutes, I discovered a sodden mess of them in a catering-size coffee tin on a splintered wooden picnic table, one of those ones with built-in benches that are an utter pain for people my size. It had been shoved out of the way behind the bins. Good.

I sent Fin a text and settled down to wait. All sorts of things could still go wrong and kill this plan dead. There could be any number of smokers on the staff, just for a start.

There weren't, or if there were, the lad I wanted to talk to got his smoke break first. He came past the bins, wearing his jacket over a long, water-stained apron. A motion-sensor light flickered on. This close I could see the jacket was fake, with the PVC or whatever it was worn away at the elbows.

He stopped, startled to see me sitting there.

I spoke first. 'How would you like to earn a hundred quid?'

'Fuck off,' he said reflexively. 'I'm no fucking rent boy.'

He was still standing there though, and he was bright enough to stay out of grabbing distance.

'Relax, you're not my type.' I tried to look as friendly as I could. 'And believe me, I've never had to pay for it.'

Thankfully that was true. I was going to have to stick as close to the truth as possible, if this was going to work. Like I say, I'm a bad liar.

He was still looking wary. 'Then what do you want?'

'Do you know who drives that Jag?' I waved a hand at Tom Kelley's car.

'Yeah.' He scowled. 'He's a right prick.' There was a hint of challenge in his voice.

'An utter wanker,' I agreed. I'd hoped Doctor Tom's not-so-charming personality would work in our favour. 'And a fucking thief.'

'Seriously?' He wasn't expecting that. 'What are you? The cops?'

He reached inside his jacket and took out a lighter and a battered tobacco packet where he had a few roll-ups ready. His eyes didn't leave me as he lit one.

I shook my head. 'His family don't want to get the police involved, not just yet. Not unless they know for certain he's got what he's taken with him. I only want to get a look in his room, to see what's in there. Get some idea of what he's up to next. Do you know where to get a master key? I only need five minutes. No one will ever know I was in there.'

'Fuck off,' he said instantly. 'I'll get the sack, or nicked.'

He was still standing there though. I spread my hands and tried my best to call on my greenwood blood to persuade him.

'I'm not going to take anything apart from some photos. You can come with me, to be sure. If anyone sees us, you start shouting. Raise the alarm. You say you heard a noise and caught me sneaking around. You won't get the sack, believe me. You'll be a fucking hero.'

He liked that idea. 'Five hundred.'

I shook my head. 'One fifty.'

'Three hundred.'

'Two hundred, final offer.' And the daily limit on my debit card. I held his gaze and shrugged. 'Or I see who else works here. I'm sure someone might like a bit of a bonus. Or I wait until he moves on, and try my luck at the next place he stops.'

The lad took a long drag on his ciggie, still looking at me. He breathed smoke out through his nose. 'He spends most of the day in his room.'

I decided that meant we had a deal. 'He's got to eat, hasn't he? Does he come down for dinner?'

'Oh yeah.' The lad sneered, though not at me. 'Table for one, seven sharp. No one at adjoining tables unless that's absolutely unavoidable. He's not here to make idle conversation.' He dropped his nasal imitation of Tom Kelley's patronising voice. 'Tosser.'

I nodded. 'That sounds about right. Does he take his time with his dinner, or just eat his food and leave?'

He squinted through another cloud of smoke. 'Him? No fucking chance. There'll be something wrong with his meal, or the wine, or something else he wants sorting. He was bitching about the candles on the tables last night. Said they were scented, which is utter bollocks.'

'So if I was out here at, say, five or ten past, do you reckon you could get me upstairs without being seen? Two hundred quid for five minutes in his room,' I reminded him.

He came over to drop his cigarette butt in the coffee tin, before stepping back out of reach. 'Money up front.'

'Fuck off,' I said amiably. 'I'm not sitting out here till midnight with my dick in my hand.'

He grinned. 'Worth a try.'

Though I could hear he wasn't entirely serious about ripping me off. I began to think this might actually work.

He looked over his shoulder towards the kitchen. 'I better get back.'

I stood up and took out my wallet to give him a quick glimpse of the thick wad of notes. Him staying out of my reach meant he was too far away to try snatching it. 'See you out here just after seven then.'

He nodded. 'Deal.'

I let him walk off. I braced myself in case he'd gone to fetch someone else, to try getting my wallet off me or to threaten me with the police. I heard a door close. There were no footsteps or voices coming my way, so I texted Fin a quick thumbs up.

I headed out of the car park and back to the Land Rover, walking as fast as I comfortably could. Fin readjusted the seat and got out of the driver's door as I approached. I got in and checked the seat was where I wanted it as she opened the passenger door.

'Well?'

'He went for it.'

'Seriously?' She shook her head. 'What are the odds.'

I was having trouble believing it, and this had been my idea. 'In our favour, apparently. It's a shit job, but it's the only work he can get around here. I'm guessing he doesn't drive, and it must take forever to get anywhere from here by bus. He's bored and he's pissed off. I'm offering him some excitement and two hundred quid. What's not to like?'

'Do you think he'll keep his mouth shut?'

'As long as he does till I'm out of there. It doesn't matter after that. It would be my word against his, and anyway, he doesn't even know my name. He's not going to either.'

'What if we come back and the police are waiting in the room?' she demanded.

'Then I say we were passing, and stopped to see if we wanted to eat here. We recognised the Jag, and I asked the lad to show me Tom Kelley's room. I just wanted to talk to him about the damage at Talbot House. Let him know that his family are trying to find him. Letting me into his room was all the lad's idea. I'm very sorry, officer, I should never have agreed. It was really, really stupid of me. I can only apologise.'

I would be in a shitload of trouble, there was no doubt about that, but I'd drag the lad right down with me. Good luck to the cops trying to sort that mess out. Easiest way out would be giving us both a caution, official or informal. I was more concerned that Kelley would try to insist on 'pressing charges', and good luck to any copper trying to explain that was a cliché off TV. Any further action would be up to the Crown Prosecution Service.

'If they arrest me, I go no comment, until they charge me or let me go.' It would hardly be the first time. With any luck the CPS would live up to the nickname a foreman I once worked for had for them. He was desperate to stop thefts of copper pipe and wire from the site, and everyone knew who was responsible. Ah, but there was no evidence that would stand up in court, the CPS said. Couldn't Prosecute Satan, the foreman said.

Fin must have seen something in my face. 'What is it with you and the police, Dan? I know they gave you a hard time up in Derbyshire, but that was sorted out, wasn't it?'

I didn't like the edge I heard in her voice. I also didn't want to have this conversation just yet. It didn't look like I had much option though. She knew there was something I wasn't telling her, and putting that off would just make it worse.

I stared through the windscreen. 'I've got a criminal record. When I was still living at home, I pleaded guilty to breaking a man's arm, and got a suspended sentence and community service. He was a badger baiter. My dad and I caught a gang of them digging up a sett on the nature reserve. They'd already set their dogs on a pregnant sow, and killed her.' I couldn't hide the surge of fury I always feel when I remember that night.

Unsurprisingly, Fin was appalled. 'Oh—'

I held up a hand. 'One of them went for my dad with his spade. I took it off the prick and thumped him with it. Not as hard as I wanted to, but hard enough to put me on the wrong side of using reasonable force. So any time a copper looks me up on their computer, they see a thug who can't control his temper.'

And a loner who keeps moving from job to job, and who can't hold on to a steady relationship. I was hoping working at Blithehurst would do something about that first one, but I didn't give much for my chances of Fin helping out with the second. Not after this.

I shrugged. 'Cops don't give someone like me the benefit of any doubt.'

I'd had enough run-ins with short-arses drunk enough to try taking on the biggest bloke in the pub to know that. Some of those incidents were officially on file as well, just to convince any copper they were right about me.

Fin took her time before answering. 'I see. Thanks for telling me.'

She sounded as if she was going to take a while to decide what she thought about what she'd just learned.

I turned the ignition. 'We've got some time to kill. What do you want to do?'

Fin leaned forward to press the screen and go back through the satnav's history. She entered a destination. 'Head for the retail park. We can get a coffee and something to eat.'

We drove there in silence. I told myself that was fine. It meant I could concentrate on the roads in the fog. We didn't talk much when we got there either. Fin checked for messages from her mum and used the coffee shop Wi-Fi to look Reedmere Bridge up on the Internet. That's what she said she was doing, anyway. I had my doubts, but I wasn't going to make an issue out of it. The truth had done enough damage for one day.

We drove back out to the hotel through the heavy rush-hour traffic. Reedmere Bridge was clearly on a well-used route. I hoped that would make us less conspicuous. I pulled onto the disused shop's forecourt. If the hotel car park had CCTV, I didn't want to hand anyone a shot of the Land Rover's licence plate.

'His Jag's still here,' I said, relieved.

There were no police cars lurking anywhere that I could see, but I guessed even the dimmest constable would realise that would be a dead giveaway, if they were hoping to catch me red-handed. If the lad had belatedly had an outbreak of guilty conscience.

'I can see into the restaurant.' Fin took the little binoculars out of her coat pocket and focused on the building's front window. The lights were on inside, to tempt passers-by to stop. The tactic wasn't working too well, judging by the largely empty car park. I supposed it was still early though.

Fin stiffened. 'I can see him. He's just sat down.'

I reached for the door. 'Be ready to leave if I come running.'

Fin nodded. 'I'll text you if he leaves the table.'

I walked across the road and through the car park towards the rear and the kitchen door. I felt as if I had 'up to something' scrolling across my forehead in neon letters. If it was, at least there was no one around to see it. My pulse still accelerated as I approached the bins. My breathing was getting quicker and quicker.

The lad was waiting by the picnic table, smoking a roll-up. He was shifting from foot to foot, looking like someone desperate for a pee. His look of relief when he saw me was a surprise.

He dropped his ciggie into the coffee tin. 'I was starting to think you were some fucking set-up. See if I would take a pay-off.'

That hadn't occurred to me, but I was glad to hear it. That should mean there were no cops in Kelley's room waiting for me. I took my wallet out of my pocket. 'Half now, the rest when we're done.'

'Cool.' He took the notes without counting them and shoved the money in a back pocket. 'This way.'

Now it came to it, he wanted to get this done as much as I did. That suited me fine. He used a card to trigger the lock that opened a side door at the end of the extension. I followed him into a corridor running past a handful of bedrooms. He walked so fast he was nearly running, and I lengthened my stride to keep up. There were no sounds of TV or conversation behind any of the doors. Good. We reached a stairwell that I could see served the new bit of the hotel as well as the original building. I looked warily around and listened for any sign of someone coming or going, from the upper floor or the hotel restaurant or bar.

'Up there.' He jerked his head as he offered me a card key. 'Number 21.'

'Come on then.'

He shook his head. 'Got to get back before someone comes looking. Leave this and the cash under the coffee tin. I'm fucking trusting you, mate.'

I couldn't hear a lie in his voice. I didn't think he was faking his anxiety. All I could do was trust him, or this had all been a waste of time. We couldn't afford to walk away. We had to find out what Tom Kelley was up to.

'Thanks.' I took the card key and headed up the stairs as quickly and quietly as I could. To my relief, number 21 was the first room at the top. My heart pounded as I tried the card key. The light on the lock turned green. I turned the door handle, and I was in.

It was a middling-sized room with a double bed, a narrow desk and two armchairs by the window. The TV was fixed to the wall above the desk, and the door immediately to my left opened into a bathroom. Thankfully the lights worked without needing the key card in one of those slots to keep the power on. I could see house-keeping had been in today to make the bed. Without a dining table to cover with his stuff, Kelley was using that to spread out his maps. I got my phone out and quickly started taking photos.

I concentrated on the modern OS maps, making sure to get several shots of the marked-up areas. I also photographed their sheet numbers, so we could be sure we got copies of the right ones. That meant moving things around, but we'd just have to hope Doctor Tom didn't notice. I didn't bother with the older maps. For one thing, there were no marks or notes on any of them. Add to that, I was painfully conscious of every passing second. We didn't need to know how Kelley had arrived at his targets. We just needed to know where he was going to dig.

Unless we could put a stop to this here and now by taking away Edward Kelley's crystal ball. Would that be enough? If he couldn't see the sylphs and hobs, would that mean he couldn't force them to obey him?

It had to be worth a try. I know I'd promised the lad I wouldn't take anything, but there had to be a damn good chance that Kelley wouldn't report it. Not and risk the police getting involved, if he had those stolen papers from Cambridge here. Besides, there was no sign of forced entry, and that lad was hardly going to admit to any involvement, was he?

I stopped wasting time debating with myself. I dropped to my knees to look under the bed. Nothing there. I ignored the desk because that drawer was too shallow to hold the crystal ball, and turned around.

There was a single unit built against the bathroom wall that had a shelf for the complimentary tea and coffee set-up, and double doors to the right. I opened those to find full-length hanging space and an ironing board on one side and a high shelf and coat hooks above a set of drawers on the other. There was a hotel safe on the shelf, but the door was open, so he wasn't using that. A suitcase sat on the top of the drawers. I opened it, and I didn't need to disturb Kelley's clothes to see the crystal wasn't inside.

There was an iron and a hair dryer in the top drawer, and nothing in the rest. There was nothing hanging up, and no sign of that black briefcase. I closed the doors and looked at the bed again. There were maps spread out, but nothing else on there. No journals, no faded documents or the stark new photocopies. I quickly checked the desk drawer. Nothing in there. Everything else including the crystal must be in the briefcase, and that wasn't anywhere in this room.

I guessed it was still in his car. There was nowhere else for him to hide it. That also made sense, if he wanted to be certain that no hob or sylph would try to steal it off him. That's what I'd be trying to do, in their place.

Unless the briefcase was in the bathroom. That would be a stupid place to keep papers, but I checked anyway. It wasn't there.

It was time I left. I had no idea how long I'd been in there, and I didn't waste time checking my phone. I did take a moment to listen at the door. As far as I could tell, there was no one outside in the corridor. If there was, I'd just have to hope they didn't know this was Tom Kelley's room. I opened the door and stepped out. There was no one to see me.

I headed down the stairs and strode along the corridor to the far end. There was a button to press to open the door and I hit it so hard a sharp crack split the silence. For one awful moment, I thought I'd broken it. A second later, the lock buzzed, and I hurried out. The cold air hit the sweat on my forehead, and I shivered as I made my way to the bins.

Someone I didn't recognise was sitting at the picnic table, huddled in a thick coat and using a vape. I could smell the fruity scent in the air. I veered away, hoping I wasn't too obviously changing my mind about where I was going. I left the car park, crossed the road and headed back to the Landy.

Fin was in the driving seat. I raised a hand to tell her to stay there and got into the passenger side.

'Well?' She went on before I could answer. 'I think that was the longest ten minutes of my life! It's okay though. He's still eating his dinner.'

Whatever tension there had been between us earlier seemed to be gone. I would be happy about that once we were out of here.

'There's a problem.' I explained about the card key and the cash. 'I don't want that boy thinking I stiffed him. What if he goes to Tom Kelley and sees what he's prepared to pay to know more about someone asking for his room number?'

I wasn't worried about Kelley going to the police, especially since nothing was missing, but I didn't want another encounter with a murderously inventive sylph.

'Give it all to me.' Fin held out her hand. 'Whoever that is out there with the vape will notice if they see you a second time. If they've gone, I can leave the stuff. If not, I'll find somewhere to wait until I see them go back inside.'

I hated this idea. At the moment, I was the only person the kitchen lad or anyone else could describe. Fin could still stay out of this. Unfortunately I didn't have any better ideas.

'Come on,' she said impatiently. 'We need to get going.'

I handed over the cash and the card. Now it was my turn to watch and wait, growing more and more anxious. Fin had left the little binoculars, but I didn't bother with them. I wasn't interested in whatever Tom Kelley was up to in the restaurant. I just wanted to get us both safely away from this place.

Fin came back, walking briskly, just as I was trying to decide if I should get into the driver's seat and adjust it in case we needed to leave in a hurry, or if that was too risky. Seeing I was still sitting on the passenger side, she got behind the steering wheel.

'All done. The vaper was already gone, and I just saw that lad heading out around the back.' She turned the key. 'Let's get home and see what your photos can tell us.'

Chapter Fourteen

Back at Venturer's House, Grandad's archive included the Ordnance Survey maps we needed. We downloaded the photos from my phone onto Fin's laptop. She started enlarging the marked-up areas as much as she could. I'd used the highest resolution setting on my phone so everything would be as clear as possible. Well, the images were sharp and focused. What Kelley's notes meant wasn't remotely obvious.

Fin groaned. 'Why can't the arrogant bastard use plain English?'

We were sitting at the kitchen table. I moved the laptop a little bit to get a better look at the map on the screen. I realised one thing about Tom Kelley's annotations in fine-tipped red and green pen.

'He's using the same weird alphabet or whatever it was that John Dee and Edward Kelley used in their diagrams. Enochian, they called it.'

Fin gave me a look. 'Can you read it?'

'No,' I admitted.

She reclaimed the laptop and clicked on the next image. 'What do you reckon this is?'

I got up and stood behind her as she zoomed in. Something on the map had red notes beside it. There was also a scrawled circle of what looked like blue biro. That didn't seem nearly so mystical.

Helen came into the kitchen with an electrical cable in her hand. 'If you hook that up to the telly in the sitting room, we can get a much better look at whatever you've found.'

We went next door. Helen and Fin used the HDMI lead to connect up the laptop, and I brought Grandad's maps through. I unfolded the sheet that had Reedmere Bridge on it, and laid it out on the coffee table.

'So where exactly is this?' Fin muttered to herself. She was using the laptop's touch pad to shift the image from side to side and up and down. 'Come on, let's have a place name.'

Printed words came and went too fast for me to read. I had to stop looking at the TV. Trying to follow such quick scrolling was making my eyes hurt.

Helen peered at the map, glancing back at the screen several times. 'That's here.' She took a pencil and drew a faint circle around a point at the side of a field where three footpaths met.

I saw that she was right. 'Are there any more of those blue circles?' I asked Fin.

'What are you thinking?' She started clicking through the photos to see what she could find. 'Yes, two more.'

She put them up on the TV screen. After a bit of fumbling, she resized the pictures so we could see all three of them next to each other, centred on the rough blue circles.

'Well, that narrows down the list of places to take a look at,' Helen observed.

'Do you think that's what Tom Kelley's doing?' Fin zoomed out on the images a little. 'Picking his best prospects?'

'That would make sense,' I agreed.

Helen was studying the map on the coffee table again. 'Those other two places are here and here.'

I looked at her faintly pencilled crosses. One was at the edge of a copse, at the junction of three fields. The other one was halfway down a field that seemed no different to any of the others that surrounded it.

'Look,' she went on, 'there's Reedmere Bridge. If you drew a circle, sort of anyway, it's right in between those three sites.'

I saw that she was right.

Fin stared at the screen. 'He couldn't number them one, two and three, just to help us out?'

'Maybe he hasn't assessed them yet,' suggested Helen.

'We need to take a look at all three of them.' I tried to remember how to put a map reference into the satnav. None of the circles were close enough to a village, or even a farm, to give us a destination.

'Where do we go first?' Fin asked. 'They're pretty remote. At least we shouldn't meet anyone who might ask what we're up to.'

Of course, the other side of that coin was Tom Kelley wouldn't be seen doing whatever he was up to either. I reckoned that could well explain why he was focused on these three sites.

Helen had other concerns. 'How do we explain ourselves if he turns up while we're there? That one's on a public footpath, but those other two aren't. We can hardly say we're just out for a country stroll. He's already suspicious of us, even if he doesn't know what he's got to be suspicious about. What if he's forcing some sylph to keep watch?'

Fin grinned. 'Like I said earlier, I bet he can't tell one swan from another, and why would he ask a sylph about the local wildlife? We can fly over there and take a look easily enough without anyone or anything being the wiser. If we make a day of it, we can take a look at all three.'

'Wait a minute,' I began.

'It has to be us,' Fin insisted. 'You can drive us to park somewhere close to each one, but you have to stay out of sight, in case Tom Kelley's around.'

'I know that.' Even if I didn't like it in the least. 'But what if he's out there with that crystal? We know he uses it to see the sylphs and hobs. What if he's looking for one of them to tell him what they know about the site? That could well be why he's keeping it in his car, not just because he doesn't trust hotels. What if he catches sight of you with it or through it, or however the sodding thing works?'

'What are you talking about?'

I realised I hadn't told Fin what I hadn't found in Kelley's room. I explained about the missing briefcase.

'We have no idea what else he can use that crystal for. Who knows what it might show him about who you really are?'

'Oh.' Fin didn't like that idea.

'That's not a risk we can take. We could put the whole family in danger.' Helen wasn't going to discuss it further, that much was clear.

I still wanted to discuss how we were going to take a look at these three places. I might not like it, but Fin had the most workable idea. 'So you need to know Tom Kelley's somewhere else when you're out there. That lad at the hotel says he's been spending most of his time in his room. How about I park up there and keep watch? As soon as you're ready to... to go, you call me to check he's still there. If he is, you—' I hesitated a second time. I had no idea how to describe what they could do. Shape-shifting? Metamorphosis? Transformation? 'Then you go and see if you can get some idea about what he's after.'

Fin nodded slowly. 'Then we go on to the next site. That could work.'

'Only if Tom Kelley stays where he is,' Helen objected. 'There's no guarantee of that. If anything, I'd say the chances get less every day, every hour. He's burned his boats with his family, leaving Talbot House in that state. Won't he be in a hurry to do whatever it is that's going to make everything he's already done worth it?'

I couldn't argue with that. Fin didn't even try. She sat for a moment, thinking.

'So we get Will to help. Tomorrow, if he's free. The sooner the better, anyway. That way we can hit all three sites at the same time, while Dan keeps watch on Doctor Tom. I was going to give him a ring anyway, to ask if he knows anything about these places. If he's ever seen anything unusual. You know he goes all over taking photographs.'

Now Helen took a moment to consider that. She nodded. 'Okay, that would work. First thing tomorrow. One thing Tom Kelley has never been is an early riser.'

Fin immediately took out her phone. Helen stood up. 'I'll put the kettle on.'

'Hi, Will.' Fin was talking to her cousin. 'No, that's okay. We know where he is. What we need to know now is what the hell he's up to.'

As she explained, I followed Helen through to the kitchen.

'Can I get you something to eat?' she offered.

'I'm fine, thanks. Just a cup of tea will be great.'

I sat at the table to drink it, thinking through as many angles of this plan as I could. Helen was busy with something in the utility room. When she came back, I put my cup down.

'Can I borrow your car tomorrow? If you don't think Tom Kelley will recognise it. If that's okay? I'll be covered on my insurance, since I'll be driving with your permission. We don't want anyone in Reedmere Bridge ringing the police because they've seen a strange Land Rover hanging around for two days in a row.'

She nodded. 'Good idea.'

'What is?' Fin came through from the sitting room. Helen explained.

Fin gave me a look I couldn't interpret. 'Fair enough. Will will be here bright and early. Let's see who's going to need the Land Rover most.'

I fetched the map, and Fin set up her laptop to see what online satellite views could show us. The first site we looked at was the one in the unremarkable field. There wasn't anything to explain Tom Kelley's interest that I could see.

Helen looked over Fin's shoulder, leaning forward. 'Is that a crop mark? Like the ones they used to find some of the ditches here.'

'This, you mean?' Fin used the cursor to follow what might be a line of darker green wavering across the screen. Whenever these satellite photos had been taken, a crop of some sort was flourishing in the field and the trees were in full leaf. 'Maybe,' she said doubtfully.

I knew that crop marks could show ditches under the ground, where the deeper soil meant plants grew taller and stronger, or buried walls meant that shallower-rooted crops dried out first in really hot weather. If there were any such signs on the satellite view, I couldn't see how that helped us. We wouldn't see anything like that walking across a ploughed field in the middle of winter. I decided not to say so, and risk sounding like a dickhead.

I traced the line of a road on the map with my finger. A side turning led to a point where a winding stream met a straight blue line that took a direct route to the mud flats and the sea. 'That looks like the closest place to park a vehicle where it won't be too obvious.'

'That's going to be muddy,' Helen said with conviction.

Fin looked at her mum. 'Do you want to take the Land Rover down there?'

'I'm not keen, to be honest, and you've driven your dad's often enough.' Helen glanced at me, apologetic, before talking to Fin again. 'I'd rather take your car and see whatever's where those footpaths meet.'

Fin nodded. 'Fine by me. I'll take the Landy and the mud, and that leaves Will with the place by the trees.'

'As long as he's okay with that.' Though I couldn't see why he wouldn't be.

'He's a good lad. He'll do as he's told,' Helen assured me.

Fin woke me the following morning with a strong cup of tea. It was still dark outside. 'Will's just arrived.'

'Thanks.' I got dressed and went downstairs to find a welcome smell of bacon as I opened the kitchen door. I'd noticed Helen had put that on the shopping list.

She put a plate of scrambled eggs on toast, beans and a couple of rashers in front of a man somewhere around my own age, maybe a bit younger. 'Same for you, Dan?'

'Yes, please.' I took a seat.

Fin was eating poached eggs on toast, and an empty plate said Helen had made her own breakfast first.

'Hi, I'm Will Saffrey, but you probably guessed that.' He grinned as he picked up his knife and fork.

'There is a family resemblance,' I acknowledged.

His hair was as pale blonde as Fin's and cut so short it bristled. It was hard to be sure, since he was sitting down, but I reckoned he was about six feet tall. He was also stocky enough to look as if he'd be useful in a fight. Not that I intended to start any trouble, but there was never any guarantee that someone else wouldn't, human or otherwise.

'Do you know anything about any of these sites?' I remembered Fin had been going to ask him that yesterday.

Will shook his head, swallowing. 'Sorry. Makes it more interesting though.'

'Not too interesting, hopefully.' I wanted to suggest everyone carried something iron, but before I made a fool of myself, I recalled that would stop them transforming into swans. I knew that much from Fin. 'If you see any sign of a sylph, it's probably best to head straight back to your cars.'

Will nodded. 'Fin told me what nearly happened here. Nasty.'

Helen handed me a full plate. 'We'll be careful.'

I'd have to settle for that. Fin's smile from the far end of the table told me she knew I'd much rather be the one running any risks than sitting watching a hotel car park.

As soon as we'd had breakfast, we set off. Everyone had a satnav as well as a map printout of their destination.

The sky was barely lightening, but at least there was no fog this morning. That was a relief, since it took me a few miles to get used to driving Helen's VW with its all-or-nothing clutch. I was the last in line as we pulled out of Fen End, which was a relief. Anyone coming up too close behind me was in for a nasty surprise if I stalled it again. The roads were already busy.

Fin took the lead in my Land Rover, setting a pace that helped us stay together. She was the first to turn off though, heading down a dark road that made me glad she'd assured me she was used to taking a four-wheel drive over rough ground. Will took another road a bit further on. The tail lights of his Renault disappeared around a sharp bend and I saw him speeding along a road raised high above the fields. That left me following Helen driving Fin's Toyota. When she turned off, I was on my own.

I hated it. I hated not knowing what was going on with each of them. I hated not being able to see for myself if there was anything to see out there. I hated not being ready to take on anything that might threaten any one of them. Okay, Fin most of all, but Helen and Will as well, even if I'd only just met him. Not that I could be in three places at once, so there was no guarantee I'd be in the right place at the right time.

I gripped the steering wheel harder. I wasn't interested in sodding logic. I should have insisted on us visiting these places one by one, just me and Fin. Who knows, the Green Man might be prepared to show himself if I was there when we explored the site beside those trees. But I was the one who had to stay out of sight while everyone else took their chances with fuck knows what possible dangers.

By the time I arrived at the hotel, I was in a filthy mood. I pulled into the car park and saw the red Jag was still there. I pulled straight out again, heading back the way I had come. There was nothing remarkable about doing that, was there? Just someone needing a safe space to turn around on a busy road.

At least online street views had helped us identify a cul-de-sac of modern houses where I could park with a decent view of the hotel entrance. Helen had printed me a sign for the dashboard saying 'Traffic Survey' and I had a clipboard with a sheet of paper on it. That was divided into columns headed 'car – driver only', 'car – passenger(s)', 'van – trade', 'van – delivery' and 'HGV'. Fin had done some Internet research. She and Helen reckoned that should look suitably convincing, if any nosy neighbour came knocking on the window to ask what I was doing. If they asked who I was doing the survey for, Will told me to say there was concern about the state of the bridge, and there'd be a letter from the council about it soon.

Between them, they seemed to have thought of everything, and they'd had a lot of fun doing it. I reckoned the local police should be grateful this family hadn't gone into planning bank robberies or security van heists. Though I supposed a swan couldn't fly very far carrying a big bag of cash.

Now this part of the plan was down to me. If someone came knocking, and I couldn't sell the lie, and whoever it was persisted with questions, I was going to resort to my most unfriendly face and tell them to leave because they were wrecking the survey. For the moment, I had a pen in my hand, though I wasn't doing anything with it. Fin had already filled in the columns with assorted tally marks, ticks and numbers. I was concentrating on the car park entrance. We'd set up a group chat app on our phones, so I could alert them if I saw that red Jag nose out into the traffic.

My hand jerked and the pen scored a mark on the paper as my own phone startled me. That was a message from Fin. She was ready to go. After an excruciating ten minutes, so was Will. Helen's message came through just before we reached the half hour. I confirmed the Jag was in the car park and there was no sign of Tom Kelley on the move.

Now they had to hurry. We'd used online maps and everyone else's local knowledge to calculate how long it would take Doctor Tom to get to any of the three sites if he left right now, just as the three of them were turning into swans. They needed time to get away as well. The obvious places to park were the obvious places for him to head for too. That gave us the maximum time they could allow. I insisted, otherwise I wasn't going to agree to any of this. At least they assured me they could keep track of the time, whatever form they were in.

I stared at the car park entrance, trying not to even blink. As soon as I saw that red Jag, I would send the alert. Obviously swans can't use phones, but I wanted that warning waiting for them the moment they got back to their cars. I wanted to hear back from all three of them. I wanted to know they were okay as soon as possible.

I wanted to do something. I thought about that Jag. If that briefcase was still in the boot, if I could get hold of it, maybe I could put a stop to Tom Kelley's plans once and for all. Then no one need risk their neck, human or swan. We could work out some way to find any mysterious buried treasure in our own time. Or we could tip off Chris at the museum somehow. Or we could leave everything well alone, and not risk getting on the wrong side of Witta and her kindred.

If, if and maybe. If Doctor Tom was working in his hotel room, there was every chance he'd have taken the briefcase inside. Even if he hadn't, how would I even get into the Jag? I know less about breaking into cars than I do about picking hotel door locks. There wasn't anyone to bribe to help me out either. Then there was the car park CCTV, and I guessed the Jag had an alarm. I'd be caught or at the very least identified far too easily.

Even if I did get away with the briefcase, it was a fair bet the police would be waiting on the doorstep by the time I got back to Venturer's House. If I still had the briefcase with me, Tom Kelley would be no worse off, and now he would know for certain who his enemies were. If I'd chucked it into the deepest waterway that I passed, that would only make things worse for me. Even the CPS would have to fancy their chances of getting a result in court. Meantime, I'd have caused a shitload of trouble for Fin and Helen. Tom Kelley was bound to retaliate, and as long as I was banged up in a cell I wouldn't be able to protect them.

So that was a stupid idea. I wasn't ready to give up completely though. What if we shadowed Doctor Tom when he left the hotel? Three swans should be able to do that between them. He would have to park the Jag somewhere out of the way to visit any of the places that interested him.

That would be somewhere without cameras and only wildlife to hear the alarm. I could smash a car window and – then what? Where was the boot release lever in a Jag? How long would it take me to find it? Was there some security system in place that meant it only worked with the key in the ignition or something like that? I had absolutely no idea, but it was a fair bet whoever designed cars like that knew all the ways to make life difficult for passing thieves who might try their luck.

One reason I drive an old Land Rover is they're nowhere near as complicated as more modern, more expensive cars. I like to do my own maintenance as far as I can. I like to have a chance of sorting out a breakdown with the tools I've got in the back, not waiting for hours for a breakdown service.

I had tools. Would brute force and ignorance do the trick? Could I just smash through the boot lock with a hammer and screwdriver? Maybe, if the lock was obvious. There was no guarantee it would be. One of the garden centre staff at Blithehurst had recently had the battery in her car key fob die while she was at work. She couldn't find any way to unlock her car without it. She'd had to call her breakdown service and have the mechanic show her which bit of the door handle to lift and twist to find an actual keyhole. No one took the piss, believe me. None of us had been able to find it.

Regardless, breaking into the Jag like that would take time. Enough time for Tom Kelley to hear his car alarm, even if no one else did. What then? Was I going to fight him, and get done for assault again? Even if he couldn't identify me, because I covered my face or I beat him senseless, I reckoned I'd still be screwed. The cops in the Peak District had taken my DNA. I hadn't been charged, so the sample should have been destroyed, but I wasn't betting any money on that. Besides, I might be confident I could beat Doctor Tom to a pulp on my own, but there was no guarantee he'd be on his own. We had no idea how many sylphs he could call on.

Unwilling sylphs. I thought about that. Could we persuade a sylph to help us, if the pay-off was breaking Tom Kelley's hold over them? I glanced down at the VW's ignition just for a second. Looking back at the car park, I ran my fingers over the fob that Helen's key folded into. I traced the edges of the buttons to unlock the doors and the boot. The thing was mostly plastic, though obviously there was metal there as well. How much plastic was enough for a sylph to handle something? How much metal was too much?

It had to be worth asking, if we could find a sylph we could trust not to go running to Tom telling tales. The more I thought about getting hold of that briefcase without leaving a trace, the more I liked the idea. Tom Kelley could claim he'd had the Crown Jewels stolen from his car, but there'd be no proof of anything. Would he even go to the police and risk facing awkward questions about papers missing from some Cambridge University library? He'd certainly have no reason to suspect Fin or her mum. So could a sylph pick his pocket and bring us the key without him realising? Or could a sylph help us find a spare key somewhere?

A fresh thought hit me like a punch to the gut. Sylphs. Shit. We were assuming Tom Kelley would be driving the Jag out to the sites that interested him. What if he was forcing a sylph to carry him from place to place? I should have sodding well thought of that. I was the one with the experience of being swept long by a dryad's magic, and a naiad's come to that. Fin and her family weren't to blame, but they could be neck deep in the shit if they'd found Doctor Tom and he could see who they really were.

Fuck! I clenched my fists and was about to smash them down on the steering wheel when I realised that risked sounding the car horn. All I could do was vent my feelings by swearing, long and loud. At least no one walked by with their dog to hear me.

After what felt like half an hour but was closer to ten minutes, my phone chimed with a message on the app. Will was back at his car. He was ready to leave. Helen checked in next, then Fin. I was so relieved my hands were shaking as I chucked the clipboard onto the passenger seat and swept the fake sign off the dash. I turned the ignition key, and stalled the VW twice in the six me-tres it took me to get to the junction.

The day was bright and clear now. The traffic had eased, and I got back to Venturer's House without any bother. Fin was already waiting for everyone else by the open gates. Judging by the state of the Landy, she'd had a very muddy drive.

'Put the kettle on, Dan,' she called over as I parked the VW and got out. 'The door's open.'

As I went in, I heard another engine. That was Will. By the time Helen ar-rived, I'd made coffee in the big cafetière that Fin had got out of a cupboard. I poured out four mugs and we sat down at the table.

'Right.' Fin stirred two spoonfuls of sugar into hers. 'Okay, there is an old, dry river bed in that field. You can just about make out the paler line of the silt cutting through the peat if you know what you're looking for. So why would Tom Kelley be interested? I've been thinking about that on the drive back. If there is buried treasure somewhere under there, I reckon there could have been a Bronze Age ritual site when the river still flowed. A place where offer-ings were made to the waters, maybe from a timber platform over the water, like they think happened at Flag Fen. There could be swords, torcs, spears, things like that. They'll be broken – that was part of the ritual – but I bet histo-rians and archaeologists would love to find something like that.'

She shrugged. 'I'm just guessing, but that would fit. There weren't any sylphs around to ask, not that I noticed.'

I remembered hearing a radio programme where an archaeologist had explained how weapons used as offerings were broken to somehow signify they had passed to the spirit world. Now that I'd met Witta, I reckoned anyone who knew anything about the very real spirits who lived in these waters might have something else in mind. Personally, I would make damn sure that a bronze sword, or anything else sharp that I was offering, wasn't left in any condition for a nereid or some other, less friendly creature to pick up and use against me.

Helen finished her coffee. 'We did need to go and see these places for ourselves. It's not really clear on the maps, but those footpaths meet at a high point locally. As high as the ground gets around there, anyway. I saw something else as well, thanks to the angle of the light as I flew in low. I think there may have been a mound there, though it's been – what do they call it? Ploughed out? Or I may just be imagining something I want to see, of course.'

She smiled and looked more like Fin than ever. Will grinned back.

'I didn't see anything out of the ordinary, I don't have any exciting theo-ries, and there were no sylphs to ask. That place definitely ruffled my feathers though. Spider sense – swan sense – call it whatever you like, that was definitely tingling.'

He was trying to make light of it, but we could all see he was unsettled.

'You didn't see anything in the trees?' I asked. 'Feel there was something in there taking an interest?'

'Maybe?' He shook his head. 'Sorry, I can't swear to it.'

'So what now?' Helen looked around the table. 'Where does this get us?'

'It would help if we could be certain there really is some treasure for Kelley to find.' Fin looked at me. 'Do you think there's any possible way to persuade one of the hobs to show us what happened in one of these places in the past?' She didn't sound hopeful.

'What?' Will was intrigued.

Fin explained what had happened to me and then to both of us, in Talbot House. Will was amazed. I waited for her to finish before saying what I reckoned.

'I can't see how that'll happen. Not without one of us signing up to be a hob's servant for life, for a start. Anyway, even if one of them agreed, how would we get them out there?'

Fin nodded. I could see she'd expected an answer like this. 'It's not as if we can stick a hob in the back of a car, is it?'

'So what do we do?' Helen looked around the table again. 'We can't spend days on end sitting outside that hotel, watching and waiting for Tom Kelley to make a move.'

'We need to find some way to provoke him into doing whatever he's got planned,' I said slowly.

'And we need to be ready to throw a spanner in the works,' Fin pointed out.

'He can't be in three places at once,' Helen observed. 'He'll have to pick one, sooner or later.'

'How can we find that out?' Fin's frustration equalled my own.

'Is there any way we could persuade the sylphs to talk to us?' I wondered. 'Without them tipping him off.'

'Camera traps,' Will said suddenly. 'Trail cams, whatever you want to call them. We could set those up at all three sites to see how often Kelley goes there and what he gets up to. I've only got the ones that record onto data cards, not the ones that transmit video, so someone will have to go and swap out the cards, but that's something we can fly in to do, trust me. That's got to be better than another round of musical cars and trying to stake out that hotel.' He grinned at our startled faces. 'What? Did you think I get prize-winning wildlife photos by accident? I use camera traps to see what's around before I set up a hide.'

'That's a great idea,' I assured him.

Will was about to say something else when there was a knock at the door.

Will was closest and he got up to open it. He took a hasty step backwards as Witta strode into the kitchen.

She wasn't masquerading as a human. Her skin was blue-green and shone where it caught the light, with a pattern like fish scales. Her eyes were opaque grey and her hair was clear, vivid green, slicked back. Like the naiads I've seen, she looked like a woman in a bodysuit rather than one who had stripped. Even if she had looked naked and vulnerable, any man with half a brain would surely think twice about trying his luck. Her hands and feet weren't remotely human. They were long and fully webbed, and each finger and toe was tipped with a translucent silvery talon.

'What have you done?' Her accusing gaze swept over the four of us.

Chapter Fifteen

My first instinct was to say 'Nothing', but that wasn't strictly true. But saying nothing clearly wasn't an option either.

'We think there are three places where Tom Kelley hopes to find buried treasure,' I said carefully. 'We went to take a look at them this morning. Well, they did.' I nodded at the others. 'I kept watch on Kelley.'

'We flew over these places as swans,' Fin added. 'We did everything we could to avoid attracting attention. None of us saw any sylphs or anything else that could have known us for what we are. Whatever's happened isn't our fault.'

Will looked at her. I could see he was thinking about whatever he had felt near that wood. He didn't say anything, so neither did I. We would deal with one thing at a time. An angry nereid was the immediate priority.

'Show me,' Witta demanded.

Fin fetched the map. Helen and I cleared the table. We all stood and looked down as Fin pointed out the places they had visited. 'Here, here and here.'

Witta tapped the map with a talon, at the site with the lost river. 'This man, this magician, he's doing something here. Something to dry out the ground. You have to stop him. I don't know what he's doing. I daren't go near him in case he can do it to me.'

She didn't sound scared. She was furious. Her gaze challenged us to refuse her, or to offer sympathy, or to do anything, really, except get on with what she was telling us to do. Her hair shifted and rippled as if it was stirred by flowing water.

'I'll go,' I said quickly. 'There's nothing he can do to me.' I hoped to hell that was true. 'I can try to get that crystal off him. He won't be nearly so dangerous without it.' I certainly wasn't going to miss this chance of stopping Kelley once and for all.

'Go!' Witta gestured towards the door.

'Wait,' Fin objected. 'You're not going out there on your own.'

'If it's just Kelley, I'll be fine. If it's not, if I see anything else, I'll back off as soon as I've got some idea of what he's doing. Then we can work out what to do about it.' I looked at the others. 'Meantime, you go and get those camera traps and set them up at the other two sites. This has got to be our best chance to do that, while we know where Kelley is. We still don't know which place will be his first target, do we?'

'That sounds like a plan,' Will agreed.

Helen nodded at her nephew. 'If we take two cars to yours, you can show us what to do. Then we can split up and set up the cameras in both places at once.'

'Hang on.' Fin still wasn't happy.

Witta clapped her webbed hands together with a deafening crack. Her hair swept itself into a fierce crest. 'You're wasting time.'

Fin wasn't about to be intimidated. She hit the map with a forefinger. 'Can you wait for Dan there? It's where I parked this morning,' she explained with a glance at me, before looking back at the nereid. 'You should be able to tell if he gets into trouble without showing yourself. You can let us know.'

How was that going to happen if they were driving around the county? Don't get me wrong, I liked the idea of some backup, but—

'Agreed.' Witta turned to Will. 'Give me a feather, fly boy.'

He looked startled, but he didn't argue. There was a blinding flash, and there was a swan in the kitchen. I blinked and rubbed my eyes while it— while he spread out a bright white wing. He thrust his beak into the lower feathers like a bird preening. One feather fluttered to the tiled floor. Witta sank down and picked it up more deftly than I expected. Then I was blinded again, and Will stood by the worktop, rubbing his arm.

Witta smiled. That was more unnerving than her anger. She stepped close and stroked his cheek with the feather. 'Stand near water and call. I'll come to you. Now, open the door.'

Will blushed scarlet and hurried to let her out. He stood with his back to us for a moment, and I didn't want to think what his problem might be. I'd met a naiad who could and would stir every lustful impulse in a man's brain and balls, either to get him to do what she wanted or just to prove that she could. I focused on wiping my watering eyes.

'What's the matter?' Fin was concerned.

'You don't see that? A bright flash when you... you—'

'When we shift?' Now she was puzzled. 'No.'

'No one's ever mentioned it.' Helen was equally bemused. 'Swan or not.'

Will cleared his throat. 'Maybe it's something to do with Dan's mother's blood?'

The three of them were looking curiously at me. I stood up.

'Is this really what we should be talking about? Come on, let's get on with this before Witta comes back.'

There was no sign of the nereid outside, or the hob or any sylphs. For the second time that morning, we set off in a line of cars. At least I was more comfortable driving my own vehicle, once I'd got the seat readjusted. The others

142

went straight across the crossroads rather than turning left, but that wasn't a problem. Since Fin had been to the lost river this morning, I could find the destination in the satnav's history.

I was glad I was driving the Landy. Once I got off the main road, the tarmac was covered with muddy clods dropped from the thick treads of a tractor's tyres. The final turn on the route took me off the raised road and down a black, rutted slope to an uneven track that the satnav was still happily convinced was a real road. It wasn't even close, as far as I was concerned.

I'd nearly reached the place where Fin had parked when I noticed a difference in the way the Land Rover was handling. The parking spot was close to the point where the straight new cut was carrying what must have been the little river's waters away from their ancient route. So close to the waterway and so low-lying, this ground should be moist at any time of year. After the wet autumn and winter we'd had, the soil should be absolutely saturated. It certainly had been this morning. I'd seen the fresh mud on the Landy to prove it. It had been for most of the way along this track. I'd felt the softness pulling at the steering as I avoided the puddles in the ruts. There was no telling how deep that water might be, and the last thing we needed was the Land Rover getting bogged down.

Now, though, I could feel the tyres hitting solid ridges under the wheels. Even with the suspension doing its best, I was being jolted hard. I found the parking spot and pulled up. Getting out and zipping up my jacket, I looked down to see the dark soil was hard, dry and dusty. I didn't think it would look like that after months of summer sun. What the hell was Tom Kelley up to?

I'd go and find the bastard and ask. The map printout was on the passenger seat. I reached over and picked it up. I took a quick look to make sure I knew where I was going, folded it up and put it in my pocket. Then I checked my phone. There was barely a signal, and no texts or messages on the group app. Still, these trousers had a zipped, waterproof mobile pocket so I put the phone away in that. If I could get close without Doctor Tom seeing me coming, getting some more video of him metal-detecting without permission might be useful. On the other hand, I wanted to keep my hands free in case Kelley put up a fight to hang on to that damn crystal.

Though I might be facing Kelley and somebody or something else. I realised there was no sign of the red Jaguar. I checked the map again. He could have parked somewhere else. No, I decided. Anyone heading here by some other route across the fields was in for a hell of a hike. It was much more likely that I'd been right earlier. The prick was forcing a sylph to take him from place to place. I had to warn the others about that. We might have got lucky this morning, but we couldn't take that risk again.

143

I opened the back of the Land Rover and found my toolbox. You never know when you might need a screwdriver, and I had a flat-head and a Phillips with me. I put them in the leg pockets of my combat trousers. Good thing I wasn't wearing jeans today. A hundred mil of pointed steel wouldn't be as effective as that frying pan, but that should be enough to stop any sylph sweeping me up and carrying me away while Kelley made his escape.

I locked up the Landy again and began walking, shoving my hands in my jacket pockets. It was another chilly day. There was a line of leafless poplar trees on the far side of the shallow channel in the ground. That marked the field boundary. I might as well take advantage of what cover there was out here. The closer I got to Tom Kelley before he saw me coming, the better.

I crossed the old route of the river to walk along the field edge. Between the tree trunks with their upswept branches I could see the field beyond had water lying in its furrows. The field where I was walking had been ploughed as well. This ground was as dry as a bone, though, with the breeze sweeping flurries of dusty soil along the dark ridges.

I wondered how Tom Kelley expected to explain that, if he planned to make some great discovery for everyone to admire. Some treasure that would make him famous. The Kelley Hoard. Unless he did just want to get rich.

I was approaching another boundary now. A straggly hedge cutting across my path divided this stretch of drained land into two. There was a wide metal gate in the corner by the trees. Once I was through that or over it, Kelley was bound to see me. The spot circled on his treasure map was about halfway along the next field. There would be no way for me to hide as I approached him.

Of course, that worked in my favour too. If he tried to run, I'd see whichever way he went. I hoped he did make a break for it. Kelley didn't strike me as a man who worked out, in a gym or anywhere else. I'm no athlete but my job keeps me fit. I might have been useless as a long-distance runner at school, but I was enough of a sprinter to be usefully fast on the rugby pitch, even if my size meant I played in the scrum. Doctor Tom wouldn't get up again any time soon if I tackled him, especially not on ground this hard. Well, he only had himself to blame for that. If he broke an arm or collar bone, that would just make it easier for me to take the crystal off him.

I reached the gate. Now I had a clear view into the field beyond. There was no one and nothing to see there except more ploughed, peaty soil. If there was a paler line of silt to show the river's path, I couldn't see where it was, now that the ground was so dry.

After a few minutes silently swearing, I realised our mistake. Witta had said Kelley was doing this, but she hadn't seen him here for herself. We'd all just assumed he must be. I might have thought this through and realised that, if I hadn't been so eager to find him and get hold of that crystal.

I stood there, trying to decide what to do for the best. Well, I'd come all this way. I might as well take a look at the place Kelley was so interested in. Wherever he might be, he wasn't here. With that line of poplars along the field edge, I was also closer to more trees than I had seen for a while. There had to be some chance that the Green Man would show himself and offer some sodding clue about what I should do.

I hoped the others had their wits about them, in case Kelley turned up where they were. I reached for the loop of chain that was padlocked to the gate and hooked over the metal post driven into the ground. Something stung my neck just under my ear. I raised my hand instinctively, before thinking slapping a wasp or a bee would be a stupid move. Then I remembered it was January. Where would a wasp or a bee come from?

I felt more needle-sharp blows on my neck, where the skin was exposed above my jacket collar. My head was being peppered too, and I keep my hair too short to do much to soften that. My jacket and trousers were thick enough to protect me, but the sound of whatever was pelting me hitting cloth was as loud as rain on a car roof.

I pulled up my collar and turned around. Hunching my shoulders, I held my coat closed with one hand and did my best to shield my face with my other arm while I tried to see what the hell was going on. The air was full of dust. No, it was soil. Not just soil being swept up by some passing breeze. The earth was being hurled at me, and this was more than the fine topsoil left by the plough. I could see peaty clods being lifted off the black ridges. They spiralled upwards, to be broken into hard, dry fragments. Those pieces were small enough to dart through the air and sharp-edged enough to do damage. My face was throbbing. I felt a trickle down my cheek that had to be blood.

What I couldn't see was what was doing this. It was easy enough to guess. Sylphs, willingly or not. They didn't want me here. Okay, I can take a hint. I tried to drag my collar further up my face and really wished I'd worn some sodding gloves. I began walking back the way I'd come. Within a few steps, I was fighting my way through a gale. I ducked my head to protect my face and staggered onwards. I focused on the ground in front of my feet. I didn't need to look ahead to see the Land Rover. As long as I followed the line of the trees, I'd reach the place where I'd parked.

How long that would take me was a different question. This was getting to be hard work. Every step took more effort. The brutal wind was getting stronger. I could feel my feet slipping on the hard, dry ground. I trod on a plough ridge and the earth crumbled under my boot, not into dust but into pellets.

The ground was as lethal as a floor covered in ball bearings. I went down hard onto one knee.

There's a reason people say the bigger they are, the harder they fall. I'm a big man, and all of my weight landed on my knee. Pain shot through the joint and up into the muscle I'd pulled a few days ago. It had to be the same sodding leg, didn't it? I heal fast, but that injury was still tender. Now it was as bad as it had ever been.

I hunched over to catch my breath as I waited for the pain in my thigh and knee to fade from that vicious shock. I had an idea while I was down there. If I couldn't see the sylphs, maybe they could hear me. Still squinting at the ground, I shouted as loudly as I could.

'The stargazer's son is not your friend. We want to break his hold over you. Whatever he's told you is a lie. He wants whatever's hidden here for himself.'

I broke off, coughing, as the words stuck in my throat. The air was as dry as the sodding Sahara. All the same, the wind eased off. It didn't die away completely, but I was able to get to my feet. I took a cautious step, testing my footing as well as my injured leg. My knee was throbbing and my thigh was burning, but I could still put weight on that foot. That was a major relief. I slid my boot forward to sweep the hard pellets of soil aside. Raising my head just a little, I looked around for any sign of a sylph.

Trying to swallow to moisten my lips and tongue, I shouted again. 'We want to help—'

Wind slapped my face and peat filled my mouth. I barely managed to avoid breathing in a lungful. I couldn't help swallowing some. I spun around to face away from the wind, trying to get away from the attack. Coughing and retching, I spat out what I could, but my mouth was drier than ever.

The gale hit my head, my back and my knees. The blows were brutal. This felt like a beating with a scaffolding pole. My injured leg buckled. At least this time I had the sense to go with the fall. That didn't help. The wind rolled me over and over. I buried my face in my arms. The wind seized my feet and hauled me around. Another gust shoved my shoulders. Now I was spinning, from head to toe. I tried to dig my boot heels into the ground, but that was impossible. As I got so dizzy I wanted to throw up, I heard mocking laughter around me.

The savage wind died back again. A peat-filled breeze still swirled around me, but I was left lying there motionless. Panting, I did my best to take shallow breaths. If I started coughing again, I didn't think I'd stop until I brought up a lung. As the dizziness receded, I lay there, waiting. I could feel the anticipation in the air around me. I could also feel the growing weight of the soil as it fell out of the air to cover me.

My eyes were stinging. I blinked and sniffed and considered my options. Whatever she had promised, Witta was no help. I had to fight my way free of this or some farmer was in for a hell of a shock when his plough dug up my corpse. Not that I'd be lying here until someone came to plant their next crop. Fin and the others would come looking for me. Sod that for a game of soldiers. There was no way I was having them lured into this trap.

I had an idea. I rolled onto my belly, staying as flat to the ground as I could. Flexing my feet, I got the toes of my boots under me. I put my hands in front of my face and took my weight on my elbows. I began inching forward, slowly and painfully. Crawling on my hands and knees would have been a damn sight easier, but that would mean the wind could get underneath me. As I hugged the earth, the buffeting began again. Violent blows tried to snatch my hands away from my face or drag my feet aside. Thumps to my ribs hurt, even more than before. I kept on crawling. Now my height and weight were working to my advantage, keeping me pressed against the ground.

I focused on moving forward. I decided that anyone who thought soldiers had it easy crossing ground like this was welcome to try it for themselves. I also realised I had absolutely no idea which way I was going. I'd lost my bearings completely. Okay, that wasn't good, but it wasn't a problem I couldn't solve. As long as I kept going, I had to hit one edge of this field eventually. Once I did that, I would follow the boundary. Whether I went left or right didn't matter. However long it took me, I'd either hit the track I'd used to get here or I'd find the old river bed and the trees.

Either way, I would find my way back to the Land Rover if it took me until sunset. I hoped it didn't take that long. I really hoped Witta was right when she said sylphs lost interest in their games sooner rather than later. I desperately hoped that whatever hold Tom Kelley had over them didn't mean he could order them to keep this up until they killed me.

As I shuffled forward, my hands hit something hard. Not solid. There was some give in whatever it was. Caught unawares, I lowered my hands and lifted my head to see. A hand seized me by the throat and forced my chin up. I struggled up onto my knees. I had no choice. It was that or choke.

Whatever had hold of me wasn't a sylph. There was some resemblance all the same. This was another human-shaped creature, outlined against the dust-filled air by faint, eerie radiance. This glimmer was the colour of a candle flame though, and this creature's eyes were as red as embers. Its gaze burned with malice as it tightened its grip. It was going to take its time strangling me, and it was going to enjoy itself.

I reached for the pocket on my thigh. The creature didn't care. It laughed, and it wasn't alone. As I wheezed, I saw more pairs of glowing eyes as faint figures circled around me. I fumbled with the button on my pocket. At least that meant the bloody screwdriver hadn't fallen out. I could feel its reassuring weight. Now I just needed to get hold of it before I passed out.

I summoned all the strength I had left to thrust my hand into my pocket. The screwdriver was handle down, of bloody course. I grabbed it and wrenched the tool free with a sound of tearing cloth. The hold on my throat slackened a fraction as the creature realised I was up to something. Too slow and too late. It let me go the barest instant before I stabbed it. I don't know what I hit but we were so close I couldn't miss.

It exploded. I was already dropping to the ground, not because I expected that to happen but because I was barely conscious. The blast went upwards and outwards as far as I could tell, with a short, sharp roar that left my ears ringing.

I sprawled face down in the dirt, gripping that screwdriver like my life depended on it. As soon as I could, I forced myself back up to my knees. As I did that, I realised a couple of things. Firstly, the air around me was clean enough for me to take a few deeper breaths. That made me cough again, and my chest hurt like a son of a bitch, but I was able to control the spasm. As that brought tears to my eyes, I felt saliva flood my mouth. I hawked and spat out as much of the peat dust as I could.

I realised the faint, flame-tinted figures had backed well away. They were still circling around me, and I still couldn't count how many there were. They weren't coming any closer though. I held the screwdriver as if I was ready for a knife fight and took a few steps forward. The figures in front of me retreated.

They didn't go far, just enough to maintain the distance between us. Just far enough to stay out of reach if I lunged at them with my lethal steel. I still couldn't see where I was going. Beyond the small clear space around me, the air was still opaque with dust. The flame-tinted figures left swirling trails in it as they crossed each other's paths ahead of me.

I'd work with what I'd got. I was on my feet now, and I was going to find the field's edge as fast as I possibly could. I walked faster and the shimmering creatures withdrew again. I made maybe ten paces before something hit me hard between my shoulder blades. These things weren't stupid. They knew they could still attack me from behind. I got the other screwdriver out of my pocket. Now I had steel in both hands. That made them back off a bit further and I quickened my pace. Then something hit the back of my head so hard I staggered. I spun around, lashing out. I didn't make contact with anything, and the mocking laughter started again.

Something white flashed through the dust-filled air above me. It was a swan. It wasn't only Tom Kelley who couldn't tell them apart. I had no idea who it was, but there was no way this was some random coincidence. No bird would fly into this mess without a good reason.

148

The swan landed on the ground in front of me. Wings spread, it circled around. I turned to follow it. Neck arched, its beak gaped as it hissed. The laughter faded to be answered by a menacing murmur.

The swan looked back at me. It dipped its head twice and then turned to jab its beak emphatically ahead.

'That's the way to go?' It was pretty obvious.

The swan dipped its head again and flapped its wings to take off. But swans need a run-up to get off the ground, and that took it to the edge of the clear air around me. Close to the flame-tinted creatures. They mobbed the bird. I felt the rush of air around me as the ones at my back raced to join the fun. I saw those white wings flail as a surge of wind tumbled the swan over. Before I could see what happened next, the swirling dust hid the bird from me.

I started running, with a screwdriver gripped in each fist. If I could catch these bastard things, I'd see if I could make another one explode. I'd got as far as realising being caught in that would do a swan no favours when I also realised that however fast I ran, these sodding things could outpace me. I didn't care, as long as I had them running scared. I just hoped I wasn't going to stumble across a swan with a broken wing, or with its long neck snapped. That thought made my throat burn with anguish.

A few more paces and a new sound split the air. It took me a moment to recognise the Land Rover's horn. Someone was sounding it to give me something to aim for. That was a good thing too. I realised I had already veered off the direction the swan had shown me.

I ran towards the noise. The dust ahead of me thinned. The red-eyed creatures grew even more indistinct. As the soil grew softer under my feet, they swooped past me. One came close enough to scour my face with a touch like sandpaper. I didn't even bother trying to stab it. I wanted to get back to the Landy, to know whoever that swan was, they were safe.

The last of the dust fell out of the air. The peaty soil under my boots squelched. I saw the Land Rover ahead. There was someone in the driving seat, still sounding the horn. I ripped open the passenger door. Fin was there. She was safe. Her blonde hair was dull grey with dirt and her face was bruised, but apart from that, she looked okay. Now relief left me breathless.

'Get in,' she rasped. 'Before someone comes to see—' She broke off coughing, and had to open the driver's door to spit onto the ground outside.

I got into the passenger seat. As Fin wrestled the vehicle into a three-point turn, I looked down at my hands. I was ten times as dirty as she was, and not just on the surface. I could feel the gritty sensation of soil against my skin, inside my clothes. It chafed under my thighs and against my back as I pressed against the seat when Fin reached the slope to get back up to the road.

Once we were on the tarmac, she accelerated away, although there was no sign of anyone coming to see who'd been sounding a car horn. There was still a lot of mud on the road, and I felt the wheels lose their grip, just a fraction, as Fin rounded a bend a shade too fast. Looking at her, I saw she was struggling to suppress a cough.

I saw a field entrance ahead. 'Pull over.'

She shook her head.

'Pull over before you put us in a fucking ditch!' Now it was my turn to start coughing.

I couldn't stop. Within seconds, I was bent double, fighting for breath, wrenching at the seatbelt. That did make Fin pull over at the side of the road. She hit the seatbelt release and I managed to open the door. I half fell out of the seat, and leaning hard against the side of the Landy, I worked my way around to the back. Fin met me there. I wasn't coughing quite so badly now, thankfully. I opened the rear door and found the six-pack of bottled water I'd stashed there ages ago, just in case. I hadn't had an emergency like this in mind.

I handed Fin a bottle. Like me, she rinsed her mouth and spat out the unpleasant results. We both drank cautiously, to soothe our dry, sore throats. My chest still ached, but there wasn't anything I could do about whatever crap I'd breathed in. Quite possibly literally crap, I realised uneasily. I had no way of knowing what that farmer used to fertilise his field. Had Tom Kelley planned on giving us some sort of pneumonia or was that just going to be a bonus? We'd have a hard time explaining what we'd breathed in to some nurse in A&E.

'Thanks.' Fin raised her water bottle to me.

'Thanks for coming to my rescue.' I spoke as quietly as she did. Neither of us wanted to start coughing again. Keeping my voice low was an effort though, as anger at the nereid tightened my throat. 'So much for Witta's help.'

'Who do you think told me and Mum you were in trouble?' Fin waved that away. 'I would have flown over to find you anyway. We got a phone call from Will. He saw Tom Kelley at the footpath site when he got there. He's been keeping watch.'

She screwed the lid back on her bottle of water. 'Let's hope he's still there when we arrive.'

So that explained her hurry. She was already walking back to the driver's door. I didn't argue. She had a better idea of where we were going, and we'd probably still be safer with her driving. My leg ached and I had been beaten black and blue, even if I was too covered in dirt for anyone to see it.

Chapter Sixteen

The drive was just long enough for me to stiffen up horribly. At least that stopped me jumping out as soon as Fin pulled up behind Will's car and Helen's VW. I very much wanted to grab Tom Kelley by his scrawny neck and beat him to a pulp. That would be a bit of payback for what we'd just been through. We'd see what a magician could do about that.

Unfortunately, I had no idea which way to go to find him. I looked at Fin.

'Will saw his Jag parked at the closest spot so he carried on driving,' she explained. 'This is the best place he could find to get close enough to keep an eye on him.'

We got out of the Land Rover. This wasn't an official lay-by, but the grass verges had been worn away on both sides of the narrow road. Plenty of tyre tracks showed people stopped here regularly. I guessed walkers knew this was a good place to join the public footpath that was clearly signposted beside the stile.

There was an actual hedgerow worthy of the name running away from the road. Fin ducked behind it and started walking, stooping low. 'Keep your head down.'

That was just what I didn't need after the morning I'd already had. I did my best, following her in an awkward, uncomfortable crouch. Thankfully it wasn't far to a thin spot in the hedge where Will and Helen were both sitting on the ground. One of them had woven a lattice of leafless sprays to hide behind. Helen had the little binoculars Fin had bought in the petrol station. Will was looking through a camera that had a lens as long as my hand. I lowered myself down beside him, trying not to swear at my various aches and pains.

I could see a distant figure walking back and forth where the ground rose to what passed for a low hill around here. Whatever had been grown in this vast field had long since been harvested to leave bare earth and a few wisps of withered vegetation. I studied the lie of the land and decided that Helen was right. There was some sort of ancient barrow or mound there. You had to be looking for it to see it, but once you did, you'd be convinced.

Fin was right as well. We were a long way off, but we couldn't have got any closer without Kelley seeing us coming. I wondered if Will's camera traps were going to be any use from this far away.

'What's he doing?'

'Pacing something out to measure it, I reckon. He's got his crystal ball with him. He was walking around, looking into it, until a few minutes ago.' Will didn't look away from his viewfinder. 'And there's somebody with him. They turned up just now. That's when he put the crystal away.'

As he spoke, I saw a second figure. Whoever it was must have gone down the far side of the slope and then come back to join Tom Kelley. Man or woman? They were too far away for me to tell as they stood silhouetted against the sky.

'I don't recognise him,' Helen said slowly. She handed the binoculars to Fin. 'Take a look.'

Her eyes widened as she saw the state of us, but she didn't waste time with questions. We were here, and we were walking and talking, so we'd survived whatever had happened. Everything else could wait.

I glanced between Fin and the two men up on the hill. If she recognised the stranger that might help us somehow.

'No,' she said, exasperated. 'I've no idea who that is.'

By sheer luck I was looking at Tom Kelley when I saw whoever had joined him turn to walk away. Kelley raised his hand. He was holding a backpack by the handle at the top rather than by the straps. He swung it hard into the back of the stranger's head. The stranger collapsed like a puppet with its strings cut.

'Shit!' Fin had seen him do it too.

'What?' Helen had been looking at her daughter. She looked up the hill, confused.

'He's just knocked that man out!' Fin sounded as if she couldn't quite believe it.

'Got it all on video,' Will said with satisfaction. He didn't move or lower his camera, staying focused on Kelley.

I looked at the others. 'Then that's assault, and we can prove it.'

'Where's he going?' Fin raised the binoculars again.

I looked back, but Kelley had disappeared beyond the hill.

'Back to his car. Making a run for it. Got to be.' Will had no doubt about that.

Fin tossed me the Land Rover's keys. 'I'll see where he goes.'

Before any of us could object, she shifted into a very grubby swan. At least I managed to turn away and avoid being dazzled this time. A moment later and she was in the air, swooping over our heads.

'That man needs an ambulance.' Helen was on her feet.

'Let's see how badly he's hurt.' Will was finally putting his camera away. 'I've got a first aid kit in my car.'

'You get that while we see what we can do for him.' Helen looked a bit queasy, but she set off up the shallow slope, determined.

As I went with her, I realised my phone was still in the Land Rover. Damn it. 'Have you got enough signal to call 999?'

She checked as we kept walking. 'Just about. What are we going to say?'

I hesitated. 'Better ask Will. He's the one with the evidence, so he'll need to keep his story straight.'

And I needed to think of a way to explain to them both why I didn't want my name mentioned anywhere near the police, without making them think I was some hardened criminal.

We reached the top of the hill. I looked warily around before approaching the unconscious man. There was no sign of Kelley. Thankfully there was no sign of anyone else approaching either. The last thing we needed was some dog walker turning up, demanding some explanation or calling the police before we'd agreed on our story. It wasn't as if we could have any good reason to stop them.

'That's where he was parked.'

Helen pointed, and I saw the trodden line of a path heading down the far side of the hill. It led away to a fence with a stile that was a lot closer than where we had parked. There was no sign of the red Jag by now. There wasn't any other car waiting there either.

'How did he get here?' I wondered aloud.

'Is he dead?' Helen's voice shook as she looked down at the motionless man. 'There's an awful lot of blood.'

There really was, glistening briefly before it soaked into the sandy earth. I hated to think how heavy that crystal might be. I really didn't want to see how much damage it had done. There was every chance it had cracked this man's skull like an eggshell. I wanted to see Tom Kelley stopped, whatever the hell he was up to, but seeing this poor sod getting murdered on his country walk was a hell of a price to pay.

The stranger was wearing black jeans and walking boots, and a grey waterproof coat, heavy enough to ward off any bad weather. He lay on his back, arms spread wide and his legs uncomfortably buckled. Not that he cared at the moment. He was around the same height as Will, with a medium sort of build. His hair was medium brown, and he was nothing out of the ordinary to look at. The sort of man you'd pass on any street in any town without even remembering that you'd seen him. Just some unlucky bastard in the wrong place at the wrong time.

I dropped to my knees beside him. I remembered any number of health and safety briefings I've had on building sites over the years. The specifics and the gruesome stories vary, but the basics are always the same. If the casualty is breathing okay, isn't bleeding from what looks like an artery and isn't about to get crushed by a JCB or similar, leave them well alone. Wait for the paramedics. They know what they're doing and you don't. You can do a whole lot more damage trying to move someone, especially if they've got a spinal injury.

That seemed like good advice. I didn't want to try lifting his head and finding I had half his brains spilling into my hand. As far as I could tell he was still breathing. I could see his chest rise and fall, just about anyway.

'Has he got a pulse?' Helen asked, apprehensive.

I felt the man's neck, but couldn't find one. That didn't necessarily mean it wasn't there. I could just be feeling in the wrong place. I settled for using a dirty thumb to raise one of the man's eyelids, as gently as I could. Doctors always look at someone's eyes on those TV medical dramas. I'd been watching a DVD box set I'd picked up in a charity shop. Pupils equal and reactive was good. Fixed and dilated was bad. That would be something we could tell the paramedics.

I also wanted to know if Fin was chasing a killer, whether or not Tom Kelley realised how much damage he had done.

'Shit!' I recoiled.

'What is it?' Helen was alarmed.

I got to my feet as fast as I could. 'We need to get out of here.'

I looked down the hill to see Will hurrying towards us with a green-and-white box in one hand. I grabbed Helen's arm. 'Come on!'

'Daniel!' She tried to shake me off.

I wasn't having that. Not after what I had seen. On the other hand, I was in no fit state to force anyone anywhere. My throat was aching with the effort of suppressing another bout of coughing. 'Please, trust me. You're in danger if that thing wakes up, you and Will, and Fin if she comes back.'

'What are you talking about?' She glared at me, but something in my voice must have convinced her. She started walking back towards Will beside me.

I let go of her arm. 'Sorry.'

Seeing us coming towards him, Will broke into a run. 'What's the matter?' he called out as we drew close.

I waited until we reached each other, about halfway along the path. 'That's not a man. That's a wyrm.'

They both looked at me blankly.

'Wyrm, with a "y". Serpent dragon sort of thing.' I looked at Helen. 'Didn't you see its eyes?'

'I didn't get a chance,' she said curtly.

154

'I didn't want it seeing you, and recognising you're not... that you're—'

To my intense relief, Will interrupted. 'What do a wyrm's eyes look like then?'

'Pale grey, but translucent, sort of like moonstones. Cold enough to freeze your blood when they're awake.' I couldn't help shivering at the memory of the two wyrms I'd met before. They'd done their best to kill me and Eleanor, and they had damn near succeeded.

Helen and Will were staring at me. She spoke first. 'What's it doing here? What's it doing with Tom Kelley?' She shook her head, clearly not expecting me to answer. 'How do we find out any of that?'

'Maybe Tom Kelley had no idea.' Will looked past us. 'If it's pretending to be someone ordinary, maybe there's a clue on the body. A wallet or something like that.'

'Is it dead?' Helen asked me.

'I have no idea. I don't think we should take any chances. Those things are sodding hard to kill, I can tell you that.' I still have nightmares about it, but I wasn't ready to share those memories.

'We need to know.'

Will darted past me. I was still too shaken to react fast enough to grab him. I went after him but I couldn't catch him either. He was too quick on his feet. I was still stiff and in pain from my knee and thigh. I managed to swallow an obscenity when I realised Helen was walking beside me.

Will reached the top of the hill. He stood there, looking around. He stared at us as we approached. 'Where's he gone?'

'What?' As we reached him, I saw he was right. There was no body to be seen anywhere.

That didn't mean there wasn't a trace left. Helen walked in a slow circle, searching the ground. 'Here!'

As Will and I went over, she was retreating, waving a hand in front of her face. 'This reeks.'

The patch of bloodstained earth looked very different now. The surface was sunken and pitted. Whatever leaves or stems had been left there had dissolved into black slime. I could taste an acrid taint in the air.

'So where has he gone?' Helen looked around, astonished.

I did the same. I was apprehensive. 'They heal in water.'

At least, the ones I'd encountered before had. There was no way to know if this creature was the same, and anyway, if it was looking for water close by, it was out of luck. I realised this was the first place I'd been since I got here where I couldn't see a river or a dyke or a drain.

'So what do we do now?' Will looked unnerved. I didn't blame him.

'We go home,' Helen said, decisive. 'That's where Finele will go as soon as she can.'

I wasn't about to argue. I wanted to know Fin was okay. I also desperately needed a shower and some painkillers.

'I'll catch up with you,' Will said. 'I still need to set up those camera traps.'

We left him to it. Thankfully Helen was a steady driver. I followed her back to Venturer's House without any need for sudden braking or other drama where my injured leg might betray me. She got out and opened the gate, drove through and parked next to Fin's Toyota. As I pulled up, she walked over. I lowered the window.

'Strip off in the utility room,' she said briskly. 'There are clean towels in a basket in there, and that'll keep the worst of the mess in one place.'

'Right. Thanks.'

I did as I was told, and went upstairs to take a shower. Then I looked under the bathroom sink and in the cupboards until I found what I needed to clean the shower, because it looked as if someone had been mud-wrestling in there. By the time I was finished doing that, I was dry.

The mirror on the wall showed me a whole lot of bruises and my knee was red and swollen. I went back to my room and strapped it with the tape Fin had bought me. I used the last of it on my thigh, and really hoped we wouldn't need to make another trip to the pharmacy. I got dressed, gathered up the rubbish and went downstairs.

'Lunch.' Helen was setting out soup bowls and bread. 'Your clothes are in the wash.'

'Thanks. I appreciate it.' I hadn't expected her to do that, but saying so risked sounding really ungrateful.

We sat down to eat together, once Helen had nuked some tomato soup from the freezer. I took some painkillers, and was trying to decide if I wanted to accept the offer of a second bowl when we heard a knock on the door.

It was Fin. I was so relieved I could have hugged her, but she held me off at arm's length. 'Not till I've had a shower.' She wasn't just dirty from our encounter with those things by the dry river. She was as sweaty as if she'd been working out in a gym.

'Where's Kelley?' I asked.

'Back at his hotel. Where's the man he attacked?'

Before I could answer her, Helen spoke. 'That can wait until we're all here. Soup, Finele? Tomato, lentil or mushroom? I can heat it up while you're getting yourself sorted.'

'Mushroom. Thanks, Mum.'

Fin surprised me by heading into the utility room. She came out wearing a towel that started late and finished early. As she headed for the stairs, I could see the soft white feathers that were so essential to her transformation clinging to her shoulders.

According to old folklore, swan maidens in human form wore shawls or undergarments with feathers woven into them. Fin had explained that was just a way to justify keeping their feathers close. People who found out would call that an eccentric custom. If they realised those feathers naturally stayed as close as a second skin without help, they'd most likely call a priest or a witch finder.

She'd told me that when we were in bed, when we spent that weekend together. When I found brushing those feathers aside to kiss her breasts more erotic than stripping any girlfriend of the sexiest lingerie. I was savouring that recollection when I saw Helen looking at me with an expression I couldn't read.

'Let me empty the dishwasher,' I offered hastily. 'I think I know where most things go.'

I did that, and Fin was showered and downstairs, eating soup, when we heard the gate being opened outside and a car coming through. It was Will.

'Tomato, thanks.' He accepted Helen's offer and sat at the table with a satisfied smile. 'I've set the camera traps up, at the hill and by the river, so we've got all three sites covered now.'

Since he wasn't covered in earth, I guessed he hadn't been attacked by whatever had hit Fin and me by the dry river bed. I still asked the question. 'Did you see anything or anyone? Get any sense of being watched?'

He shook his head. 'Not a thing.'

Helen brought over his soup. 'We didn't see anything by that little wood,' she said slowly, 'but we did feel something, didn't we? Something that didn't seem too happy.'

Fin nodded. 'Something Tom Kelley's stirred up, maybe?' She looked at me and Will. 'On purpose or by accident?'

'Where is he?' Will asked.

Fin spoke at the same time. 'So what did happen to that man he hit?'

It took a few minutes to get everyone up to date. Then it took a whole lot longer for me to explain what I knew about wyrms, and why the Green Man had steered me to Blithehurst. He'd sent me to help Eleanor Beauchene deal with the threat from the fearsome creatures there.

'That's awful.' Helen was horrified. 'No wonder you wanted to get well away when you realised what that man really was.'

'So where's it gone?' Fin looked grim. 'How can we find out?'

Will tried to look on the bright side. 'At least we can be pretty sure he – it – whatever – isn't working with Tom Kelley. Not if he tried to smash its skull open. With a bit of luck, it'll eat him and solve all our problems.'

'Or that could make everything ten times worse, if it gets its hands on that crystal.' I tried not to get irritated. It wasn't Will's fault he had no idea what we might be dealing with. I looked at Fin and Helen. 'Are there any local wyrm or dragon legends?'

'Not about any of them closer than Norfolk, or Lincolnshire, I don't think.' Helen didn't sound certain.

Fin glanced towards the door to the hall. I could see she wasn't any keener than I was to spend another evening sorting through Grandad's archive in search of stories that raised as many questions as answers. Fortunately, I had another idea.

'Let's see what Witta knows.' I looked at Will.

'Oh. Okay.' He stood up. He looked eager and nervous at the same time. 'I'll go and give her a call, so to speak.' He got up and went outside.

Helen started clearing the table. 'I'm going to have to spend a day cooking to refill the freezer.'

She didn't sound too happy about that. Though I wasn't sure that was really what was bothering her.

Fin glanced at me. 'Let us do this. We'll give you a shout when Will gets back. You sit down with a coffee.'

I put the kettle on. Helen hesitated. Then she handed Fin the stack of bowls.

'I should check my email. There are a couple of work things I need to keep track of.' She headed upstairs.

Fin and I loaded the dishwasher and tidied the kitchen pretty much in silence. There wasn't really anything to say until we could talk to the nereid. Not until Fin caught me by surprise with a hug.

'I didn't know what had happened to you, when I saw that peat blow. Then I saw that big flash, and headed for it. What on earth did you do?'

'Got very lucky.' I leaned back against the cupboard with my arms wrapped around her. 'I think it was a dust explosion. Whatever those things were, they weren't expecting that. Nor was I.'

Though every carpenter and most builders know how dangerous a really dusty atmosphere can get in an enclosed space. When the density of fine particles in the air gets high enough, it only takes a spark and then 'boom'. If I'd had any idea that sticking steel into one of those red-eyed frights would strike that spark, I'm not at all sure I would have risked it.

Fin's arms tightened around my waist. 'Let's not do that again.'

'You've got a deal.' Though I didn't think those things were going to be caught out a second time. Not if they were as quick on the uptake as the sylph we'd met here. But as long as knowing what had happened stopped them trying to suffocate us like that again, that would do for me.

I hugged Fin closer, trying not to think about seeing her vanish into those swirling grey clouds, pursued by those flame-tinted creatures. Risking my own neck was one thing. That was my choice, and no one lives forever, not even dryads. The thought that Fin could have been hurt though, or even killed, because she was trying to save me? That was something else entirely. It left me hollow inside. How could I live with myself if she was badly injured or worse? How could I keep her out of harm's way? Would she even let me try?

We stood like that till the door opened and Will came in. Witta was with him, and she was dressed as a hiker again. I hoped that was a good sign. Fin went to the hallway to let Helen know they were here. Once we were all sat around the kitchen table, I brought the nereid up to date.

She nodded. 'The water has returned to that ground. All is as it should be.'

'What were those things that attacked us?' Fin wanted to know.

Witta shrugged. 'There are more creatures of the air than sylphs, though they are all kin. I know the kindred you speak of, but I have no idea what you would call them.'

I had more pressing concerns. 'What can you tell us about wyrms around here.'

'Nothing of any substance, alas,' she apologised. 'I've never heard even a rumour of one close by. There are tales of them to the east and to the north, but they were killed before my father's time.'

I had no idea how long nereids lived, but if they were anything like dryads, that would fit with medieval legends of dragons in Norfolk and Lincolnshire. Even so, Witta had to know more about the damn things than we did.

'What can you tell us about wyrms in general?' I asked. 'If there is a barrow or something on that high ground, why would a dragon be interested in whatever Tom Kelley is doing?'

'If the man is looking for buried treasure? He may dig up more than he expects.' Witta looked grim. 'The men who lived here before the fens were drained, before the invaders led by William of Normandy arrived, they had close ties to the great serpents. You can see that in their artefacts. Some did more than merely honour the wyrms and placate them with gifts. There are tales of great leaders being buried with dragon eggs hidden among their treasures.'

'To guard against grave robbers,' Will guessed.

'Hardly.' Witta was amused. 'As far as the wyrms are concerned, that gold is merely there as bait.'

'Oh.' That was a new perspective on dragon hoards.

Witta spread her hands. 'You know about wyrmsong?'

'We do.' I'd explained to the others how Eleanor and I had both heard the eerie calls of a young wyrm that was ready to hatch, buried deep beneath Blithehurst. Those calls had summoned a far more dangerous foe to help it. 'But I didn't hear anything like it on that hill. None of us did.'

I looked at the others for confirmation, and was very relieved to see them shake their heads.

Witta shook her head for a different reason. 'A wyrm cannot rely on those of you with blood that is both human and other being close enough to be lured there when the wyrmlings are ready to hatch. Once the touch of the air enables them to shift from their first ethereal state into solid flesh, they must have meat to eat that will bind them to their hatching place. Then they can draw power from the earth as well as from the shadows. So the wyrm that watched over the eggs of a clutch would tempt ordinary mortals with tales of buried treasure, once they heard their offspring calling. Mortal greed would do the rest. There would be no survivors to warn anyone else of such dangers.'

I wondered if any archaeologists had any idea of the risks that they ran. Then I concentrated on the here and now. 'But there's no wyrmsong. Those eggs aren't ready to hatch.'

'No,' Witta agreed. 'The wyrm you saw must just have been curious about Tom Kelley. The last thing it will want is to see that burial dug up. If sunlight reaches the eggs before they are ready to hatch, the wyrmlings within will die and the eggs will crumble to dust.'

I wondered how many archaeologists had trowelled away the remnants of dead baby dragons over the years, without a clue what they were doing.

Fin was frowning. 'You said wyrms need somewhere warm and wet to lay their eggs, Dan. That hardly fits with a burial mound on top of a hill.'

Witta answered her. 'Somewhere warm and wet *enough*. That ground would have been suitable before the land was drained. Just barely,' she allowed, 'but that risk would be worth it for the wyrm to put those eggs beyond the sea's reach back then. My father's people and the serpent kind are mortal foes. If sea folk ever learned of wyrm eggs hidden too close to the shore, they would raise storms to drown them in salt water. The naiads would flood the rivers to help. They would wash the ground itself away to get to the clutch if they had to. Then they would sweep the eggs into the depths, where the wyrmlings would die in the dark and the cold.'

'Do we think Tom Kelley knows any of this?' Helen looked around the table. 'He can't, surely? Not and risk rousing a dragon.'

'Why did he attack that man,' Fin countered, 'if he had no idea who or what he really was?'

'Could he have seen something through the crystal?' Will wondered.

'If he did that must have been a hell of a surprise.' Though I couldn't see how we'd ever find out what Kelley did or didn't know. I was starting to wonder if it really mattered.

'What do we think he's going to do now?' Fin's expression said she had no idea.

I was in no mood to waste time on more questions we couldn't answer. 'There was nothing about dragons of any sort in that book I read about John Dee. I don't think they're any part of what he's planning.'

'The wyrms were driven out of these lands long before the stargazer's day.' Witta sounded as though she agreed with me.

'Not all of them,' Will objected. 'Not if one's been hanging about for... how long? Seriously? Since some Anglo-Saxon warlord was buried up on that hill?'

Witta shrugged. 'You and yours live for decades. Me and mine see centuries pass. Even so, a wyrm can lie sleeping and hidden, so we would never suspect it was there. Dragons measure their lives in millennia.' She shook her head. 'My kin won't be happy to hear that this one has shown itself.'

'Hang on,' I objected. The last thing we needed was more people involved in this. People who saw humans as bystanders who weren't necessarily innocent.

Witta's eyes flashed grey-green like a stormy sea. 'I don't answer to you.'

No, she didn't, and I couldn't think how to persuade her to cooperate. Which was just great.

'So what are we going to do?' Fin sounded exhausted.

I knew how she felt. I gestured at the window. It was already dark outside. 'Tonight? Nothing. We all need to sleep after the day we've had. Witta, please can you see if Tom Kelley's still at his hotel? Can you let us know tomorrow if he goes anywhere tonight?'

The nereid took so long to answer that I thought she was going to say no. Then she nodded. 'We will talk in the morning.'

That sounded a bit ominous, but I'd take it for now. I looked at the others. 'With any luck, he'll be freaked out by what he's just done, or whatever he thinks he saw. He doesn't know there were any witnesses and he thinks no one knows where he is. He should stay put, at least for tonight.'

I hoped like hell I was right about that.

Will stood up. 'I'll check the camera traps first thing and then come over. Good thing my diary's pretty empty at this time of year.'

'Speak for yourself.' Helen tried to make a joke of that and failed. 'I really must do some work tomorrow,' she said apologetically.

Witta rose to her feet and looked at Will. 'Let's go.'

As the door closed behind them, I looked at Fin and Helen. 'Let's go and have dinner at The Wheat Sheaf, my treat. I don't know about either of you, but I really need a break from all this.'

So that's what we did. It turned out that Helen had been waiting for a chance to ask me all about my childhood and where I'd grown up. That wasn't exactly relaxing, but at least it wasn't fighting murderous sylph-things. She tried to hide it, but I could see she wasn't too impressed to find out I'd dropped out of university after a year. I decided this wasn't the time to explain about my criminal record.

Chapter Seventeen

Thanks to a good meal, as well as the two bottles of wine that we shared between us, I slept far better than I expected. I was still awake early though, and given my aches and bruises I was in no mood to stay in bed.

I got up quietly, got dressed and went downstairs to make myself some toast and tea to go with my painkillers. It was a clear, dry day, so I put my jacket on and went outside to cough up another lungful of the crap I'd breathed in from yesterday's dust storm. After that, I decided to wash the mud off the Land Rover. I'd seen where Helen kept a garden hose, and there was an outside tap on the utility room wall. As long as I took it slow and was careful, I could do the job well enough and stay dry. There'd be no need for Helen to do any more laundry for me.

Once I'd got the Landy clean, I put the hose away. I went over the windows, the lights and number plates with a rag. After that, I fetched the vacuum cleaner out of the utility room. I could hear the shower running upstairs, so I didn't think I'd be disturbing anyone too badly by now.

I opened the utility room window a crack for the power lead and plugged the vacuum in. Back outside, I fitted the fine nozzle attachment to the cleaner's hose and took my time getting every last speck of dirt and peat out of the carpets and seats.

Fin appeared in the kitchen doorway as I was finishing up. 'Do you want me to unplug that for you?' Her voice was a little hoarse, so I guessed she was still coughing up muck like I was. The bruise on her face looked a lot worse this morning.

'Thanks.' I walked to the utility room window to take the plug off her.

She came outside to join me as I rewound the flex. 'I think I know what attacked us yesterday. I found a story in one of Grandad's books about things called Lantern Men. They're a sort of will o' the wisp, but instead of leading people astray to drown them in the marshes, they used to attack people carrying lights, to leave them stranded in the darkness.'

'And now Tom Kelley's stirred them up again.' I carried the hoover back inside and put it in its place in the utility room. 'As well as pissing off a wyrm, and that's going to piss off whoever Witta tells about what's going on.'

I'd been going over everything that had happened as I worked on the Landy, from all the angles I could see. I always find it helps to be doing something with my hands when I'm trying to find answers to problems.

'So…?' Fin looked at me, unsure where this was going.

'At the risk of sounding like some project management bollocks poster, we have to start making things happen instead of scrambling around catching up after they do. We need to take some initiative instead of just stumbling into fights with things like those Lantern Men. We have to stop hoping that a hob or a sylph or anyone else is going to give us the answers we need. We definitely can't wait for Tom Kelley to do whatever he's got planned and just hope to hell we can clear up whatever mess that lands us with.'

Fin nodded. 'Or wait until Witta and her people do something that we're all going to regret.'

'You picked up on that?' It was good to know I wasn't being paranoid.

'It was pretty hard to miss.' Fin looked at me. 'So what are we going to do?'

I realised we were alone in the kitchen. 'Where's your mum?'

'Working.' Fin wrinkled her nose. 'And I should be back in Bristol by now, and they're going to need you back at Blithehurst sooner or later. Just because we can tell my sister and your boss what we're doing without freaking them out, it's still not fair that they're having to pick up our slack.'

I guessed she had spoken to Blanche. I realised I'd been here for what, nine days now? I needed to call Eleanor with an update. I should also speak to my dad. If I could think of some way to explain what had happened yesterday without completely freaking him out. I had a better idea of what he must go through when I told him I was fighting monsters, now that I'd seen Fin heading into danger, leaving me behind and helpless to follow her. I kept remembering seeing her swept away into that turmoil of wind-blown peat. I didn't like that one bit.

'So what are we going to do?' she asked again.

I hesitated. 'You know I said we have to stop asking for help? There's one last thing I want to try. I want to see this other place that Kelley's interested in. The site by the trees. I haven't been there yet. Maybe the Green Man will show himself if I do. Maybe I'll get some idea of what you've been sensing there.'

Fin nodded. 'Okay. Do we want to wait for Will, or what?'

'He said he'd be here first thing.' I glanced at the kitchen clock. 'Do you think he knows what that means?'

Unless something had happened to him, of course. That was another reason why I wanted to get whatever Tom Kelley was stirring up dealt with. I was used to only having to take care of myself. Keeping track of three other people and worrying about them as well was getting exhausting.

Fin picked up her phone from the table. I waited as she found Will's number, and I breathed a sigh of relief when he answered her call. Her side of the conversation was limited to saying 'okay' repeatedly as he explained himself.

'We'll see you in a bit then.' She grinned as she put the phone down. 'He says he's sorry, he's had a late start. I think he may have been a bit distracted. Apparently Witta called around first thing to let him know Tom Kelley didn't leave the hotel last night. So he's heading out to check the camera traps now, and then he'll come straight here. Witta will keep an eye on Doctor Tom in the meantime. He's going to call her to join us when he gets here.'

'Fine.' So Witta knew where he lived. I wondered if Will had any idea how deep the water he was getting into might turn out to be. But that was none of my business, and I wasn't going to wait around while he caught up with whatever he had to do this morning.

'I'm going to take a look at those trees.' I was still wearing my jacket. I took my keys out of the pocket. 'I want to see if I can expect the Green Man's help or not. Either way, the more we know, the better. Then we can work out what to do.'

'I'll come with you,' Fin said quickly. 'Just let me get my coat and tell Mum.'

She headed up the stairs. I thought about trying to find a reason to go out there on my own. I couldn't come up with anything convincing by the time she came back down again, so we went together. Fin gave me directions, and the place was easy enough to find. Thankfully, there was no sign of Tom Kelley or Will.

There was even less to see than there was at the other places on Tom Kelley's map. A space where three fields met had been left to a small copse of ash and alder trees. The trees were some distance from the closest point on the narrow back road, and there was no sign that anyone came here regularly. We were almost certainly trespassing, but the chances of anyone seeing us looked remote.

'These are well established,' I observed as we walked towards the spinney. 'I guess the extra farmland that clearing them would get him wouldn't be worth the farmer's effort.'

'That and leaving them be will be doing a lot to keep the ground here dry.' Fin pointed to the brimful dyke dividing the fields. 'This corner would be a lot boggier without them.'

'True enough,' I agreed. Trees do suck up an awful lot of water.

We got closer to the copse, and I frowned. I was growing increasingly uneasy for no apparent reason. I also realised that we were walking more slowly.

Fin glanced at me. 'So you can feel it too? Have you ever felt anything like this before?'

'No.' All I knew at the moment was that I very much wanted to leave here. To leave and never come back.

I gritted my teeth and looked hard at the trees. There was no sign of the Green Man's presence. Maybe if I got closer. I forced my feet onwards, though every step felt like wading through mud. The sensation was so vivid that I even looked down, to see if I was sinking into the ploughed soil.

'Dan, are you all right?' Fin was concerned. 'You're sweating.'

I was, and for no good reason. This morning wasn't as cold as the past few days had been, but it was still January, and my jacket wasn't that thick. I looked at Fin. 'You're not?'

'No.' She looked at me intently. 'This place gives me the creeps, but you're feeling whatever's here a whole lot more than the rest of us.'

Movement caught my eye. My heart pounded. I saw a hare sitting at the edge of the undergrowth that fringed the trees. It was a big one. It drummed on the ground with one hind leg. I expected it to leap away, to vanish into the trees after sounding that alarm. It stayed put, staring back at me.

'What's it doing?' Fin whispered.

I couldn't answer. My mouth was dry, and not because something was searing the moisture out of the air like yesterday. Adrenaline was racing through me, and forget 'fight or flight'. I wasn't about to fight anything. I just wanted to run. I drew a deep, shaky breath and forced myself to look up at the leafless branches of the trees. There was still nothing there. The Green Man wasn't going to help me. I had to solve this puzzle on my own.

Before I even realised what I was doing, I had turned around. I started walking back to the Land Rover. It took all my determination not to break into a run. Even so, I was going faster than Fin was comfortable with, even with my sore leg curbing my stride.

I got into the driving seat and waited for my breathing to slow down. Gripping the steering wheel helped stop my hands shaking. Fin sat in the passenger seat, half turned sideways and waiting for me to talk to her.

I only had one thing to say. I couldn't think of anything else until I said it. 'Whatever the hell is in there isn't something we want Tom Kelley digging up.'

'Not if just the feeling of it scares you so much.' She looked through the window towards the trees. 'What do you suppose that hare was doing?'

'No clue.' I couldn't see how that was relevant.

'There are folk tales about women who could turn into hares,' she said slowly. 'Witches, mostly.'

'Have you ever met one? Someone who could turn into a hare, I mean, not a witch necessarily.'

166

'Not that I know of, but that's no proof. We don't exactly have support groups. "Hello, my name's Finele and I can turn into a swan." But I'd be a fool to dismiss the possibility, wouldn't I? Me of all people?'

I appreciated her trying to lighten the atmosphere. Thankfully the sense of dread that had shaken me so badly was fading. 'After everything that happened last year in the Cotswolds, I'm not going to discount the idea of witchcraft either.'

'So where does that get us?' Fin sighed, frustrated.

I was glad to hear that. 'This is exactly what I was talking about. We don't know what we're doing. New things keep cropping up, and there's no easy way for us to find out what's really going on. We need to focus on what we know, and solve the problems that we can actually tackle as quickly as we can.'

Fin nodded, decisive. 'Agreed.'

I turned the ignition key and we drove back to Venturer's House. Will and Witta were already there, sitting out in the garden despite the chilly day. Helen came down from her studio and we settled down around the kitchen table for yet another conference. As far as I was concerned it was time for less talking and a lot more action.

'Any news about Tom Kelley?' I looked at Witta and then at Will.

The nereid shook her head. 'He's still at the hotel, and one of my sisters is keeping an eye on him. She'll send word if he moves, as soon as he moves.'

That was good to know, although it told me that she was already involving other people in this. Other people with concerns of their own which we didn't necessarily share. There was also no knowing how far and how fast word would spread, or what news was spreading. We needed to put a stop to Tom Kelley's treasure hunt before things got completely beyond our control.

'There was no sign of him on the camera traps,' Will said cheerfully. 'Though that little wood's going to be a great place to go if I want to take some shots of hares. There were three of them out there last night.'

'No!' I said before I could stop myself. That startled me as much as everyone else. Even Witta was taken aback.

I tried to explain. 'Those trees...'

Seeing I was struggling, Fin quickly told them how strongly I had felt whatever could be sensed there. She told them about the hare that might or might not have been watching us. She mentioned the stories she remembered about shape-shifting witches. Will looked at Witta.

'Don't ask me,' the nereid retorted. 'I'm hardly going to come across one unless she goes for a swim.'

I managed to get a grip. 'It doesn't matter. We know what we need to. Firstly, we're not going to find any help from the Green Man there. Secondly, we really don't want Tom Kelley disturbing whatever's in those trees. So let's move on. At least that helps us work out what we have to do.'

'Which is what, exactly?' Will asked warily.

'Get Tom Kelley arrested for illegal archaeology.' I didn't imagine that would be the actual charge on the paperwork, but it was the best way to say what I meant. 'Nighthawking, isn't that what they call it?' Personally, I'd call it vandalism and stealing.

'How do we do that?' Helen was curious rather than sceptical, which was a relief.

I nodded at Will. 'You get the evidence on your camera traps and you go straight to the police and get them to call the county archaeology people – whoever Chris in the museum was going to ring about Kelley metal-detecting on the hillfort here.'

'Okay,' he said, 'but we still don't know where he's going to dig first.'

'So we force his hand. We make sure he starts digging where we want him to, and we make sure he gets caught with something valuable that he can't explain away.'

'We're not going near that little wood, I take it?' Fin looked thoughtful. 'So is the burial mound our best bet, or the dry river bed?'

'We want to leave the burial mound well alone, don't we?' Will looked around the table. 'I don't fancy fighting a wyrm.'

'Tom Kelley caught it by surprise.' But Fin clearly wasn't convinced we could do the same. 'At least those lantern sylphs won't attack him at the lost river bed, but they're bound to give us trouble unless we can get rid of them somehow.'

Helen raised a hand. 'Those what?'

I let Fin explain the Lantern Man folk tale. When she was done, I spoke up.

'It has to be the burial mound, and not just to avoid those fire sylph things.' I looked at Witta. 'How soon will your people want to do something, now that they know there are wyrm eggs buried on that high ground?'

'They're already arguing about what to do,' she admitted. 'I'm not sure how long they'll hold off.'

'You said they'll use storms and floods.' I looked at the others. 'How much land is going to end up under water if they go ahead? How many homes and businesses? How much collateral damage are we looking at?'

No one suggested getting the map to work that out. We all knew it would be horrendous. I could see my own feelings reflected on Fin's face, as well as

Helen's and Will's. We'd all seen the news on the telly, and far too often lately, when supposedly once-in-a-lifetime floods wrecked people's houses and liveli-hoods when rivers burst their banks after unexpectedly heavy rain. We couldn't be responsible for that. None of us even wanted to think about the risks of innocent people drowning.

Witta leaned back in her chair. She laid her hands on the table, palm down. As she spread her fingers, the webbing between them shone in the sunlight coming through the window. 'My people will settle for nothing less than know-ing those eggs are destroyed.'

I nodded. 'Which is why we want them dug up. You said it yourself. They'll crumble to dust as soon as the sun's light and warmth reaches through the soil to touch them. That won't be a problem. Once the county archaeologists or whoever have good reason to believe there's an undiscovered burial on that site, they'll be in there like dogs after a rabbit.'

'I'm not so sure about that,' Helen observed. 'Most digs these days are about checking for archaeology that building work might wreck. Developers have to pay for that now, so the work gets put out to tender, and then some commer-cial archaeological outfit will do the digging.'

'Oh.' I tried to remember what else Chris at the museum had said. 'Won't this barrow be an ancient monument? Wouldn't that get the authorities in-volved? Won't they want to do a dig if it looks like Tom Kelley found some treasure?'

Helen shrugged. 'That depends. We don't know if anyone even knows there's a barrow there. I'll see what I can find out.'

'Thanks.' I was happy to leave her to it, since she clearly knew a lot more about these things than me. I looked at Witta. 'We have time to work out how to persuade someone there's something there to dig up. We know those eggs are nowhere near hatching. That means the wyrmlings inside them are still ethereal. '

Witta held my gaze, unblinking. 'You don't think the wyrm will have some-thing to say about that? Now that it has been roused?'

'I'm sure it will,' I agreed, 'which is why we need your people to kill it for us. Can they do that, if I lure it close enough to the shore? Somewhere where a storm surge won't damage anything else too badly. Will they agree to that?'

Witta sat still for a long moment, then nodded. 'Since the wyrm has already been roused, it has to be dealt with. We cannot leave it roaming loose. We cer-tainly can't let it guard those eggs until they hatch.'

'How are you going to do something like that?' Fin demanded. 'Come to that, why does it have to be you doing the luring?'

'Because you two will be at the police station with Will.' I looked at her and Helen. 'You'll be backing up his story, and telling the cops about Tom Kelley wrecking the window seats in Talbot House. You'll tell them he's suspected of stealing valuable papers from a Cambridge University collection. You're upright local citizens. You know the people they'll want to talk to, to confirm the things you're saying. You can give them Mike Kelley's phone number and no one will think twice about it.'

Helen raised a hand. 'You still haven't explained how you plan to provoke Tom into digging for some supposed burial site. I'm sure we can convince the police that he's lost his grip on reality, because honestly I think he has, but Tom's not stupid. He knows how much trouble he would be in if he was caught nighthawking. Why would he be so reckless?'

'Because we'll convince him if he doesn't act, and act now, someone else will beat him to it.'

'How?' Helen persisted. 'Why should he believe a word we say? Even supposing we can convince him to hear us out. You said yourself he'll probably bolt if he realises he's been found.'

'He'll believe a sylph.'

'But sylphs can't lie,' Fin objected.

'Exactly. That's why he won't ask any awkward questions when we persuade one to tell him that Will found some piece of treasure up there on that hill when he was out taking photos. Something he's going to take to the portable antiquities people.'

Will grinned. 'Where am I really going to get hold of something like that?'

'That's where I'll need a hob's help,' I admitted.

'What's that going to cost us?' Fin was looking more and more dubious. 'And how do we persuade a sylph to play along? The last one we met wasn't exactly friendly, was it?'

'What do they want more than anything else? I'll promise that I will break Tom Kelley's hold over them by getting that crystal away from him once and for all. I'll make sure that no one else can ever get hold of it.' I looked at Witta. 'How deep are those depths you were talking about? Where your people drop wyrm eggs to die?'

'Not deep enough for something like that,' the nereid said wryly. 'Not once word spreads that it's down there. You know those stories about people throwing things like a magic ring into the sea, only to find it again when they're gutting a fish? There are good reasons why there are so many of those tales. Sooner or later, one of my father's people will want to throw something that troublesome back on the land, to be someone else's problem. Either that, or someone will realise its value in the right – or the wrong – hands. They'll trade it for something they want from a dryfoot. You'd be surprised at the deals that get done in seaside car parks, with humans who have no clue who they're really talking to.'

That was sodding inconvenient. 'Okay, I'll think of something else.'

'You keep saying "I".' Fin glared at me.

'There's no need for more than one of us to be in this level of debt to the hobs and the sylphs,' I said firmly. 'Besides, if things don't go exactly to plan, you and your whole family have still got to live here. You don't want them to have any excuse to hold a grudge against you. If they end up pissed off at me, well, I'll be going back to Blithehurst, or back home. We know hobs don't travel, and if any sylphs come after me, they'll have dryads to deal with. If that doesn't make them think twice, I'll get the Green Man involved. I'm sure he'll back me once he knows what was at stake here. We know he doesn't want to see wyrms loose across these islands again.'

I spoke as confidently as I could. It wasn't as if I was lying. Maybe I was ex-aggerating a little, but I was pretty sure the Green Man would realise I'd done what I had to in order to get this job done. Whether or not he'd be happy about it was another question entirely, but I'd deal with that when I had to. What I might end up owing the Blithehurst dryads was something else I didn't want to think too much about. My mum would definitely be furious with me.

Helen raised a hand again. 'This plan is all very well, as far as the broad brush strokes go, but there are a lot of details to work out before we can decide if this is a good idea.'

'That's where I do need your help. All of you.' I smiled at Fin.

She didn't smile back.

Helen got up from her chair. 'I'll put the kettle on.'

Chapter Eighteen

When we finally finished talking, I stood up. 'Right, I'll see if I can persuade the hob to help us.'

Fin got to her feet as well. 'I'm coming too.'

Will looked at her, puzzled, as he started gathering up the plates from lunch. 'I though we just agreed what everyone was doing. Especially the things Dan has to do on his own.'

'Only once everything kicks off,' Fin said stubbornly. 'There's no reason why I can't help now.'

Helen reached for her daughter's hand. 'I really don't think that's a good idea.'

'If any of this is going to work, we need to get moving. You know what hobs are like.' Witta was getting impatient. 'He'll twist Dan's words as far as he can, and ask for whatever he thinks he can get away with. If two of you are there, that gives him more chances to argue and delay, not to mention trying to play one of you off against the other. Let's just stick with the plan.'

No one answered her.

'Right.' I managed a smile. 'Wish me luck. I'll be back as soon as I can.'

I walked out of the kitchen door and drew a deep breath of clear, cold air. Then I heard the door open and close behind me. My heart sank. I turned around, expecting to see Fin. Witta was standing there instead.

'Have you thought of some way to convince the hob?' I asked warily.

'No.' She began walking towards the side gate. 'I need to talk to my people, to let them know what's going on.'

I walked with her. 'Don't you want to wait until we know if the hob will help? If we can find a sylph to play along?'

If either one or both told me to get lost, we had a serious problem. We had absolutely no Plan B. That was pretty much the only reason Fin had finally agreed to Plan A.

'You need to persuade them, and we need to do this today.' The nereid glanced at me. 'Whether or not you can make this work, my father's people will go after that wyrm, now that they know it's been roused.'

'You made that crystal clear,' I reminded her.

'You should be grateful. The wyrm will sense their anger and lie low until you provoke it past bearing. Otherwise it would see your schemes to get Kelley arrested stopped dead.'

'You said that as well.' I wondered who she thought would end up dead, me or Doctor Tom?

'Then listen to me now,' she said forcefully. 'You have to get this done, and it has to be today. The best you can hope for is me persuading the fiercest of the sea folk to wait and see if you can bring the wyrm to them. The sooner I share this scheme of yours, the better the chances are they will hold off, at least to give you the time you need. If you don't want to see floods rising as far as that burial mound by morning, you had better not fail. Time and the children of the tide wait for no man, not even a dryad's son.'

I had no answer for that. We walked along the gravel track in silence. When we were about halfway to the hillfort, Witta halted. In the blink of an eye, she transformed into her natural appearance. Before I could say anything, she dived into the dyke. There wasn't even a ripple as she disappeared.

I looked around for any startled dog walkers. There was no one in sight. That was a relief. On the other hand, I felt very exposed alone on the ridge. I felt very alone, full stop. This was the flip side of insisting I had to be the one to do this, to try to keep Fin and the others out of danger. If I screwed up, there would be no one else to blame.

I kept walking towards the hillfort. It was deserted. I looked at the trees and felt my tension ease just a little. Even with the branches bare of leaves, this felt more like home than anywhere else around here. I walked into the centre of the thicket and sat down.

'I need to speak to the hob of the long isle,' I said quietly. 'Please.'

There was no need to shout. If he was here, he would hear me. I sat down on the dead, dry grass and waited. The only sounds were the soft rattle of leafless twigs in the breeze and the distant rustle of the sedge. I didn't check my phone for the time. I didn't move. I would stay here for as long as it took for the hob to answer me, or until I came up with another way to set our plan in motion. The birds came and went, content to ignore me.

'What do you need so badly, greenwood?' The hob was sitting beside me, as if he had always been there.

'I need your help if I am to stop the stargazer's son forcing you and the sylphs, and any others that he can see, to do whatever he wants.'

The hob grinned with sly anticipation. 'Then let us—'

I spoke over him. 'I want to stop him doing far worse. He's roused a wyrm. It was sleeping as it guarded a clutch of eggs in a place where he went looking for treasure. I don't think he did it deliberately. I don't think he knows what he's doing. That doesn't mean he hasn't put every one of us in danger.'

I looked at the hob. 'The daughter of the tide knows about the wyrm. That means her people know. You must know what they'll do if we don't deal with it before they can. To do that, we have to deal with the stargazer's son first of all. We need to do that as quickly as we can. There's no way to know what he will do next. There's no way to know if he will make some alliance with the wyrm.'

Sat around the kitchen table, we had debated what Tom Kelley might be doing while he was holed up in his hotel room. We'd agreed it was a fair bet that he was searching through his papers for something to explain whatever he had seen through his crystal ball up on the burial mound. Will and Witta had raised the possibility of him trying to do some deal with the wyrm. Fin and Helen couldn't believe that even he would be so stupid. I pointed out there was no way we were going to get any answers on that, and it made no difference to our plans either way.

But I was willing to use the idea to scare the hob, if that would persuade him to help us. Not that I had shared that with the others.

The hob looked at me thoughtfully. 'How can you thrust such a spoke into the stargazer's son's wheel?'

I explained the laws against digging up archaeological sites as best I could, and how Will would go to get the police involved as soon as he had video of Tom Kelley digging up some treasure from the mound. 'While he's being questioned, and hopefully locked up, I can get hold of the crystal. I know where he keeps it.'

The hob glowered. 'What will you do with it then?'

'Whatever is agreeable to you and yours, and to the sylphs. Whatever we need to do, to put it beyond any mortal's reach, so it cannot be misused again.' We might as well see what solutions they could suggest, since Witta had poured cold water on my original idea.

The hob narrowed its golden eyes. 'We will discuss that further, greenwood. You are getting ahead of yourself. What can you use to tempt the stargazer's son to such folly?'

'If you can pass through soil and stone, and if you can handle gold and silver, can you find us something long buried that we can use to lure him?' I really hoped I was right about what hobs and sylphs could do. Witta thought I probably was, but she couldn't be entirely certain. If any of this was impossible, we had some serious rethinking to do.

I looked down at the ground. 'Is there anything still buried here that you would be willing to give us? To lend us,' I corrected myself quickly.

I had no idea how deep ground-penetrating radar went, or whatever else geophysicists use. I was betting that hobs could do deeper. We just needed him to agree to help.

He shook his head. I felt sick. I desperately searched for some way to persuade him. Before I came up with anything though, the hob spoke up.

'I would do what you ask if there was anything of that kind to be found here. Alas, I always returned any lost treasures to their owners, or waited to pass such wealth to those who deserved some good fortune.'

I tried not to show just how relieved I was to hear that. 'If I could show you where such things are buried, could you fetch something for us? Even if it was a good distance from here?'

At least Witta had confirmed that while hobs prefer to stay close to the homes they have chosen, they aren't actually limited in how far they can go. Though they need a compelling reason to go further afield, she had warned us. I could believe it, thinking of the hob at Talbot House spending her endless years hidden and alone rather than move away. Hopefully a wyrm waking up would be reason enough to at least make a day trip.

The hob cocked his head. 'My legs are shorter than yours, long shanks. How long will it take me to walk there? Will half this land be drowned before I arrive? Even a wyrm cannot hold back the sea when the waves come in search of an enemy.'

I chose my next words carefully. 'Would you be willing to let a sylph carry you there? I need a sylph to help if this plan is to work anyway.'

I explained why we needed a sylph to convince Tom Kelley that his treasure was about to be discovered without him. The hob took a long time to think that through. He replied with a question for me.

'What if the stargazer's son simply takes his map to these diggers and convinces them he has proof of what they seek? Without digging, so he won't be confined.'

I was momentarily glad that Fin wasn't there with me. She'd have said 'I told you so', and I wouldn't have blamed her. She had raised exactly this possibility herself.

'Then I will still deal with the wyrm. Then I will find another way to take the crystal back from the stargazer's son. I will promise you that.'

The hob folded his arms and stared at me. 'How will you deal with the wyrm? I don't see you riding a mighty charger into battle and wielding a fearsome sword.'

I couldn't decide if he was serious or taking the piss. I had to answer him though. He was crucial to that part of the plan as well.

'Could you – would you – fetch me an egg from the clutch?' I didn't wait for him to answer, talking fast. 'They are nowhere near hatching, I promise you that. If you can bring one to me, I'll take it away with me, in my vehicle.

The wyrm will come after me. It'll have no interest in you. As long as I'm in the Land Rover, the wyrm won't be able to get to me. It'll chase me though, and I'll lead it to a place where the daughter of the tide and her people will be waiting. A wyrm on its own won't be able to fight the sea.'

Witta had agreed that I should be safe as long as I was inside the Landy. I'd promised Fin that I would lob the wyrm's egg out of the window as soon as the sea folk showed themselves. Then I'd be out of there as fast as I could accelerate, while they drowned the bastard thing as well as the wyrm that wanted its egg back. Fin still wasn't happy, but she couldn't come up with any better ideas.

The hob blinked. 'No wonder you are so ready to make such bold promises to me and mine, greenwood. There's every chance that you'll die before you can make good on what you owe us.'

That wasn't exactly reassuring, but I couldn't think about that just now. 'Can you do it? Will you do it?'

He nodded slowly. 'On your own head be it. On one condition.'

'What?' I asked warily.

'You give me the stargazer's crystal, as soon as you have it. Before I give you the wyrm's egg.'

That was clearly non-negotiable. I didn't have a problem with saying yes. The sooner the crystal ball was out of our hands, the better, in case the police turned up at Venturer's House asking questions. I reckoned there was a good chance Tom Kelley would start throwing around all sorts of accusations. The police would have to make at least some show of following them up, even if they thought he was a nutter. But the hobs weren't the only ones with an interest here.

'As long as the sylphs agree.'

The hob nodded slowly a second time. 'It would only seem fair.'

So far, so good. I resolutely refused to think about being pursued by a furious wyrm. 'Now I need to talk to a sylph. Can you tell me how to find one who knows the stargazer's son is their enemy?'

The hob smiled, and that made me more uneasy than anything he had said so far. 'I can do that, greenwood. Do you think we have been sitting here weaving garlands of grass and daisies while we wait for your kind to save us?'

I wasn't sure what he meant by that, but I didn't get a chance to ask. The hob vanished, and I drew a deep breath. So far, so good, I told myself again.

But how long was I going to have to wait? I looked around. Did I even have to wait here? Sylphs weren't like hobs. They went wherever they pleased. Well, within limits. We weren't going to be taking the chains down from the Venturer's House windows any time soon, so I couldn't go and wait indoors.

176

'Good day to you, son of the greenwood.' A sylph appeared in front of me.

The hob was sitting beside me again, as if he had never moved.

'Hello.' I studied the sylph. They looked just like the one we had met before, but I had no way to know. I had no idea if they all looked the same. There was only one way to find out. 'Excuse me, but have we met before?'

Asking if they had tried to blow us up or set fire to the house wouldn't exactly be diplomatic. Now I'd got this far setting up our plan, I couldn't risk the sylph taking offence.

'We have, and I am pleased to see you don't hold a grudge.' They smiled, though that wasn't exactly reassuring. They nodded at the hob. 'Our friend tells me you intend to frustrate the stargazer's son's desires.'

The sylph sat cross-legged, hovering in the air a foot or so off the ground. I tried not to let that distract me as I explained the steps we needed to take for a second time. The sylph sat and listened without comment. They stared at me with unnerving intensity. When I stopped talking, their head moved a fraction as they spoke to the hob.

'Bold indeed.' That vivid blue gaze came back to me. 'Very well, but we must act swiftly. Tonight. The sons of the sea and the daughters of the tide will not wait if you fail them.'

'You'll help?' I hadn't expected this to be so easy.

'We will be no man's slaves.' The sylph's eyes flashed with anger. 'You offer us at least the hope of freedom. There can be no certainties, but this scheme has more to recommend it than any we have been able to devise.'

That sounded as if more than just the sylphs had been trying to find a way to escape Kelley's control. I guessed that's what the hob had meant about not sitting around weaving garlands, waiting for someone else to save them.

'You think we can do this?' I asked before I could stop myself.

'I think at the very least, you will throw everything up into the air. Who knows what opportunities may present themselves amid such upheaval?' The sylph smiled with sly satisfaction.

I decided not to pursue that. 'This place where we think there's buried treasure for our friend here to find. It's where a river once flowed.' I tried to think how to give directions to the field. It wasn't as if I could give the sylph a map reference. 'There were some of your kindred there. Their eyes were red—' I couldn't think of a way to describe the things that had attacked me without risk of accidentally insulting the sylph.

'I know where you mean, and who tried to drive you away.' The sylph looked down at the ground. 'They will not trouble you again, as long as the stargazer's son has no reason to order them to serve him.'

177

I could have sworn the creature was embarrassed. 'You've been following us? Me, or Fin? Did Tom Kelley tell you to do that?'

'No.' The sylph stood up and stretched out a hand. 'Bring the swan's son with you. If I am to say I saw him holding some treasure, I must see him doing just that.'

'Can't I bring it to the burial mound and give it to him there?' I still wanted to keep the others out of this as much as I could, for as long as I could.

The sylph ignored that. 'We will meet you by the lost river. Master Hob?'

As soon as their fingers touched, both creatures vanished. I drew a deep breath and tried not to get angry with myself. It was my own fault. I should have asked my questions one at a time, and got a clear answer before I moved on to the next one.

I started walking back to the house. I decided the sylph had most likely answered my last question. They had been watching us on their own time. That was the only thing that was really relevant. If they had been trailing us and reporting our every move to Tom Kelley, we might as well give up now. But they wouldn't do that without direct orders. Not now we knew they were looking for a way to stop him, just as hard as we were.

It didn't really matter how they knew about the field with the lost river. They might have been following me, or Fin, or have gone there with Kelley some other time. What mattered was the sylph could take the hob there.

That still didn't mean we could trust them. I'd seen enough TV and movies to know that 'the enemy of my enemy is my friend' is a load of bollocks. They hadn't warned us about the lantern sylphs. If they had actually been there when Fin and I were attacked, they hadn't lifted a pale, glittering finger to help us.

I reached the side gate to the house and hesitated. I wished the sylph hadn't said I needed to take Will with me. I had my keys in my pocket. I could open the main gates and head straight for the field with the lost river in the Land Rover. Right, and Fin would be coming after me in her own car before I even reached the crossroads. Plus I'd have pissed her off even more than I already had. Not just her. Helen and Will deserved better from me as well.

I knocked on the back door and went into the kitchen. There was no one there. After a moment of confusion, I heard the television in the sitting room. I walked through to the front hall.

Will must have heard me coming. He opened the door as I reached for the latch. Fin was on her feet behind him. She pointed the remote at the telly and switched it off. It had served its purpose as a distraction while they waited. Helen appeared at the top of the stairs.

'They've both agreed to help,' I told everyone. 'They want to see Tom Kelley stopped as much as we do. More so, I'd say. The sylph's taken the hob to the lost river, so I have to go and meet them. You need to come with me, Will.'

I looked at Fin. 'I'll give you a ring when I get there, okay?'

She nodded. She looked a little self-conscious. I could guess why. Some part of her had been hoping that the hob or the sylph would say no to our plan. Then I wouldn't have to risk my neck being chased by the wyrm. I couldn't blame her. That thought had been lurking in the back of my mind as well.

Will was sitting on the bottom stair, getting his boots on. He looked up at me with that cheery grin. 'Right. Let me get my bag and let's do this.'

Fin came outside with us to open and close the gates to the yard. She didn't say a word.

Chapter Nineteen

Will and I sat in silence as I drove away. Neither of us spoke until we were more than halfway there. Rain spattered the windscreen and I flicked the wipers.

Will leaned forward, looking up at the sky. 'I thought it was supposed to stay clear today.'

I was in no mood to talk about the weather.

Will tried again a mile or so further on. 'How's your phone battery? We should check. I know mine's okay. I put it on charge while we were waiting for you to come back.'

I fished my phone out of my pocket and handed it over. 'Take a look. There's the charger. Plug it in if it needs a top-up.'

'It can't hurt.' He fussed about with the wire and the socket for a bit. 'I'll put them both on silent. May as well be on the safe side.'

'Good idea.' I tried to think if there were any other precautions we should be taking.

We drove on for another mile or so. Finally Will said what was really on his mind. 'What do we do if we find Tom Kelley there?'

'I beat the shit out of him. We take his car keys. We take the crystal and whatever else we can find in the Jag. We call Fin to come and get you. I go with the hob and the sylph to get a wyrm's egg, and that part of the plan goes ahead. If Kelley does go to the police, you and Helen and Fin swear blind that he's lying through whatever's left of his teeth. We were together at the time, playing cards or something like that, so no one gets caught out trying to remember what's on the telly.'

Will laughed. Then he realised I was absolutely serious. Of course I was. I'd thought this potential problem through while I was walking back from the hillfort.

'I've got some work gloves in my toolbox,' I went on. 'You'll need to fill them with stones and chuck them in a river or a dyke somewhere. DNA and all that.'

Will shook his head. 'You don't get rid of things by dumping them in water around here. There are pumps and sluices that keep everything on the move, and meshes to catch the crap.'

'Let's hope we don't find him there then.' Something else had occurred to me. If Kelley was there, and if he saw the sylph and the hob through that damn crystal, it was a safe bet that he would order them to tell him what was going on. We could be walking into all sorts of trouble if Doctor Tom knew we were coming. Shit could happen even if he didn't.

'We need to carry a screwdriver each regardless. In case those lantern things turn up.'

'Right.' Will was sounding a lot less cheery now.

To my relief, we arrived at the parking spot to find no sign of the Jag or any other vehicle. We got out and I looked around warily as I opened up the back and found my toolbox. Thankfully there was no sign of murderous flame-tinted sylphs. I still stuck the flat-head screwdriver in my pocket and handed Will the Phillips. Then I got out a couple of pairs of work gloves. I'd just realised Tom Kelley's face wasn't the only thing we mustn't leave DNA or fingerprints on.

'Should I call Witta?' Will was looking in the direction of the cut that carried water away towards the sea. 'Find out what she can tell us about what Kelley's up to?'

A spatter of rain struck my face. I looked up at the sky. Dark clouds were gathering and the wind was getting up. It was cold enough for me to wish I'd worn my heavy coat. 'Let's just get this done.'

We walked across the field. It was much heavier going now that the soil wasn't so dried out. I still pushed the pace on. If we were here much longer, we'd lose the daylight. We reached the gate and I unlooped the chain.

'Let me get the data cards out of the camera traps first.' Will went past me and did whatever he had to do with the little black boxes he'd hidden among the poplar trees. He walked back to join me, tucking something into an inside pocket and zipping up his coat again. He shivered. 'So where are they?'

'Waiting and wondering where you are, swan's son.' The hob appeared between us.

Will jumped as if someone had just stuck a pin in him.

'You should hurry.' The sylph was standing just out of reach. 'The sea folk are not going to wait if you delay.'

The hob looked up at me. 'Where am I to look for these treasures?'

Shit. I had no idea where the rituals Fin had guessed at might actually have happened, and this was a sodding big field. Come to that, I couldn't say for certain there was even anything here. What if John Dee's map was complete nonsense?

The hob laughed at me. 'Rest easy, greenwood. I can follow the memory of the river.'

He walked away, looking down. If there was some pale line of silt, I couldn't see it. The rest of the ground might be darker now the soil was moist again, but the light was fading fast. A moment later, I blinked. The hob had disappeared.

'Dan.' Will's voice shook. That's quite an achievement, when you're saying a name as short as mine.

'What?'

He pointed. I saw shadows gathering beneath the poplar trees. No, those weren't just ordinary shadows. Indistinct shapes were moving around in the gloom. Here and there, I saw a head or a shoulder outlined with a candle-coloured shimmer. A glint of flame came and went, and I realised one of them had just blinked.

'You said they wouldn't attack us.' I tried not to sound as if I was accusing the sylph. I also wasn't sure who I was trying to reassure, me or Will.

'I never said they would not take an interest.' The sylph was shining more brightly in the dusk, so it was easy to see them shrug. 'They have as much reason as I do to detest the stargazer's son. Be warned. If you fail, they will not be nearly so forgiving as me and mine.'

I was glad I was carrying a screwdriver in my jacket pocket. Though I didn't like the idea of these vicious things finding out where Fin and Helen lived. Would the sylph tell them?

'Will this serve, Master Greenwood?' The hob was by my side.

He raised his hands. He was holding a torc: one of those solid necklace things you see in museums. The ones that aren't a complete circle, but have a gap at the front so it can be opened up a bit to put it on. This one was a thick rope of six twisted gold cords that ended in loops decorated with swirls and criss-cross patterns made of fine wires. The sylph moved closer, and the metal gleamed warm and inviting in the soft light.

'Wow.' Will was awestruck.

'Right. Thank you, Master Hob. This will do very well indeed.' I swallowed hard and quickly put my gloves on as he offered it to me. It was heavy in my hands as I took it, and I had no idea how much it could be worth. Enough to land us in a shitload of trouble if we were caught with it and no good explanation.

'Could you—' Will said suddenly. 'Could you show us what happened here? What this place used to look like? When people were making these offerings?'

'No.' The hob looked at Will as if he was a complete idiot. 'How could I do such a thing when I wasn't here to see?'

'Oh, right.' Will was disappointed, but he wasn't quite ready to give up. 'What else is down there then?'

'Nothing that you have any need for,' the hob said severely.

'Nothing we will let you have without paying a suitable price.' The sylph's smile was chilling.

'Nothing that you'll be able to explain getting hold of without a lot of awkward questions, and probably getting yourself charged with trespass and theft,' I pointed out.

We were wasting time and losing what little daylight remained. The clouds overhead had got thicker, and it was starting to rain properly. I looked at the sylph. 'What do you need us to do now?'

'Take this to the hill where the warrior of old lies buried with the wyrm's eggs.'

They vanished, leaving me and Will in the empty field. That didn't mean we were alone. The lantern sylphs at the edge of the field were growing more distinct. It was hard to be sure, but I reckoned they were getting closer.

'Let's leave before those things change their minds about whatever they agreed to,' I suggested.

'Right.' Will nodded.

We didn't exactly run back to the Land Rover, but we didn't hang about. I refused to look over my shoulder to see if we were being followed.

'They're coming after us.' Will's voice was unsteady as he turned to loop the chain over the gatepost.

'Just taking an interest.' I held on tight to the torc, though I was ready to drop it and go for my screwdriver if I needed to. With luck these things wouldn't explode this time, not without peat dust filling the air.

I could feel faint warmth on the back of my neck by the time we reached the Landy though, and the torc was reflecting glints of red light behind me.

'Put your gloves on.' I handed it to Will as soon as he was ready to take it, and found my keys. 'Get in.'

For a moment, as we both put on our seatbelts, the lantern sylphs surrounded the vehicle. Red eyes glowed in the dusk. Then I turned the key in the ignition, and they vanished. Will heaved a sigh of relief, and I felt like doing the same. Instead, I concentrated on getting the satnav up and running, turning the Land Rover around and getting back to the tarmac road.

Will sat turning the torc over and over in his gloved hands. 'How the hell do you put something like this on?'

'Very carefully?' I glanced at it before concentrating on the road again. 'I'd say there's a bit of flex in it, given how it's made. Enough to force the ends open wide enough, as long as your neck's not too thick. You wouldn't want to do that too often though. The metal will get brittle where it's stressed. You can already see some big cracks in the back of that.'

I may be a carpenter by trade, but I've picked up the basics of metalworking over the years.

Will studied the fractured gold. 'You don't think that was done deliberately? As part of some ritual, like Fin said?'

'Maybe.' I used my indicator as we approached a junction even though there were no other cars around. I was driving so carefully at the moment, I would have passed the official practical test first time. I was also very glad that I'd cleaned the Landy's lights and plates that morning. That's just the sort of thing a bored copper will pull you over for, if he sees more mud on them than he likes. 'Just make sure you keep that out of sight.'

Will rested it in his lap. 'It's a hell of a thing to do, isn't it? Offering something like this to the gods or whoever.'

'It certainly makes a statement. Shows everyone what you can afford to give up. Like burning fifty quid notes to light a cigar.' As well as showing whoever or whatever else was taking an interest that you were prepared to give up something you valued to gain their favour – or to be left alone, I shouldn't wonder.

I suddenly remembered that we'd promised to ring Fin. That I had promised to ring her. I was guiltily relieved that I was the one driving. 'Give the others a call, would you? Let them know how we got on.'

Will got out his phone. 'I'll ring Aunt Helen.'

I didn't blame him. He brought her up to speed with a quick conversation. After that, we drove on in silence. The rain fell harder. Will checked his phone to see what the time was and reached for the radio. We caught the end of the weather forecast. Apparently an unexpected area of low pressure was forming unusually rapidly in the North Sea. It was going to be a dark and very stormy night.

At least the rain was keeping any dog walkers or other hikers at home. Will gave me directions to the closest parking spot to the barrow. There was no one else there. We parked and I erased the satnav's history. Now no one could tie me to the lost river field. Maybe I was getting paranoid, but I wasn't about to take any chances.

We walked up to the burial mound. Will was carrying the torc. I was looking in all directions.

'See anything?' he asked nervously.

'Not so far.' I didn't say the wyrm could probably appear out of the ground at any moment, and there'd be nothing we could do about it. I didn't think that would help.

'The creature is not here.' The hob appeared, walking beside me.

Strolling next to Will, the sylph looked up at the sky. 'It will hide itself elsewhere, for fear of the sea folk realising this is where its eggs are hidden. Until its clutch is threatened, when it will come for you.' Those cold blue eyes glanced at me. 'Let us hope the sea folk come to your aid in sufficient strength. Let us hope this storm does not escape their grasp before the wyrm is dead.'

'Hang on.' Will was taken aback. 'You're saying they're whistling up this bad weather?'

The hob nodded. 'This will not be a night for flying, swan's son. Stay close to the ground and preen your feathers.'

Will looked at me. 'Witta never said.'

The possibility had occurred to me as we drove here. Storms don't usually come out of nowhere to leave the Met Office's billion-pound super-computer looking stupid.

I shrugged. 'Does it make any difference?'

The hob chuckled. 'You are a braver man than most, Master Greenwood.'

'Either that or more foolhardy.' The sylph halted and looked at Will. 'Start digging, swan's son.'

He looked at me. 'What with?'

The sylph hissed, exasperated, and glared at us both. 'If I am to tell the star-gazer's son that I saw you digging here, that I saw you with this treasure in your hands, then that is what I must see.'

This was my fault. 'I've got a folding spade in the Landy. I'll be as quick as I can.'

I ran back down the hill, swearing under my breath, and got the spade out of the back. I ran as fast as I could to rejoin them, unfolding the tool as I went and making sure the locking nut was secure. My heart was pounding as I reached the barrow. Not from the run up the incline. The locals might call this a hill, but no one from anywhere else in the country would. I was sweating despite the cold wind because Will and I were running a hell of a risk right now. Forget the wyrm. If anyone else turned up and saw what we were doing, we'd be the ones who got arrested.

I handed him the spade. 'Get busy.'

He handed the torc to the hob and started digging. At least the rain was softening the wintry ground. He'd barely turned over three spadefuls when the sylph raised a hand.

'That will suffice.'

The hob laid the torc in the broken ground and looked at Will, impatient. 'Now pick it up.'

Will did as he was told. The sylph smiled in a way that made me very uneasy and took the golden torc out of his hands before either of us could say anything about it. Lifting the ornament up as if it didn't weigh a thing, they slipped it around their neck. Or rather, they passed the torc through their neck in an ethereal state and then turned solid enough to wear it. At least they didn't have to bend the already cracked metal and risk breaking it completely.

Now the sylph was a young warrior standing before us. He had dark hair and a short, untidy beard. Only his eyes were the same: merciless, featureless blue. He wore some sort of dark trousers under a long pale tunic that flapped in the strengthening wind. His checked cloak was fastened on one shoulder by a dangerously long pin with a metal ring on the end. No one would be looking at that. Don't ask me where the light was coming from, but the torc glowed in the gathering dusk. It looked amazing.

The sylph looked at me. 'Now I can show the stargazer's son exactly what he will lose unless he comes here to stake his claim to these spoils. Otherwise, so I will tell him, my kindred will swiftly gather to adorn themselves, now that we know where such delights lie to be found.'

'He has to actually dig something up to claim whatever's here as his? Until he finds something for himself? It won't count if he orders a hob to fetch things for him?' I'd been relying on the sylph using their supernatural charm on his greed and ambition to persuade Kelley to get his own hands dirty, but this was much better.

'He does, and any of my kin will say the same. Just as they will admit to our love of all that glitters.'

I could also see from the sylph's smug smile that they were enjoying letting me know they knew the best way to lure Kelley here. Fine by me. They were welcome to their little triumph. Just as long as they could tempt him out to start digging in this filthy weather instead of waiting for the storm to pass.

'Wait a minute.' Will was thinking about something else. 'You mean you can fetch things like this out of the earth yourselves. We didn't need to... to trouble the hob?'

What he actually meant was we didn't need to put ourselves in some massive debt to the hob.

The sylph laughed, carefree as birdsong. 'We cannot pass through solid stone as our friend here can, but sandy soil such as this does not hinder us too badly. You should have thought to ask,' he chided us both.

I glanced at the hob. He shrugged.

'It is not for me to tell you such things if you lack the wit to consider it.'

There was something else in his expression though. I reckoned he would have found a way to involve himself in whatever we were doing. I hadn't forgotten what he had said about trying to find an escape from Tom Kelley's control.

'It doesn't matter,' I said to Will. 'We just need to get Kelley out here and catch him digging on camera.'

'Your wish is my command,' the sylph said, still mocking us.

In the next breath, they were their usual pale, androgynous self. The instant after that, they vanished. The torc tumbled to the ground.

'Where did it go?' Will asked, alarmed. Without the sylph's eerie radiance we were standing in near darkness. The rain was getting really spiteful.

'I have it.' The hob stood turning it over and over in his hands, just like Will had done on the drive here. The little creature was all but invisible in the darkness and his expression was unreadable. 'What will you do with this now?'

'Surely it is for you to decide what becomes of it, Master Hob. We have no claim on it.' I glanced at Will and was relieved to see him nod emphatic agreement.

The hob smiled. So that was the right answer. Good, though I didn't suppose we'd have found out what trouble the wrong answer would get us into until after we'd dealt with Kelley and the wyrm.

'I will lay it with the rest of this fallen warrior's treasures.' The hob vanished and the torc went with him.

A tiny part of me was sorry to see it gone. Much more of me was relieved that there was no way we could be caught with it in our possession.

'Do you suppose the sylph was showing us what he really looked like?' Will wondered. 'The man who owned the torc, I mean.'

'Don't know. Don't care,' I said briskly. I had been wondering what sort of puzzle the hob might be setting for some archaeologists, if whatever was buried here was from some drastically different century to the torc. That was just as irrelevant. 'Come on. We need to get round to the camera traps before there's any chance of Kelley turning up.'

'Wait a minute,' Will said stubbornly.

I started counting in my head. I'd give him sixty seconds and no more.

The hob reappeared when I was on forty-six. It was too dark to see if he was surprised to see us still there.

'What do you want of me now?'

'Can you tell what's down there?' Will was persistent, I had to give him that.

The hob's eyes gleamed. 'The men of old dug a deep pit and lined it with oak to make a chamber. They laid their honoured warrior to rest in a well-crafted coffin of ash wood. He was dressed in his finest garb, with his belt buckled with gold and garnets. He wore rings just as fine on his fingers and glittering brooches fastened his cloak. A feast must have marked his passing from this world to whatever awaits. There are cups and bowls of copper and silver as well as a great bronze bowl for cooking. A harper must have sung of his deeds, so those who mourned might remember him in better days. A fine lyre and a bard's stool were set at his feet. There is coin, and jewellery for trade, in case he must pay his way on some unknown journey in the darkness. He had a mighty shield to guard his flank, and he was armed with spear and sword as well as the knife at his belt, for fear of unknown foes.'

The hob scowled. I reckoned if he hadn't seen this burial actually happening in those days long ago, he had seen a funeral very like it.

'Why did the wyrm let them bury him with iron weapons?' Will asked suddenly. 'Wouldn't that be a problem when the eggs hatch? If they were left to hatch, I mean.'

The hob's scorn told Will he'd just asked something really stupid.

'A wyrm can be sure that such iron will be a mere stain of memory in the soil by the time its spawn are ready to rise. Before that day arrives, it knows the dark metal will ward off me and mine, as well as any other who might seek to destroy its clutch before memory of such a burial fades away, as the years pass by.'

Witta was right. Wyrms really did think in thousands of years. I was more concerned with the here and now.

'Can you tell us if there's any treasure close enough to the surface for the stargazer's son to find?' It had occurred to me, too late, that we should have suggested the hob bury the torc just deep enough to convince Tom Kelley he'd unearthed it for himself.

I reckoned we could take that chance. In this dark and cold and rain, he was hardly likely to recognise it as the same thing he'd seen briefly around the sylph's neck. The torc Will was supposedly going to declare to the portable antiquities people first thing in the morning.

The hob grinned at me. 'There is now, Master Greenwood. I scattered a few precious trinkets to whet his appetite. No need to thank me.'

'There may be no need, but I'll thank you all the same.' Now I was convinced the hob was on our side. I wished I could be as certain of the sylph. 'Come on, Will. We need to get a move on.'

The hob put an end to this conversation by disappearing. So that was that, for the moment anyway.

We headed back to the Land Rover and drove around to the place we had parked before. We walked up to the gap in the hedge where we'd lurked and seen Tom Kelley catch the wyrm unawares. I was still wondering if it would turn up and kill him. Hopefully not, if it didn't want to draw attention to the burial mound. I wasn't concerned for Kelley. He could take his own chances. What I didn't want to risk was any chance of a wyrm getting its shape-shifting hands on that crystal and the lore that could force hobs and sylphs to do as they were told.

Will was carrying his bag of assorted kit. He found his camera traps and brought them over to me. 'I need to change these data cards. Stand with your back to the weather, will you? Hold this.'

He handed me a pen light and used me as a windbreak as he worked quickly and efficiently. Then he gave me a small flat plastic box. 'Take these, so there's no way they can get mixed up with the rest. I'll erase whatever's on them when we get back to Aunt Helen's. I'm not getting the laptop out in this shit.'

I stuck the box in an inside pocket. We definitely didn't want there to be any evidence that Will and I had been anywhere near the burial mound tonight.

Will put the camera traps back in position. Then he got a different camera to the one he'd used before out of his bag, and set it up on a small tripod. He'd promised us this one had night vision video capability as well as a zoom and a date stamp that would catch Tom Kelley breaking the law clearly enough for any court in the land. He had a waterproof cover for it, with stubby sleeves sticking out at the sides for him to put his hands through. He also had a waterproof poncho with a hood for himself, and a thin padded mat to sit on. He peered through the camera's viewfinder and adjusted various things until he gave a grunt of satisfaction. Then he got a couple of cereal bars out of a side pocket of his bag and tossed one to me.

'Now, we wait.' He didn't sound bothered at all by the prospect, despite the lousy weather. He ate his cereal bar and looked through his camera every so often. Clearly this wasn't the first time he'd spent a night like this.

I managed to find myself some shelter a bit further along behind the hedge, and ate the cereal bar. Since I had nothing else to do, all I could do was think of all the ways this could go horribly wrong. We still didn't know if Doctor Tom knew he'd attacked a wyrm. If he was panicking about that, he might never come back here, in case it tried to eat him. All we could do was rely on the sylph. If they couldn't persuade him to do this, we were wasting our time, at least as far as getting Kelley arrested. The hob and the sylph would hold me to the rest of our bargain, and the sea folk definitely wouldn't wait. I still had to get the crystal off Kelley and get the wyrm egg to the coast.

I stood and waited and did my best to do that thing where you tense and relax all your muscle groups in turn. I'd be no use to anyone, whatever happened, if I ended up too stiff and cold to move. I did my best to ignore the assorted aches and scrapes I'd picked up over the past few days, and wondered if Will had any painkillers in his bag.

'He comes.' The hob was back beside me.

I moved back to the gap in the hedge. I had Fin's petrol station binoculars in my pocket but they were no help. Rain spattered the lenses as soon as I lifted them up. As soon as I wiped them dry, more droplets hit the glass. I gave up and put them away. At least I had the excellent night vision I'd inherited from my mum to help me.

'Here he is,' Will said slowly. He was glued to his camera now.

I raised a hand to shield my eyes from the rain and tried to see whatever was going on. A figure appeared up by the mound. At this distance, in this darkness and rain, I couldn't have said who it was. It could only be Kelley though. The sylph beside him was a dead giveaway and its radiance helped me see what was going on a bit better. I breathed a little easier.

'He's looking around,' Will commented.

'For the wyrm, do you think?' I really hoped Witta and the others were right when they said it would be staying away for the time being at least.

'Whatever he's doing, it makes him look really shifty,' Will said with satisfaction. 'He knows he's up to no good.'

I squinted at the distant figure. 'Is he using his metal detector?'

'He most certainly is.'

Excellent. That was going to drop the bastard even deeper in the shit. We watched Kelley walk around in slow circles. The sylph stood motionless, watching him.

'Is he there on his own?' I asked Will suddenly. 'As far as your camera's concerned, I mean.'

'He is.'

As Will spoke, we saw Kelley drop to his knees. He bent forward, busy doing something on the ground. A moment later, he beckoned to the sylph and held something up.

'What's he got?'

'Can't see, but whatever it is, it's shiny.' Will stayed focused on the view through the camera.

The hob spoke up. 'There were coins brought by the Frankish men. I strewed them just below the bite of the plough.' He sounded oddly wistful.

'Okay, he's put that in his pocket,' reported Will. 'Now he's seeing what else he can find.'

We watched Kelley make another slow circuit. He dug something else up. Then he picked up his metal detector again. Another find was followed by another sweep. I started to wonder if he was going to be here all night. If he was, we had a serious problem. I really believed Witta when she said her people wouldn't wait, and the wind from the sea was getting stronger.

Chapter Twenty

Maybe the worsening weather finally convinced Kelley to call it quits. By my count he'd pocketed at least six finds. Good. That should make it hard to argue he'd succumbed to one-off temptation – as he took a country walk out here in the middle of the night, in the pouring rain, when he just happened to be carrying a metal detector. Even the CPS couldn't believe that, surely?

Kelley dismissed the sylph with a gesture and headed away down the other side of the hill. The night closed around us, darker than ever. Will started packing away his gear. I helped him get the data cards out of the camera traps for a second time.

'Are you sure you got all that?' I was still apprehensive. Something could still go wrong. 'Make sure you make several copies of everything as soon as you've downloaded it.'

Eleanor takes care of Blithehurst's IT. She always says data needs to be saved in at least two places, ideally three. Minimum.

'I have done this before, you know. Well, filmed frolicking fox cubs, but the principle's the same.' Will was amused.

Belatedly I appreciated him not telling me to piss off. He'd have been entitled. 'Time to make a phone call then.'

'Right you are.' He got out his phone and looked at it, surprised. 'I've got a text from Aunty Helen.'

I swallowed hard and tried not to think of dire possibilities. 'What does it say?'

He seemed to take a stupidly long time to read the message. The wait was worth it.

'The barrow here is a scheduled ancient monument, apparently. She managed to look it up online.'

'Great.' Then Doctor Tom was really in the shit. 'Okay, let's get the authorities involved.'

Will scrolled through the contacts, looking for a number. He pressed the screen and raised the phone to his ear. A moment later, he nodded, 'Yes, I—'

He broke off and looked at me. The light from the screen showed me his confusion. A moment later, he lowered the phone.

'They're shut.'

I stared at him. 'The police?'

'Wisbech station is closed. They're only open nine to five, apparently. The message suggests other numbers to call.' He raised his phone again.

'Hang on. Let me think.'

My first thought was how the hell had we failed to check something that sodding obvious? We all lived in the countryside. We knew more and more local police stations were being closed year on year, and the ones that were left were having their hours cut back. So why hadn't we checked? Because we'd been busy agreeing there was no way this could be called an emergency to justify dialling 999. Then we'd debated whether or not the cops would send a patrol car out or not. If they did, that would be a bonus, but we decided we'd better not count on it.

My second thought was never mind about any of that. What mattered was what we did now.

'Okay, the important thing is we get you on the record first, reporting what Kelley's done, and pretty much as soon as he's done it.' Because we wanted the authorities watching and waiting to see if he did declare anything he had found. Even if he got in touch with the portable antiquities people first thing tomorrow morning, we wanted him facing some very awkward questions about metal-detecting without the landowner's permission. Without permission from Historic England, now that we knew he'd need that here as well.

'Shall I ring the police in Cambridge?' Will raised his phone again.

'Let me ring Fin.' I got out my own phone. Then I changed my mind and held out my hand. 'Let me use yours.'

He passed it over. It wasn't the same handset as mine, but Fin was in his call log. She answered at once.

'Do you need picking up?'

If the police were on the way, we'd agreed I needed to be nowhere around. After all, my next task was breaking into Tom Kelley's Jag. So the story was going to be Fin had dropped Will off here for a night's photography.

'It's Dan,' I said quickly. 'Listen, the Wisbech police station closes at five. Yes, I know we should have checked, but never mind that now. Do you have a number for Chris who works at the museum? Great. How about you ring him and tell him Will just called you to say what he'd seen? Say that he tried to ring the local cops, but that didn't work so he's wondering what to do for the best. He's worried if he rings the coppers in Cambridge, it could take days for someone to notice the report. Meantime, who knows what Tom Kelley might dig up and take from here? See what Chris thinks you should both do.'

As I spoke, I was looking at Will. He gave me a thumbs up.

'Okay,' Fin said slowly. 'Yes,' she went on more decisively. 'That's a good idea. Chris will know who to call, and he's already suspicious about Doctor Tom. He'll know how to get things moving.'

'Great.' I was about to end the call.

'Wait a minute,' Fin said quickly. 'Mum's had an idea. She thinks this is the time to ring Mike Kelley and tell him where Tom is staying. She'll say we were passing and thought about stopping there for dinner and we saw his car. Obviously, if Mike rings him now, he'll just take off again. So she's going to suggest he sets off from London first thing tomorrow morning, so he can catch Tom when he's having breakfast or maybe even when he's still in bed. What do you think?'

'Sounds like a plan to me. The more things he has to occupy him tomorrow, the better, while Chris gets the archaeology people and the police lined up. And we want as much time as possible before he realises the crystal is gone. Just ask Helen to hold off until I let you know I've got the crystal though. In case Mike is too angry to wait and calls him anyway. We can't risk losing track of him now.'

'Fair enough,' Fin agreed.

'Can you come and get Will as soon as you've called Chris? So he can get back and download the video as soon as possible.'

'Of course.' Fin said something else, but I didn't hear what it was.

The sylph was back. They waved a glowing white hand in the darkness and the phone I was holding went dead.

Those merciless blue eyes fixed on me. 'Now you must make good on your side of our bargain, son of the greenwood. If you fail us, you and yours will live to regret it.'

The hob stood beside the sylph. Their silvery radiance made him a golden-eyed shadow even darker than the night that surrounded us. I didn't need to see his expression to know he agreed with the sylph on this.

I had no intention of not doing what I'd promised them. I'm not suicidal, or even just stupid. 'Has he gone back to the hotel by the bridge?' I asked the sylph.

We'd agreed that they were best placed to keep track of Kelley once he left here. The sylph nodded. 'He has.'

'Right.' I turned to Will as I got out the Land Rover keys. 'You'll be okay here till Fin arrives, won't you?'

'Give those to him,' the sylph said curtly. 'With everything else that you carry that's metal. I will take you to Kelley's lodging.'

'That's not what—'

194

'Use the wits your mother gave you,' the hob interrupted me. 'Our friend can carry you there unseen and carry you away just as swiftly. You have no need for your vehicle until you have to flee this place with the wyrm's egg.'

I really wanted to argue, but unfortunately they were right. With the sylph's help, there was no danger of anyone seeing the Land Rover anywhere near the hotel. If I needed to make a quick getaway, this would be the fastest escape possible. The only risk was some copper finding my vehicle with no good reason to be parked out here if they did come out to see what Kelley had been doing. That had to be a slim chance, all things considered. If we were unlucky, we'd just have to make up some bullshit and challenge the police to prove different. We could say there was some confusion about who was picking up Will. That could wait. I began emptying my pockets.

'Here.' Will offered me the nylon drawstring bag his rain poncho had been packed in.

'Thanks.' I filled it with keys, phone, screwdriver, penknife, wallet and loose change. Then I tied up the neck and stowed it on top of the Landy's off-side rear wheel. That was taking another chance, but this was turning into a night of calculated risks.

'Okay.' I was about to say something else to Will when white mist enveloped me. I was relieved to find travel by sylph is a lot less stressful than being swept along by a naiad's magic. That had felt like being waterboarded. This time when my feet hit the ground again, I felt breathless and a bit light-headed, but otherwise I was fine.

I looked around. We were in the furthest corner of The Ring of Bells' car park, well away from the hotel. Tom Kelley's Jag was over by the fence. So far, so good. I turned to the sylph. Okay, now there were two sylphs. They were both dim outlines, barely visible in the electric lights, even to people who could see ethereal creatures.

One of them vanished. I looked at the one who remained. As far as I could tell, this was the one we'd been dealing with. 'Were you able to do as I asked?'

Their faint blue eyes flickered. 'I was.'

The lights on the Jag flashed as the central locking unlocked itself. It was as easy as that.

After sitting and watching the car park, and wondering about ethereal creatures and key fobs, I'd gone online to see what I could find out about breaking into vehicles. It turns out there are gadgets that can intercept and block the signals sent from a key fob to open a car. When the locks don't release, people just press the button on their key again. The doors open when they get a fresh signal generated by the algorithms and electronics, so the car owner doesn't think any more about it. What they don't realise is the thieves didn't just intercept and block that first signal. They also recorded it. The car still has it registered as a valid code to unlock the doors. The thieves can follow the car and wait for a quiet moment when the driver has left it parked somewhere. Then they play back that first code and they're in.

Hackers need the right hardware and software to do stuff like this, but I didn't bother reading up about that. I had a sylph. Of course, breaking into the Jag like this meant I had to explain radio frequencies and related stuff to the sylph. They were aware of such things in the air obviously, in the same way that my mum was, but steering clear of humans meant they'd never really thought about what these signals did. They'd certainly never considered using them for themselves. Thanks to me, that genie was now well and truly out of the bottle. The way the sylph had cut off my call to Fin showed they were already exploring other possibilities. I had very deliberately not mentioned mobile phones to them at all.

I'd have to worry if I was going to regret sharing this knowledge later. Right now, I had things to steal. I looked at the sylph. 'The CCTV?'

For an instant, the sylph blazed as vivid as a camera flash, and that wasn't just going to dazzle people who could see the ethereal world. A bit more Internet research had told us that really bright light should temporarily blind the hotel's CCTV. Though we weren't sure how long 'temporarily' might be. So there was no time to waste.

I ran across the car park and opened the Jag's boot. There was the big briefcase. I tried the catches. It wasn't locked, which was a massive relief. I'd been prepared to force my way in, but I'd counted on having my penknife and a screwdriver with me. I opened it up, and yes, I still had my gloves on. I took out the crystal ball and put it down on the floor of the boot for a moment. Sorting quickly through the papers tucked away with it, I ignored the black leather journals, maps and photocopies. What I wanted was anything that looked like the old Kelley documents I'd seen in the Sedgeport Museum archive.

'What are you doing?' the sylph demanded.

I closed the briefcase and picked up the crystal as well as the creased pages with their faded ink. It wasn't easy closing the car boot without dropping something, but I managed it. I turned to the sylph. 'Okay, lock it up.'

The Jag's lights flashed. There was nothing to tell Kelley he had been robbed until he went looking in his briefcase. Then, if he wanted to do anything about it, he'd have to admit someone had taken things he had stolen himself.

The sylph reached for me. Before they could touch me, I took a long step back. 'Take me to the house where the swan's daughters live. Bring the hob of the long isle to meet me there.'

The sylph's eyes narrowed. 'Why?'

'It's not enough to take the crystal from the stargazer's son. We need to destroy whatever lore makes it possible for him to use it to see you, and to control you all. We want to see him punished for every one of his thefts.'

I was going to explain in more detail, but I barely got those words out before the world turned to white fog around me. When the mist cleared, I was standing on the patio behind Venturer's House. I took a deep breath, and guessed that meant the sylph was willing to go along with me for the moment at least. I'd have to wait till they appeared with the hob to be certain though.

I'd better check that the pair of them turning up wasn't going to cause more problems. The only car in the yard was Helen's VW. I walked to the side gate and looked out into the lane. No other cars were parked outside the front of the house. I headed back to the kitchen door and knocked. 'Helen?'

She opened up. I didn't need to explain what I was doing there. Bringing Kelley's stolen papers here was a possibility we had discussed earlier. We hadn't counted on it being possible though. The more steps there are in any plan, the greater the chances are that something will take an unexpected turn. That was why I hadn't mentioned doing this to the sylph or the hob. That and we didn't want to give them anything else to argue and bargain over.

Helen didn't waste time with questions. 'Fin and Will are heading straight to Chris's house, to show him the video. Will's going to give him a copy. Then he can email it to the people who need to know.'

'Great.' I went inside and put everything I was carrying on the table. The crystal ball threatened to roll straight off and crash onto the floor. I grabbed a tea towel and twisted it into a circle to give the sphere something to stand in. It was an eerily beautiful thing. Whatever it was made of, it certainly wasn't ordinary glass, not to my eyes anyway. Reflections of unknown people and places slid and shimmered across its surface. I hoped such visions were limited to those of us who could see the ethereal. Tom Kelley needed Edward Kelley's rituals to use it, didn't he? That's what we needed to find now.

'I rang Mike Kelley,' Helen went on. 'He'll be coming up to Reedmere Bridge bright and early tomorrow. He's absolutely furious with Tom.'

'That should keep the bastard busy.' I shoved the work gloves I was still wearing in my jacket pocket and began laying out the Kelley documents across the kitchen table. Some looked like the closely written sheets Fin had found in the Sedgeport archive. The alphabet was familiar but I couldn't tell if the language was Latin or something else. I couldn't read any of it. There were printed pages from some ancient book with columns of dates and numbers and symbols, with handwritten notes scribbled in the margins. Other pages had comparatively simple diagrams with more illegible notes around them. A couple of sheets of paper had really complicated arrangements of circles surrounding stars and heptagons that decreased in size down to a central five-pointed star. The symbols and words written on those were crisp and precise and I couldn't make sense of any of them.

'Leave the door open, please. They should be here any minute.' I certainly hoped so. Meantime, I used table mats and the salt and pepper to stop the old papers being blown about.

'Okay.' Helen shivered and wrapped her cardigan around herself as she used a wooden wedge to keep the door just a foot or so ajar. Then she came to look at what I was doing. 'What are those?'

As I'd separated out the old papers, several A5 cards had slipped out from between them and fallen to the floor. Helen bent down to pick them up. She stood up, alarmed.

'This has got Fin's name on it, and her birthday.'

'Let me see.' I took the card from her and recognised the layout of a central square surrounded by a diamond and triangles from the papers Fin had looked at in the museum. I'd seen the same thing in the illustrations in the John Dee book. I hadn't thought it could be important, so I hadn't said anything about it. These weren't old though. The card was new and the ink was fresh.

'It's some sort of horoscope, I think.' Though I had no idea how to read any of those numbers or symbols either.

'Well, this one's about Mike, and here's Angela.' Helen's voice rose. Now she was angry as well as upset. 'And this one's about me.'

I didn't blame her for being cross. I wouldn't like the idea of someone like Tom Kelley thinking he could somehow predict what I might do. I wondered uneasily how accurate something like this might be. This sort of astrology wasn't like the column in the local paper advising Leos that the time is right for a change while warning Capricorns against making rash decisions. Could there possibly be anything in it? I went through the old documents a second time, but there were no more cards to be found.

'There isn't one for me or for Will. Even if these could give him some idea about things you or Fin might do, he won't have a clue what we're up to.'

Unless I had left more of these cards in that damn briefcase in the Jag, of course. But I still didn't think Tom Kelley could have drawn up any horoscope for me. Neil or Kate at the pub might have told him my name without thinking anything of it, because why would they have any reason to keep it a secret? There was still no way he could have found out when my birthday was. No one around here knew the date, let alone the year, and I don't do social media. Even if I did, I've read enough warnings about identity theft and online security not to post anything like that for anyone else to read.

I hadn't expected to find a reason like this for keeping my personal data private. It made me more determined than ever to land Tom Kelley in deeper shit than he could possibly climb out of. That meant he needed to be the one caught with these stolen papers, not me. Where was that bloody sylph?

Light shone outside on the patio. Helen looked up from the cards in her hand. 'Come in.'

The sylph and the hob walked into the kitchen. The hob looked warily around. I wondered if he was remembering this house as it had been in a different century.

'Good evening to you, Mistress Swan.'

'You are very welcome, Master Hob.' Helen put down the cards. 'Do you mind if I close the door?' The wind was sending a fair amount of rain in through the gap to spatter on the tiles.

'By all means,' the hob said graciously.

I was relieved to see that he trusted us that far now. Helen kicked the wedge free and closed the door.

The scowling sylph had no time for such politeness. 'Why are we here, instead of delivering the wyrm's egg to the people of the sea?'

'We want your help with two things. Two things that will help keep you and yours safe for the foreseeable future.' I gestured at the crystal. 'Master Hob, we need you to hide this for us, just for a little while. We will put it out of reach for good, so that no one else will be able to misuse it. But we need to deal with the wyrm and its egg before we can do that, as we agreed.'

The hob looked at me for a long moment. Then he nodded. 'I can hide it away, for a short time. I will not be made the guardian of this perilous thing, though,' he warned.

'You won't be.' I pointed at the incomprehensible papers laid out across the table. 'We also want to see the stargazer's son punished for stealing these, as well as for raiding the great warrior's burial ground. First though, we want to know if either of you can read the stargazer's writings. We can't understand any of this.'

I looked at the sylph and the hob. They knew my mother's blood made me a lousy liar. They would know I was telling the truth.

'If you can find the pages that explain how mortals can use the crystal to see you, and to compel you and yours to act against your will, then we will destroy those papers. We can't promise no one else knows such secrets, but we can at least destroy the knowledge that's been used here to abuse you and your people.'

The hob looked at the sylph. The sylph shrugged. They both walked over to the table and peered intently at the pages.

'A little space, if you please,' the hob snapped.

Helen and I backed off. The hob and the sylph continued studying the papers. I guessed that meant they could read them. I tried not to get impatient, or at least not to let it show. I wanted to get this done, and not just because the gale outside was lashing the house with rain that said the storm was getting worse. The last thing we needed was Fin and Will turning up with Chris from the museum in tow while we had these stolen documents laid out. Of course, I didn't have my phone, but I should have asked Helen to text them a warning.

The sylph pointed with a pale, glittering finger. 'Destroy this, and this. That will suffice to keep us safe.'

'Okay.' I took a step towards the table.

'Let me,' the hob said quickly.

Before I could see which pages the sylph had picked out, the hob laid a long-nailed, swollen-knuckled hand on each one. The ancient paper twitched and crackled. It was already a faded beige. Within seconds, it darkened to ruddy brown. Another second, and it was breaking into fragments. As the hob withdrew his hands, those shards crumbled into floury dust.

The sylph gestured, and a very small, very precise vortex swept up the dust and carried it to the door. 'If you please, Mistress Swan.'

Helen looked amused as she went to open the door. The tidy-minded whirl-wind carried the dust outside and she shut the door after it to keep out the cold and wet. The sylph gestured at the table. The documents pulled themselves out from under the mats and other things that weighed them down. After swirl-ing around for a moment, they shuffled themselves into a neat stack which dropped into the centre of the table.

Now there was no way to know which pages had been destroyed without sorting through them all and trying to remember what had been spread out where in the first place. The sylph's cold blue gaze challenged me to try it.

I wasn't interested in playing games. I looked at the hob. 'Please will you ask the hob of the house at the crossroads to help us now. If these papers are found inside the house, everyone will see the stargazer's son must be the thief who took them.'

The hob surprised me with a grin. 'I will ask her, though I make no promis-es on another's behalf. I will stow this away first.'

He picked up the crystal and hurried out, barely pausing to bow to Helen as she opened the door for him.

The sylph looked at me. 'If you wish to show that you trust us, you could take those chains down from your windows.'

I looked at Helen. 'It's your house.'

She thought for a moment and nodded. 'You can take down the ones in here. Then I can stop opening and closing this door every five minutes.'

I went to the front window first, and then to the back. Unhooking the chains from the cup hooks was easy enough. I collected them all and dropped them on the floor by the Aga. The sylph and the hob were already keeping well clear of that.

I wished the job was more complicated. I really could do with something to occupy my hands as well as my mind. Listening to the wild weather outside, I was starting to think this had been a bad idea. We were trying to be too clever. We could have just burned those papers. No one else would ever know. We should have done that. I should be on my way to the coast with the wyrm's egg by now. That should have been my priority, before Witta and her people drowned half the county.

The hob appeared beside me. The female hob was with him. She looked slowly around the old house's kitchen, taking in every detail of the low, uneven ceiling and scuffed floor tiles. She turned to the hob of the long isle. Her expression was smugly superior. He was glowering at her.

'Good evening, Mistress Hob,' I said quickly before one or the other of them said something to screw up our plans. We had to get this done and fast.

Helen followed my lead. 'You are very welcome.'

The female hob smiled with satisfaction. 'Good evening to you, Mistress Swan, Master Greenwood.'

I wasn't going to waste any more time. 'Can you tell me, please, if anyone has been into the Kelley house – into your house – to tidy up the mess he left?'

She looked at me, thoughtful. I expected her to ask why I needed to know. Instead, she nodded. 'The innkeeper's wife has cleaned the kitchen and the bathroom. She has tidied his bedroom and washed the linens. The rest is still as you saw it. I do not blame her for that. I heard her talking to her husband. She has been told to leave everything else as it was.'

The house-proud hob might not hold Kate responsible, but she clearly wasn't happy about that.

I waved a hand at the table. 'The stargazer's son stole those papers. They are valuable. If they're found in your house, he won't be able to deny he's the thief. As long as he's not the one to find them. It has to be his brother or sister, or maybe the innkeeper's wife, in some place where she hasn't looked since he left the house. Then he can be punished.'

'I believe I can arrange such a discovery.' The curl of the hob's lip promised nothing good for Tom Kelley.

I could live with that. 'Thank you.'

'I believe I should thank you.' The hob glanced from me to Helen. 'I am told you have ensured the stargazer's son can no longer see us, that he can no longer command us.'

'We believe so. We certainly hope that he'll stay far away from here from now on.' I sincerely hoped the arrogant sod would end up in prison, but I wasn't going to risk promising that.

'Very well.' The hob surprised me with a sweet smile that transformed her wrinkled little face. 'I hope we meet again, Master Greenwood, so I may settle this debt between us.'

She went over to the table while I was trying to work out what to say to that. She reached up and the sylph gestured. The papers slid across the table to fall into her hands. Both hobs vanished without any fuss.

I breathed a sigh of relief. Now all the stolen property was out of our hands, for the time being at least.

'What about these?' Helen held up the horoscope cards.

I hadn't realised she had kept hold of them. Then I was glad that she had.

'Burn them. We don't want anything left that can tie us to whatever Tom Kelley's been up to, when the police or anyone else starts asking questions.'

I'm not sure if Helen heard everything I said. The sylph came up behind me and laid a cool hand on my shoulder. The kitchen dissolved into white mist.

Chapter Twenty-One

Back at the burial mound, the night was so dark that even my mother's blood was no damn use. Even cats need some light to see by. I wouldn't have been able to see my own hands without the sylph's faint glow beside me. The wind was so strong that I staggered to stay on my feet as it smacked into me from all directions. The rain drenched me in seconds and stung my face.

'Wait here, greenwood.' The hob was somewhere close by in the blackness.

I guessed he'd disappeared, not that I could know for sure. I waited. There was nothing else I could do. The sylph waited with me. That cold blue gaze didn't waver, staying fixed on my face.

'What?' I challenged. 'You think I'm going to back out, after all this?'

The sylph didn't answer. I took my gloves out of my pocket and pulled them on.

'As soon as I leave here, go back to the hotel. Keep watch on Tom Kelley. If he leaves, follow him, so we know where to find him. If he stays, see what you can hear when his brother turns up in the morning. Go and tell Fin what happens, whatever happens.'

I wasn't asking, I was telling. I'd also had enough of using stupid nicknames.

The sylph still didn't answer.

'Here.' The hob was standing in front of me. He held out something for me to take.

I cupped my hands automatically. He gave me something hard and heavy. Then he and the sylph both vanished.

'Great. Thanks.' The ferocious wind snatched my words away.

I'd thought I was cold before, but the touch of the wyrm's egg was like nothing I'd ever felt. Arctic didn't begin to describe it. I shut my mouth before I bit my tongue. My teeth were chattering so hard that the effort of stopping made my jaw ache. The egg was also astonishingly weighty for something that was supposed to have an ethereal creature inside it. I'd carried bags of cement that felt lighter, even though it wasn't much bigger than a litre bottle of water.

Unsurprisingly, it was egg shaped, as far as I could make out from feeling it. It was also completely silent, and that was a relief. This egg was nowhere remotely near hatching. I knew that much from our experience at Blithehurst. The wyrmling under the ruins there had started singing to call for help nearly a century ago. It had stirred several times through the decades before an older wyrm heard it. Whether or not the egg was its own, the creature had come to find out what was going on. That early warning gave the local naiad enough time to enlist me to help Eleanor Beauchene, even if the resident dryads had had other ideas. A lifetime measured in millennia didn't always work to a wyrm's advantage.

The cold cutting through my gloves was making my hands ache. I suddenly hoped that carrying this sodding thing wasn't going to injure me. If it did, how the hell would I drive? I wasn't just thinking about frostbite. I remembered a science lesson at school where Mr Smith dipped a daffodil in liquid nitrogen. He smacked it on the bench and the flower shattered like glass.

Really wishing I hadn't remembered that, I began walking down the slope towards the Land Rover. I had to assume it was still parked where I'd left it. The bastard sylph could at least have told me that much. They could have taken me straight to the Landy, instead of bringing me up to the top of the mound to be soaked to the skin while the hob fetched the bloody egg. They could have stuck around long enough to show me where the path was in the darkness.

As I stumbled on the rough ground, I really wished I had a torch, even if I'd have to hold it in my mouth. There was no way I could carry this egg one-handed. Then I trod on something loose that skidded away under my foot. I turned my ankle and fell down hard. As I hit the sodden ground, I lost my hold on the egg. It rolled off into the darkness. I had no idea where it had gone.

I sat up and sat there for a few moments, swearing viciously. As I ran out of curses, the pain in my ankle eased. Cautiously flexing my foot, I decided I'd only wrenched the joint, rather than injured it with a bad twist or a sprain. In even better news, the cold sensation quickly faded from my hands. I still wasn't anywhere close to warm, but my fingers weren't numb any more. I didn't even feel pins and needles as the sensation returned. That was a massive relief.

Then I felt a shiver run through the ground beneath me. It wasn't right underneath me, but the tremor was close enough to be scary. I knew exactly what that was. Wherever it was lurking, the wyrm had realised someone was screwing around with its eggs.

Where was the fucking thing? I groped around in the darkness, but that only got me enough mud coating my gloves to stick my fingers together. I felt the ground tremble again. I made a quick decision and stood up. My ankle was sore, but it was bearing my weight so that was good enough. I headed down the slope as quickly as I could without risking another fall. At least when I reached the hedgerow, the twigs and the remnants of autumn's leaves gave me some shelter from the incessant wind and rain. It also meant I could find the proper footpath, worn smooth by dogs and their owners.

The path took me straight to the Land Rover. I scrubbed the mud off my gloves on the grass as best I could and went round to the off-side rear wheel.

The nylon bag with my keys and everything else was safe and sound. I unlocked the back, tossed in the bag and grabbed the big torch I keep in there. I switched it on as I ran back up the path. Now I could see where I was going, though the light made the night around me seem far darker, if that was even possible.

I reached the gap in the hedge and slowed down. Now I had to remember the line I'd taken coming down from the burial mound. I scanned the ground with the torch, sweeping the beam from side to side. Finally the sodding rain made itself useful. Water gathering in a hollow reflected the torchlight back at me. Looking closer, I found what looked very like my own boot prints. Good enough. I followed my tracks back up towards the mound. Now I was scanning the ground for any sign of the egg.

I nearly missed it. The torchlight slid over something that looked as transparent as a soap bubble, barely outlined by a rainbow sheen. With rain drops clinging to my eyelashes, I was already dazzled by reflections from the torchlight. I couldn't wipe my face without risking getting mud in my eyes.

I blinked and shook my head as I swept the torch beam from side to side again. This time I saw it more clearly, for an instant at least. I hurried over, and for a moment I thought I'd lost it again. How could that be? Then I realised I was looking straight through it. Either that, or the egg had some ability to mimic its surroundings, to protect itself. As soon as I laid a hand on it though, I could see it clearly enough.

I unzipped my jacket. I was already so wet that didn't make any difference. I put the torch down and picked up the egg with both hands. Sliding it inside my jacket meant I could hold it in the crook of my arm. Doing the zip up again was a struggle, but I managed it. I picked up the torch and headed down the hill again.

I felt another tremor through my boots. For a second I thought about turning off the torch. Then I realised that was just stupid. If another person was chasing me, doing that would make me harder to see out here in the night, but a wyrm was something else entirely. It was after me because I had its egg, and I didn't think there was any way for me to hide. I needed to get back to the Land Rover, so I was surrounded by metal. That was the only way to be safe. I needed the torch to do that as fast as I could.

I hurried on, trying not to imagine what might be lurking just out of sight in the darkness beyond the edge of the yellowing beam. Something was draining my torch battery, I realised with a sinking feeling. That sensation added to the brutal cold of the egg thudding into my gut. The pain was making it hard to breathe.

The torch light lasted until the Landy was in sight. That was good enough. I forced myself to run the last few metres. I'd left the doors unlocked to make the fastest getaway, so I dumped the egg on the passenger seat and dropped the dead torch in the footwell. Stripping off the muddy gloves, I ran around to the other door. As I opened it, the courtesy light came on. I looked across at the egg. It was almost invisible again. Just the faintest gleam of reflected light outlined it, and I could see straight through it to the seat.

I tossed the gloves down on the floor beside the dead torch. My hands were filthy and clumsy as I fumbled with the keys and my seatbelt. That was just from the ordinary chill of the rain. I managed to get the engine started, and turned the heat and the fan on full blast. Thankfully the ache in my belly was fading, and I took a few deep breaths. Right, it was time to go. Just one more job and this endless day would be over. I could go back to Venturer's House for a hot bath and something to eat. I was surprised to realise I was incredibly hungry.

I switched on the satnav. Witta had told me the village to head for, close to a nature reserve out on the coast. I quickly set up the journey, got into gear, hit the lights and switched the wipers on at top speed. Then I put my foot down.

After less than half a mile, I realised I couldn't go nearly as fast as I wanted to. Even using the headlights on full beam, the night was pitch black. Glare bouncing back from swathes of rain sweeping across the narrow road made the visibility even worse. The satnav map display was showing me where the road went, as well as the route I needed to follow, but I was struggling to see the turnings until I was right on top of them. A few more bloody sign posts would help.

I didn't dare lose my way. There was no telling what sort of insane detour the satnav would recalculate for me. I had to get to the coast as fast as possible. I also needed to sodding concentrate. Thinking about what could go wrong, I'd nearly missed the next turn completely. As I wrenched the steering wheel round, I felt the rear wheels lose their hold on the road. For one heart-stopping moment, I thought I was going to end up in a dyke. I gripped the wheel and steered into the skid. The tyres gripped the tarmac. Okay, but that had been far too close for comfort.

I tightened my hold on the wheel to stop my hands shaking and eased off on the accelerator. Thankfully the next stretch of road was straightforward. The rain slackened a little, and I saw a hump-backed bridge over a waterway ahead. Then I saw the wyrm.

It reared up out of the dyke, looming over the bridge. I couldn't tell what colour it was in the darkness, but the rain glistened on its scales in the head-lights. As a serpent dragon it looked far more like a snake than anything with wings from a fantasy TV series. A snake whose body was as broad as my shoul-

206

ders. Its fangs weren't twin prongs like a snake's though. Its mouth gaped to show me murderous teeth like a dinosaur's in some museum. It ducked down, to put its head level with the bridge's parapet. Its eyes glowed bone-white, cold and menacing, and its long, forked tongue flickered as it tasted the stormy air.

I had nowhere else to go. An emergency stop risked a fatal skid. There was no point in me stopping anyway. There was no room to turn the Landy around on this narrow road without ending up in a ditch – dyke – whatever. Fuck it. Why should I stop? Witta had assured me the thing wouldn't be able to get to me inside the vehicle. Medieval knights had killed wyrms wearing chain mail and plate armour. I was surrounded by a damn sight more metal than that.

The wyrm lowered its head, stretching across the parapet. It twisted around to look at me, with its great head hanging in the centre of the road. The rest of its body looped up and back down into the water, disappearing into the darkness.

I floored the accelerator. Either it would move, or it wouldn't. If it did, at least now I could be sure it was following me and its precious egg. That's what we wanted, right? If it didn't move, we would see how it liked getting two and a half tonnes of solid West Midlands engineering crashing into its face.

The monster reared away. That was a relief. It had occurred to me at the very last minute that the Landy might be mostly metal, but the windscreen was made of glass. Laminated glass, but that would still end up cobwebbed with cracks. The whole thing might even fall into my lap. Either way, I'd be driving through this foul weather when I couldn't see where I was going. That would soon end in disaster.

For the moment, I had other things to worry about. I'd hit the bridge hard and fast. I felt all four tyres leave the ground. All I could do was hold the steering wheel as straight as I could and hope I didn't hit mud or a pothole when the Landy made contact with the tarmac. I snatched a glance at the satnav. If the road decided to make a sharp bend about now, I was royally fucked.

There wasn't any mud, or a hole or a bend. The Land Rover touched down on the road with a thump that jarred me from my arse to my shoulders. The tyres gripped, and the Landy sped away. I wasn't about to relax though. As I drove on, I was snatching glances in the mirrors to see what was happening behind me. I soon saw the wyrm. It was looping along the road and coming after me fast. Then I couldn't see it at all, but a great surge of water out of a dyke came splashing across the road behind me, glinting red in the Landy's rear lights.

I drove on as fast as I dared. My heart was pounding as I tried to watch the road ahead, the mirrors to see what was coming after me, and the satnav screen at the same time. I had been soaked through with rain. Now I was sweating like a pig, although my mouth was as dry as a bone. The Landy was far too hot and stuffy and the windows were misting up. I reached for the fan and the heating controls. What I needed was a blast of cold air to keep me alert.

Something thudded into the Land Rover's back door, hard enough to jolt me forward against my seatbelt. Bastard thing! I accelerated, just for a short stretch. It wasn't enough. I caught a glimpse of dark scales in the wing mirror. This time the wyrm slapped a heavy coil against the side of the vehicle. The Landy skidded sideways and I had to fight the wheel to stay on the road.

As I risked a bit more speed and checked my mirrors again, I saw steam or smoke or something rising from the wyrm's flank before it slid away into the water-filled dyke. So hitting metal did hurt it. Witta had been right about that. On the other hand, it looked like we'd seriously underestimated how much pain the wyrm was willing to take, when it was determined to retrieve its egg. We should also have remembered there was water everywhere for it to dive into and heal.

The wyrm attacking wasn't my only problem. By now I could see the blue edge of the coast at the top of the satnav screen. Getting this much closer to the sea meant I'd left what little tree cover there was far behind. The storm was coming straight off the water towards me. Ever more ferocious wind hammered on the Landy's windows, shaking the whole vehicle. The rain was coming down in bucketfuls and the wipers couldn't keep up.

Still, I didn't have far to go. A bit further on, and I realised I was on the low road we'd seen on the map. This route was cutting through the reed beds where the fens yielded to salt marsh. That meant I'd nearly reached the nature reserve.

Unfortunately, I wasn't sure I was going to make it all the way. The feedback from the road through the steering wheel changed abruptly. I realised the vehicle was aquaplaning where water was flooding the road. I eased off the accelerator, but that didn't make any difference. Two and a half tonnes and momentum were doing the work now. I fought the temptation to stamp on the brake. That couldn't possibly help, and if I did that just as the wheels got some grip, I'd crash and it would be my own fault.

The tyres bit tarmac. I let out a breath I hadn't realised I'd been holding. I checked the mirrors. No sign of the wyrm. I slowed down just a little, with my foot agonisingly careful on the brake. Then the wipers stopped working. I couldn't see the line of the road ahead. I flicked the controls off and on. Nothing. I slowed down a whole lot faster, block-changing down the gears.

The satnav died and so did the headlights. Now I couldn't see anything at all. Fuck. I slowed down some more. Then I stamped on the brake and the clutch to stop completely. The wyrm was on the road right in front of me. I could only just make it out, mostly thanks to its glowing white eyes. I eased the clutch up to the biting point and carefully pressed the accelerator to keep the revs up. I had no idea what was wrong with the Landy's electrics, but I'd bet if I stalled the engine, I wouldn't have a chance in hell of getting it started again.

So what was the wyrm going to do? Obviously it wanted its egg back, but I had no idea how it thought it could manage that. I snatched a quick look at the passenger seat. I'd assumed the egg was still there since I hadn't heard it thud to the floor. Yes, it was safe and sound. Now there was no other light, I saw it was outlined by a dim, eerie radiance. I could feel the cold still coming off it. Even more creepy, I could see a faint scaly coil inside the shell, like the curve of a new moon seen through high cloud.

The rain drumming on the roof eased off. I didn't have time to be glad about that. The wyrm was coming towards me. It writhed along the road until it came right up to the Land Rover. Rearing up, it arched its neck and lowered its head over the bonnet. I could see it was being very careful not to touch any metal, but its nose was inches away from the windscreen. It opened its mouth and I got a close-up view of those terrifying teeth. Then its forked tongue delicately tapped the glass.

I wondered if it was making the same calculations as me. Its head was probably flat enough to get a fair way into the Landy if it smashed the windscreen with its nose. The surrounding metal would most likely sear its skin and scales, but that would surely be worth it, if it could reach its egg. Could it pick the egg up with that long, muscular tongue? Would it be able to open its jaws wide enough to use its teeth? Would it take a moment to bite my head off first?

The wyrm withdrew. Not far though. It reared up tall in front of the Land Rover. Its head was raised twice as high as the roof. I couldn't see the rest of it, but I guessed it was coiling up, ready to strike. I reached down to undo my seatbelt and fumbled for the door handle. Diving out of the driving seat looked like my only option. If I got really lucky, the wyrm might be more focused on getting away with its egg than taking its revenge on me. I didn't reckon much to my chances, but it was the only hope I had.

The wyrm shivered in the darkness. It disappeared. At least, I thought it did. Then I blinked and I realised the monster had shifted into its human form. As far as I could tell, the creature looked the same as it had when Tom Kelley had flattened it with a smack around the head with the crystal. An ordinary man, standing there in the storm in his black jeans and grey jacket. Maybe it was trying to look less scary. If it was, that wasn't working. Those translucent white eyes were still glowing insanely bright. I'd never seen anything look so inhuman.

The wyrm looked at me and smiled, not showing its teeth. Raising its right hand, it gestured towards the passenger seat. Then it held up both hands, cupped as if it held the egg. Maybe that's why it had shifted form. Hands would definitely be more useful in this situation.

It drew its hands towards its chest, arms bent and shoulders rounded as if it cradled a burden. Keeping its right arm crooked around the imaginary egg, it extended its left hand towards me, palm upwards. It gestured again, and its smile broadened. Its meaning was clear. If I gave back the egg, I could leave without any further attack from the wyrm.

Chapter Twenty-Two

I sat gripping the steering wheel, considering my options. I was very, very tempted to hand over the sodding egg. It was blindingly obvious the alternative was getting a face full of wyrm through the windscreen. Add to that, I had very nearly reached the coastline. Witta had said the sea folk could kill a wyrm, as well as wash its egg away to be lost for good in some deep part of the North Sea. Wasn't I close enough for this to be their problem now?

Only there was no sign of the sodding sea folk, and our deal was I'd give them the egg. Not that I'd get it close enough for them to go chasing after it themselves. When you make a deal with ethereal creatures, you need to stick to it, in every detail.

Add to that, I had no idea how quickly the wyrm could get away from here with its precious burden. If Witta's people couldn't catch the monster, they'd really be looking for someone to blame. That someone would be me, and it would be hard to say I didn't deserve it. I might very well drop Fin, Will and Helen in the shit with the sea folk too.

There was also no way to know if I could trust the wyrm. The one I'd encountered at Blithehurst had been entirely ready to kill the humans that it duped to get what it wanted. If this wyrm killed me and got away, a whole lot more lives than mine would be lost. And I didn't want to sodding die.

I tensed my feet inside my boots and refastened my seatbelt. I reached for the handbrake. Could I make a decent racing start before the wyrm realised what I was doing? The Land Rover was a lot bigger and heavier than that backpack with the crystal ball had been. The wyrm hadn't fancied being hit by the vehicle when it was in its monstrous serpent form. Would being run over by the Landy do enough damage to its shifted human shape for me to get away? I had to be close to the nature reserve by now. That's where Witta said the sea folk would meet me. I pressed my boot down on the accelerator.

A massive wave appeared out of nowhere and crashed right across the road. The foaming water swept the wyrm off its human feet and carried it away into the salt marsh on the other side of the tarmac. I saw there was something else in the water besides mud and sand. Something long and large and phosphorescent. I caught a glimpse of an enormous eye. Then everything was gone, vanished into the darkness.

I got the Landy moving. Not nearly as fast as I had been planning to, but I had to get off this exposed stretch of road. This looked like my only chance. I swore as I realised that was going to be easier said than done. The surge of water wasn't draining away back into the marsh. The tarmac was awash, at least a foot deep. I eased the vehicle forward more slowly. If I went too fast, sea water would get into the engine. That wouldn't just stop me here and now. The Landy could be wrecked for good.

I drove on a bit further, but the water got deeper. The sea wasn't simply rising steadily either. I could hear waves slapping against the passenger side of the vehicle. I couldn't see if there were any leaks letting water in through the door seals, but that was the least of my worries. The rain might have stopped, but the wind was still brutal. These buffeting waves were getting stronger and I still had no lights or satnav. Even if I had lights, I wouldn't be able to see where the road went under this muddy water. If I strayed off the tarmac into the marsh, I'd be irretrievably fucked. A Land Rover might be the original off-road vehicle, but that reputation is still based on being able to see where you are actually driving.

Things got worse. I could feel the wheels shifting underneath me as those waves hit the passenger door even harder. Once the water got deep enough, the Landy would start to float and nothing I did would matter. I accelerated cautiously. I focused my attention on listening to the engine's revs and feeling for the contact with the road. I made more progress. That was good. Every metre was getting me further away from the wyrm and whatever was fighting it.

A huge wave smashed into the front of the Land Rover. Water swept right up the bonnet and onto the roof. It left the windscreen smeared with wet sand, and seaweed was tangled around the wipers. The engine coughed and died. Another wave hit just as hard at an angle and shoved the back end of the vehicle around. The sea surged around me, with foam high enough to reach the top of the windows. Now water was definitely getting inside. I could feel cold wetness soaking my feet. The next wave spun the Landy around completely. I was facing back the way I had come.

The sea foamed with eerie light, so bright I could see an almighty battle underway. The wyrm had reverted to its serpent form. That wasn't doing it much good. It was fighting something out of a medieval sailor's worst nightmare. Pale tentacles wrapped tight around the wyrm's black body. The boneless loops dragged its writhing coils under the water to meet whatever was down there. The wyrm's head was still free though, and it wasn't going down without a fight. The monster thrashed this way and that, biting big lumps out of those clinging limbs. The unseen creature's gaping wounds bled dark for a few seconds before the seething water washed the gore away. Where it was forced to let go, the wyrm still paid a price. Suckers ripped away its scales, leaving great gashes in its hide.

The sea folk attacked those wounds mercilessly. I couldn't count how many there were in the water, but there were a lot of them. From what I could see, they looked like Witta in her nereid form, though they seemed darker-skinned and larger. They weren't swimming so much as riding the waves. Foaming breakers obediently lifted them up so they could drive long spears deep into the wyrm's injured flanks. Whatever those weapons were, they couldn't be iron though. Without that advantage, I knew the wyrm would take a lot of killing.

The monster's head whipped around and its jaws closed on an unlucky attacker's waist. The wyrm ripped its victim up and out of the water. The attacker's arms flailed wildly, their weapon falling away before they could think to use it. I remembered Witta saying the sea folk couldn't transform themselves. This attacker would never pass for human, that much was certain. What looked like thighs weren't legs that would ever walk on land. Instead of feet those fish-scaled limbs ended in twin-finned tails. Not that it mattered now. The wyrm bit the poor bastard clean in half and the ragged remains flew away into the darkness. Then another great swell of foaming water spun the Land Rover around, and I lost sight of the fight.

I had my own problems to worry about. The rising sea was up to my arse. I was sitting in a puddle and I was colder than ever. The vehicle was definitely floating now. It wouldn't be doing that for long. The engine block would make the whole Landy nose-heavy. When it started sinking, it would go down fast. I had to make sure it didn't take me down with it.

I undid my seatbelt a second time. I had to get out of here and swim for whatever safety I could find. I certainly wasn't counting on any help from the sea folk. As I looked out of the driver's window, all I could see was wind-ruffled water. I had no way of knowing how deep it was. All I could tell was this flood had now drowned the salt marsh and the road completely.

I looked at the passenger seat. The wyrm's egg was still there, sitting in its own puddle. I thought its glow was fading. To be honest, I really didn't care what happened to it now. If these sea folk wanted the sodding thing, they could dive down to fetch it. Let them work out how to get it out of the Land Rover's wreck.

I had to get out of here. I was still shivering so I didn't think I had hypothermia just yet, but the cold was definitely making me clumsy as well as sapping my strength. First things first. Trying to open the doors would be stupid. My best bet was kicking out the windscreen. That would be most vulnerable at the corners. I shifted in my seat, trying to get my legs up above the dash, to use my boot heels on the glass on the passenger side. It wasn't easy, but I got into a position that I hoped would work. I gripped the sides of my seat for more leverage and drew a deep breath to make a first try.

A hand knocked on the passenger window. A dark green hand with a claw on its thumb and lit by phosphorescence in the water. A face peered through the glass, scowling at me. His hair was a wind-tangled crest, and I couldn't tell if he had a beard or gills or both, but this sea dweller was unmistakably a he with shoulders and pecs like that. He was also big and muscular enough to make me look like Captain America before he got the super-soldier serum. That still didn't mean he could open the Land Rover door against the pressure of the water outside.

I tapped on my own window, down in the bottom corner. The merman or triton or whatever he called himself nodded swift understanding. Whatever his weapon was made of, the handle end easily smashed the glass. I twisted around, reaching for his hand. It was going to be a tight fit for someone my size, getting out through that window. I could see there were jagged edges of glass to cut me as well. I was desperate enough not to care.

The merman slapped my hand away. He was reaching for the wyrm's egg. He didn't care about the broken glass, even when it gashed the silvery fins that stretched from his elbow to his armpit. He threw his weapon away to get a second hand to the egg. With a guttural exhalation, he heaved and lifted it up. Then he threw himself backwards, carrying the egg out through the window. There was a thud on the door panel as he pushed himself off to swim away.

Bastard! Utter, fucking bastard! Fury warmed me for a moment. Then I scrambled towards the window anyway. I still had to get out before the Land Rover sank. The vehicle lurched and I fell forward onto the passenger seat. I barely braced myself with my hands in time to stop my face going into the water. For one heart-stopping moment I thought the Landy was about to topple over. Then I'd be trapped inside to drown. About a nanosecond before panic overwhelmed me, the vehicle rocked again and settled on an even keel. It wasn't settled on anything solid though. It was drifting through the water and getting faster. Some current must have caught it. Where the hell was I going to end up?

I saw movement through the windows. I realised the sky had finally cleared. There was enough starlight and moonlight to show me two or three mermen on either side of the Land Rover's bonnet. There must have been more at the back, shoving it along. They weren't finding it easy, and not just because of the weight. One appeared at the passenger door and reached up to push against the broken window's frame. His face twisted with pain, but he stayed with it as far as he could. The shards of glass weren't the problem. When the merman pulled away, I saw welts and torn blisters across the palm of his hand. Shreds of dark skin were stuck to the metal. That didn't stop another one taking his place.

They were forcing the Landy through the water fast enough to raise a bow wave. Foam surged along the sides. All I could do was sit tight and go along for the ride. I had no idea where they were taking me.

The wheels hit the ground with a jolt that threw me forward into the steering wheel, nearly winding me. I barely managed not to headbutt the dash. By the time I had got my breath back, the sea folk had disappeared. I was completely alone and I had absolutely no idea where the fuck I was. The water was still level with the door sills, and even if it wasn't, I wouldn't be driving anywhere. My poor Landy was as dead and drowned as I sincerely hoped that sodding wyrm was by now. Fuck. I had some savings, but I hadn't planned on having to buy a new vehicle any time soon. I didn't think I'd have much luck trying to make an insurance claim. Describe the accident. Well, there was this serpent dragon in the middle of the road...

That would have to wait. I reached down and groped around until I found the dead torch in the passenger footwell. The water reeked of weed and mud as it lapped against my cheek, and I kept my mouth tight shut. I used the torch to knock out the remaining bits of glass from the broken window. Since I was able to take my time, I got myself out and up onto the roof without injuring myself. I was relieved to find the Land Rover stayed steady as a rock while I was hanging off the side. Whatever it was standing on was good and solid at least.

That was it as far as any good news went. The skies might have cleared, so I could see a fair distance, but all I could see was dark water in every direction. I had no idea which way to go to find dry land, even if I was prepared to risk wading, and most likely swimming. Without some sort of clue, I could end up heading out towards the Wash and the sea. Assuming I didn't drown when I stepped into some unseen dyke.

I looked up. The stars should help me work out which way was north, at least. Before I could find Polaris though, I saw white wings against the dark sky. It was a swan. There are no words to describe my relief. The bird circled overhead and flew down to come in low. I shifted to the edge of the roof to let her – or maybe it was him – land. I really needed to learn how to tell Fin and her relatives apart.

Whoever this was, the bird didn't land. They circled the Landy at the same level with my head and flew away into the darkness. If I was supposed to get some message from that, I had no idea what it was. Sit tight and wait to be rescued? I really hoped I'd got that right, even if it would mean an embarrassing conversation with the RNLI or whoever appeared. I was sure they'd be very polite, just as I was sure they'd leave me in no doubt whatsoever that they thought I was an utter moron for going out for a drive in that storm.

I wasn't left wondering for long. I soon saw a boat coming towards me. Like before, that was as far as the good news went. It wasn't a bright orange inflatable with a noisy outboard, or a sturdy RIB with a life-jacketed crew, lights and warm blankets. A tall figure shrouded in a long dark cape poled a long, low punt silently across the waters. If I hadn't been so cold and exhausted, I'd have been absolutely terrified.

As it was, I just sat there and waited. It wasn't as if I had any other options. If I was dead, and this was some ferryman come to carry me off to whatever came next, then dying hadn't been painful enough for me to notice it happening. I only hoped Fin would tell my mum and dad what I'd done to foil the wyrm.

What? Get a fucking grip, Daniel. I must have been closer to hypothermia than I realised. I focused on the approaching boat and braced myself as best I could on the wet, sandy metal of the Land Rover's roof. The boatman trailed his pole in the water to slow his boat, and I saw the vessel was skilfully made from a single massive tree trunk. I also knew there hadn't been any oaks this size growing anywhere around here for thousands of years.

The boat slid alongside the Land Rover with barely a thump. The ferryman drove his pole straight down into the water on the far side, to hold the boat steady. He pulled back his hood and smiled warmly. He was taller than me, and bearded, with long grey hair and a weathered face. A silver glint lit his deep-set eyes, and I felt some indefinable sense of power backing his presence. Whoever he was, any ordinary human would be very unwise to cross him.

I cleared my throat. 'Thank you.'

He looked even more amused as he watched me climb carefully off the Land Rover and into the boat. I opted to sit at the far end, looking at my rescuer. That should be the best way to keep everything balanced, and it seemed rude to turn my back on him. As soon as I was safely aboard, he shrugged his cloak off his shoulders and leaned into the task of punting the long, narrow vessel away. He raised his pole with a swift, flowing movement, gripping it hand over hand as the water dripped off the wood without splashing him. Then he clasped the top and drove the whole length of it down hard, using the considerable strength in his legs, his broad back and his shoulders.

With his cloak tossed back, I could see he was wearing leggings and a tunic that looked a lot like the clothes the dead warrior had worn, though I couldn't tell their colour. If he wore a torc, that was hidden by the cloak at his neck. He was also very slightly transparent. Looking up from my seat in the bottom of the boat, I realised I could see the stars in the sky above us shining right through him. That was distinctly unsettling.

I decided to think about something else. I ran my hands along the sides of the boat. The wood had been shaped and smoothed with expert skill. This would be fine work for a modern carpenter with power tools. To achieve this with bronze or maybe even stone tools would take a master craftsman. Not for the first time, I thought how wrong it is to look down on people in bygone ages. You can't call them unskilled, when they could produce something like this. I rubbed the wood again, and felt some oddly comforting sense of kinship with whoever had made this superb vessel. The tension racking me eased.

Reeds appeared around us. We were heading into a channel that cut through some shallows. I twisted around to see where we were going and saw an embankment rising out of the water. There was a landing stage jutting out of it, and there had to be a proper road running along the top. I knew that because Fin's Toyota definitely wasn't a cross-country vehicle, so there was no way it had got there without one.

The headlights were on, and she was standing by the open car door with Will beside her. I could see the tension in them from here. As the punt approached the landing stage, they both took an involuntary step back.

I turned to my rescuer. 'Thank you.' That seemed wholly inadequate, but I couldn't think what else to say.

He smiled as if he understood. Then he looked at me with penetrating intensity. His eyes shone as bright as stars. 'Tell your liege that more than the waters are rising.'

I saw his lips were moving but his words seemed to arrive inside my head without bothering my ears.

The boat glided to a halt by the landing stage. He used his pole to hold it steady again. Will and Fin overcame whatever doubts they had and hurried down the slope to the planks. They each offered me a hand as I stood up cautiously in the boat.

Before I accepted their help, I looked at the boatman. I knew his message must be for the Green Man, but I wanted to know more. 'Who shall I say is sending this news?'

He looked thoughtful for a moment. 'There was a time when mortals called me Wade.'

At least I think that's what he said. But Will and Fin were reaching out to help me and I really wanted to feel solid ground beneath my feet. I took their hands and between them they hauled me safely ashore. I found my arms were shaking and my grip was surprisingly weak.

I turned to see the boatman was already poling away. I looked at Fin. 'Did he say his name was Wade or the Wader?'

She was startled. 'I didn't hear him say anything.'

Will was staring past me. We watched the boatman growing more and more translucent as his vessel slid across the water, barely leaving a ripple. Within a dozen strokes of his pole, he had faded to a misty outline. A gust of wind rattled the reeds and the last trace of my rescuer was scattered to drift away on the night air.

Fin turned on Will. 'Who was that?' she demanded.

'I don't know,' he protested. 'Witta just said she would send us help to find Dan and get him back safely. Ask her.'

Clearly I wasn't the only one who'd had a stressful night. 'I'd say he must be the Master of Fords and Ferries that the hob was talking about.'

I had no idea what that might mean, but at least it stopped the two of them having a row. They both looked at me as if they were astonished to hear me speak.

'Can we please get back?' Now my voice was shaking as well as the rest of me. 'I'm absolutely knackered.'

That spurred them into action. Will helped me up the grassy slope while Fin ran on ahead. She opened the car boot and lifted out a big nylon bag. It held towels wrapped round a hot water bottle, and my clothes from the other day, the things Helen had washed and dried for me. I stripped off my wet, muddy clothes, down to and including my underpants. Fin and Will each grabbed a towel, drying my back and arms as I rubbed my chest and legs. There was still enough sand sticking to me to scour my skin, but I didn't care. That was better than feeling so cold and numb. I just wanted to get somewhere close to warm again.

Will bundled everything back into the bag while Fin helped me into the dry clothes. All I had on my feet were socks, but that didn't matter. I wouldn't be driving anywhere else tonight. Will got into the Toyota's driving seat and Fin got into the back. That left the passenger seat for me, and I pretty much fell into it.

'Mum sent soup and coffee,' Fin said behind me. 'Do you want some? Either?'

I shook my head. 'I'd end up wearing it.' I'd gone beyond hunger to feeling unpleasantly sick.

I have no idea which way we took to get back to Venturer's House. With the car heater on, I was soon dozing off. I tried to stay awake. Once I was asleep, there'd be no waking me, and I couldn't see the three of them lifting me out of the car without someone regretting the attempt.

The best I could manage was lurching in and out of my doze as the Toyota rounded bends and braked for junctions. Even so, arriving back at the house took me unawares. Opening my eyes to find we were parked by the patio, I made an almighty effort and managed to get out of the car and through the door.

Inside the kitchen, Helen took one look at me and shook her head. 'Shower. Bed. Now.'

I nodded. Doing anything more than that was beyond me. Getting clean took absolutely the last of my energy. I was still damp when I dropped into my waiting bed. The last thing I registered was Fin slipping under the duvet beside me. Not that I was in any fit state to do anything about that. I didn't even have time to regret the lost opportunity before I was fast asleep.

Chapter Twenty-Three

I woke up alone in bed, and rolled over to see bright daylight around the edges of the curtains. The house was silent. I reached for my phone to see what the time was. Then I remembered where my phone was. It must be as dead as the Land Rover. Where had that been abandoned? I had no idea, but I needed to find out. My phone would be a write-off, but I had other stuff I needed to get back, like my wallet for a start.

That made me think how expensive this trip was going to turn out to be. I'd have to buy a new phone just to begin with. I wasn't due an upgrade for another six months, after losing my last phone fighting a different murderous monster. Then there was a good chance I'd need to replace the Landy. They'll take a lot of abuse, but there are limits. Even if the vehicle could be salvaged, it would take a lot of time and work and money to get it back on the road.

It hardly seemed fair. Heroes in folk tales like Tom Hickathrift got to kill dragons and keep their hoards of silver and gold in days gone by. If the local hob turned up with a bag of treasure to reward me now, all I'd get would be some very awkward questions when I tried to turn any of it into usable cash.

Since there was no point lying there and getting depressed, I got up. I was about to get dressed in my good jeans and my last clean rugby shirt when I saw the pile of clothes on the seat of the armchair. Someone had washed and dried everything I'd worn yesterday, along with doing the rest of the laundry out of my holdall. I wasn't sure how I felt about that. I decided just to be grateful.

Wearing my old jeans, a T-shirt and a sweatshirt, I went downstairs. The house wasn't just silent, it was empty. No one else was in, though I supposed I shouldn't be surprised. It was already gone midday. I found a note on the kitchen table.

Bread in the crock, bacon and eggs in the fridge, beans in the cupboard. Help yourself to anything else you fancy, Helen.

That was very welcome as far as it went, but it didn't go nearly far enough for me. Where was everyone? What were they doing? There wasn't anything much I could do to find out though. I had no phone and no vehicle. I didn't even have any dry boots, though I did see the ones I'd been wearing yesterday were standing by the Aga packed with old newspaper.

I opened the back door and looked outside. Both Fin's and Helen's cars were gone. I looked down the garden. It was a nice day, sunny and quite mild for the time of year. I stood and waited, but there was no sign of the hob. Not of either of the hobs we had dealt with. That didn't mean they couldn't see me, of course. I waited a bit longer. Nothing happened. No sylphs put in an appearance, and I realised I wasn't sorry about that.

I closed the door and thought about getting my laptop out. If I looked up Fin's number in my contacts, I could call her on the landline and find out where she was. I decided to have something to eat first. I was too hungry to think straight. So I took care of that, and felt a whole lot better for some food.

After I'd eaten and washed up, I went to see if I could find anything about my rescuer in any of Fin's grandad's old books. All I learned was that Wade, or possibly Wada, was a character from Old English folklore who cropped up in Norse myth as well. Back in the day, his story was so well known that no one bothered writing it down. But stories get forgotten if they fall out of fashion and there's no one retelling them. By the time scholars realised The Tale of Wade had been lost, it was too late to get it back.

There were a few tantalising remnants to be found in passing references. Wade was the son of a human king and a mermaid, with mystical ties to the water. He had a boat that may or may not have been magical. Okay, I'd seen that for myself. He was the father of Weyland, the smith who made Beowulf's sword and chain mail. Beowulf, who killed monsters until one of them killed him. Did any of that have anything to do with the message Wade had given me for the Green Man? I decided to leave that for another day. I'd had enough of monsters for the moment.

I was sitting at the table with another mug of tea, thinking through what still had to be done here and now, when there was a knock at the back door. It felt a bit odd to answer it. This was someone else's house, after all, but I was the only one here.

Witta was standing outside on the patio, in her human guise. She held out the nylon drawstring bag that I'd last seen when I chucked it in the back of the Land Rover. 'May I come in?'

I took a step back from the doorway. 'If you like.'

My first impulse was to ask her what the hell had happened last night. How did she think her people had lived up to their side of our bargain? My anger faded as fast as it flared up. What was done was done. As long as everything really was done with.

'Is the wyrm dead?' I tried to unknot the bag's string.

'It is, and the egg you brought us will never hatch. May I help?' Witta held out a hand.

I shrugged and gave her the bag. She flexed her fingers and her hands transformed to her nereid form. Just her hands, not the rest of her. She used her long talons to tease the knot loose. I noticed that the webbing between the fingers on her right hand was shrivelled and discoloured, like plastic film that's got too near to some heat.

'There you go.' She handed the bag over, and her hands returned to as close to human as they usually got.

I could still see the burns that she must have got from touching something metal. From opening up the Land Rover, I guessed. 'Thanks.'

I began laying my stuff out on the table. The screwdriver was fine, and my penknife would survive with a bit of care and some WD-40. I didn't think there was any way to resurrect my phone, but I might as well try that bag of rice trick before I gave up on it completely.

I opened up my wallet and laid out my bank cards and driving licence. A quick wipe and they should be fine, fingers crossed. Those sodden receipts could go straight in the bin, but I could be grateful that the couple of tens and fivers I had been carrying were polymer notes. The wallet itself was nylon, so that just needed a good rinse to get the salt water out and then it could be left to dry.

Then I realised what was missing. I looked at Witta. 'Have you got any idea what happened to my keys?'

'Will has them. He'll be here any minute now.'

That was a relief. I'd need my house and workshop keys when I got back to Blithehurst. Once I'd worked out how I was getting back there. Hire car? Train? I wondered where the closest station to Blithehurst might be.

'What's he doing with them?'

Before she could answer, there was another knock on the door. It was Will. He grinned. I managed not to ask what he had to be so cheerful about. 'Come in.'

He offered me my keys. 'The Land Rover's at Uncle Simon's. I got a mate with a van to take me over there, after Witta showed me where to find it, and he gave me a tow. I've got everything I could find out of it. That's all in a box in my boot. I said it was completely my fault. I told him I'd said I was going to be out that way doing some night shooting. When you heard that the sea defences had given way, you came looking for me. Only I'd changed my mind about where I was going, but I hadn't bothered to tell anyone. So as far as everyone's concerned, I'm the one to blame—'

I held up my hand to interrupt him. 'Who's Uncle Simon?'

'Oh, sorry. Fin's dad. He's got plenty of room at his farm. He says it's no bother.'

Oh great, now Fin's dad would think I was a complete idiot. Someone who'd been trying to be a hero and nearly ended up dead of stupidity.

Will was still talking. 'You can leave the Land Rover there till you decide if you're scrapping it or going to try to restore it. He reckons there's a decent chance of getting it running again. He says he'll drain all the fluids and get the pressure washer on it to get rid of the sand and the salt. Then he can put it under cover in his workshop to dry out. Then you can see what's what.'

His cheerfulness faded. 'I'm really sorry about it though. Listen, if there's any sort of reward going for catching Tom Kelley, you can have my share. That's a promise.'

'Thanks, I appreciate it.' I wouldn't be counting on that though, not any time soon, or at all. I didn't want to talk about the Land Rover, or think about the hassles that lay ahead for me dealing with it. 'So what did happen about Kelley? Where's Fin?'

'She went to Cambridge with Chris this morning. He's only got a motorbike, so she offered him a lift. Said he'd be safer if the roads were wet or icy, as well as more comfortable. He said she should tell the Historic Environment Team everything she knew about Kelley. He hit the roof when we showed him the video last night, so Fin said she'd seen him snooping around the hillfort as well.' He glanced at the clock. 'They should be back here soon.'

Mentioning Chris reminded me of something I'd thought of earlier, while I was drinking my tea. I looked at Witta. 'So the only thing we still have left to deal with is that crystal, isn't it?'

She nodded. 'The hob here doesn't deserve to be burdened with guarding it. We need to put it out of reach of everyone who might misuse it.'

'I've had an idea about that.' I looked at her and at Will. 'I reckon the safest place for it is in the museum at Sedgeport. If it's locked away in a display cabinet, then no one can get their hands on it, human or anyone else, and you'll know exactly where it is. You can drop in there every so often to check. But it needs to be handed over by someone with no ties to any of us. There needs to be a convincing story behind the donation that has nothing to do with the Kelleys. That way, even if someone gets curious about the same stories or whatever old papers Doctor Tom found, they'll have no reason to think that crystal ball in Sedgeport Museum has anything to do with John Dee or Edward Kelley.'

Will nodded slowly. 'That could work. Yes, I think that's a good idea.'

The door opened and Fin walked in. Chris from the museum was with her. I swept the things I had spread out across the table back into the nylon bag. I wasn't interested in answering questions about how my wallet had got soaking wet last night.

Witta stood up. 'Leave that with me,' she said briefly. 'I think I have an idea.'

Before Will or I could work out how to ask her what she meant without giving anything away, she skirted quickly around Fin and left.

I don't think Chris even noticed. He wanted to talk to Will, stumbling over his words in his eagerness to share his news. 'Tom Kelley's been arrested. Handcuffs and everything. There's a major crackdown on theft from archaeological sites at the moment. I don't even know if he'll get bail. He's definitely facing serious charges, and he could well end up in prison.'

Fin was putting the kettle on. 'I think the handcuffs were because the police turned up at The Ring of Bells this morning to find him and Mike having a row that looked ready to turn into a fist fight.'

'That won't do him any favours with the cops.' I was pleased to think they'd seen Kelley at his worst. With any luck, they would be less impressed with his money and status after that display. Ideally, he'd piss them off even more by demanding to be called Doctor Kelley, and generally being an arrogant shit. I liked the idea of him spending a night in a custody suite cell.

Fin looked at me. 'Mum went up to The Wheat Sheaf to help out this morning. When Mike Kelley told the police about the damage at Talbot House, they sent someone over here with him to take a look, and to get statements from Neil and Kate.'

I nodded. 'Right.' I wanted to know if that meant the stolen papers that the hob had hidden had been found, but I couldn't ask that with Chris here, any more than Fin could tell me.

'So what did Tom find in the field exactly?' Will asked him innocently.

'Merovingian coins,' Chris said with relish. 'The Merovingians were the kings of the Franks who established themselves after the Roman Empire collapsed. I've been looking them up. Their territory ended up as France – that's where we get the name from – though they actually held a whole lot of land that stretched well into what became Germany. They were the dominant European power after they defeated the Visigoths down in the Iberian peninsula, as well as the Burgundians closer to home. They had quite a sophisticated legal and political system. You know, the Dark Ages is a really misleading term that needs to be got rid of—'

I held up a hand to interrupt. 'So how did money from what, sixth or seventh-century France end up in a field in the Fens?'

'Well, that's the however-many-thousand-pounds question, isn't it?' he said, looking very bright-eyed for a man who couldn't have got a lot of sleep. 'There could be a hoard down there. Who knows how big, or what might be in it?' He laughed. 'Or someone had a hole in their pocket when they were just passing through, and they lost their life savings, Tom Kelley picked the coins up, and that's all there is to it.'

I wanted to say 'How about a burial?', but I didn't think I'd get away with 'lucky guess' when the dead warrior turned up. 'So there'll be some sort of dig to find out?' I asked instead.

'I wonder what a geophysics survey will show.' Fin looked hopefully at Chris.

'You've been watching too much telly archaeology.' He shook his head, regretful. 'For a start, geophysics stuff like resistivity and magnetometry doesn't really work on mounds. They're for finding things like pits and ditches and buried walls. No, the first thing the Historic Environment Team will do is take a good look at Tom Kelley's bit of digging, record anything else that's there to be found now there's some daylight, and fill the holes back in.'

'That's it?' Shit. I hoped none of the hobs or sylphs were listening to this conversation.

Chris shrugged. 'It's a scheduled ancient monument, and these days, they're left well alone even if no one's taken a look at this place since some antiquarians had a bit of a ferret around before World War One. I checked. We've got their reports back at the museum.'

'Seriously?' Fin persisted. 'When there could be, I don't know, something like the Sutton Hoo treasures down there?'

Chris shrugged again. 'A lot will depend on what else might turn up where Kelley was digging. If there's something really interesting, a university team might apply to Historic England for permission for a limited research dig, but that would have very strict conditions attached. The only way a whole site like that gets dug up these days is if someone's about to put a road or a high-speed rail link through it and that's hardly likely around here.'

He grinned, then suddenly looked anxious. 'We mustn't say anything about this though, not to anyone. If word gets out, the whole site could be wrecked by scavengers before it's been properly assessed.'

'No one will hear about it from me,' I assured him.

'Or me,' promised Fin as she poured hot water into the teapot and a cafetière.

Will sighed. 'Better take down my Instagram posts.'

Chris looked aghast. Will laughed. 'What sort of idiot do you think I am? Of course I'll keep quiet. Why else do you think we came straight to you when we realised what was going on?'

Chris looked relieved, as well as embarrassed. He couldn't work out what to say, but thankfully before the silence got too awkward, the door opened and Helen came in. I saw her quickly register who was here.

'Well.' She smiled at everyone. 'This is a lot more excitement than we're used to, isn't it?'

'How are Neil and Kate?' Fin asked as she put mugs and milk on the table.

'As startled as the rest of us.' Helen brought the coffee over while Fin brought the tea. 'Tom Kelley won't be coming back to Talbot House any time soon. Still, as long as Neil can get the repairs organised, and everything is put straight again, it'll be available for lettings by the start of the season.'

She poured herself a mug. 'Mike and Neil have gone off to see a man about the woodwork. Kate and I went over to the house for a proper look round, to make a list of what needs doing. We found a whole lot of old papers in a cardboard box. Not newspapers, but handwritten letters and the like. That must be something Tom left behind.'

Chris looked like a dog that had just heard a whistle. 'Where are they, these papers? Still at the house or did Kate take them to the pub?'

'Still at the house,' Helen said, unconcerned. 'Mike will see what he can make of them later.'

Chris was already on his feet. 'I should take a look. Excuse me.'

'Text me when you want a lift back to Sedgeport,' Fin called after him.

'I'm not sure he heard that.' I looked at the closed door and wondered how the hell we were going to deal with the remaining wyrm eggs if we couldn't get some helpful archaeologists to dig them up. I was just glad Witta hadn't stayed long enough to hear the bad news. Her people weren't going to like that at all.

Helen was laughing. 'The hob in the house was following us in and out of every room. It was really distracting. Then I realised she wanted me to look under the bed in the room where Tom had been sleeping. I think I made it look fairly natural. I said I was checking for stray socks. Kate said herself that she hadn't even looked under there when she was tidying up earlier in the week, she's been so distracted by all this. Anyway, she's the one who opened the box, and we decided she should give it to Mike when he and Neil get back. I'm sure Chris can tell him what to do about it.'

And Chris would know who to contact in Cambridge to drop Tom Kelley even deeper in the shit, I thought with satisfaction.

Helen looked at me. 'You did mean it when you said you didn't want to do the woodwork over there, didn't you?'

I nodded. 'I haven't got the tools here, and anyway, I need to get back to Blithehurst.' Though I still hadn't worked out how I was going to do that without my Land Rover.

Helen looked a little taken aback. 'I suppose so, now everything's sorted out. But you can stay for a few more days, can't you? You haven't exactly had much of a holiday here.'

That was an understatement. It was hard to believe how much had happened in the past ten days. I looked at Fin.

She was smiling. 'You could make your visit the full fortnight.'

'Why not?' I agreed. 'That'll keep Blithehurst's records nice and tidy.'

So that's what I did. Fin and I had a couple of days out. We visited the cathedrals in Ely and Peterborough, since there wasn't a whole lot else open for visitors in January. The weather stayed cold and dry, so we wrapped up well and visited a nature reserve where there was sod all to see at this time of year, but I learned a lot more about the Fens.

I learned a whole lot more about Fin's family when Helen invited her sisters and the cousins who lived in the area over for a family dinner. Fortunately, they were far more interested in hearing about the hobs and the sylphs and Tom Kelley's crimes to start interrogating me. They were startled to hear about the wyrm, and they didn't like the idea of that buried clutch of eggs any more than I did. Unfortunately, none of us could come up with a plan to deal with them without landing ourselves in prison.

Still, we were able to enlist them all in keeping an eye on the site, as well as an ear once I explained about the wyrmsong. At least we reckoned we had some time in hand to find a solution. The eggs were still silent and the wyrm that had guarded them was dead. For the moment, Will had been able to convince Witta that arranging any sort of archaeological dig took ages and endless paperwork. Since he was telling the truth about that she had no reason to doubt him.

The nereid had been as good as her word when it came to putting the stargazer's crystal out of reach. Fin and I went out for a curry with Chris the evening before I left. He told us about an old lady who'd just brought the museum a battered suitcase that had belonged to her grandmother. Gran had been a fortune teller with the travelling fairs before World War One. Apparently King's Lynn once had a famous ironworks that built fairground rides, after starting out making agricultural machinery and steam-powered water pumps. Anyway, the old lady's suitcase was full of posters and bits of costumes and tarot cards and all sorts of props including a crystal ball. Chris reckoned the collection would make a really interesting new exhibit.

We agreed, and I hoped anyone who glimpsed weird reflections in the crystal thanks to some nereid or sea folk ancestor would have the sense to keep their mouth shut. With luck, they would have already discovered that sharing anything like that almost always caused hassle.

On the drive back, we wondered who the old lady was, and how she knew Witta. We agreed that couldn't have been the nereid herself masquerading as human, not with that other stuff to back up her story which Chris was bound to research and verify. I wondered how good that long-dead fortune teller had been. If she'd had a parent or grandparent who wasn't human, she could well have had some sort of second sight. That might be the old lady's link with the sea folk.

On my last day, we drove over to Fin's dad's farm. Simon was a friendly, no-nonsense bloke about six inches shorter than me, and he was a lot more optimistic about the Landy's prospects than I would have been. It had cleaned up far better than I expected, and it looked like Simon would enjoy the challenge of getting it running again. He was already talking about stripping out the wiring loom and replacing that once everything had dried out. Perhaps the vehicle wasn't a complete write-off after all. It would give me a good reason to come back here as well.

When we said our goodbyes Simon shook my hand very firmly indeed as he looked me in the eye. I didn't need any supernatural insight to know that if I didn't do right by his daughter, he'd follow me to the ends of the earth to make me regret it. It wouldn't matter how much bigger than him I was.

Fin drove me back to Blithehurst. She said that was the least she could do. She had one condition, so we went to Staffordshire by way of my dad's house on the Warwickshire-Oxfordshire border. Fin and I told Dad and my mum about everything that had happened. Then Fin went out for a walk with my mum, while Dad and I cooked a meal.

I told him I knew how much it had worried him when I'd got caught up with the fight to stop the wyrm at Blithehurst. I swore I really hadn't meant to do it again. He said it didn't sound as if I'd had much choice. That made me feel a bit better, but there was plenty left to talk about. We both wondered what else might be stirring under the ground undisturbed by archaeologists, or going unseen in the depths of the rivers and seas. We had no idea what Wade's warning might mean, but it couldn't be anything good. I didn't reckon I had better count on the old fairy tale tradition of the woodcutter's son successfully facing three challenges and then getting his reward.

When Fin and Mum came back, Mum was holding a white swan's feather. She put it behind the clock on the mantelpiece. She didn't say anything, and neither did Fin, so nor did I. Mum could tell Dad what it meant after we'd left.

A week or so later, Fin rang me. I was taking my lunch break in the manor house kitchen, using the Wi-Fi to look at second-hand vans for sale in the area. I needed some sort of vehicle at least temporarily.

'You've got your new phone sorted out then. How are things?'

It was good to hear her voice. 'Fine. Everything okay with you and Blanche?'

'Yes, we're fine. Listen, make sure you check your email. Mum sent me a link to the local news website this morning and I've just forwarded the story to you.'

I could hear Fin was finding something funny so I guessed a wyrm hadn't turned up to eat some unfortunate archaeologists. 'What's it about?'

'Apparently there's been a spate of cars being broken into lately. They haven't been damaged, so the police think someone's using an electronic gadget to open the central locking. Maybe kids, they reckon, since not much has been taken, and nothing that's valuable. Cushions and picnic blankets are being stolen, along with plastic cups and things like that.'

I grinned. Then I wondered just how much trouble I had accidentally started. 'Do you suppose the sylphs are doing that for the hobs, or they've taught them how to do it for themselves?'

Fin laughed. 'Hard to say. Mum says she's seen several sylphs around, as well as at least three hobs. She's lit the fire pit for them a couple of times, and they seem very happy about that. The hob from Talbot House has been round to complain about the mess the carpenters are making over there, but Mum says she thinks she's actually looking forward to the new season and plenty of holiday rentals coming in. She's said a few things that make Mum reckon she finds having visitors in the house interesting.'

I supposed that made sense. 'It's not as if she can watch telly, is it? How's everyone else?'

'Fine. Will's talking about going on holiday to the Norfolk Broads with Witta when the weather gets warmer. Chris is excited about something the archaeologists found up at the burial mound, but he keeps telling me that he really can't tell me anything about it.'

Maybe there would be some sort of dig after all. 'Has he heard any more about what's happening with Tom Kelley?'

'Not a thing, but apparently these cases take absolutely ages to get to court. He won't get away with anything that he did though.' Fin sounded more serious. 'Have you told Eleanor about everything that happened? Have the dryads there had much to say?'

Thankfully I was on my own in the house so I didn't have to worry about being overheard as I answered her. 'They're relieved to hear the wyrm guarding those eggs has been dealt with, but they weren't thrilled to learn another one had turned up so soon after the trouble we had here.'

'Is there any way they could warn us if they hear any hint of something else stirring?'

'I can certainly ask. Eleanor suggested I ask if they can put me in touch with the naiad who sometimes visits the river here. Meanwhile, she's hitting the books in Durham to see if she can find any clues to what we might have to worry about.'

'Let me know how she gets on. Let me know if the naiad turns up.'

The connection crackled and I wondered if that was one of the dryads listening to our call. 'Are you still there?'

'Yes.' Fin paused. 'I was wondering, how would you like to meet up in Stratford-upon-Avon some weekend in March or April? Go and see some Shakespeare. Book a nice hotel.'

'I'd like that a lot.' I smiled.

'Okay then. I'll look at the RSC website and see what's on.'

Now it was my turn to pause. 'I got a parcel from your mum yesterday.'

'Really?' Fin was surprised.

'Sheepskin slippers. Size fourteen.'

'They must have taken some finding.'

I could tell Fin was pleased.

There was another silence.

'I'd better get on,' Fin said after a moment. 'I just wanted to check in.'

'Good to hear from you, any time. I'll see what's on in Stratford, and let you know what I like the look of, okay?'

'Okay then. Bye.'

'I'll talk to you soon.'

I put the phone down and realised I was still smiling. I might not have got the treasure after the wyrm was dead, but I was starting to think I had got the girl.

Still, I would be happier if I had some idea if we were going to find ourselves caught up in any future challenges. I'd been walking in the woods here every day since I'd got back. I hadn't seen any sign of the Green Man. I wondered how long it would be before I could pass on Wade's warning. I wondered how soon I might find out what it meant.

Acknowledgements

This story started with some casual information that I didn't think much about when I added it to *The Green Man's Foe*. The folk tale that inspired Finele as a character is from Cambridgeshire, so it made sense to say that's where her family lives. Afterwards, I found myself wondering what Dan would make of the Fens if he ever visited her there. While I was thinking about that, the archaeologist Francis Pryor had a book published looking at this region and its long, complex history. That's a fascinating read which started me on the path to writing the story you have just read.

East Anglia isn't a part of England that I know well, so we spent a week's holiday near Ely last November, to see what inspiration I might find. As you can see, that trip was very worthwhile. I recommend visiting the area, its local museums, historic houses and churches. This book owes a particular debt to the Wisbech and Fenland Museum, founded in 1835, both as the inspiration for the Sedgeport and District Museum, and for the books of local folklore I found for sale there. The National Trust nature reserve at Wicken Fen supplied me with further essential information. As you might imagine, staff at both places were intrigued when I explained the reasons for my interest.

A paradox of contemporary fantasy fiction is the need for stories to be rooted in reality in order for readers to find the supernatural believable. My thanks to Sue Rumfitt, whose knowledge of the highways and byways of the area made her an ideal reader to assess the sense of place. Philip Cresswell's Land Rover expertise is very much appreciated, as is Julia Cresswell drawing my attention to *The Tale of Wade*, and to the Prittlewell burial. With regard to the archaeological details, I am most grateful for the notes and corrections provided by Sheila Raven, Archaeology Finds Specialist and professional jeweller. You can find her work at CuckoosNestGallery on Etsy. As always, any errors or infelicities that remain are my responsibility.

As with the previous books, the team I work with have done an outstanding job. This achievement in a time of unprecedented upheavals, distractions and uncertainties should not be underestimated. My sincerest gratitude goes to Cheryl Morgan of Wizard's Tower Press for her technical and production work, and to Toby Selwyn for his invaluable editorial input. Once again I am utterly delighted with the way Ben Baldwin has turned my words into such compelling and fabulous artwork.

Last but very far from least, I would like to thank the readers and reviewers whose enthusiastic recommendations to fellow fantasy fans have made this independent, small press series such a success!

About the Author

Juliet E McKenna is a British fantasy author living in the Cotswolds, UK. Loving history, myth and other worlds since she first learned to read, she has written fifteen epic fantasy novels so far. Her debut, *The Thief's Gamble*, began The Tales of Einarinn in 1999, followed by The Aldabreshin Compass sequence, The Chronicles of the Lescari Revolution, and The Hadrumal Crisis trilogy. *The Green Man's Heir* was her first modern fantasy rooted in British folklore, followed by *The Green Man's Foe* and *The Green Man's Silence*. She also writes diverse shorter stories that include forays into dark fantasy, steampunk and science fiction. As well as reviewing for web and print magazines, she promotes SF&Fantasy by blogging on book trade issues, attending conventions and teaching creative writing.

www.julietemckenna.com

@JulietEMcKenna

The Tales of Einarinn

1. The Thief's Gamble (1998)

2. The Swordsman's Oath (1999)

3. The Gambler's Fortune (2000)

4. The Warrior's Bond (2001)

5. The Assassin's Edge (2002)

The Aldabreshin Compass

1. The Southern Fire (2003)

2. Northern Storm (2004)

3. Western Shore (2005)

4. Eastern Tide (2006)

Turns & Chances (2004)

The Chronicles of the Lescari Revolution

1. Irons in the Fire (2009)

2. Blood in the Water (2010)

3. Banners in The Wind (2010)

The Wizard's Coming (2011)

The Hadrumal Crisis

1. Dangerous Waters (2011)
2. Darkening Skies (2012)
3. Defiant Peaks (2012)

A Few Further Tales of Einarinn (2012) (ebook from Wizards Tower Press)

Challoner, Murray & Balfour: Monster Hunters at Law (2014) (ebook from Wizards Tower Press)

Shadow Histories of the River Kingdom (2016)   (Wizards Tower Press)

The Green Man (Wizards Tower Press)

1. The Green Mans Heir (2018)
2. The Green Man's Foe (2019)

THE GREEN MAN'S SILENCE